About the Author

J.P. Roarke practiced trial law for about three decades.
He has written two other books, several short stories, and
a number of poems. He lives with his wife in the
Coachella Valley, in Southern California.

For Jeannie, Lou and Laura

J. P. Roarke

FROM THE VILLAGE OF LUCCA

AUSTIN MACAULEY
PUBLISHERS LTD.

A CIP catalogue record for this title is available from the British Library.

ISBN 9781785547102 (Paperback)
ISBN 9781785547119 (eBook)

www.austinmacauley.com

First Published (2016)
Austin Macauley Publishers Ltd.
25 Canada Square
Canary Wharf
London
E14 5LQ

I owe a great deal of thanks to several people for their help with this work, including the late Sarah Getty, the great Wyn Cooper, and the hardworking team at Austin Macauley, including especially Larch Gallagher and Greg Carter. I also wish to mention, and thank, the women who provided inspiration for the story. The first braved far more than her share of pains for as long as I've known her; and the second, whom I never had the privilege to meet, suffered enough slings and arrows that she became an almost mythical part of our conversations over the years.

If there be nothing new, but that which is
Hath been before, how are our brains beguil'd,
Which labouring for invention bear amiss
The second burthen of a former child!
O! That record could with a backward look,
Even of five hundred courses of the sun,
Show me your image in some antique book,
Since mind at first in character was done!
That I might see what the old world could say
To this composed wonder of your frame;
Wh'r we are mended, or wh'r better they,
Or whether revolution be the same.

William Shakespeare, Sonnet 59

PRELUDE

Twenty-five years after his greatest heist, an old thief struggled to make his way up a driveway. He was headed towards an old Packard, but his age made it difficult. There were beads of sweat on his forehead by the time he was half way there, so he stopped to catch his breath and frowned at the sight ahead. An ugly oleander had grown into a rough hedge that crowded across the driveway's curving border all the way up to the road. Thick branches rested against the left side of the Packard, matching scratches in what was left of its dull paint.

The gravel road at the top was used by neighbours' cars on their morning commutes to work, then again when they came home each night. Their passings roiled wakes that billowed up and out, then settled onto the hedge, the driveway, and everything else within fifty feet of the roadway, including the Packard. All its surfaces—the scratched paint, a crumpled fender, and the dented bumpers—were covered in light brown, though sunlight still made its way through to old chrome and these days made the old thief squint.

He shielded his eyes and huffed forward again. It was steeper here. His steps shortened and his shoes scuffed the driveway, stirring little trails of dust which coated the polish he'd applied the night before, right after he'd ironed his shirt for the thousandth time and chose among pairs of shiny trousers. His nightly ritual of laying out the next day's things had taken longer, but then he'd first had to make arrangements for today. They were unusual, complicated and hard to remember, but each was very important; Joe's friend Arlo had written them down for him. The list was in his pocket, and though he didn't have the energy to pull it out he tried to run through it again in his head.

One, laun ... The laundry thing. His, hers, the boy's. Two, the sheets. Four ... no, three, bleach ... no ...

Demands of the incline took his focus from the count, so he stopped at the rear bumper to try again.

One, lowd ... laund ... the laundry thing. Two, sheets. Three, bleach ... no ... bath ... "Merda," he swore, and he gave up. Shielding his eyes, he shuffled sideways between the bush and the driver's side of the car. Stiff branches streaked dust against the back of his pants, and the door swept more broadly across the front. He scowled at the mess while forcing the door then contorted himself into the front seat. Gravity and the branches slammed the door shut.

"Mer—" he began, but the impact of the door's closing brought a spastic interruption. He stiffened, cleared his throat and jerked his head left, though there was nothing to draw his attention to the left, to the right or anywhere else for that matter. The movements had no purpose or physical cause. They were merely old habits to which thousands of repetitions had given independent life.

A tic.

Over time Joe had learned to decorate the thing with a repertoire of manly after gestures: following the throat clearing, head jerk conjunction he'd add symmetry by yanking his head in the other direction, and then, depending on his mood or the tic's appearance in conversation, either frowning, sighing, waving his hand abruptly and in any case uttering a suitable curse—as if the little parade was simply an overdue release of frustration. Done correctly it added *gravitas*. So he thought, anyway.

But it was really just a tic.

With the most recent spasm past, he struggled to take an old set of keys from his pocket, flipped to the one with the worn 'P' emblem, and shoved it forward until the familiar metals joined their opposites. He hesitated before turning, for these days there was an irritating coincidence to this operation. Only now that the family claimed he was failing had the car's reliability begun to suffer. Joe found it impossible not to connect the two. The Packard had for decades stood ready to help with escape from the family home, something he did for almost all of the twenty-six years before his wife Rose died last fall. The only exception was Christmas time, when she'd insisted he play the role of a well-behaved husband. His jaw tightened. *That* memory still rankled.

"It's Christmas! You've got a family!" she yelled the first year they came to this country, and she waved an iron skillet near his head. Joe had leaned recklessly into its likely arc, daring her to swing, for he was more firmly violent then, while she was just more firmly Italian. But she was no fool. Rose learned early to avoid beatings by swooping between attack and retreat as suddenly as an amusement ride: a year after they arrived she even began using an ally from beyond the grave. Lowering the skillet and her voice she stepped into his face and pleaded, "Seppe. Your mama. She's gonna be here."

"She's dead!" he shouted, but Rose glanced around cautiously, and then shrank her words to a whisper.

"She come, Seppe! An' she want you here a' Christmas."

"She's dead!"

Things only got worse. Over the next few years, Rose began to tell details of conversations she was having with the dead woman. "She no' like what you do, Seppe," she whispered one year, looking ominously over her shoulder. "She say if you no' stay here for Christmas someday we should do somethin'—"

"She's dead, Rose."

"—She say to me the money should not go to the *stronza*—"

"Did you tell her I gonna cut off your hands if you touch it?"

"—No but she say some day she gonna make you blind. She—"

"She's dead!" he shouted again, and he'd followed that with a 'mild' beating.

Rose withdrew for a while, but as the years passed religion edged her into deeper waters. After returning from St. Vincent's one evening she drew into his bed, rubbed his chest and spoke as if to a favourite child. "Your mama was in church today—"

"Christ, Rose!" he sighed.

"—She was at the back, and she waved and I see her, and I met her and we spoke, then she came home with me, and she come in our house, and she's here, Seppe, to help me, Seppe—"

"Come on, Rose!"

"—She tell me what you doin', Seppe! Your mama say to me where you been ..." she'd continued, her voice rising against her will, "She tell me you been with the *meretricie*—"

"Shut up, Rose!"

She curled her finger in front of his eyes and yelled. *"Those women are mignotta!"*

"God damn it, Rose," he shouted, but her tone wisely retreated to a whisper.

"She says she want you *here*, Seppe, with me, *mio caro,"* while caressing his arm, his chest, or his cheek, and tightening anger within herself.

That marked the beginning of the end, as far as Joe was concerned, for it was then that Rose began to complain to others: the butcher and baker, the priest and parishioners at St. Vincent's all learned of his whoring and gambling. The priest even made a special trip to warn Seppe about afterlife repercussions from such behaviour. Rose was triumphant at that—God himself had sent a messenger to validate her complaints. Even Arlo, who'd helped with Joe's great theft decades before, became mildly religious about it, and urged Joe to seek protections offered by the church.

And, being a pious man, Joe relented. Each December he began going to confession and, at least during Christmas, played the well-leashed husband. Not that it was easy, but for at least a week each year Joe chafed at home while his women wondered what the hell he was doing.

Joe pumped the Packard's gas pedal out of frustration. After all of that he'd lost everything because of them—*everything! His own wife and daughter!*

He took a deep breath and turned the key. The starter turned slowly, but the sickly rrrr, rrrrr noise slowed to a stop. Several irritating clicks followed, then all was silent. *"Merda,"* he sighed again, and his thoughts went back to the list.

One, lowd ... laund ... the laundry thing. Two, sheets ... no ... Bleach ... no ...

He lost count over another memory that always bothered him. For almost forty years now Rose' reaction to his greatest feat had grated at his soul. It had been his Everest. His Magnus opus. *The* theft of his life.

It hadn't begun badly. When she saw him afterwards she fussed over his injury with the perfect note of feminine tenderness while he poured out details of the heist. But when he told what he'd done to the woman who'd been there she recoiled and was suddenly pale.

"But she stabbed me!" he said, incredulous at her reaction. Feeling every inch a wounded knight he pulled out the best piece, knelt before her and said reverently, "*La Crime* is now yours, Signora Martini." But Rose turned away as if from a foul smell.

He sighed again, thinking of how she deserved what he finally gave her that day. And yet the wake of that recollection brought back memories of how cold Rose became, how, to the very day she died, she'd never been her old self, and how then, later, Joe learned that she'd infected their daughter with the same poison.

He tried to go through the list once again, but resentment tugged him back. The ingratitude was astounding. His wife and daughter had accepted the home he bought and clothes he furnished, the cars and trips and most of the jewellery, yet did what they'd done! Even whores showed him gratitude—*they* were always grateful, and there were always plenty of whores—until, of course, the money was gone.

His jaw tightened while thinking of it. On a fittingly stormy July morning he'd driven up to the bank to retrieve one of the more valuable pieces, but when he opened the so called 'safety' deposit box in the supposedly safe young bank … *it was empty! Even the necklace! Every last bit was gone!* The tic had shaken Joe like an angry puppet. When it subsided he threw the box against the door and stormed out to confront Giannini.

Amadeo nervously checked the records. "Only your wife Rose 'as been here, Seppe. No one else."

"When?" Joe demanded.

"Not two months ago," Amadeo insisted.

"Two months!" Joe shouted, thinking *my dead wife came in here?* Giannini turned the book and pointed to the entry:

Rose Martini, 3 Maggio, 1929.

The signature brought a cold sweat. The writing was his daughter's!

"Din't you know, Seppe?" Giannini asked anxiously.

Joe brought out the tic to buy himself time, but it was like tepid water. Calling police would bring questions of origin, and those would be answered with prison. He forced a better show of the tic; then shrugged as if realizing it were no matter. "Yes, of course. Now that you mention it, she did tell me …" he said. "I've … had other things on my mind."

Amadeo was relieved. "You sure everything is all right?"

"Yes, yes." Joe pulled himself up and left. He lurched aimlessly in the rain until he found a bar, stayed there until the place closed, then wove the Packard home, somehow without incident—until he'd had trouble seeing in the dark and hit the garage.

His daughter and son in law rushed out and found him, bleeding and cursing. After hearing what had happened they explained what they'd done, how they'd honoured Rose' last wish by donating the remaining pieces to St. Vincent's! He could have killed the *stronza* then, but her ape-like husband knew about him, and warned what would happen if he didn't behave.

The new budget allowed for no whoring or betting—*none*. He was on an allowance now, his car could no longer approach the garage, and to add insult, they insisted he do *chores*—shopping, cleaning and the like!

His anger settled itself back to the plans for this evening. *One* ... "Shit," he murmured, losing count. He turned the key once again. The signal reached the motor more weakly this time. A lesser turning noise sounded, and wound down even more quickly.

"Non mi rompere le palle, non mi scazzare i coglioni!" Joe swore, but as the starter spent its last turn one cylinder caught. Smoke exploded out the tailpipe. A split-second's silence followed, then another explosion, then more in stumbling succession, and the Packard began to rock back and forth on its ancient springs. After a minute the engine was running on six cylinders, after another maybe seven. The lines on Joe's face relaxed a little. He waited to let the car gather strength, and in the lull his thoughts went to his daughter's further and final treachery.

He detected it last month, when after they left he searched their room for extra cash and stumbled upon the papers. *The papers!* He thought bitterly, with a lumpy rev of motor. He'd set a meeting with Arlo at Tony's café to work out their murders. Arlo was reluctant, but he'd trapped himself with too many stories about the cousin who caught a man in bed with his wife. The killings for which said cousin served time were always related with the same knowing look that said, *within my family there are such men*, followed by that same sigh that said how weary he was of the life.

And yet, even then Arlo tried to get out from under it. "It costs money," the big man said, studying his cigar as though it was the problem.

"I'll do it myself," Joe snapped.

"You're too old, my friend."

"You'll help me, won't you?" Joe demanded, with hands curled into fists.

Arlo took a quick puff, let it out nervously, and through the smoke finally said, "I will speak to my cousin." He called Joe the next day. They had spoken, *but*—and Arlo made it clear this came from the cousin— he now suggested compromise. "Maybe first you sit with them like you do with me. Tell them what you need to say."

"I tried that," Joe said impatiently.

"Not since you found the papers," Arlo said, a little too quickly. He steadied himself and went on with more reserve. "You need to talk with them, Joe. *Really* talk. Don' get angry or upset. Maybe even practice, then talk."

Joe was disappointed at the suggestion, but took it to heart. All the following week he practiced and he brought it up during the next Saturday dinner. It was a thoroughly unpleasant failure. Tension appeared with the first words and his tic tripped up the rest. Joe cleared his throat and jerked his head so much that he looked like a wind sock. His daughter and husband exchanged obvious glances; Joe burst up from the table and stormed off to his tiny room.

He met Arlo once more at Tony's. Arlo was even more nervous as he explained his cousin's final suggestions, but they seemed good ones. He even knew where to bury the bodies so that no one would ever find them. Arlo helped Joe write down the important parts on the list. They would do it tonight. It brought a scrap of the old excitement back into Joe, and more relief than he'd felt in months. There was pride in the plan, faith in his old skills, and even a little gratitude for his friend, for Arlo had at least traced the necklace to a collective store

19

run by St. Vincent's. Getting it back would be his next priority.

Joe restarted the sequence in his mind but immediately lost track, and with resignation pulled the paper from his pocket, unfolded and read it to himself:

1. Laudanum, first husband and wife, then son.

2. Lay out plastic sheets—two on floor, one in tub.

3. Knives and saw—Arlo, the husband; Joe, the wife and boy; all in the tub, all on plastic.

4. Pieces into trash bags.

5. Clean everything with bleach.

6. Follow Arlo to hills.

The Packard's engine was at a motorboat burble now. Joe checked the gauges. All seemed ready. His left hand gripped the clear plastic steering wheel while his right shifted the chrome stalk, then he pressed the pedal. The engine noise swelled, and the car crept off oleander like a ship off its dock. He turned onto the small road and made his way to its intersection with the larger. Within moments the heavy car was rolling easily towards the expressway, dust sailing off behind.

Traffic was light at the intersection but the signal changed to red as he approached. He stopped between a shiny new Cadillac and a yellow beer truck, and peered out of his dirty windshield. A woman in a Volkswagen minivan was on the other side of the intersection, waiting for the signal to change. Joe squinted and stared. The woman was younger, and reminded him of Rose in her early years. The face had the same shape, and her hair the same grey streaks. His mouth tightened inward with frustration at the memory.

One, laud—

The tic hit him. He cleared his throat and turned his head, and using the motion to check to the left his eyes caught the green signal for cross traffic. With the sun's reflection off the Cadillac's chrome Joe mistook it for his own light. He nodded obediently and stepped on the accelerator while trying to remember. *One, laud ... the laundry thing*—he began, as the Packard began moving ahead. *Two ... sheets; three ... bleach ... no ... knives ... wait ... Merde! One, laud ... the laundry thing*, he thought to himself.

He was almost to the other side when he realized the minivan hadn't moved. *Two, sheeting*, he thought, but as his mind worked the list his eyes registered the driver's expression. Her eyes were open wide now, her mouth too, and her hand was coming up. *Is she ... waving? What the hell does she want?*

There was a burst of skids a split second before a violent explosion knocked the Packard sideways. Joe's eyes lost sight of the woman and the minivan, but his mind went on with fading momentum. *One,* he thought, but the number came without meaning. He heard dim shouts and tried to turn his head, but the voices faded to a tiny pinpoint of murmur, the murmur faded, and the light went out of his eyes.

Nathan Locke made many mistakes in his life before the big man had the good sense to marry a tiny woman named Lou. The nickname was one of few informal parts of the young woman, who made up for her small size with great strength and strictness, and who, despite fierce organization of her world, could show a charming smile whenever she wanted to. Given her looks it was understandable Nathan fell for her, but given his nature it was remarkable she did for him.

His father had been an excellent Idaho carpenter (one of two skills Nathan inherited) who spent most of his life drunk (that being the other), until one unsober morning, while on their way to church, the elder Locke drove the family into the Snake River. Only Nathan survived, and with the first war rumbling closer the seventeen year old and a drinking buddy lied their way into the Navy. The rigid military was probably good for both men, but shortly after armistice each was discharged for drunken brawling; Nathan landed more or less on his feet, and in between drinking binges found carpentry work with a local construction company.

Nathan first laid eyes on Lou after he and his friend had taken in a Hickok Saturday matinee and decided to experience some of the Wild Bill world on horseback. She was helping guests mount up at her Father's riding stables, and was dressed, despite its mostly western theme and tack, in a thoroughly English outfit—tailored white shirt, English boots and tan breeches. One look at those breeches and Nathan forgot all about Wild Bill Hickok. Lou Norred was surely the most beautiful woman he'd ever seen, though she also turned out to be one of the most stand-offish. Nathan was, however, as determined as a stubborn man can be, and though he'd never once before sat even a Western saddle he signed up for every one of her English jumping classes.

That was a strange sight, the line of young English-clad female riders interrupted by a tall Levi-clad construction worker, but he was a decent looking and polite young man who dismounted to replace knocked down cavalettis with an old-fashioned courtesy that grew on Lou. But Lou was nothing if not cautious. Nathan asked her out after his first class and, though she refused, asked again the next week, and the next, until finally, after a month of gauging his manners and demeanour she finally agreed. He took her in his dusty pickup truck to see the movie *You Can't Take It With You,* and though she told him at dinner that he drank too much wine, and allowed only a kiss on her cheek when he dropped her at her door, she agreed when he asked her out again the following week, and agreed again every week after for the next month.

By that point Nathan was thoroughly smitten. On their fifth date he took her to another movie called *Sweethearts* and at dinner after, with his third glass of wine, he signalled the waiter, who immediately brought in a bouquet of flowers. Nathan then got out of his chair, down on the proverbial knee, and in front of a dozen other patrons asked for her hand in marriage.

It didn't go as he planned.

"I'm not marrying anyone with drink on their breath," Lou said coldly.

"It's just wine, Lou," he said, getting up, embarrassed.

"Which wine are you talking about?"

"What do you mean?"'

"Is it this expensive bottle you're serving me with or the cheap one you drink before you pick me up?"

"Come on, Lou!"

"I won't marry anyone who needs liquor to ask for my hand."

"It was just a little."

"You've been having a little every time we go out, and every time you come to class."

Nathan was quiet, thinking, but then he said, "I can change."

"Sure you can, until we marry, then you'll change right back because you think you can have it whenever you want. It doesn't work that way, Nathan."

"I promise."

"Promises mean nothing when you're drinking. Will you climb Everest for me too? Swim the ocean? It's saying you'll follow any new road as far as you can see it, which really just means until it bends."

He thought about her words for a moment, then nodded, took the forty dollar bottle of wine, and turned it over in the wine bucket. As the liquid gurgled out, he drained his glass in the bucket and pulled his water glass close to replace it.

They dated three more times, with him stone cold sober on each, before he proposed again. This time she accepted, and two weeks later she announced to the disbelief of family and friends that she and Nathan had run off and done it. They were married. Just like that. Her Father especially was dismayed, but Nathan surprised them all—everyone but Lou, that is, for during the five weeks he was student and suitor she was sure she saw something they couldn't.

And her instincts were right. Nathan never took another drink; he worked longer hours and spent every remaining minute with her. They spent little time with others, but were occasionally seen on walks together, usually her talking and him listening, and the two always holding hands. And though their differences sometimes led to quarrels, the magic of compromise allowed her firm hand to straighten some of his crooked lines, and his patient one to soften her edges, until it was clear the marriage had made its halves a better whole.

Their first major challenge came with the birth of their child, because Molly came with the twin difficulties of cerebral palsy and an extra chromosome. They were good parents and tried to adjust, often in ways that meant more work and less sleep, until Lou became convinced they'd made another mistake. "We need to stop this," she said when he came in just after midnight.

"Stop what?" he sighed, slipping off a dirty boot. The lines around his eyes were deep with fatigue and perspiration.

"Our hours, yours especially."

"Remember what you said about schools? This is the only way we can get her into the private system, Lou."

"They've got decent programs in public schools now, and we don't need this house ..." she said, putting her small hand on his pant leg. It was bleached with fume and cement. "We can move back to an apartment. We can even get a trailer. We need more rest, and more time together."

"That'll come, baby. We just need to stick with it a little longer."

She insisted, but he resisted, for selling the home was a greater step back than Nathan could stand as a man, and they had their second big argument. When tempers cooled, neither retreated so much as simply changed tactics. He tried to take more time off, and she kept hinting here and nudging there. In the end they stayed in the small home with the big mortgage, and Molly went to the better school.

But Nathan took their talk inside himself, and kept it brewing there, until the day Joe Martini died.

His spirits were as high as ever that day, for he was on a mission that had taken two years of effort. It was a little thing that started it. While searching for a used stroller for Molly he and Lou wandered into a collective, and idling along behind he caught her eye drift across a glass case, blink back, and suddenly, *bang*, there it was, a brief glimpse of genuine admiration that showed she'd

25

seen something she really, truly admired. But it was a fleeting moment, for in the next second she caught him watching and reined herself back to a 'I'm fine with what we've got expression', as if nothing had happened.

He gunned his truck and grinned, thinking back on it, but then set his jaw. Their first argument still bothered him.

"I can fix it," he'd said about a twelve year old Auburn, on her first birthday after their marriage. The paint was chipped and the leather torn, but it ran better than their truck.

"We can't afford it Nathan," she sighed.

"I'll put in a little more time on weekends and we can pay it off in … five, maybe six months."

"We talked about this, Nathan. We're going to have kids. Our plan—"

"The president said two cars in every garage, honey."

"He brought us this depression—"

"You won't have to use the bus anymore," he interrupted.

"The bus is fine."

It was early enough on their path together that he slipped into an 'I'm the man' tone, which was the worst thing he could have done. Though less than half her husband's size, Lou was easily as stubborn as he, and the argument lasted several days.

Nathan forced his mind back to the collective, and to the smile he'd seen Lou smile that day, as he pulled onto the expressway. On this matter he wouldn't be swayed. Besides, he'd done it. He had squirreled away more than enough money, for a month after they were in the collective he went to Lou with the special project his boss asked him to work. "It's two years of just five more hours a week," he promised. "Then I get promoted to

26

foreman with shorter hours and more pay," he said, without telling her the raise was already coming into his pocket.

"It's already too many hours!"

"I'll never have to work as much again."

"They always say that," she said, eyes flashing with disappointment.

"They mean it this time."

"They *always* mean it!"

It took seeing her reaction, which was hard, and siphoning off the extra money for two years, which was easy. A smile crept to his mouth. He'd even made enough to begin a search for what he knew was a pipedream: his wife's everlasting wish to someday find a childhood friend, someone named Laura. There'd been only two mentions of the name, only one in which she'd added the girl's last name—Spinali—but as with her expression in the collective, Nathan tucked it carefully into his list of '*things I can do for my beautiful wife*', or rather, things he could try. Two days ago he'd suggested they splurge on birthday dinner at her favourite restaurant. He'd have the one present brought in on a desert plate. She'd open it, the smile would reappear, and before she could assemble objections he'd explain not just his financial plans, but that he'd begun the search for Laura.

He made his way into the collective's dirt lot, filled with excitement, and strode through the old wooden doors and stepped across to the counter. It was still there, resting among a group of newer pieces which paled next to this one. *Hell of a thing,* he thought, as he saw it again. The owner approached, eyeing his soiled jacket and Levis warily.

"May I help you?" she asked. Her blonde hair was neatly coiffed.

"I'll take that," he said, and he pointed.

For a moment she seemed unsure whether he was robbing her. When it appeared he wasn't she said, "It's ... it's on hold."

"I know. I paid a deposit."

She blinked at that, but retrieved a card from behind the necklace. "Are you Nathan Locke?"

"Yes Ma'am."

"It's a pretty expensive piece ..." she began, but he was pulling a thick fold of fifties from his pocket. She retrieved a felt board, lifted the necklace and arranged it in a graceful arc on the soft black.

"It's such beautiful work," she said.

Seeing it this much closer he felt a little unsteadied. The single emerald wasn't particularly large, but it was the deepest, shiniest green he'd ever seen, and was bordered on either side by three glittering diamonds of lessening size, and the silverwork! His carpenter's eyes settled on the tiny rope and filigree arcs that lifted and clutched the stones with elegant precision.

"Who made it?" he asked, counting out the money.

"I don't know. St. Vincent's consigns me pieces from time to time, and sent me several a few months ago."

He put the last bill on the stack and stood back. There was a year and a half of fifties on the glass counter, and the roll was down to a single folded remainder. He'd use that for dinner this evening. He'd give her the meal, and the present, and the deposit slip showing the rest of the money, and she'd give him back the priceless smile, and if she wasn't too tired later, maybe more.

The woman found a box of blue velvet, pinned the ends and middle of the necklace into an arc, and tied the box with a silver ribbon. She put it in a brown paper bag.

Nathan felt a little wild as he left the store. He made it to the expressway and hurried past other cars, and was well ahead of them as he drove into the intersection at Magdalena. He was imagining what he'd tell her when it happened, and never saw the Packard. Lou's smile, and how it brightened his world, were his last thoughts.

PART ONE

Arizona, 1968

CHAPTER ONE

April 14, 1968

People sometimes returned to Laura as memories do in dreams, so vivid they were alive, right there in her room. When she awoke they'd break apart and mostly disappear, but shards remained to litter her mind—parts of a face, a sentence someone spoke, an emotion they left. She clung to these bits, even ugly or frightening ones, as you might to an only friend, fitting both bad and good into a mosaic she'd started years ago. It began as a simple story with a modest plot, but years of confinement and thousands of dreams added enough body and soul that it gained life of its own, one with far more mood and much greater vitality than her own dismal world. Over countless solitary hours, months and years its fiction became her truth, its truth became her refuge, and when moonlight arrived to light up her friend, she'd tell it to her friend, and her friend would listen.

Last night the dream was of the captain and their first time together. God, how long ago was that? He was at his table, reading a paper when she was brought in. When she woke after she remembered the smell—a fragrance so different from that in her room, so fresh and clean despite the touch of spilt wine. The captain ignored her at first, and she stayed by the door, watching as his hand reached out to something—what was that? In the dream she realized he was eating, oblivious to her, and as it went on she remembered the wonder of that moment, the Why am I here while he hasn't finished his meal? He picked up a knife, hacked a chunk of dark bread, then cut a slice of soft cheese, dipped the bread in his wine glass, folded it around the cheese and with the wrap in one hand returned to the newspaper.

Her eyes went to the knife. It was silver and glittered, and small, but in the dream it grew until she saw its serrations clogged with bits of cheese. Then the dream changed and it shrank back, back to the table where it waited with everything else—the smell, the cold of the room, and she held her breath as the captain ate. She kept her breathing quiet, drawing in air softly, letting it out slowly, hoping she might somehow disappear into thin air, but then he finished.

He stood, wiped his hands on his pants and looked her over. "Let's get you started," he said. And in the dream she remembered that other instant of wonder, the question that came and went so quickly in her mind, whether the words meant some small relief or some great anxiety, but then he took a rope from the chair and came towards her, and the dream answered itself.

I was a young lawyer when I first began work on Mrs. Locke's case. My boss said her friends used to call her Lou, but she'd outlived most of them and I more often heard her addressed as 'Mrs. Locke'. That's what I called her, when we finally met. She was in her last years, trying to carry out a promise she'd made nearly seventy years before to a friend everyone assumed was probably long dead. It was the kind of childhood thing kids make—to be pals forever, to never give up on the other—but some combination of heart or DNA or whatever makes us do such things made Mrs. Locke hold onto the promise until her father, her husband, her daughter and her prime were long gone. She probably figured there was nothing left for her to do in life, though the better part of her must have known that by then it was far too late.

That's what I concluded when I first read her file, and I was in no mood to waste time on another geriatric whim. Most of Father's clients were wealthy older folks who had no idea what a lawyer was really for, and rich enough that they didn't have to care; in addition to their real estate and trust predicaments, which I had become pretty good at unravelling, they liked having young lawyers drive them to appointments, do their shopping, and pick up their dry cleaning. It added importance to the mundane parts of their lives, I suppose. One of the last clients I had before getting Mrs. Locke's assignment insisted I take her toy poodle out for daily walks.

"James will give you her leash and a plastic bag, and some tissues to clean up after her," she said, with the same tone you'd use to tell a child to tie their laces. I wasn't particularly patient in those days, and to be honest was the boss' somewhat arrogant son. So I asked if she shouldn't have James do it, instead of paying five hundred an hour for me to. She replied, "How about you quit talking back and just do what you're told?" So I walked out on her.

She called Father and he called me, and down from Mt. Olympus came the lesson that clients worth a quarter million in yearly fees were entitled to have a first year lawyer do anything they wanted, including walking their poodles. And since Father was not someone you crossed unless you had a survival plan ready, I became a dog walker. Barely a year into my legal career I was already sick of it.

Until I realized what was really in store with Mrs. Locke's case my only reprieve from the boredom was another old client named Melchior Quarrato, who'd killed someone and wanted me to help with his defence. His wife answered a knock on Christmas Eve of '66, and found a particularly insolent delivery boy there with a package from the Quarrato's son. The gift was Mr. Quarrato's old service revolver, cleaned and fitted into a lovely rosewood case with six rounds of ammunition. While Mr. Quarrato fetched a tip Mrs. Quarrato caught the dishevelled rat try to pocket a silver ashtray from the foyer. There was a struggle, during which she fell and hit her head. She died on the spot. When Mr. Quarrato returned the delivery boy was laughing, so he loaded two Christmas bullets and fired both. I would second chair his trial on murder charges, but then Mrs. Locke took up her old promise, and took my trial away.

"For a *missing person's* case!" I complained when Mr. Oneal, my father's partner, gave me the news. "I've done everything on Mr. Quarrato's case. I'm ready. He's expecting *me* to be there … to help try it." It was self-serving but true. Once Mr. Quarrato found out I was a vet too, not a Guadalcanal hero like him but a brother of sorts, he began asking for me, even called to talk at odd hours. I'd done most of the groundwork on his case so far, attended all the hearings, completed all discovery and finished most of the preparation for the upcoming trial. Though untested, I was eager and ready to help one of our firm litigators handle the trial.

"Charlie can take another associate to work on Mr. Quarrato's case," Mr. Oneal said firmly. "I need you to help me."

"It's just a missing person case! Anybody could do it! A private investigator could do it!"

"She's tried three, but none of them got anywhere. Her friend has been missing almost forty years."

"So it's hopeless! Her friend is gone, dead, lost! Tell her to save her money."

"She doesn't care about the money. She's already given us a retainer."

"Give it back," I snapped.

Mr. Oneal looked at me sharply, but for the moment said nothing. "I know what you've done on this case," he finally said, sadly, "but your father wants me to help her."

With that I knew my trial was gone. Father was the involuntarily retired founder of our firm, a fighter who cut through the morass of Phoenix lawyers and cases to become an icon in Arizona's legal world. A request from him was like a command from George Washington. I let out a deep sigh, but Mr. Oneal went on.

"Your father grew up with her father, Hank, and knew Nathan, her husband. They *both* asked Maurice for help on this a long time ago, but then Hank died, Nathan was killed, and she spent the next three decades helping her daughter."

I sighed. "What was wrong with the daughter?"

"Molly had a lot of problems, cerebral palsy, Down's syndrome. But she died three months ago, so Mrs. Locke looked up your dad, and he understood enough that he wants us to help her, without charge, if need be, though she insisting on paying," he said, leaning back in his chair. "She's paying three times our usual rate, with a million retainer—"

"Good Lord!"

"And she'll pay another million if we find her, even if that happens tomorrow."

"*Two million* for a missing person case!" I said, feeling bitter that such an outrageous fee would become the obstacle coming between me and Mr. Quarrato's trial.

"She's not … *wealthy* wealthy," Mr. Oneal added. "Your father got her a large settlement on her husband's case, and her father had something. She's probably got about five million, but says she'll spend it all to find her friend. I told her the retainer is too much, but she's convinced more money brings better effort. I said every one of our clients gets our best, and she told me," he said, allowing a wry smile, "that we probably give that bullshit to everyone."

"How long have you known about this?"

"Your father called last week." He hesitated, eyeing me. "I had a lot of trouble figuring it out—I don't think he's doing so well."

"What do you mean?" I said, more from politeness than interest. Father and I were estranged, and my feelings about him were so strong that I was only mildly sympathetic when his retirement was forced by early Alzheimer's. Mr. Oneal's mention of his condition, though, reminded me of how strange it was that the two men ever became partners. Father—the "great" Maurice Rankin—grew up on the streets, while Oneal came from a world where you wore ties in elementary school. Their paths crossed in law school and despite differences—or maybe because of them—they became friends, then partners, then best men at each other's weddings and eventually even godfathers to each other's children. It was always assumed one of them would ultimately eulogize the other, and lately it seemed clear Mr. Oneal would be the one speaking; I'd heard rumours that Father's long time house maid was a stranger to him now, and that despite being told not to, Father sometimes snuck out, still dressed in pyjamas, to ride his horse. Twice he'd gotten lost, and search parties had to go out and find him.

"I had trouble understanding what he was getting at, but it's clear he considers Mrs. Locke's matter unfinished business." Mr. Oneal continued, "We have the investigators' notes and a file on this from twenty-five years ago, but there's not much in either. I spoke with his doctor last night, and this morning Mrs. Locke came in and explained the rest."

"And who's this friend she's looking for?"

"A daughter of Italian immigrants, a woman named Laura Spinali. They landed a couple hours east of here in the early 1900s. It's where Maurice lived before you were born. He and Mrs. Locke's family knew the girl, but they're all gone except for her and Maurice. We'll go back over the usual steps, but probably need to track down the heirs of witnesses, check old records, papers, and periodicals. Maurice's assistant suggested we pay him a visit to find out more, thinks seeing us might help settle his mind, but the doctor says we should do it soon."

"Where is he?"

"At the ranch in Virginia. We'll fly out to see him tonight." He glanced at his watch as I stared. Everyone knew I had no desire to see my father again, but it didn't seem to matter to Mr. Oneal.

"I've set up a meeting for you with Charles and his staff in thirty minutes," he said. "Give them the Quarrato matter, and set up a meeting for them with the client. Then go home. Pack three days' worth of things and be back here in two hours."

CHAPTER TWO

He led her through a maze of doors and corridors, and finally outside. The sun was blinding. She stumbled and fell before they got to the hose. That day it happened once, but in the dream she fell over and over again. Each time he pulled her up, but then she'd fall again, and he'd pull again, and it kept happening until the dream collided with reality. He pushed her against the wall, let out enough rope to be out of the spray, then disappeared in the stunning water.

The stream came so hard and cold, and so delicious. She rubbed her hands through her hair, trying to separate its matted strands, but her fingers caught, and in the dream she couldn't get them loose. The captain tossed her a bar of soap and began to yell.

"Your face!" he shouted over the spray. Her hands came free, and she obeyed. She began with her forehead and cheeks, her nose and chin, then moved lower, between her neck and the top of her gown. In the dream she remembered how the rest began, how water cascaded farther down and wet the gown against her body, how she tried to stop it by bending forward to let the gown hang loose, and how the water's spray defeated her. That struggle became the dream, and losing it took over her mind. The gown changed from friend to enemy, and he was changed with the effect. He *became distracted by, then intent on spreading it, until he finally shouted for her to remove the gown.*

She grunted refusal but he focused the spray so it came sharp as an icy sword. Then, finally, she held up her hand to surrender. From there the dream was all memory, and filled her mind with the feeling of that day, until she woke. Then the dream broke apart and its pieces drifted away—all but one fragment, the memory of her gown, dirty and rumpled and wet, tossed to a well of sandy ground.

It was still dark when we landed at the Shenandoah Airport. We were greeted by an attractive young Japanese female dressed in western clothing whom Mr. Oneal introduced as 'Jenny'.

"I will be at your disposal," she said, in perfect English. I don't remember much else of what she said, but I definitely recall that although I was in a foul mood then, Jenny struck me as one of the more beautiful women I'd ever seen. She was short, perhaps just over five feet tall, dressed in a long leather skirt and trim blouse, with long dark hair and a reserved appearance. She led us to a gleaming silver Bentley. As we drove out of the airport it became clear that she knew why we'd come, and that she wanted to help, but just exactly how she knew that or precisely what we'd accomplish out there wasn't yet clear to me.

Frankly, I didn't much care; the farther I got from my old client Mr. Quarrato, the more irritated I became at any involvement with the new one, and the closer I came to seeing my father the more resentment I felt for him. As the Bentley turned off the freeway and into the countryside surrounding his ranch I wasn't thinking of the aging Mrs. Locke anymore, or even the old Mr. Quarrato—just the fact I'd see Father again.

He had been as much an icon as Mr. Oneal still was, though in a wilder, even violent way. His crumbling faculties eventually side-lined him from trial work, but their pinnacle—or nadir, depending on your point of view—was the defence of a doctor charged with murdering his wife. Enough of the prosecution's case went public that everyone called for the doctor's scalp, but Father's brutal courtroom tactics destroyed enough preconceptions that the doctor was found not guilty.

It was one of those seeming miscarriages where a guilty client walked, and enough bedlam ensued after the verdict was read that the bailiff, whom my father had represented in a divorce, took him and the doctor down a back stairway to avoid a riot waiting in the hallway. The only problem, and what seared things into everyone's memory, was that the dead woman's sister was waiting in the stairwell with a loaded revolver. Before the bailiff could react she shot her brother-in-law dead; then she handed the pistol to Father and spoke the next day's headline: "Now you can get me off."

But however others viewed him; to me he was mostly the parent and rarely the pal, always pushing so hard that I never felt like a satisfactory son. It grew so bad that I resented not just his strictness but even his success, especially after mother died in an accident. That happened after an argument they had. I knew it wasn't Father's fault, but for some reason I blamed him for it. My mother was a very kind and tender woman, but when she died, rather than softening his role to add some of her gentler influence, Father just hardened his own. He was strict, even rigid, in everything: I was always doing chores—the yard, the floors, the dishes; there was no television allowed in our home, just a lot of books; we never wore jeans, always slacks; and it was never 'Dad' always 'Father' or 'Sir'.

For a while after mother died I felt sorry for him, but pretty soon my resentment overwhelmed everything else, and by the time I became a teenager, we were battling, almost all the time. Often it was over issues I kindled, mostly because Father never changed his ways. He planned out everything, my chores, homework, college, my career, and would have done the same with my choice of law school had I not finally exploded.

It happened the day after my acceptance to Yale law school came in the mail. I saw that more as an escape from him than an opportunity for a great education, but he insisted on an Arizona school to keep me close. We argued for hours but he wouldn't budge, so the next day I went down to a Phoenix recruiting office and enlisted in the army instead.

He was sure I'd lost my mind, but it took being away for those three years before I truly found any part of it. By the time I got out he'd aged immeasurably; he was much greyer, far weaker, and backed off enough that he finally, grudgingly agreed when I went to Yale for law school. I worked summers as a clerk in Father's firm, but for Mr. Oneal and not him.

The last time I saw him he and Mr. Oneal were preparing for Father's last trial, working in the large conference room with coffee in the mornings and whisky late at night. I remember walking past the night before his final argument and seeing Father's profile looking up at Mr. Oneal. It was sad, not because he was losing a case they thought he'd win, but because his granite profile had cracked. He looked broken, and it got worse after the verdict.

I purposely stayed away even after it was announced, and after he left the firm I never flew out to visit. This trip would be the first time I'd seen him in almost two years.

The ranch he retired to was in the parts of the Virginia foothills that are broken only by white fencing. As we drove along Jenny pointed out the first part of his property, but we passed another five miles of oak studded meadow before the trees cleared, horses began to appear, and the fence parted for a large but simple front gate. We entered under a 'Rankin' sign done in metal lariat script and rocked along more than a mile of what seemed to be pasture, then dipped back into another three miles of oak and scrub brush before the drive opened towards a brick estate set in moss-draped oak. The grounds glowed with lights that showed a number of outlying structures built in the same Georgian style as the main house, including a huge brick barn off to the left.

As we drove up I noticed a man seated casually at the bottom of the broad front steps. He was dressed in worn western gear and a dingy hat. At first I thought he was a hired hand, but it was Father. He looked much thinner than I remembered, and seemed to hesitate when we got out of the Bentley. He eventually recognized Mr. Oneal, then embraced him, as if everything was fine, but didn't recognize me.

"Father," I finally said. He squinted at me; then shook his head. I wondered if he was angry, but he was confused. I started forward to embrace him, but he backed away, as if startled. So I just shook his hand; he seemed more comfortable with that, but still didn't recognize me. He turned to lead us into the main house, but slowed as he approached the broad front porch, paused before the first step and stared down, as if it was somehow unfamiliar. He backed away, then turned around and waved us to the car.

"Jenny, let's go around back," he said. She nodded; we got back in the Bentley, but when she put the car in drive he changed his mind again, and told her to take us to 'the ridge'. So she turned and we drove back out the long driveway, and headed further down the road. After a mile we turned onto a small road which led up the eastern hills. For the next twenty minutes the Bentley's headlights swept back and forth up a long set of switchbacks.

I remember how quiet it was, that drive. I tried a couple times to ask Father how he was, but he held up his hand as if he needed silence to guide our travel, and peered forward with a little anxiousness. It was strange, seeing him that way, but it seems we were headed the right direction, because Jenny got no further instructions from him until we reached the crest, passed two turnouts and finally got to a long area of grassy overlook.

"Here!" he called out. "Here, here!" he said again, but Jenny was already slowing the Bentley. She turned off, drove us bumpily over a stretch of thick grass and stopped on a downhill slant just as the first rays of sunrise broke from behind us.

Father burst out of the car, shouting, "Come on," over his shoulder, and started towards the edge of the crest. We caught him at the top of a slope that fell away to forest, then dropped two thousand steep feet to a meadow at the valley floor. I still remember him looking out at that remarkable view, and appreciating why he liked it, even at that time of morning.

The dull light showed shades of fresh growth everywhere along the twisting river that was in the bed of the valley, but there were grey bits of upturned trees along the water's edge, partially enveloped by a meadow that rippled in the breeze.

I remember it was cold. Very cold. I remember distinctly the early chill a breeze that cut over the ridge and right through my clothes. I was dressed in a business suit, and before long was freezing. Father wore nothing but Levis and a shirt worn thin as tissue, yet he seemed unaffected by anything but his age—and the dementia. He looked emaciated compared to how I remembered him from the office, and tired, but he didn't shiver once while we were up there. No, his problems seemed mostly memory and weakness, but not the cold. He forgot so much, and had to rest his weight on one leg and to shift from time to time, but he never seemed cold.

It was still quiet once we got out, as if we were waiting for something—for what I didn't have any idea, and for several minutes the only sound was the breeze rushing past. I eventually looked at Jenny, wondering what the hell we were doing. She shook her head as if warning me to be patient. But then, finally, even Mr. Oneal tried to start things by pretending to cough. It was a little thing, and Father didn't respond. It was Mr. Oneal's turn to look at Jenny. She shrugged as if then even she was unsure what to do.

Mr. Oneal tried again. He turned to Father, and asked, "Are you with us, Maurice?" Father shifted weight from one leg to the other, but it only creased his trousers to another pattern. Nothing else happened. After several further seconds Mr. Oneal glanced at me, then put his hand on Father's shoulder and said, "We came to help Hank Locke's daughter."

That finally did something. Father nodded slowly, but from the dazed look on his face I wondered if he picked up anything but the tone of what Mr. Oneal had said. He was quiet again.

Mr. Oneal tried a third time. "Can you help us find Louisa Locke's friend Laura? Laura Spinali? Her mother was Sophia Spinali?"

That did something. Father nodded more firmly, and without turning towards us said the last name softly: "You mean Sophie, not Sophia."

"That's right, Maurice," Mr. Oneal said encouragingly. "You called me a couple weeks ago and said something about her being beaten, and that her daughter Laura was born with some problems?"

Father glanced at his bare wrist as if he had a watch on. "I talked to a fella ... maybe an hour ago," he said, and a little clarity seemed to come into him. He turned towards us, about to speak, but the movement brought the first rays of morning sunlight to his face. He squinted, then shifted his ragged hat to set a wedge of shade across his eyes. But that simple act broke the moment. He looked around, as if searching for something, then turned his head back to the valley, leaned forward and peered, and was quiet again.

"Maurice," Mr. Oneal said softly, "do you remember Laura Spinali?"

"Of course," Father said, regaining a little focus. He repeated the first name—"Laura"—to himself, and that repetition brought him even further back. But his face tightened, and he suddenly seemed sad. "That poor girl," he whispered. He turned away and was quiet, then brushed roughly at his eyes.

"Maurice?" Mr. Oneal asked.

Father waved backwards to keep us away, then crouched down and clutched at his face. He was crying.

I was stunned. I'd never seen my father cry, but here he was weeping at the mention of a girl's name. He coughed roughly, obviously embarrassed. Jenny knelt

46

and put a hand on his shoulder. She pointed into the valley.

"Would you look at that," she said.

We turned and looked, and there was something – something moving, down on the floor of the valley, dark forms, on the far side of the river, some kind of animals, all the same basic size and shape. Even at this distance you could see some raising their heads.

Father's hands came off his face. "That mare's ready to foal," he said. He hitched himself up and stood, and leaned forward for a better look. "There's a couple more over there," he said, motioning. He pointed out more foals, then older animals, then looked beyond them for a perimeter, a fence. He eventually pointed to a split rail fence in the distance. It was old, and broken in places.

"We need to get to fencing," he murmured, glancing up at the sky.

"It's not your herd," Jenny said softly.

"Doesn't matter."

"I thought you can't ride anymore," I said.

Jenny frowned at me, and a little indignation came into Father. He began to speak, but hesitated, eyes still on the animals. They seemed to distract him. He went quiet for another moment, then he whispered, "I've seen this before." His voice came up. "I know I've seen it before."

What? I thought. This made no sense. Of course he'd seen it. But Jenny simply asked, "Have you, Maurice?"

"… I swear to God I know this place."

"Do you?" she said, as if talking to a child.

I was losing patience. This seemed a waste of time. "Don't you live right down there?" I said. Father whirled on me.

"What are you talking about?"

I stammered, "I'm sorry … I thought … me …"

But Jenny patted his shoulder again. "Look again, Maurice," she said, and she took his arm and turned him. He went back to the view, and almost immediately he began to nod.

"I know this place ..." he said. Suddenly he cried out, "It's that picture! It was what? It ...it was ...sixty years ago? Must've been ...wait. They'd just hung the fella who shot President Garfield. It was ..."

"You mean... That was 1882," Mr. Oneal said.

"About then. I was ... eight. My first boss had an old National Geographic. It was open on his desk, and there was a picture of this valley ..."

I groaned inwardly. Father was in the land of *non compos mentis,* on a subject that made absolutely no sense.

"... First time I ever realized there was more to life than Arizona desert. It stayed with me for weeks—hell, it vined in and out of me all those early years. Goddamn. This is it!" he exclaimed, and waved both arms towards the grandeur at our feet. "It's Virginia!"

"Quite a sight," Jenny agreed patiently. Father turned towards her.

"We should go here, Jenny."

"We are here, Maurice," she said patiently, and she patted his shoulder tenderly.

"What the hell you talkin' about?" he asked in a low voice.

"You're here. We're at the edge of the Shenandoah Valley, Maurice. You're here. You live here."

Father looked surprised, then disappointed. He looked disconsolately at his boots. "This thing gettin' worse?"

"You'll be all right, Maurice," she said, taking hold of his hand.

I began to wonder who this woman was, not just because he seemed to rely on her, nor because she was attractive, but she was one of only a handful of people I'd ever known to address Father by his first name. For some reason it made me sad. I still remember feeling suddenly sorry for the old man.

Jenny motioned Mr. Oneal to speak. He took an offhand tone.

"Say, Maurice, do you remember whatever happened to Sophie Spinali's daughter, Laura?"

For several seconds there was no response, but then Father nodded without looking at us.

"You came … you came to help with Hank's daughter?"

"That's right," Mr Oneal said, a little eagerly. Father kept nodding, but his face tightened with resolve, and he seemed to cling to the question now. He looked at the non-existent wrist watch again, and spoke with a harder edge. "I spoke with the guy about an hour ago."

"With who, Maurice?" Jenny asked.

"Arlo …"

"Arlo what?" I asked, pulling a pad and pen.

"Arlo something … I talked to Arlo maybe an hour ago."

"Who's Arlo?" Mr. Oneal asked, but there was no reply, until Father turned slightly, and stunned us.

"Arlo Moffatt. He said she murdered someone."

"Who did, Maurice?" Mr. Oneal asked.

"I told you," he said. "Laura did it."

CHAPTER THREE

This dream wasn't finished with her, and kept going for days. They sometimes stayed for weeks, but the very next night this one brought back every detail of how the captain looked later, much later, how the pale stripe of his uniform widened along his thigh and narrowed along his calf, how his undershirt was stained and bunched above a pale fold of belly, and how his half-opened trousers showed a dirty triangle of underwear below his belt. There was even the smell, that mixture of sweat and wine. And then, of course, the realization that despite the matting of her hair and her soiled gown, those months later he still found her attractive. And finally, there was that foolish wonder, her naïve confusion of attraction with affection.

"You want something to eat?" he offered, his words crowded with food. He motioned to a broken wedge of cheese and a tear of Pueblo bread.

She shook her head towards the concrete floor, then gave him a nervous glance. The sight stuck with her all these years, how the tangled glow of dirty hair caught sunlight from the window and made him appear angelic. The halo didn't fit him; but that was something she had yet to learn.

"You aren't hungry?" he mumbled.

She shook her head again. This time her eyes strayed along the limestone floor to the bed, and she wished for her room, and the wall in her room. But there'd been a little recklessness inside her that day, and it came out as resentment.

"What's the matter?" he'd demanded. She didn't answer. He poured more wine but was watching her as he did it; his glass filled too quickly and red spilled over the rim. He fumbled the bottle upright, and then frowned back at her as though she'd done it. "Oh, Christ, tell me."

She fought for control, but her eyes welled. He took a long drink while watching her. She brushed at her face. He caught the gesture and put down the glass like a gavel. "Why are you crying?" he demanded.

She shook her head at the floor.

"Tell me!" he shouted, and he threw a piece of the bread. It bounced off her shoulder.

She struggled against saying anything, but anger took hold and she bent. The grunts came out, acrid noises that loosened more tears.

His jaw began to shift irritably, even before she finished. "You bitch," he interrupted. He shoved himself to his feet. "Ungrateful bitch." She shrank to the door, but he came after her.

When she woke the dream broke apart and began to slip away, leaving only pieces of what happened next. Those parts would go into her story and be told to her friend, those fragments of what he did, what she felt, and another glimpse of the knife, there behind his halo.

Standing there on the crest I wrote '*murder?*' on my notes, but for several moments the only sound was the wind.

"Who did he say she killed, Maurice?" Mr. Oneal finally asked. "Where did this happen?"

Father turned back to the valley and nodded to himself. "They've got him out west—" he began, but his voice trailed off, and several more moments went by with frustrating silence. Jenny finally tried to draw him back out.

"How did you meet her family, Maurice?"

"Whose family?"

"Laura Spinali's."

"At the whorehouse," he said immediately.

"What whorehouse?" Mr. Oneal asked.

"Corporal Mays' whorehouse."

What? I thought, writing but confused.

"It was the corporal's place, Isaiah Mays. His daughter turned it into a whorehouse."

I exchanged looks with Mr. Oneal. He drew in a deep breath. "Go on. What else do you remember?"

But we'd gone on too long.

"I'm tired," Father said, and he turned towards us.

"That's enough for now," Jenny said, and she helped him back to the car.

I was sure then that the trip was a waste of time. What clarity was left inside him had come out so briefly and unpredictably, that an hour on the freezing crest provided absolutely nothing to tell whether Laura was even still alive. And what was this about her having murdered someone?

I was disgusted with what we were doing. I wanted to forget about the Spinalis, to wash my hands of Mrs. Locke, and get back to Mr. Quarrato and my trial. But Mr. Oneal wasn't put off. After Jenny drove us back she put Father into bed and made us breakfast, and though at that point I was ready to give up, Mr. Oneal began to tick off a list of assignments.

"I want you to find out who in government or the private sector might have any records of brothels in Maricopa County before the First World War. Check every newspaper that was in or around Maricopa County then, every hospital, every clinic, every law enforcement agency; check all the city police and county sheriff departments, and see if there are any law firms still around from those days, and whether they had any clients by the names Spinali, Mays or Locke. Check the Army, see if they have anything on a Corporal Isaiah Mays who retired about that time—the father I mean, but also his family—"

"The army won't release anything."

"You still have friends there, don't you?"

"They can't access those materials."

"Then check out the legislation President Johnson just signed—the Freedom of ... something act. It's supposed to have a new process for getting information from the government. Figure it out. Make an application, petition, or whatever is needed. Make it broad as possible, and make one on every conceivable agency."

"That could take months!"

"So start now," he said, without so much as a shrug. "And look for other sources. Find somebody who knows of a historical record of Maricopa County, maybe even who could help find descendants of people who lived around there in those days. There have to be stories floating around somebody's family about a whorehouse, and maybe the people who lived there."

"Aren't we wasting time? I mean, we have better things to do, don't us?"

Mr. Oneal stared at me. "We have a client your father has endorsed, and she's paying a generous fee. So quit thinking about Mr. Quarrato and start concentrating on this. Figure out where else we can search, what other sources we might check, and what other help we may need. Call the office, put together a team, and hire new associates if you need to. I want time and effort spent on this, and right away."

I felt frustrated and angry, and probably sorry for myself. This meant months, maybe a year's work on a hopeless cause, while Mr. Quarrato's case was in the hands of someone who didn't know the first thing about him, and had no need for yet another trial.

"Why don't we just contact the man he mentioned, 'Arlo,' and get what he had?"

"Do that too. Have someone—"

"Mr. Moffatt is dead," Jenny said from behind us. She was bringing in a silver tray of coffee and service.

"But ... Maurice said he talked to him ... he said 'an hour ago'," Mr. Oneal said.

"Maurice doesn't think of time as we do anymore," she replied, filling our cups. "The conversation he's referring to took place about twenty years ago. He spoke with Mr. Moffatt—Arlo Moffatt was his name—in the late forties, I believe."

"How do you know this?" Mr. Oneal asked.

"We lived here after the war. I don't remember the whole story myself—I was only four or five—but my father helped Maurice find Mr. Moffatt, and told me about this later. I remember the story."

"What did he know about the missing girl Laura?"

"I'm not sure of the details, except I believe Mr. Moffatt knew a great deal about the Spinali family."

"You know about the Spinalis?"

"Only that they came from Italy."

"What about Mr. Moffatt?"

"That I know more about. He was a criminal, a murderer and a thief, but he's dead now."

"What was his connection with the Spinalis' daughter Laura?"

"I only know that he knew of the family, and that he knew a lot. But that was …" she shook her head.

"What about the murder?" I asked. "Father said Laura murdered someone."

"I think he's confused. Mr. Moffatt was the murderer."

"Who did he murder?"

"A family. He murdered an entire family."

"Where was he?" Mr. Oneal demanded. "Where did Maurice find him?"

"He was in a prison on Alcatraz Island, in San Francisco. Maurice got permission from the governor and flew out to speak with him."

"But Moffatt's dead now?" I asked.

"He was executed, but before he died he told Maurice a lot about the Spinali family."

"Did Maurice keep notes, maybe keep a file?"

"I wondered about the same things, and searched, but no. There's nothing."

"Do you really think Father may still be able to tell us?" I demanded. My eyes narrowed over her. I continued to wonder at how easily she used his first name, and how she fit into Father's life. She was obviously an employee, but her western clothing, boots, long skirt, though understated, seemed higher quality than that.

"It is hard for him," she said as she poured herself a cup of coffee. "He has his moments, but it is becoming more difficult."

"So we really have nothing," I blurted.

"I said it is more difficult, not that we have nothing," Jenny said quietly, sitting at the table. "It will be hard, but you may have more luck if he asks you to return to the hillside."

"You're kidding!" I said. "We spent almost an hour up there this morning and got nowhere! How will going back help anything?"

"You know of Corporal Mays. You know of Mr. Moffatt. These things came from the effect the hillside has on him."

"You said Moffatt's dead!"

"But he had a son who may know something. Mr. Moffatt's wife and son lived in San Francisco while he was on the island. She died the year after her husband was executed, but the son was in his fifties then, and may still be alive."

"In San Francisco?" Mr. Oneal asked.

She shook her head. "No more. He moved back to Italy after the parents died."

"How do you know all this?" I demanded, but Mr. Oneal held up his hand.

"Do you know how to reach him?"

"I have a number, but they would not speak with me. When Mrs. Locke's daughter died last year she spoke with Maurice, but even then it was hard for him. He tried to tell me about the missing woman—the girl named Laura--but with difficulty. But I remembered my father telling about this search that took place years ago, and about the man in prison, and his son. So when Mrs. Locke contacted Maurice last year I found a law firm in Naples, and they had an investigator who found the man's son—Moffatt's son—and obtained the number. We called … I called, but Mr. Moffatt's son refused to help, or even speak with me. There are still some papers on this in Maurice's library, but I think you'll have to go to Italy to find out what he knows." Her face soured. "He was not a nice man."

"Will you help us find him?" Mr. Oneal asked her.

"Of course," she nodded, "but you will have to go." And they both looked at me.

CHAPTER FOUR

Laura's dreams affected her story just as the story affected her dreams; each nourished the other for days at a time. For the past week the captain came back every night, and every day she worked more of him into the story. Tonight she dreamt of the last night in his bed, of how he made no move to send her away, of his slow-moving breath as he slipped back to sleep, and how, as she held to his chest and his breathing relaxed, the seed of hope came into her; how her eyes flickered up and she grunted a small noise, how his eyes opened slightly, and how violence and hunger were gone from them. And in the dream she remembered thinking that he was satisfied.

Then the noises came back to her, the flexing noises she made, so careful and quietly, how the little sounds paused and began again in small efforts—until he sighed. She remembered how then she'd stopped, but how by then it was already too late.

The side of his mouth curled, and he snorted with disdain. She reacted without thinking and flexed out more sounds, and that set him off.

His eyes opened fully, the disdain fell into disgust, and then he made the sound—quick, sharp, and guttural. She tried blocking it out, but the sound echoed past her defences. He made it again, louder and harder, then again and again, until the echo roared into every cell of her mind. It went on until he tired, and shoved her away, then he sighed and closed his eyes. When he finally slept she slipped off the bed, backed to the wall and, watching him silently, she cried. But at least then she was more careful. Her tears came without noise. They rolled down her cheeks and dripped off her chin, and the only sound was his snoring. And she lifted her head until she could see what was on the table, and decided what would happen.

Today she'd add more to the story, and tonight she'd tell more to her friend. The others would hear and seem reassured, though they understood only the tone, only the murmur, only the feeling.

Jenny set Mr. Oneal up at a desk in the living room and put me in Father's study, where I began to make telephone calls. I called the firm and enlisted three associates with some of my tasks. When I returned to the living room to report on my work, Father was there, seated in a heavy leather chair opposite the desk where Mr. Oneal worked. He looked rested and relaxed, with a cigar and a tumbler of whisky on the table beside him. Jenny sat on the arm of his chair, and, to my surprise, had her hand on his shoulder. It seemed too affectionate, inappropriate, at least to me, but no one else seemed to care. Father was talking. Mr. Oneal was listening; he motioned a pad and pen to me. I took them and sat nearby.

"Go on," Jenny said softly.

"… Hank and I were out of work again. So one day this coloured woman Mays—"

"M A Y S?" I asked. Jenny gave me a warning look, but it didn't seem to matter. Father nodded at my spelling and went on.

"That's right. Her father was Corporal Josiah Mays, of the 54th Cavalry. You know about them?"

The 54th Cavalry! I certainly did. Every veteran does, but I couldn't believe what he was saying. "Buffalo soldiers?"

"Right, Fort Wagner men."

"Fort Wagner! Come on! That was where—"

"Paul!" Mr. Oneal snapped, but it still made no difference. Father waited for the interruption to pass, then went on without a hitch, gathering momentum, nodding his head to emphasize points, looking and sounding much better than before.

"… That's right. Fort Wagner. He got shot there but lived, got shot worse again at San Juan, so they retired him to an old army ranch in Apache Junction. Threw in a couple boxcars next to the siding where they'd drop off broken down stock for the rendering plant. The Corporal fixed the box cars into a diner that served everyone around there, but knackers cuttin' up deadwood horses right out the window of a biscuit and egg place weren't always the greatest for business," he said, now even chuckling, "and Corporal Mays thought some of the horses didn't look so bad off, so he offered to take them for half of what the knacker charged. He could take any horse that weren't bound up with colic and turn them around until their own dam wouldn't remember 'em, and he did. He took the old stock to the ranch and fixed 'em up, then sold them back to the army. Did so well the place came to be called *The Buffalo Horse Ranch.* But then he died and his daughter Isabel had a hard time selling off the horses, wanted to keep them …as *pets*," he said, and his brow wrinkled at the extravagance.

"She was a soft touch, started taking in other hard cases too, mostly women in town who'd been beaten by men or broken by life, I guess, did with them what her daddy had done with horses, fed them, housed them, gave 'em nice clothes and good manners, unless they got old or lazy. Then she'd take a big knife and kill them."

"What!" I cried.

"Just making sure you're awake," Father said, grinning.

"You feeling better?" Jenny asked.

He nodded, then turned to me, and his eyes narrowed. He seemed to catch who I was. "How you doin', Paul?" he asked, as if nothing was wrong.

"Fine, Father," I replied, very unsure of our footing. Father was not often pleasant with me, unless some explosion was just around the bend. Not that he was usually unpleasant, but there was always formal distance between us, something that kept his status as my 'father', never my 'dad'. But now he seemed almost friendly, and his energy was back. Maybe it was the rest, but his strength looked more like I remembered. He was a little thin, sure, but sharp again.

"I'm fine, Father. Go on," I said again, checking my notes. I'd written *"... Brothel—check Maricopa County sheriff. Check health department. Army—Josiah Mays ... White house, ranch? Horses, 20—100 acres, maybe more (?). Other women there. Daisy ..."*

He settled back in the chair and went on.

"But there was a problem keeping horses as pets. Without the money from selling stock Mrs. Mays had to make it some other way. The diner didn't bring in enough, so Daisy, the whore who helped run it, suggested that with all the rooms the ranch had, and the half dozen women who'd been in the trade before, she could start a string of working girls. First Mays

61

wouldn't, but she was stubborn, not stupid, and so long as everyone understood there'd be no fightin' or killin', she agreed.

"The women liked it because of how Mays ran it; she made sure they were treated right and wore nice clothes, and of course they had a good home and good food. Before long the ranch became the best whorehouse in Arizona." He paused, smiling. "The women were proud of it, when most of 'em never figured for pride again. And the men! Man, did they ever come! By the time Mays died every man in Maricopa County had ridden there, without once sittin' a horse."

"How'd you come to be up there?" Mr. Oneal asked.

Father took in a deep breath. "It happened one morning. Hank Norred and I were friends. We met in the shanties. Hank was twenty-four, thereabouts, already married with a nine year old daughter we called Lou— who eventually grew into your Mrs. Locke. I was a little smarter than her daddy, but not by much—least I didn't have kids yet," he said, and he shot a glance in my direction. I stared at him, unsure of what he was thinking, as he went on.

"We were both out of a job, lookin' for work, and we'd heard of the Mays' place, how they didn't have just whores there, but horses too, and a real workin' ranch. So we went. And one day Mrs. Mays and her girls were out on her porch sipping tea and these two dirty kids came walking up her drive. She looked down and yelled, 'What you doin' on my property, boys?' And Hank said, 'Well, Ma'am, I thought you might want to know you got some fencing' down by the road there, and your horses goin' to get out', and Daisy said, 'Horses broke out again,' and Hank offered that we'd fix the fence for free, and if the work was good maybe she could use a couple extra hands? And Daisy asked him, 'What kinda pay you want?' and another of the women said, 'And from which of us you gonna want it?' and they all laughed. Hank said thanks but he was married. So Daisy said, 'Some of our best customers are married.' He said he wasn't married that way and they laughed and said 'We'll see,' like they'd heard that before.

"But Mrs. Mays said sure and we got jobs, mostly fencing and taking care of the horses, but it was good work, and suddenly we weren't bad providers." The tip of his jaw elevated itself for a moment, but then he seemed to catch it as a brag, and tightened it back.

"How did Laura come to be up there?" Jenny asked softly.

"Laura," Father said, and his voice slipped into a sad and confidential tone. "Hank's daughter Lou came home from school one day with a black eye. It was the first day Laura came to her school, and the way she talked and looked, there was a near riot over her. There weren't any special education programs to help kids with that sorta thing, so she was stuck in a regular school with regular kids and teachers, when nothing regular ever fit her.

"But she tried. She raised her hand a couple times in class that first day, but the teacher couldn't understand her grunts, and those sounds set off the rest of the class. A few made pig noises, and laughed at her, and the teacher," he said, shaking his head, "she just smiled like it was kids being kids. So Lou stood up and tried to tell everyone she understood and that Laura had the answers, but the teacher told her nonsense, and gave the whole class a lecture that amounted to saying Laura was *retarded*—" and he said the word with a harder edge.

"Lou stayed at recess to try to explain Laura's side to the teacher, but while she was in there the other kids were out with Laura, out on the playground, and had that poor girl surrounded. They were yellin' 'pig girl' and making snorting noises, tried to make her eat dirt, and pushed her around in a circle until Lou came out and lit into 'em."

He paused, shaking his head. "It's how she got the shiner. Hank had to visit the school later that day. The teacher told him *Lou* was causing trouble, and that if she kept it up she was going to go with Laura into Madonna."

"Madonna?" Jenny said, looking in my direction. I wrote it down.

"That's right. Back then it was called *The Madonna Home for Wayward Girls*. It was for runaways or kids whose parents wouldn't keep 'em. Some of the women from the ranch knew it, and said it wasn't so much a home as it was a jail, with locked doors and doctors more like wardens. But ..." He hesitated, and was quiet. The silence went on for several seconds, and he looked lost.

"Maurice," Jenny said, "you were telling us Mrs. Locke got in trouble because she stood up for Laura?"

He nodded slowly, and seemed to catch the thread. "That's right," he said slowly. "And she told us...about what happened that day, and Mrs. Mays got the idea of getting Laura and her family as more take-ins, even before she found out about what happened to Sophie." He hesitated. It went quiet again, and now the quiet went on more than a minute.

"So what happened to her?" Mr. Oneal asked.

"To who?"

"What happened to Laura?"

Father didn't answer. He was looking down at his boots, and seemed gone again.

I sighed. We were wasting time again. It was frustrating, waiting for some relevant fragment of his mind to drift into his speech. He seemed to grasp at something, but just as quickly lost it, and slapped his leg in frustration. He looked up at Jenny, then glanced at the window. "Maybe we can go up the ridge?"

I groaned, but she patted his shoulder and got up. "Sure, Maurice. I'll get the car," she said. He caught her eye, and something familiar seemed to pass between them. The next thing I knew we were in the Bentley, headed back up the mountain.

CHAPTER FIVE

It was a new dream of an older memory, one with some parts already in her story, but others she'd forgotten. The gaunt men were all around her again, in their dusty breeches and with dirty weapons, staring mostly at her. She stared back, until two officers made their way through the crescent.

"Are you white?" one demanded. He was young and brown, with knife-cut hair. She didn't answer. He took hold of her hair with both hands and yanked the halves to a parting. "You're white!" he announced.

She jerked back, and spat in his face.

"Goddamnit!" he yelled. He struck her with his fist. Her knees buckled. Blood began to run from her nose, but it wasn't enough. When she got to her feet he pulled his revolver and cocked it at her forehead.

"Wait!" the other officer commanded.

"For what?"

"If it's white they'll want it."

"How much?" he asked, his gun still trained.

"Ten if it's female," the officer said, and he pushed the man's revolver down. He pulled a paper from inside his shirt, and scanned the first page. "Male or female?" he demanded.

No one answered. It was impossible to tell.

He motioned. *Another soldier grabbed her arms, a second dropped and held her legs, and a third pulled a knife and held it to her neck. She struggled, cutting herself against the blade as she burst out with fierce grunts, but the lieutenant grasped the front of her shirt and tore it down, exposing her breasts and torso.*

Gasps rose from the circle. Her breasts were full and upturned, but what caught their attention was her disfigurement. Her upper torso was bent heavily left, with the skin tightly taut outside and heavily pleated inside.

"What the hell is this, some kind of injury?" the lieutenant exclaimed, running his eyes over the pleats before they moved back to her breasts.

Then came the part she left out of the story. It was loud and clear, but her friend would never hear it.

"Got to be the Mongoloid," the officer said, looking at his list. She hated that word as much as the tone, but remembered both.

"What the hell is a Mongoloid?"

"A retard. A freak. A retarded person. Like that," he said, motioning.

"How old would you say she is, Janoff?"

"Fifteen, maybe ... seventeen, Captain."

"She's got to be the one they want. Jesus! They'll pay twenty-five dollars."

Low whistles. "Who in God's name would want that?"

"Give her a bath and we'll take her," one of the men called out. There was a ripple of agreement from the others.

The captain read the paper and eyed her, and then he said her name.

67

"There it is, Maurice," Jenny said in a soft voice. We turned. Sunlight had chased dawn off the valley floor and left warmth, and with warmth the herd had spread. We stared, fascinated by the beautiful sight, and except for a breeze rustling the long grass, it was still. After a while Father squinted to get his bearings, leaned back and began talking about the animals.

"It's a mostly young herd," he began, but then he stopped, leaned forward, and exclaimed: "I rode that horse!" The conviction seemed to stagger him. He swayed unsteadily, and Jenny grasped his arm. His head turned towards her, and just that little distraction only added to his confusion. He looked at us, around us and at the shiny car, then back down and at the horses, but without seeing anything familiar. His eyes wandered along the shapes below without remaining at any, then passed across the waving mustard and went upstream, past the broken tree trunks and up the valley, up to its farthest parts, where sunlight changed the river from deep blue to glittering silver.

He finally shook his head and turned to Jenny. "I can't find the damn thing."

"It's there," Jenny said, pointing. I had no idea what they were saying.

"Where?" Father asked, but she turned, and pointed. We all turned, and finally saw. Halfway up the valley, in lodge pole fencing that broke from foothills in a zigzag towards the river, there was a break. A horizontal rail had been broken; both ends angled down into mustard, and on the other side of the opening a mare and foal were grazing peacefully. Father turned as if to leave, "We need to fix that fence."

"It's not yours, Maurice," Jenny replied softly.

"What?"

"The herd isn't yours."

"Doesn't matter," he replied as if by instinct, but she held his arm. He stood, confused again, but now looked down, embarrassed. She let the silence hold him for several seconds, then turned him unsteadily back to the valley and broke it herself.

"Do you hear me, Maurice?" she asked, and she put her arm around his waist.

"Yes," he answered uncertainly.

"Do you remember the Spinali family?"

"'Course I do," he said, and his eyes rose to the distance.

"And their daughter Laura?"

"Sure," he said, but with the name he bit his lip.

"Is she still alive?" Mr. Oneal asked.

Father shook his head and then glanced at his wrist. "I talked to somebody about that ... maybe an hour ago."

"Can you help us find her?" Jenny asked.

"What did I tell you so far?"

"You said she went to the school. You said the teacher and kids were cruel, and that Lou—or Louisa— when she was young Mrs. Locke tried to defend her."

Father nodded slowly. By the time the movement stopped his face held a frown, and the frown stayed while he began to speak. He started slowly, but seemed to gain momentum as he progressed.

"Lou came home late one night, beat up, clothes torn, and told what happened.... She'd fought the other kids in the school, ones who were torturing Laura; but she went too far and said the sheriff had to come and was going to send her and Laura both away. So she took Laura and they ran all the way back to the More'n Other."

"Where?" I asked.

"Where what?"

69

"What is the More'n Other?" Jennie asked him.

"A part of Shanty Town," Father shrugged. "It was where you lived if you weren't allowed anywhere else, everyone there was poor, some more 'n others. Laura's family lived in the more 'n other part, a place with shacks of cardboard and tin. Laura took Lou there when they ran away from the school that day. It's where Lou met Laura's daddy, Gino; and her mother, Sophie. Lou told us about it later, 'bout her folks, but mainly 'bout this girl she met in school. She said Laura was a beautiful child, in the face, I mean, but she'd been injured somehow, with a twisted spine that turned into her throat, like she was always looking over her shoulder; and that broken little girl was always looking over it to watch out for her broken mother," he said sadly. "Lou told us Sophie was even more beautiful than Laura, but lay there half dead, couldn't talk, didn't move hardly at all."

That little part had somehow given him strength, and now he went on in a rush.

"Lou said she asked them what happened to her. Laura's daddy didn't want to tell, but Lou's askin' was always like somebody drilling for oil. So Gino let Laura say what happened but made Lou promise not to tell, not knowing the other problem with Lou."

"Which was?" Mr. Oneal asked.

"Which was that the only trouble Lou ever had keeping secrets was that folks she told never learned to keep their mouths shut."

We smiled at that, but Father seemed serious.

"Where was the school going to send them?" Mr. Oneal asked, motioning to me. I pulled my pen and a pad.

"Madonna," Father said, and he spat with contempt and sharp accuracy just ahead of his boot. "But after Lou told us about Laura and what happened to Sophie the Spinali family became the next life mission for Isabel Mays. She set out to find Sophie and Laura and take care of that family as much as she ever had any whores or horses. We were all goin' out to the More'n Other the very next afternoon, to pick up the whole Spinali family and bring 'em back."

Jenny smiled. My father nodded. Even I felt some sympathy, but then he said, "But we never went, because of what happened with the stampede."

What! I thought, as it got quiet again.

"Tell us," Jenny said.

Father looked around as if to see if anyone else was there, then took in a long breath. "She's dead, you know."

What! I thought.

"She's dead," he sighed.

"Who is, Maurice?" Mr. Oneal asked quietly.

I glanced at Jenny. She waited with the rest of us, but after several moments of quiet she pressed Father's arm and said, "Go ahead, Maurice. Tell us about the stampede. What happened there?"

He looked around again, then lowered his voice.

"Well...The very next morning there was fog lyin' around the ranch like an old blanket. Mrs. Mays and the women came on the porch and sat down with cups of hot tea in the very top of it, with little curls of smoke comin' out of their cups. Then she hollered to me and Hank to let out the horses, so we went up to the barn and started bringing 'em out to the top of the pasture, three and four at a time, back and forth between the barn and pasture until the whole herd was there, sixty-some odd horses, with their heads and manes poking up out of the fog," he said, looking down at the animals below. A smile played with the edge of his mouth, and his voice relaxed to a more normal tone.

"Those old horses were always like kids when they were let out, not sure at first what to do with being out of their stalls, then they'd get excited and start milling around in the herd. After a while one would trot a rickety trot for a little ways, and another would follow and try to kick him—just playing—and run off a ways, and the one kicked would say hell no you don't and start after him. Then a few others would follow and maybe two seconds later every last horse was at a dead run."

He paused, patted the side of his right leg once, then again, and took a deep breath and went on.

"When they ran like that they weren't sixty horses any more, they were a herd, one big river of animals that poured down toward the road, mostly hid under the fog. And we all stood there, because it was a sight to behold, Mrs. Mays and the women stood up and watched, and we all did, we watched and listened, because you could hear the horses even when they were hidden under the fog, and you could feel the ground shake. And we all stood there, admirin' that world, until Mrs. Mays screamed."

He hesitated, frowning across the valley before going on.

"She screamed, and some of the whores screamed, and they pointed, and we turned and looked down where we fixed the fence that first day. And—" He stopped, fighting for control of his voice.

"There was a cart down there with a mule, and a guy maybe a little older than me. He was holding a small woman in his arms, holding her like a child, holding her up to see, and there with them was a pretzel of a girl sitting on the fence. The li'l pretzel was Laura and the others were her parents, her daddy Gino holdin' up his wife, Sophie, to let her see what was happenin'. But they were right at the spot we fixed that first day, right where those horses were headed.

"Lou had told her about Mrs. Mays' horses and what sometimes happened those mornings, how the sight and sound and feel of the horses would go right into you, and Laura thought it might help make her mother better." He shook his head helplessly. "Laura forever hoped for some miracle with her mother, and thought maybe if Sophie saw the horses, and heard them runnin' and felt their thunder, that maybe it'd wake her, or at least that maybe with all that excitement she'd get better. And so she talked her dad into it, and Gino borrowed the cart and they came. So there they were, looking and listening over the top of the fog, as those horses tore down at them, not knowing a train was headed their way..." He stopped, his voice choking.

Jenny stared at him sadly. "Tell us, Maurice."

He nodded, took another slow breath, then went on with resignation. "Everyone was running, Mrs. Mays and the whores and me and Hank and his girl Lou, running down through the fog and yelling as loud as we could, but there was no way they could hear over the noise of the horses, and they couldn't see us. They had no idea. They just stayed there at the fence, watching the tops of the herd where the mist was thinner and the horses' heads would be flying above it, and listening to the thunder when the horses disappeared into thicker patches. And after a while the fence surely started rattling, and shaking, and Laura had to get down to the ground, but the ground shook to where they could barely stand. I came out of a thicker piece of fog just as the horses came out of one fifty feet from the fence, the whole herd at a dead run, headed straight for that little family.

"By that point Gino knew. He started yelling something, but Laura just stood there, holding her mother's arm."

He turned away, and it was quiet.

"What happened?" I demanded, but he didn't answer.

"Go on," Jenny said, and she patted his arm.

He nodded, smiled wearily, and said, "All right," then waved his arm in a slow circle overhead. "Those horses turned at the last second like they were tied to a spike, wheeled 'round with the closest not three feet from that fence, wind and hooves and tons of horse rattling it to pieces and ripping up clods of dirt and grass, knocking the family down just a few feet away, roaring by, and we got down there, and Laura was helping her mother up, and then she pointed and said something I couldn't understand, but we turned to see what she was pointin' at, and Mrs. Mays and the whores turned, and we watched the horses take their thunder back up through the fog until they reached the top and slowed and stopped, and they stood there, snorting and sweating just as the sun broke out from behind the hill, and light stretched across the meadow, and lit the steam coming off the tops of their backs, and lit the little clouds of their breaths, and lit their manes and tails and the little hairs on their backs like some kind of pretty picture."

He looked down, and went on with a more tender voice. "Laura was making noises … saying something to Sophie that I couldn't understand and pointing up the hill, trying to get her to see it. But Lou always understood, and she told us Laura was tellin' her mother there weren't much prettier things in this world than horses, especially when they were moving but even when they weren't, and she hoped the sight was fillin' her mother with enough wonder and beauty that it might

74

help her, just a little. She wanted that more than anything, but ..." his voice broke again, and he struggled fiercely to control it, "but Sophie was past that. She never caught any of it."

He stopped, unable to go on, and looking exhausted again. It was quiet for several moments.

"But who's dead?" I finally asked, for he'd never answered that question. Jenny shook her head towards me, but I could all but see the story slipping away from Father's mind. His face tightened, as if he was trying to hang onto what he'd just said, then he reached out into the air as if to grab onto it, to somehow keep it in his mind, but just that movement upset his balance. His body jerked unsteadily, and I reached forward to catch him. He fell sideways into my arms, looked around, puzzled at his surroundings, and then looked up into my face without any sign of recognition. He murmured hoarsely, "She never caught any of it," but the words had come from only the force of repetition, and I knew then he'd already forgotten the story.

The next days were long ones. We started each morning by five and finished each night after midnight, Mr. Oneal drafting letters while I scoured old records, and prepared subpoenas. The third morning Mr. Oneal shifted me to the telephone to find businesses and agencies that dealt with immigrants, military families, prostitutes or even horses in Maricopa County while he worked with Jenny to coax more from Father's disintegrating memories. I did the work with increasing frustration, sure now that we were wasting our time. Father had, after all, said "she" died, though Jenny and

75

Mr. Oneal thought he could have been talking about Laura's mother instead.

I suppose that while I felt some sympathy for my father, by then too much had passed between us for that to erase my irritation at losing Mr. Quarrato's upcoming trial. Mr. Oneal and Jenny saw my restlessness, and I suppose that's why on the seventh day they took me with them when Father asked to be taken up to the crest again. At first that trip seemed as pointless as before. He started to speak about Laura but stopped almost immediately, distracted again by the horses. We were there late on an October morning, and the sun had once again warmed the herd. Some horses had wandered to the cooler shadows of pine on the western edge of the meadow, some had waded into shallow flats of the river, and the distraction seemed too much for my father. He became obsessed again with studying their enclosure; when he spotted the fence he followed it until he found the break, and that in turn convinced him we needed to get "fencing." This time was more difficult than the last, and it was only after a half hour of coaxing that Jenny got him started on Sophie Spinali.

But even that was hard. Father waved his hand towards the valley as if to keep us quiet, but finally began to speak in a sad voice:

"Sophie ... she was ... well, I had a friend once, Ben, whose horse got spooked by a rattlesnake. His boot caught in a stirrup and the horse dragged him three miles over rocky ground. Never could walk straight again, but Sophie made him look like Wild Bill Hickok. She couldn't eat without being fed, couldn't move without being carried, couldn't smile or even seem alive, but Laura ...was ... devoted to her."

He hesitated, then went on with a rush of conviction. "That little girl did everything for her mother, fed her, bathed her, and told her stories, day after day, week after week, even though Sophie did so little back that we sometimes wondered if she was still alive, until every so often she'd breathe and remind us that she was. Nothing seemed to help, not Laura, not Mays, not the other women's attentions, but everyone tried. So Mrs. Mays had a doctor out. Gino said no to that at first, 'cause he couldn't afford a doctor, but she told him the doctor was out to see her and she was in better shape than he thought, and since she'd already paid him rather than throw away a chance at good medicine how about he let him look over Sophie? So he did."

"Who was he?" Mr. Oneal asked, glancing in my direction. I pulled out my pen and paper.

Father softened with this subject. "He had orange hair, was just out of school."

"What was his name!" I snapped. They all turned towards me, and I lowered my voice. "I'm sorry, but Father, what was the doctor's name?"

Father stared back at me, then shook his head and demanded, "What are you doin' here?"

Jenny took his arm. "Paul's helping find Laura, Maurice. He's helping, now tell us who the doctor was."

"What doctor?"

"The one Mrs. Mays had out to help Laura's mother."

He frowned at me and turned back to the valley. "Wisler," he said, and the name seemed to settle him. "He used to come out couple times a month for what those women needed, but once Mays got Laura's family up there he spent a long time with Sophie. When he was done he took us outside, said he didn't think what was broke could be fixed, but that he'd find other doctors who might know more and wouldn't charge Mrs. Mays. Gino flat asked him if it'd help. Wisler stood a minute without answering, then said as soft as a man could that even in a hospital she probably wasn't long for this world."

He paused, staring down into the valley.

"Maurice?" Mr. Oneal asked. "Doc Wisler, what was his first name, and where was he from?"

Father replied absently. "Doc Wisler?"

"Yes, where was Doc Wisler from?"

"He was ... from ... from Tempe. Wisler was from Tempe ... and his name ... was ... Don ... or Bob or some three-letter name like that." He sighed. "But Gino changed after hearing what he said about her not being long for his world, like he wanted to give up, but Mrs. Mays wouldn't let him. She had Daisy's man Lalo out, the man who ran the diner, because they were into Indian remedies and astrology. They decorated the room with bits of feathers and pictures of movie stars and did some singin' and dancin', but none of that did any good either. So Mrs. Mays had Gino move Sophie up to the ranch house. They were already in a real nice room she had made in the barn, but the whores offered to give up one of their rooms for Sophie and Gino, and Mrs. Mays gave Laura a big couch downstairs. Gino wouldn't do it at first because it was charity, but a few days of fighting all those women and he was a goner. He got Mrs. Mays to keep a tab he could work off with extra help around the farm, but that was one of a lot of deals she never got around to keeping." He paused, calmer now, then glanced back and smiled at us as if nothing was the matter.

"It was good for them, for a while. Laura'd sit with her mother each night and grunt out stories about how the day had gone, or about the horses, or about the Corporal and whatever else came to her pretty little mind. Lou asked her one day whether all that talk might

78

be useless, whether Sophie really even understood her sounds. She was trying to be nice, I suppose, but kept picking at it like a sore." He smiled, and the smile fell into a chuckle. "Laura bloodied her nose over that one, but Lou had a temper too and the girls knocked each other up pretty good that day. But they had the talk friends do after a good fight, and the next morning Lou gave everybody the Grand Canyon version of what they'd learned.

"They both realized—this was when they were maybe twelve or thirteen, mind you—since fair really just shows up in fairy tales that we all got to look out for each other in the unfair parts of life, and since Mrs. Mays would never give up on whores or horses in their unfair patches, Laura sure as hell wasn't ever giving up on her mother in hers. Then Lou said—and she used at least a dozen nevers telling us—she said we shouldn't never, never give up on each other, no matter what. And if any of us grownups ever had the chance we should handle such things just so, and … it was good, for a while …"

His voice trailed off. It took some seconds, but I could see his smile fade, and the look of confusion return, and then a little dread came into his eyes.

"Maurice?" Jenny asked. Father didn't respond. Within the shadow of his hat I could see his features had turned grey.

"Father?" I heard myself say, and I walked over next to him. But he was quiet.

Mr. Oneal spoke more gently. "I guess that's why Lou spent all this time, all these years, looking for Laura."

At first Father didn't reply, but then he turned towards Mr. Oneal, and his words came hoarsely. "Looking for who?"

"For Laura," Jenny said.

"You were telling us how Mrs. Mays told Lou and Laura to look after each other," Mr. Oneal offered, but Father shook his head. He was no longer with us.

"How'd they talk to each other?" I asked, taking his arm. I still remember how thin it felt beneath the shirt. I felt suddenly sorry for him again, so very sorry. I said softly, "I mean, Father, how did they communicate with Laura's speaking problems?"

He seemed to recognize my voice. He pulled his arm away from me, and replied with a rougher tone. "Hell if I know," he said curtly, but then his mind seemed to slip back into the question. He looked out over the valley, smiled a little, then turned to face us.

"Lou figured out Laura's sounds almost from day one, and every day spent time tellin' us what Laura said, like she was Columbus reporting back to Isabella. She went on and on about how Laura was a princess, how her folks were famous back some place with somethin' called 'Uffizi' … and how Laura was educated, how she knew four or five languages and could even talk to horses."

Mr. Oneal looked up suspiciously, but Father just shrugged.

"That's how Lou's daddy got started with the horse business."

"Does this have to do with Laura?" I sighed.

"That's who I'm talkin' about," he said sharply, but there was still a softness in his eyes. "Mrs. Mays saw the two li'l girls loved horses, Laura especially, and how she took to Next Question, and how he did to her. 'Course some of that was 'cause Mrs. Mays showed them how to feed a horse carrots and apples without losing your fingers, and Laura took to not losing fingers every chance she got. Next always knew when that little carrot and apple girl was coming, when they was goin' to have … conversations." He seemed to hesitate at how this sounded, then tried to explain. "She'd sing or grunt out stories while feedin' him and even when the carrots was gone Next would stand there listenin' and when she'd stop talkin' he'd nicker back, and they'd go back and forth 'til Mrs. Mays'd start yellin' for her to get workin'. It got to where we'd hear the nickering and know Laura's was takin' a breath while tellin' stories to her damn horse. Never figured how any livin' thing could take that much talk, but ole' Next sure could from her. He loved her as much as everybody did, I suppose—" He shook his head wearily, but he'd become relaxed with the subject of horses, and we stood there listening, letting the story unfold.

"—it didn't take Mrs. Mays and those whores more than five minutes to fall in love with them girls, 'specially that li'l pretzel Laura, and come that first Christmas Mays surprised everybody by givin' her Next Question." He shook his head, still impressed by the gesture. "Next had been the Corporal's horse and was always Mays' favourite. Sometimes at night she'd be out to the barn to spend time with horses, yellin' 'bout how you doin' tonight, how's your leg, oh my you got a li'l sore, don' you, and she'd always end up with Next, askin' him if he remembered this or that 'bout President Thee-o-dore Roosevelt and the Buffalo soldiers at San Juan. Laura would come out of the house and stand there with them, gruntin' right along while Mrs. Mays yelled and ole Next'd nickered, and the rest of us couldn't get a damn bit of sleep for all the noise."

Jenny smiled. "How did Lou react to Laura getting a horse?"

"Wasn't a problem. Mays gave Lou Ain't—"

"Ain't? "

81

"Ain't was the last horse Mrs. Mays got from the Army. When I got her off the wagon and Mrs. Mays looked her over she yelled that this horse was nothing but an old nag. Lou got the way kids do around big brown eyed animals and started insisting she ain't a nag." He dipped back to imitation. "*She ain't! She ain't!*" he said, then he sighed wearily. "Arguing' with Lou on just about anything could be a day's work, and since we needed time to sleep everyone just went with the name Ain't."

"What about the other horse, Next Question? Why was he called that?"

"'Cause he always did what anyone asked," he said simply. He stopped, suddenly looking very tired, but then a smile flickered over his face.

"That was a great time for Laura. Next Question was as good a friend as Lou to her, never once made fun of her sounds, and now she had two best friends, including a big one that followed her around. She was proud of that, wanted everyone to see how he accepted her. One day she even took him into the house to show her ma, took him up the stairs, to introduce 'em." He rolled his eyes at the memory. "We felt the ground shake that day. Mrs. Mays came in and peeled paint off over it, yelled loud enough to be heard in Phoenix. So Laura took him outside, but left a window open so he could stand with his head in the kitchen while she did downstairs chores and told stories."

He stopped again, exhausted now, and stared down at the ribbon of water. Some of the horses had waded in. After a while he turned around, frowning at me. "What are you doin' here?"

I stared back.

"He's trying to help find Laura," Jenny offered. But it was as if he hadn't heard.

"What do you want from me?" he whispered.

I shook my head. "Nothing, Father. I'm …I'm just trying …"

"Why aren't you working?" he demanded.

"He is," Jenny said, patting his shoulder. She glanced my way, then tried again to help. "Paul is trying to help you and Mrs. Locke find Laura."

He eyed me suspiciously, and I stepped back, unsure of what to do. Jenny held his arm. "You were talking about Laura, and a horse Isabel Mays gave her," she said, but he'd lost his bearings. Father stared at Jenny as if he barely recognized even her. After a few more minutes of trying we had to give up. We took him back down to the ranch, Jenny took him to his bedroom, and I went back to the library to work. And that was the last time I'd accompany my father to the crest.

Mr. Oneal joined me in the library, and we had just got back into the paperwork when Jenny came in with news that there was a call from the law firm in Arizona. Mr. Oneal left to take it, and after several minutes he returned, looking unusually solemn.

"What is it?" I asked. He patted my shoulder and took a seat facing me, studying me, then shook his head sadly. "What?" I repeated.

"Mr. Quarrato died."

The words hit me like a fist. "What!" I cried

Mr. Oneal sat, facing me, and spoke quietly. "He had a heart attack, a bad one. His daughter got him to the hospital, but they couldn't save him. I'm sorry, Paul. I know you liked him, and worked hard for him."

"I should have been there," I said bitterly.

"It wouldn't have made a difference." He said it in soft words, but just then, just there, after everything else, the effort at consolation was of no use to me.

"You don't know that!" I snapped. I'd reached a breaking point, and it let out some of what was inside. It was directed mostly at Father, but I threw it at his partner. "You've got us all wasting time with a senile old man! With a hopeless case!"

For the next several minutes Mr. Oneal sat and listened while I ranted and raved. When I stopped to catch my breath he asked if I wanted to fly back for the funeral. It just got me going again.

"What good would that do? I should have been back there, instead of wasting time on this case."

"We're not wasting time, Paul, and you couldn't have made a difference. Charlie is one of the best trial attorneys in Arizona."

"We're all wasting time!" I sputtered. "This work ... this ... is useless! All it needs is a good shrink for Mrs. Locke."

Jenny spoke in a quiet voice, "Don't forget about Laura."

"She's probably dead," I cried, "and you're forgetting she may have murdered someone."

"Murdered?"

"You heard me!"

"Didn't Mr. Moffatt use the word 'killed'? He said she "killed" someone, not that she murdered him."

"You're splitting hairs."

She didn't reply to that, but sat, smiling sadly towards me.

"So what have you come up with so far?" Mr. Oneal interrupted.

I stared at him angrily without answering, and in the quiet felt my anger ebb. He was right. It was obvious even to me that we weren't nearly finished.

"Come on, Paul. Tell us what you found so far."

"A lot of nothing," I sighed, and I reached wearily for my notes. "There are six law enforcement departments and about ninety medical facilities in Maricopa County. Most of the police agencies won't give out information without a subpoena, but a couple at least checked all the way back to nineteen hundred and told us they never heard of anyone named Spinali or Mays. I had them try a few other spellings, but there's nothing."

"File a John Doe lawsuit with as many theories as you can think of and start issuing subpoenas. What about the medical?"

John Doe lawsuits! I thought wearily, but I kept my mouth shut.

"Paul, what about the medical? Have you done anything to check them?"

"Of course. We've contacted all the medical facilities closest to Apache Junction. Six go back that far, but only two of those agreed to check their records without a subpoena: they don't have anything on patients named Spinali or Mays. They gave me the names of former directors and we're tracking those down, but if their facilities didn't have any records I'm not sure what that will turn up."

"What about the place he called 'Madonna'?"

"It's the first place I called. They're a dead end. It's a small facility, just eight or nine patients. The director's been there almost thirty years and couldn't recall anyone named Spinali. He's going to call another staff member who worked there even before him, but it doesn't sound like she was ever there, either."

"Keep at the list. Someone must have something. Find out who Dr. Wisler was. Add him and all the medical facilities to the John Doe lawsuit and follow up your calls with subpoenas for every one of the medical entities as well."

"Even the ones who cooperated?"

He nodded. "People look more thoroughly when they're ordered to. Another thing, if Laura is the kind of person Maurice described she might have gone on to become a care giver or social worker. Have someone check Maricopa's nursing homes, retirement facilities, maybe even the religious orders to see if they heard of her. And he said she liked to tell stories. Maybe she wrote some of them down. Check the newspapers, too, and every magazine and book publisher she might have had access to back then. And check to see what charities and churches were around then, and whether they had any programs to help poor or disabled people, and find out when the state or federal government began to fund indigent patient care, and if it was going on back then add more government records requests. Speaking of which, what's happening with government records, anyway?"

I sighed at the mountain of work he just added.

"What else are you doing, Paul?"

I frowned. "I have the office working on petitions under the new act. It's called the Freedom of Information Act, FOIA for short, and we're filing applications for every department of every branch of the military service to find out what happened to the Mays' facility, and the people who lived there. It may be months before we get any answer."

He nodded, thinking, then replied, "Don't give them any extensions. If they don't respond promptly file a motion, a lawsuit if you have to, anything to keep the fires burning."

"We're submitting more than a dozen of these requests!"

"Then file a dozen lawsuits, if you have to."

"You know we've probably already spent ten thousand of the firm's time just this week on this?" I protested. "You're going to add more than ten times that on litigation."

His voice hardened a little. "Did I mention that we've been given a non-refundable retainer?"

I straightened. "Yes ... sir."

"So you know that what we're being paid would easily cover more than a few lawsuits."

"Of course, but—"

"But what?" he snapped. There was suddenly a tense cloud over the room.

"Perhaps we should discuss what else might be done besides lawsuits?" Jenny interjected.

I stared back, not wanting to go on, but there had been something else, a titbit that was interesting but useless.

"What else have you done?" Mr. Oneal asked me.

Part of me had wanted to keep it to myself, but I told him. "I checked with veterinarians—there are twenty-seven in Maricopa County—one had a grandfather who knew about Corporal Mays' herd—his grandfather did work for them. He said Mays *was* at Fort Wagner, by the way, and told me the Buffalo Ranch was the fanciest bordello in that part of Arizona. I got the distinct impression the grandfather may have traded services up there. But he never heard of anyone named Spinali, or Norred, or Rankin, for that matter."

"Nevertheless, that's something," Jenny said.

"Not really," I said, "but he said a woman named Dickerson ran a general store back then and knew everything about everybody in the area. She's dead, but had a daughter, and we're trying to track her down."

"What else?" Mr. Oneal asked.

"That's pretty much it."

"Make sure everything anyone else can handle is delegated before you go."

"Go where?"

"To Italy, to find Moffatt and talk to him."

"You can't be serious!"

He motioned to Jenny. "She contacted a law firm in Rome. One of the partners is a man named Marcel Scipio; he has a couple of investigators. They let Moffatt know we'll pay for whatever he has to say."

"Why doesn't the firm there question him?"

"He's got his own share of legal issues and doesn't trust the Italians. But his problems are expensive, and he'll need money. I want you to take some, go and try."

"How much do I pay him?"

"Fifty thousand, American—"

"Jesus!"

"Only if you need it. Start lower but go higher if you have to, and dole it out, in pieces, I mean; let him know you're holding something back as a prize if what he says checks out. And remember, you're dealing with someone who's probably dishonest, and may be pathological about it."

CHAPTER SIX

Something interrupted Laura's story yesterday, something that made her forget about its characters and plot, about the dreams that gave it life, and even about the friend who came at night to hear it. For the first time in years she ignored it all. It was the same for the other women; every routine and train of thought was interrupted, and in every room the air changed from monotony to expectancy. Everything seemed to stop, because of news that came through the copper pipes and concrete one day. They all heard.

Another young woman was coming to join them.

"How old?" they heard the judge ask. They all knew his voice.

"Can't be more than fifteen," the sheriff's voice answered. He'd plucked a hitchhiker from the roadway. "Says her name is Free Bird." All three men laughed with genuine amusement. "She says she's on a pilgrimage."

"A what?"

"There's some rock and roll thing in New York next year. She wanted to take the whole year to get there, to get in touch with the world, so last night I got her in touch with my friend Richard." The laughter fell to coarser levels.

They asked what she looked like, and each woman imagined the judge and the doctor leaning forward. The sheriff described her face as "nice" and her figure as "very nice", and said she hadn't given him any trouble at all. The judge suggested he work with the doctor to file papers. The sheriff and doctor agreed to take care of it the next morning. That subject faded, and the men's words drifted to golf.

The news was like an earthquake to the women. It brushed aside every thinking scrap and mundane habit of the past weeks, and filled all their minds with memories of what it had been like to come here, and then, too, with a little delicious dread that what happened to them might happen to the newcomer.

For Laura it was the same but different. She felt the all-consuming interruption, but what took up the space of the story and overpowered every other thought, what made the early night so restless, wasn't just the memory of what arrival had been like for her, but how this newcomer would react when they met. Would she understand?

Probably not.

Might her old plan rise again, like Lazarus?

Almost certainly not.

Jenny drove me to the airport in the wood and leather of the Bentley. Mr. Quarrato's passing and my arguments with Mr. Oneal left me in no mood for conversation, but she insisted on explaining more about Moffatt.

"He comes from a family of crime. His grandfather was an embezzler, his father was worse; he was executed for the murder of a family—a mother, father and child.

He is wanted by *Guardia* for extortion, but may have done more the authorities don't know of—"

Do I need a gun? I wondered sarcastically.

"—Mr. Scipio doesn't think he himself is very dangerous, but you should keep that in mind."

I had no desire to hear more, let alone to deal with such a person, but she went on.

"Mr. Quarrato's funeral will be next week, and I have arranged for your flight from Pisa to Phoenix. You'll have seven days with Mr. Moffatt."

That seemed the end of what she felt needed to be said, and I didn't reply. The car got very quiet.

"You do not get along with your father and his partner?" she finally asked.

I glanced at her and frowned. "No ... I mean I do like ... Mr. Oneal. I respect him. But—" I couldn't think of anymore to say.

"And your father?"

"I like him fine," I lied.

"You do not like something else about your life, then?"

"You ask a lot of questions."

"I am making conversation."

"Can we talk about the weather?"

"We could discuss flowers, colours, songs, if you prefer."

"How about we not talk at all?"

"That's strange to hear. I thought you were a lawyer!"

"How about you just shut up!" I snapped.

She smiled as if nothing was the matter but went quiet, and we drove in silence until I began to realize how stupid I was acting.

"I'm sorry," I finally said. "It's just that I worked very hard to try to help Mr. Quarrato."

"And to obtain your first trial?"

"That's right," I said, reddening. "I worked on it every day for almost a year."

She didn't reply. I felt embarrassed, but for another while neither of us spoke.

"Look," I finally blurted, "my father was not the easiest man to be around after …"

"After your mother died?" she said softly.

"Even before that, but especially after. He could be a bastard about things …I mean, he was a good provider, I suppose, but he was so goddamn strict—and I'm not just talking about organizing every inch of what I studied, the books I could read, the music I listened to, every goddamn thing in my life. It was hard to breathe around him."

"You didn't enjoy your upbringing?"

"It wasn't what you'd call fun. Breakfast was like going to court every day. I had to shine my shoes and wear a tie, even during chores, and god forbid we'd ever have a good time. I don't think we ever … *did* things together—I mean, went to a game, read a book together, *anything*. I had friends in school whose parents were good people and didn't have to be nearly as strict—they did well, studied, but went to parties, to movies, had a life."

"And yet here you are, Paul. A young man who served in the military, completed law school, and has gone into a good profession."

"Right. He raised a complete fucking bore!" I snapped.

She glanced at me, then was quiet again. Neither of us spoke for several seconds.

"Must be nice being able to use a Bentley to drive around in," I finally offered.

"It is very nice."

"Father must like you. Otherwise he'd have you driving around in a Jeep, maybe a truck, maybe even on horseback, but not a Bentley. What do you have going with him, anyway?"

She glanced at me as if she knew exactly what I was saying, yet seemed to relax. "This is my own car, Paul."

"*Your* car?" I said, before I could catch myself. "I'm sorry, but I thought—"

"I have my own money, Paul. I am not supported by your father, and not employed by him."

"But then why are you here? What do you have going on with him?"

"An old debt," she replied, and she said nothing further about it. We drove the rest of the way without saying another word.

When we got to the airport she parked in the private terminal. They were still fuelling the plane, so she got out, took a file from the back seat, and went inside with me. We had coffee and tea while waiting. Sitting there my curiosity got the better of me.

"What debt?" I asked.

"I beg your pardon?"

"The debt you mentioned? The reason you're helping my father? What's that about?"

She took a sip of tea, then put the cup down quietly without answering.

"If it's personal, don't tell me. But … I was wondering what you meant. Forget it!"

"It *is* personal," she said quietly. She took another sip, then leaned forward. "However, it concerns you, in a way."

I nodded, even more curious.

She glanced at me. "My father was a gardener. He lived in Phoenix. It's a difficult place for gardens, because the land and climate are not friendly, but he

93

worked very hard, and became very good at it. He worked for your own parents, and for others, and became successful enough to buy a small home. Then he married my mother, and they were going to start a family. But the war came and Japanese in the West were moved to camps. Father and mother had to sell everything. There were men—speculators—who bought from the Japanese for small amounts because of how quickly they had to sell. Your father told mine not to sell, but instead to sign over everything to him in a trust. "It seemed foolish to others. They said my father was *baka* to do this, but he believed Maurice. He signed everything over, and went to the camp. Your father took his time to sell the home, avoiding the speculators and using the regular market. He made a profit which he then invested in the war economy. It was a small amount which became a large amount, and my parents became wealthy while they were interned."

"Well … at least that's something."

"It was certainly that, something, yes, but my parents were taken to a place known as Heart Mountain, in Wyoming. That's where I was born. But it is cold there and my mother was very weak after she gave birth. She suffered a great deal. Your father tried to get them released, but the government wouldn't allow it. He tried to get them moved to Arizona, but the government wouldn't allow that either. He finally hired another lawyer to help. That was Mr. Oneal. They brought a suit which went before the Supreme Court. Mr. Oneal wrote well in his papers and your father spoke well in his arguments, so well that everyone knew the government would lose, and that the Court would denounce the internment. So the day before the Court was to announce its decision all Japanese were released; everyone was released."

She'd said all this with such calm that for a moment I wasn't sure I'd heard correctly. But then I realized I had. I stared at her in disbelief. "I never heard of anything like that happening."

"You can check if you don't believe me. The decision is called *Endo*."

"Well, at least when they got out they were rich."

"My father did not think so, because on the same day *Endo* was decided my mother passed away."

"Jesus!" I sighed.

"Shikata ga nai."

"I beg your pardon?"

"It is a Japanese saying–it could not be helped. People had reasons for what they did, some had very good reasons, yet still many died. It was neither fair nor unfair, unless you are the sort to expect fairness of life. But at least your father helped; he and Mr. Oneal both helped."

"My father never said anything about … any of that."

"Your father is not a proud man, but he has his pride."

"You're not making sense."

She studied me before speaking. "Maurice focuses on battles to be faced instead of those already fought. He may not speak of the past, but since you said some things yesterday which misunderstand him, I mention it."

"Jesus," I said again, feeling a little ashamed.

"You feel guilty?"

"No I don't," I said, but I did.

"It can be a mistake to feel guilty about mistakes."

"I don't feel guilty," I insisted, studying her face. She seemed a little disappointed at my reply, but then went on as if she wasn't.

95

"I am sorry," she said. "I sensed that you do feel guilty, but perhaps I was wrong. I just thought back to a thing my father taught me when my mother died. *I* felt guilty about her then, because of how my birth had weakened her. The guilt grew inside me until one day my father asked me why I was unhappy. So I told him, and my father told me to save guilt for mistakes made when I could have done something."

I stared at her. She was so serious, and lovely, watching me with those dark eyes. I nodded, and said, "Thank you."

"You needn't thank me. I said this for your father, because I will always be in his debt." She patted my arm and looked up at the clock. "It is time. Here is Mr. Moffatt's file. Take it and go, Paul, and help your father help Mrs. Locke."

CHAPTER SEVEN

Laura had neglected the story for seven days now, because the newcomer was here. It was the same for everyone. It was quiet most of the time, but the quiet had a thrill in it, as everyone's thoughts were on Eight. The men called her that—Eight, just Eight—no one had addressed her as anything else since that first week. She was placed in the room next to Laura's, but she wasn't there for long. Being new she was in demand, and being in demand she was gone almost every day. The pipes let everyone hear everything that happened. Laura put her ear to the wall, but just now no sound came through the concrete and copper, and there was only the thrilling quiet.

Was Eight sleeping? She wondered. Not likely.

Had she learned her lessons? It usually took at least one or two weeks to realize that compliance brought calm, that calm allowed for thought, and thought permitted learning. Right now it was still, so maybe eight had already learned.

The whole process had begun early the first night. An orderly came into the room next to Laura's. She heard him take out one of the beds, then return an hour later with the lighter footsteps of Eight, and they all heard her for the first time.

"What's happening?" was her first question. Her voice had that blend of thin confidence over nervousness that every newbie's did.

"The doctor will explain," the orderly replied. He tried to force small talk, but it didn't take and he finally left. Then it was quiet until the others came.

The doctor was first. They heard him introduce himself.

"Why am I here?" Eight asked him.

"I'm afraid you're very sick."

"I feel fine."

"This illness doesn't show that way. Look ...see that?"

"See what?"

"Your skin. See? This paleness, lack of colour? But if I do it here, see that? When I squeeze here it's red, but over here it's pale—"

"That's weird. What is this?"

"It's a desert contagion that affects the blood and lymph glands. We're going to run some tests, but I can see it on your skin, your face, and your cheeks—"

"What the fuck is a ... contagion?" she asked, and a little fear had crept into her voice.

"A lot of people get it out here because they haven't built up resistance. Most people drive right through. If they stay in their cars, keep the windows rolled up, they don't have a problem, but if you're outside and you haven't had it or been inoculated, you can get it. It's why you want to keep your windows closed and your AC in recirculate when you're in a new desert, and another reason it's not a good idea to hitchhike around here."

"Is ... it serious?"

"It can be, but we can treat it. It takes a little while but we'll get you back on your feet. You'll be on your *way in no time," he said, and then they heard sounds of instruments on a metal tray.*

"I really feel fine. I can have a doctor check me later. I'm just going to go."

"I'm afraid we can't release you until we get you better. The Board of Health won't allow us to release anyone who might infect the public."

"So when can I go?"

"It will take a little while. I know you want to go to ... what is it called? Woodbridge?"

"Woodstock!" she exclaimed, and she began to gush, using expressions Laura had never heard before. Words like 'cool!' and 'far out', with meanings Laura gathered only vaguely from Eight's tone.

"That shouldn't be a problem," she heard the doctor say, and there was the sound of a wrapper being torn.

"What is that?"

"It's part of your treatment. I'm starting you on it right away, so you can get going."

Eight sounded somewhat reassured. She went on nervously about the Woodstock thing, and those who were going to perform. She was particularly excited that someone named Shankar was coming, but after two or three minutes her words began to slide into each other. She slurred on with more strange expressions. The doctor offered wine and something to eat.

"Far out," she repeated drunkenly, now more pleased than before. It was quiet for several minutes, then the other noises began.

The sound drew Laura away from the wall, and she tried to force herself back into the story. But that was impossible. After a while the sounds stopped, she heard the doctor leave, and it was still until the orderlies came and took Eight away.

Laura looked up at the tiny window. It was nearly opaque with dirt, but you could tell there'd be no clouds tonight. Moonlight would make its way through grime and light the wall, and her friend would come. She'd smile in anticipation, and Laura would smile back and try to tell the story, and maybe, for the time being at least, forget about what was happening to Eight.

I spent the next day and a half using the Italian law firm Jenny mentioned—and the promise of ten thousand American dollars—to finish the task of coaxing Federico Moffatt into meeting me. It was difficult, not only because there was a warrant out for his arrest, but because the law firm's investigator said he demanded a thousand dollars just to set up a meeting. He insisted I bring the other nine thousand in cash, with me. I agreed, and the investigator delivered the down payment and set up the meeting in a town called Lucca, about an hour's drive west of Florence. I had less than a day to get ready, and spent it on long distance calls and going over Moffatt's file, then left at four the next morning.

I still remember that drive. Everything seemed so different, not just because I was traveling the autostrada in the dark, nor because I was going to meet the criminal son of someone who from all accounts had been a complete bastard, but because of what Jenny said about my father. That was a particularly selfish time of my life, I suppose, and thinking back I know I resented a lot of the attention my father got from others But Jenny had spoken with so much respect about what he'd done—and had seemed so composed and attractive as she said it— that the words somehow added a little melancholy to the euphoria of being in Italy for the first time, maybe a little shame, as well, I guess, and maybe something else.

I arrived at the appointed meeting place still thinking about Jenny and my father, and early enough that it was still dark. It was a small café on a large square. The place was still closed, but there were two dingy plastic tables with loose-hanging blue and red *Cinzano* umbrellas out front. Each table had two chairs and a dirty vase with a wilted rose. There was a large and rumpled cardboard box on the stoop. I took a seat and waited.

About fifteen minutes had passed when I heard a faint clattering of hooves from my left. The sound came up one of the cobblestone streets into the square, until an ancient baker's wagon appeared, drawn by an old draft horse. The horse clopped to the front of the café and stopped, nodding its head. Two men climbed down from the wagon. One took a full box from the back of the cart and handed it to the other, then took the empty box from the stoop, put it in the cart, got back up and clicked the horse on. The other unlocked the front door, turned to me and said something I couldn't understand—except for the word 'espresso', to which I nodded and said *si*. He took the fresh box inside. Ten minutes later he brought out a cup of coffee.

Moffatt was almost an hour late. He was a fat man, balding, in his thirties, wearing shiny gabardine slacks and a thin sport coat. He was sweating despite the morning cold, and beneath his arms perspiration had soaked through both his shirt and coat. He shook my hand with a damp palm, but demanded his money before taking a seat.

"You have information?" I asked.

"The money first. You were to bring nine thousand dollars." It was cold enough to see the puffs of his breath, but he pulled a handkerchief and mopped his brow.

"You already got a thousand to show up, but you're late. I'll give you another five if you have anything worth listening to," I said.

"Then we 'ave nothing to discuss," he said, and he began to leave.

"All right," I snapped. I pulled an envelope from inside my coat, counted out four thousand and laid it on the table. "The rest when we're done, depending on what you have to say."

He snatched up the bills and stuffed them inside his coat, and after calling to the café owner to order wine and a croissant, glanced around us at the empty square, then surveyed my own suit. "Where are you staying?"

"At the Vecchietti. Where is Laura Spinali?" I asked.

"That I don't know."

You're kidding! I thought. *Then why am I here?* I began to get up.

A frown crossed his eyes. "If you leave you will not find out the best parts."

"Such as?"

"Such as what others would pay a great deal to know, my friend. There is much more to learn about her family, much I know about the Spinalis."

"Go on," I said, retaking my seat.

He held up his hand as the owner brought a carafe of wine and his food. "First I drink. Then I talk. Then you will pay?" he asked.

"Depending on the talk," I said impatiently, but he took his time. He had two quick glasses and the pastry; then produced a cigar and box of wooden matches from inside the jacket. He lit the cigar, took a deep puff and waved out the match, and glancing over his left shoulder said, "Well, then, I will first tell you about my father and Seppe."

"Who?"

"Seppe. A common thief my father knew," he said. I was dubious, but pulled a pad and pen from my pocket.

"It was the *diaspora,* as you say, the depression?" he said, speaking with a mixture of Italian and British accents, and mopping his brow from time to time. "It was a bad one, very bad." He motioned around the square. "Half these shops were shuttered; the rest stood open but empty. But my father," he said, crossing himself and rolling his eyes heavenward, "he was one of the lucky few who had a job, a good one, in a bank. It allowed him to make just enough to stay here and feed his family, until Seppe … forced him to crime." He took another sip of the wine. "You know about my father?"

I pretended I didn't, but Jenny's file had shown this man's father was an embezzler and extortionist before he graduated to the triple murder of a family in Northern California. He was caught, convicted and executed in San Quentin's gas chamber. His sweating son across from me looked around again, then leaned forward to flick his cigar ash towards the vase, but it was too soon and none of it fell. He frowned and went on. "Seppe was a bad man, a man of violence man who forced others into crime, and he did so with my father."

"And this has what to do with Laura Spinali?"

"Was she not the disfigured daughter of Gino and Sophie Spinali?"

"Yes, so?"

"Were not her disfigurements caused by damage during the mother's pregnancy?"

What! I thought.

Seeming pleased at my surprise, Moffatt collected himself, leaned back and spoke with feigned expansiveness. "I'm going to tell you about the child from her beginnings, firstly, why she was born the way she was."

He l lowered his voice. "Seppe, the man I told you about, was the best thief in Lucca, but also the worst and most cruel. He used people like my father. He knew Father worked in Lucca's biggest bank, so he gave him a list of those who still had homes—estates, villas, vineyards with workers—and demanded Father check on their accounts to see if they had anything left. He promised to share what he stole in exchange for information about what they had."

"And that's what you call being forced into crime?"

"Seppe was not a person one said no to. A few tried, even the Monsignor at the Cattedrale, but everyone in Lucca knew what happened to him." He took another swallow of wine, then picked up the napkin and daubed his lips, forehead and cheeks.

"Are you going to enlighten me?"

He shrugged with an obvious air. "The churches were among the last to have money, so Seppe became religious. Each week he went to a different church service to see if it still had anything of value—mostly gold or silver chalices, plates, candlesticks and the like—and if it did he'd return that night to steal. When he saw the golden cross and chalice on the altar of the Cattedrale he returned after dark and knocked. The Monsignor answered, holding one of the great candlesticks from the altar. Seppe got on his knees and cried, 'I have sinned greatly, Father, and need to confess. I am afraid I will die in the morning.'

"'How can this be?' the father asked him.

"'It is a difficult story, Father, one I must tell in confession. I'm sorry, so sorry to disturb you, but I have only a few hours of this life remaining before I die!

Please, dear Father, forgive me for asking, but I must 'ave your help!' And he begged over and over to be given confession."

Moffatt sat back and forced a smile. "It was a good lie, and well done. The Monsignor let Seppe inside and led him towards the confessional, but the altar was bare! The Monsignor had locked the valuables in the sacristy. Seppe pulled a knife and demanded his keys, but the old bastard waved a finger and began lecturing him! 'You cannot live in evil and expect the Lord's blessings, my son,' he said. So Seppe put the knife to his throat and said, 'The blessings I expect are in your sacristy, Monsignor,' but still the Monsignor still wouldn't obey. So Seppe struck him to the floor, and when the Monsignor cried out more he took the other candlestick and broke the man's knees."

I sighed. Moffatt had this phony air of experience which I saw among some in the Army, a facade that usually masked a coward. Worse, he'd already been given five thousand dollars—for nothing, as far as I could see, and was wasting my time. But I stayed, and sat there, listening.

He drew on his cigar, but it had gone out. He pulled another match from the box and tried to relight it, but the end of the match broke. "Merda!" he sighed. He pulled another and was able to light it. That seemed to calm him.

"And then," he replied, with pride glittering in his eyes, "Seppe took the candlestick which was still lit and dripped the wax, first in one eye, then—" He paused again, waving his hand to let my imagination complete his sentence, "And the Monsignor finally gave up the keys."

"You're wasting my time," I said, sure now this man was lying for effect. I began to get up.

"I am not!"

"You haven't told me anything about the Spinalis yet, except to say they may have been on some list."

"And they were! Please, sit, and you will pay me. I promise! You will be so pleased you will want to reward me with even more."

"Not likely," I muttered, but I retook my seat. "Get on with it. Were the Spinalis on the list?"

"I will—" He stopped and shrank back into his seat. A mounted *Guardia* was trotting into the square. The officer slowed his mare towards us, but just then the café owner came out. He waved, whereupon the officer nodded and reined left to head up the side of the square. Moffatt remained crouched and said nothing as the officer clattered along, eyeing the shops as he went. Near the corner he twisted back, and seeing the café owner wiping the next table, waved backhandedly.

When the owner went back inside Moffatt finally sat up.

"You're afraid of the police?" I said quietly.

He brushed a little ash from his sleeve. "Uniforms have a way of enlarging the egos of little men."

"I always found police to be very helpful."

"They did bad things to my father."

"Is this the father who murdered three people?" I asked, unable to help myself.

Moffatt glared at me, then leaned forward until his chin was just short of the brown rose. "That was Seppe's doing."

"Another crime he forced your father into?"

"You don't understand!"

"Quit wasting time. Tell me about the list."

He took a swallow of wine, daubed his upper lip and went on. "There were three names on the list. Father tried to help each one by understating what little they had, but—" He stopped mid-sentence, motioning behind me.

I ignored him. "Go on."

"Signore, the butcher's daughter." I turned. A statuesque brunette was clicking towards us in angry red heels. Her tight sweater easily followed the walking movements of her bust. As she approached Moffatt whispered, "*There* is proof of God." He sat up and called out, "*Hey bellissima! Sei splendid a stasera.*" The woman flashed a coy smile, then turned away as if bothered by a small insult. Moffatt chuckled and sat back.

"What about the Spinalis?" I demanded.

"My father tried to help them too," he said, turning back. His eyes settled on the brown rose between us. "He told Seppe their account was like the others, with not much to begin with and now even less. They had almost nothing. But Seppe had seen Gino Spinali buy meat from the butcher, and thus knew they had a box."

"What? A safety deposit box?"

"No! Banks were no more secure than churches in those days, but even before the *diaspora* wealthy families had thick sided wood and leather boxes— chests, they are also called—filled with treasure. They're adorned with carvings and fitted with heavy metal hinges and clasps. A strong man would have trouble lifting an empty one, and two men would have trouble carrying a full one away. They became a better alternative to a bank, and far better than one's mattress. Seppe knew the Spinalis must have one, not only because the husband was able to buy meat, but because the wife was a Durer and his Father a jeweller."

He took another swallow and wiped his lips. "But to target them! My father was brave but Seppe's attentions on the Spinalis put him in fear. The Spinalis stretched back to the Renaissance, and however carefully it was done, theft from one of that heritage would mean there'd be more than just an occasional *Guardia* trotting his horse after them. Any acquaintance, even a man as respectable as my father might well be imprisoned, and if by some chance Seppe lost his temper while in the home! If anyone was hurt!" Moffatt grimaced. "My father tried to talk him out of it. But he couldn't. And Seppe went, and—"

He stopped and sank back into his chair. I turned. There were two *Guardia* coming into the square now, on foot, still fifty yards ahead, but neither turned as the first had. Moffatt flicked his cigar at the vase, but his hand shook. This time the ash broke, but it fell in a crater beside the vase. "My money!" he whispered, motioning to give over the rest.

"We're not finished."

"Give it to me!" he cried.

"When we're done."

"Another day then, Signore," he said, scrambling suddenly out of his chair. He disappeared inside the café. I got up to follow him inside, but by the time I entered he'd left through a back door.

CHAPTER EIGHT

The quiet was broken several times in the past weeks, mostly by sounds that fell in the same order: a clang of the heavy far door, footsteps in the hallway, the thinner clang of Eight's door, and finally, voices in low murmur which ebbed into the other noises. The first night's voices were those of the judge and the sheriff, with occasional dull replies from Eight. The next night's were from orderlies, two of them together, with sounds of paper and glass; they stayed longer, but still the sounds developed a regular rhythm. Now the sounds were familiar, no longer new and exciting, and the other women returned to their own thoughts and routines.

But at the beginning of the second week Eight began her first transformation, and the rhythm exploded. Laura was narrating the story to her friend when it broke. The judge was there. Eight muttered lowly, something about his weight. He became officious but her voice climbed quickly over his. He became angry, she began yelling. Laura exchanged knowing looks with the face in her wall. Such a mistake.

Sure enough, the far door opened, and other footsteps approached, Eight's door burst open and the raised voices of orderlies took over. There were shouts and slaps, followed by screams and blows. It went on for a while, then stopped, the door slammed and the steps went away. When the far door shut Eight began to make smaller, tired and helpless sounds until it was quiet again. But this quiet was different, more the sort that just waits for the next sound.

The doctor came in just after dawn.

"You don't like it here?" he asked.

Laura heard the bed creak.

"This is bullshit," Eight said dully. "You're ... you're ... letting ... people come in to ... fuck me. You're supposed to be a Doctor ... you shit! You ... prick! This is bullshit. You ... you ... you're a pimp!"

It was quiet for a few seconds, then the doctor spoke.

"Why would I do that? Look, I'm quite fond of you. And I respect you, Eight. I have no desire to interfere with what you do with your other visitors, or with the rest of the staff. That's entirely up to you."

"I ... I ... want ... to go home. I want ... to leave. I'm ... fine! I want to go."

"You will, but it's too soon. I can show you the test results, Eight. You're sick, my dear, you're ill, seriously ill. There's no question about it."

"Then call my ... parents. They ... have doctors who can take care of me."

"I thought you said they'd never understand you."

"They'd understand this just fucking fine. Let me ... let me ... call my father. Please!"

"We don't have phone service here, Eight." A moment of silence passed before the doctor's voice started up again. "I tell you what," he said. "I'll run some more tests—"

"I ... I ... don't ... want more tests."

"We'll see how you're doing—"

Laura heard the sound of paper being broken open.

"I don't ... please ... no ... I don't want another—"

"You still want to go to the concert?"

110

It got quiet again.

"There. Now would you like a glass of wine?" Laura couldn't make out what Eight replied, and thought it strange that he left right away. But a half hour later he came back with another man whose voice she couldn't recognize. The doctor left, but the other man stayed. And early the next morning there'd been another noise, something which signalled the next stage of transformation. Laura was in the story when it came, first low, then it climbed up and sank down, and rose and fell.

Eight was crying.

It took two days to set up another meeting with Moffatt. While the Italian law firm made the arrangements, a large package arrived from Mr. Oneal. It contained a letter, several hundred pages of subpoenaed records, a small cassette player and a few cassettes.

The letter was from Mr. Oneal. He expressed some frustration with their efforts thus far. Early returns from subpoenas produced thousands of records from several sources, most of which were still being reviewed but had so far produced nothing of relevance. The stack sent to me included real estate documents on Corporal Mays' ranch and arrangements to transfer and buy back army horses. Although some of the real estate documents were interesting, none of them brought us any closer to finding out what had happened to Laura Spinali.

Mr. Oneal suggested I try to find any surviving Spinali relations who might have some ideas about what happened to Laura. He ended with a paragraph explaining that my father's condition was deteriorating. He'd recorded some conversations with him, and asked that I listen to them, and see if there was something they'd missed.

I had coffee brought up to my room and keyed up the first tape. It was a bit of a shock to hear Father's voice; he was much hoarser than when I'd last heard him.

The recording had been switched on in the middle of a sentence, and from the wind noise in the background I could tell it was recorded on the same hilltop crest as before.

"… dear old Mrs. Mays had a new mission now, to make sure Sophie got what she needed. Gino was poor but still proud enough to fight charity, but with Mays and six whores working on him he got a little of that Bull Run feeling—"

"What does that mean?" Jenny's soft voice interrupted.

"It means he didn't so much give up as he got massacred," Father said, and with that I assume he lost his train of thought. It was quiet for several seconds, then his words started up as if farther away from the recorder. "See that mare down there?" he asked.

"Which one?" Jenny replied.

"The chestnut? He looks exactly like Next Question. What a god's horse that was, full of heart, always did what you wanted—not sure if I mentioned, but that's how he got his name. We were up on the porch one day after letting him and the other horses out, and Mrs. Mays' whores came out with their tea. Laura rolled her mother out—she always brought her to watch the horses, hoping someday it would make a difference …" His voice trailed off.

"She brought her mother out?" Jenny pressed him.

Father coughed, then went on with more hoarseness. "Laura was in a new dress, and Mays yelled out, 'Bet nobody at that damn school told you what pretty thing

112

you are?' Laura turned red but Lou looked up and nice as you please said, 'She's a princess, Mrs. Mays!' Mays worked at keeping a frown, but asked, 'You girls take care of each other?' and Lou started in with one of her encyclopaedia explanations about her helping interpret Laura for those who didn't understand her, while Laura would tell her back stories about how Sophie's family was famous back in some country called Florenz, how there was a palace there called Uffizi, and after about an hour of Lou's talk Mrs. Mays yelled out how Lou had just set the world record for the longest 'yes' answer in history. But then Laura grunted something that stopped her. So Lou said "Laura wanted to know how come you yell so much, but she said it like a spring flower in winter snow, and it broke up Mrs. Mays." He laughed, but then the tape went quiet, and it was clear that once again my father had lost his way.

Jenny finally spoke. "So everyone was out again watching the horses?"

"What are you talkin' 'bout?"

"You were telling us that the girls and Mrs. Mays and the … whores were out there with you and Gino, watching the horses?"

There was no answer, just a low hiss of wind.

"What else can you tell us about Laura?" Mr. Oneal's voice asked.

For several moments there was nothing, but then Father finally spoke.

"She killed someone once," he said. And then he said nothing. For the longest time after, the only sound was the wind.

"Who?" Oneal asked.

Father didn't reply.

"Who did she kill?" Jenny asked quietly.

Still there was no answer.

"Maurice?" Jenny said, "You were talking about Laura and the women, and Gino—"

"There was a problem with Gino and those women," Father interrupted, and he went on sounding disappointed. "He was a good-looking guy, I suppose— little thin, but had those sad eyes, and that Italian accent was like catnip for the women. One day we were mucking stalls and Rita and Miss Pete came out and said they wanted to learn to ride. Said they needed lessons in a way that made me think what they wanted didn't have much to do with horses. I wouldn't bite, but Gino said he'd be happy to teach 'em. They laughed even though it wasn't funny, and Miss Pete asked how he'd like them to pay while her eyes gave him one of those married men are some of our best customers looks, and … Gino … well, two things I remember about him that morning were how when I tried to get away from the women he kept talkin' to 'em, and how later on I saw him come out of the ranch house when he had no good reason to be there."

There was a quiet pause, then he started up again. "Every so often after that, when we were mucking or fencing, Gino'd say he needed to go check on Sophie, and he'd disappear into the ranch house for a while, but then I'd see Mrs. Mays or Laura had Sophie out on the porch, or Laura would come out after having washed or fed her mother and make noises and signs Lou explained was her asking where her daddy was. We just answered by saying we weren't sure, but one day Hank got tired of lying and told her—not in big letters, but he said Gino had gone up to the house to check on Sophie. Laura's eyes went down to slits and she started off up there— first walking, then broke into a run. The whole barn held its breath for about ten minutes when that happened, even the horses kept quiet, until we heard a gunshot come from the house."

He sighed deeply, then went on. "We ran up there and inside, ran up the stairs, and here was Lou blocking our way, looking beat up herself and cryin', but fightin' to keep us in the hallway. I started to go past her, but she began screamin', telling us we couldn't go. She tried to stop us, but then Laura came out. She had the Corporal's old Smith and Wesson. She was arguing with Lou, then finally Lou said Gino had been in the room, cheatin' on Sophie with Miss Pete and Rita, all three of 'em buck naked, and so Laura shot him. When we got in the women had cleared out but there on the bed was Gino, bleeding from a hole in his chest. And suddenly a big man's voice booms out 'Don't touch nothin'!'

"It was the sheriff comin' out of Daisy's room wearin' nothing but his moustache. He saw Laura holding the gun and said to Daisy 'get my cuffs'. But Mrs. Mays came banging up the hallway and yelled 'the hell you say!' The sheriff says 'Isabel I've got to arrest this child' and Mrs. Mays shouted 'Since when do you arrest folks for accidents.' The sheriff said 'Since when did a girl shoot a cheatin' father by accident?' and Mrs. Mays took the gun from Laura and yelled, 'Accidents happen whenever the hell they need to 'round here, Chester. You know, I can feel one comin' on now.'

"'Now, Isabel!' he said.

"'Don't you *now* me,' she said, and she waved the Smith and Wesson toward his southern parts, and yelled, 'This thing is always goin' off when it shouldn't. I'll be goddamned if it might not happen again any second.' And the sheriff tried to yell but Mays was the county expert at yelling, and she cocked the gun with both hands and shouted that he ought to get the hell back in

Daisy's room and finish his business so she can clean up this accident."

He paused, and his voice took a softer tone. "Laura's daddy lived, but she wouldn't let him anywhere near her mother, the women, or even Lou after that, made us take him out of the house. So Doc Wisler tended to him there in the barn, right up until he died a week later—"

"Doc Wisler?" Mr. Oneal interrupted, and he asked several questions about medical staff who worked at the Mays ranch. The tape ended without more explanation, but it was clear this must have been what Father was referring to when he said Laura had killed someone. *But her own father?* I thought. And yet it made sense.

I worked that evening on the subpoenaed records. None of the real estate transactions gave any clue to what happened to Laura's family, and none of the law enforcement agencies in Maricopa County had records of anyone by the name Spinali in their files. There were medical records from various sources, including a general practitioner named James Wisler, M.D., which mentioned Laura's parents. They showed her father was treated for syphilis, then some months later for a gunshot wound from which he eventually died.

There were also lengthy records of her mother Sophie, including an initial note of December 14, 1911 that said she appeared 'to be in persistent vegetative state dating to severe blunt force trauma which happened several years ago', that she required 'daily care for feedings, bathing, and the most simple of life tasks, all of which are provided adequately by her daughter', but that the daughter—not named in the record but obviously Laura—'herself appears to suffer from some sort of severe Chiari malformation, spina bifida, possibly syringomyelia and marked speech pathologies, but communicates with interpretive assistance of a friend', who I assumed was Mrs. Locke. I wasn't sure what the rest of that meant, except that it gave us no further clue on what happened to Laura Spinali.

Although learning more about her family from another source raised some feelings of sympathy for these long dead people, I still put this entire assignment in the category of dog walker projects. But now, for some reason and for the first time I can remember, I felt less angst over not having been there for the other client, Mr. Quarrato, and more interest in Mrs. Locke's world. It was ironic, because while the greater part of me knew this cause was hopeless, another part—some nagging, inexplicable and irritating part—told me there was something in what I'd read, something that I was missing.

CHAPTER NINE

Parts of the wall had changed overnight, and were darkened with the mould and mildew which thrived in the dank rooms. Laura tried to protect her friend from them by balling her fist and rubbing at it, then wiping her fist against her gown. But with the new visitor there'd been too much distraction, and with distraction the darkness had spread. She was sorry for that, for having been distracted, for having allowed the darkness to grow, but after listening to Eight's crying for three uninterrupted days she hadn't been able to stand it anymore, and in the midst of her story and with her friend right there in front of her she'd stopped, poised herself, and with every bit of enunciation she could muster raised her voice to articulate three syllables:

"Hello, Eight."

The crying kept on.

She said it again, then tried using Eight's other names—

"Hello Free Bird. Hello Ellen Parker,"

Neither produced a response.

She tried to grunt more loudly,

"Eight? Eight? Can you hear me? I'm Nine. I'm here, in the room next to you."

The weeping slowed. She grunted again, still more loudly, yelling, "Eight? I'm in the room next to you. I'm Nine. I can help you. Would you like to be friends?"

But Eight's crying resumed, now more fearfully. So she stopped.

During the next days the orderlies came to Eight's room every morning, staying just long enough to give her medicine. Then she was taken to the office. She protested feebly for a few days, but then that faded and after a while the other sounds resumed, doors opening and closing, other men's voices, and after she was brought back the orderlies would return.

It fuelled Laura. Now she began to ignore her friend and to devote new strength to an old plan, changing and refining it just as she did her story. She used the best part of morning energies on its major parts and later, weakening hours for simple refinement. But each night her guilt came back, because each night the moonlight streamed in and her friend returned, and each night the evidence of her neglect appeared as darker grey on the walls.

Moffatt scheduled our second meeting at the start of what was to become one of the worst weeks in my life. It took place at a café on the Arno River, near my hotel in Florence. I assumed he chose it for the front view of anyone approaching, including any *Guardia,* and for doors out back to elude them, but that turned out to be only partly the case.

Once again I made it there by daybreak, but once again he was late. This time I waited over an hour and a half before he finally arrived. He was dressed a little better than before, in a pale blue suit, but nervous and sweating just the same. He ordered another wine and croissant breakfast, and after finishing the pastry lit another cigar. He still said little until I pushed him, but then again he first demanded more money.

"First the information," I said.

"First the money, Signore. A first payment to begin this meeting. Another five thousand American."

"You haven't come through for what I already paid you," I snapped, but he sat back without another word, so I gave him the money, with a curt warning. "You won't get more unless you have something truly useful."

"You already have much that is useful—" he began, but his voice trailed off as he pocketed the money. It seemed to satisfy him at least somewhat. He took another sip of wine and sat back. "You want to know what happened to the Spinalis?"

"Not just them, but any relatives who might be around, and of course, particularly the daughter."

"There were no other relatives, Signore. Gino was the last son, and the daughter Laura was the last child. And her future was set by Seppe before she was born."

"What are you talking about?"

"The daughter was barely a month from being born, but the beating that ruined her mother affected her as well."

"I thought the mother … she was normal before this happened? Her health had been good?"

"It was," he said solemnly, "and my father tried to keep it so. She came from the famous and more arrogant Durers—"

"You mean the Albrecht Durers?"

"The very same, but without the typical Austrian arrogance—Sophie was a minor saint in Lucca. She taught children, worked in the hospital, volunteered everywhere, and became much loved. But then she became pregnant, and because her strengths were not in childbearing she lost the first pregnancy, and weakened greatly with the second. It was a bad time in Europe, the *diaspora,* I told you, and she and Gino had already lost much—the vineyard, their workers, nearly even the home. When Sophie became ill Gino began to worry through their belongings, selling them bit by bit, for food. It's why he was at the butcher's, and how they came onto Seppe's list." He took another sip of wine, relit his cigar and drew deeply, and while exhaling a cloud of blue smoke glanced around him. Our café was along a cobblestone promenade of shops that bordered the river. The stores were deserted except up to the right, where the owner of a grocery was loading fruit onto storefront tables.

"So … what happened?" I pressed him.

He glanced around again, then leaned forward and lowered his voice. "Seppe was in the square one day when Gino came down. Seppe followed him. He saw Gino buy fresh meat, expensive," he said, nodding for emphasis, "and Seppe went in after; struck up conversation with the owner, who boasted about a ring he'd received to create an account—he even showed it to Seppe! This wasn't just any ring, but one with the best gold work and the size of ruby one sees only in museums. He knew it must have been made by Gino's Father—he was a jeweller, you see—and since my father told him Gino had next to nothing in the bank they both knew Gino must have a chest, and that it must be somewhere in the villa. So Seppe waited through the following week until Gino left again to go to market, and broke in. And Sophie was there."

"Sophie was pregnant …?"

He nodded with a grim smile. "Her second pregnancy, and Seppe played with it."

I felt suddenly cold. "Meaning what?"

He shrugged. "I will tell you, but first you must understand that Gino left Sophie with nothing but a dog, thinking its barking would warn thieves off. But there were always dogs in such homes, and they were always barking. When this one went crazy at the break-in, Seppe killed it. Once inside he searched the lower floor, even the kitchen, and tore everything apart in his search, but it wasn't there."

"And Sophie ... she was in the house while this was going on?"

"She was upstairs, unwell with the pregnancy, but had to know what was happening. Not finding either the chest nor any valuables to speak of below Seppe was angered, and began to let his frustrations out, pulling books from shelves, breaking pictures, smashing windows, splintering fine wood—by the time he went upstairs he didn't care if Sophie heard. But then he saw the tiny woman, and perhaps from a sense of pity, for a while at least, he controlled himself. He forced himself to be polite, and when she nevertheless resisted, because he had plenty of time, he tried to reason with her. It was only when patience and reason failed that he began to play with her."

"What do you ... You mean he raped her?"

"Seppe was no rapist," he said, shaking his head as if such impressions were important. "He *played* with her, in the way Seppe sometimes did." He let that hang while taking another swallow of wine. Then he patted his face with the napkin, drew again from the cigar, and sat back. "But that was only when all else failed. He told my father he introduced himself quite politely, told her with great courtesy why he was there and what he wanted, and not only promised not to harm her, he even built a fire in the fireplace to bring warmth into the cold house, and brought her hot tea to drink. I can assure you that all would have been well except that Sophie refused to cooperate. Worse, when she heard the commotion downstairs she'd armed herself with a letter opener that she hid under the covers." He shook his head knowingly. "One could say she brought this on herself."

"Why would one say that?" I asked, thinking, *one could say you're an ass.*

"Because, had she simply pointed him to the chest all would have been fine; he would have left her alone, but though it was obvious he hadn't come simply to leave, she demanded he get out. Seppe tried to remain calm. 'Don' waste our time, Signora Spinali,' he told her. 'I only come for some of your things. Just tell me where your chest is. I will take some things and go.' Then she made matters worse. She denied having valuables, and even having a chest, which Seppe took as an insult to his intelligence, but he—and you have to give him credit for his effort to be peaceful—sat beside her and said as pleasantly as one could, 'I told you, Signora, don' waste my time. I know these are lies and we both know you have a chest. Just tell me where you keep it, I will take a few things and be gone.' And her third mistake ... well, the third was to repeat the words of the second, and to use the letter opener. Before Seppe could react it was in his shoulder."

Moffatt leaned forwards, and taking his wine glass in both hands shook his head gravely at it.

I remember at that point wanting to get up and leave. Not that I was afraid of hearing what happened next; it's just that this was unnecessary detail about disgusting and brutal behaviour towards a completely innocent woman. But I stayed put. Moffatt raised his glass and swallowed the contents, and went on while refilling it from the carafe.

"He almost killed her right there. He knocked her back and got to his feet, pulled the blade out, and seeing a cane next to the bed, a fine one with silver horse head—probably made by the father in law as well—took it, held it by the stock and using the horse head on her belly, and began the game he told my father about. He asked her—'*You think here is your child's head?*'—and while already badly hurt she turned dully away. So he moved the horsehead to the far side of the belly and drew her towards him, and back and forth began to play the game, and it went on until it led nowhere, and thus to still more frustration and anger. So he screamed, 'Where is the chest!' and struck her with the cane. She began to lose consciousness, but then, for a moment, her eyes went by chance to a far corner of the room.

"Seppe turned and saw a large stack of blankets covering something. He removed them, and it was there: a chest—not a big one, a very small one, but very fine. It took him a while to break open, but he succeeded, and suddenly he and my father were wealthy beyond any dreams. So he finished the beating—"

"Even after he had their chest!"

"I told you, Seppe was not one you said no to."

"He sounds like a complete bastard," I snapped. Moffatt simply shrugged.

"And he did share the spoils with your father?" I asked him.

"Of course," he said matter-of-factly, as if that little bit of morality was self-evident.

"And how did your father end up at Alcatraz?"

"That has nothing to do with the Spinalis."

"If you want this money," I said, patting my pocket, "you'll tell me that and a whole lot more. I want everything. If Seppe and your father had all that treasure, how did they end up as they did? What happened to him, anyway?"

He paused to finish his wine, then emptied the carafe into his glass and signalled the waiter for a refill. "For a long while things were very good. Seppe and my father took their families on the best ship to America, lived in the best hotels, ate the best food, and then took a train all across to California, where they settled in a grand home. Seppe spent time at the most fabulous races and with the best whores money could buy, but then other women came between Seppe Martini and his money, and my father committed his crime—"

"You mean … your father killed Seppe's family!"

"That was the priest's doing. My father was simply the tool by which he did it."

I sat back, stunned, as he focused on his wine. Then his eyes came up, and widened over my shoulder. I glanced behind me. Two *Guardia* were strolling towards the grocery. Moffatt motioned for his money, but I shook my head. He leaned down and spoke in a low voice. "The family's death was necessary because the daughter helped her mother not just with the forgery of Seppe's signature; she donated the remainder of the Moffatt fortune to a charity. St. Vincenz," he said, spitting out the name. "Worse still, Seppe discovered the women had gone to a lawyer and prepared papers that would have sent Seppe and my father to prison. Seppe wasn't around at the end, so my father had to finish it, had to kill all of them, even the husband had to go because he … talked them into it, and then the priest."

"But there was a ten year old boy …"

"Just so," he said, with another despicable smile. Glancing again towards the grocery he stiffened. He sank back down into the chair and lowered his head. The officers were approaching. They nodded in our direction and entered the café. When the door closed behind them Moffatt shook his head. "We will have to meet once more. But you will pay me now."

"Not until you finish!" I said, pulling the other envelope from my pocket. I held it in my hand. "What happened to Seppe?"

He replied with his eyes on the envelope. "An accident. A stupid accident. He was on his way to meet my father, when he was struck and killed in an accident. My father had to do everything, *everything!* He had to do the killings, go to St. Vincenz to deal with the priest, only to be arrested and taken off."

"How did they catch your father?" I wondered aloud.

He reached for the envelope. I let him take it, and he whispered one last bit before walking off. "The body. He was dealing with the priest's body when they found him."

CHAPTER TEN

The plan had progressed slowly, but was already far better than the last one. Like that effort this one would require an ally, and a successful alliance would require communication. Laura needed a breakthrough with Eight, but first had to retrieve the understanding of her night-time friend. The friend had been so patient about so much neglect, and Laura felt so much guilt that last evening she'd begun a penance. With her friend in moonlit silica she'd tested the wall and begun to explain. Her friend seemed reserved, even cold, and when clouds hid the moon, she'd left.

And yet somehow the effort helped. This morning Laura woke with new reserves and more determination to complete the plan, but she knew first she must please her friend. So this afternoon she balled her fist and cleaned the wall. If her friend returned tonight she'd touch her tenderly, with a gentle stroke of her fingers on the concrete cheek. She expected more reserve, but her imagination would furnish a smile. Then she'd grunt another heartfelt apology for what happened before and for the next hour would explain everything. Then, if things went well, her friend would smile back, as if her death had made no difference.

A startling surprise was waiting for me at the hotel. An intent policeman and distressed manager met me at the door with news that my room had been broken into and ransacked, a wall safe forced and the contents taken. I'd put all the rest of our money in the safe. I spent the rest of that morning at the police station, where a maid and janitor said they had noticed someone enter the elevator shortly after I left for the meeting with Moffatt. Their descriptions sounded too much like Moffatt for there to be any doubt in my mind. It was why he'd been so late to our meeting. He'd waited for me to leave, then went up, jimmied the door and had his way with the room. The police captain chided me for having dealt with a known criminal and was dubious about ever catching Moffatt, but after I explained my purpose he offered to help me set a trap.

We used Signore Scipio's investigator to set up another meeting, pretending we had no idea Moffatt was involved in our theft. If he was caught the police agreed to cooperate in helping me obtain further information, especially since I was willing to waive the charges in exchange. We set it at an old café on the Piazza Della Repubblica. Two officers dressed as waiters and I were there well ahead of time, but more than two hours passed without any sign of Moffatt. We tried again the next day, but Moffatt didn't bite.

I went back to the hotel that day, disgusted and disheartened, to find an urgent message from Mr. Oneal, asking that I call. I did, and could tell the instant I heard his voice that something was very wrong.

"Your father took a horse out yesterday morning," he said sombrely.

"I thought he couldn't ride anymore."

"He can't ... he's not supposed to ... but ... he did, and he'd gone. We're assuming he went into the hills. We've got search teams on horseback and a helicopter to look for him. Jenny made reservations to get you back here, if you can make it to the airport by this afternoon."

It took almost a full day to get back to the Shenandoah Valley, but when I called from the Roanoke airport Father's oldest hand, an aging cowboy named Tito, told me he was still missing. A taxi dropped me off at the ranch, where Tito was waiting with others in two jeeps. Tito was a small man, lean and lined, and only frowned when I asked if they'd found Father. We drove in silence over the highway to a fire road, followed that over increasingly rocky uphills for several miles, then came to a small clearing where the road ended. There were others waiting with saddled horses and radios. We rode from there farther up, over thin, rocky trails into the hills, crossing narrow valleys and small pastures, stopping occasionally as Tito received radio messages from search parties well ahead of us. After riding almost two hours we paused at a stream to rest and water the horses. We were there, standing in a small, sombre circle when a call squawked into Tito's radio. He spoke briefly, then ended the call and, while striding to his horse, said, "Found him."

I heard myself ask, "And?" but Tito only shook his head.

I have only vague recollections of the next hours. I recall riding ever up over increasingly difficult terrain, stopping occasionally as Tito got bearings over the radio, and that we eventually reached a steep valley in which the footing was concealed by thick grass. Up ahead a fence line led steeply down the left side of the valley and at an angle up the right. Halfway up the right the fence disappeared behind a cluster of horses and riders. The sight filled me with dread, and I've never been able to get the next moments completely out of my mind; I still remember moving through the waist-high grass while cicadas hummed around us, remember the horses' hooves struggling for holds on the rocks hidden beneath us, and the creak of leather tack as we drew came closer.

There were six or seven people up ahead, and at least as many horses. They were gathered around a break in the fence, with a crossbar that should have gone up to the next post, but was broken. Its longer piece hung down from the left and disappeared into the grasses. On the right another jagged piece stuck out near the top of the next post, as though snapped by a large animal. Beyond it a gorge dropped down slightly, and flattened to a tiny meadow. Two bare backed horses ate lazily in the golden grasses, oblivious to any of us. And on the right, just beyond the broken fence and the group of dismounted riders, lay the body of another horse.

Mr. Oneal and Jenny came out of the group already there. She'd been crying. I dismounted and went over to them. The footing was steep, rocky, and precarious. And it was cold. With her voice breaking, Jenny said, "He must have been freezing out there," and touched my shoulder to direct my attention. I looked back at the fallen horse. Its head lay in a dried pool of blood, and then I saw my father.

He lay partly covered by the body of the horse, his upper body naked and protruding from under the withers, his lower torso and legs hidden beneath them. His skin was white, his features swollen, and his right arm lay over a rifle.

Mr. Oneal and Tito came up behind me.

"He must have been riding this fence," Tito said, motioning to the left side of the gorge, where a few places showed the grasses had been disturbed. "Looks like he saw the break and was headed towards it, but his horse slipped in the rocks and caught a hind leg. Must have rolled, and for some reason Maurice couldn't get clear."

"He must have … what, shot the horse to try to save himself?"

"Put it out of its misery," Tito said, motioning to the animal's hindquarters. The horse's leg was badly broken.

It took six men to move the carcass before we discovered more of what had happened.

Father's right boot had slipped completely through the stirrup and caught just above his ankle, and beneath the very rear of the horse they found a very large and very dead rattlesnake.

Father wore only pyjama bottoms and a hat. They wrapped his body in a blanket and laid him carefully over a horse, and we made our way back down. I don't remember that part, and the rest of that week is a blur. Jenny and Father's staff handled the funeral arrangements. The ceremony was held at the ranch and drew a crowd of lawyers, politicians, office workers and ranch hands. When all the reminiscences concluded and the last of those in the wake departed it was nearly midnight. Mr. Oneal, Jenny and I remained for a while in Father's study with a last brandy. They took the easy chairs and I sat behind his desk, and we sipped, not saying much of anything for a while.

Father's death was one of those things I somehow never expected, even when a lot of him was already gone. Maybe somehow I took his whole life for granted, but sitting in his study I kept thinking back to the last time we were on the crest, when he'd staggered and I'd steadied him, and how he'd looked at me.

"He would have liked what Tito Fuentes said," Jenny offered, interrupting my thoughts. It's true. He would've liked the break in mood his old hand had offered. Tito had told a story about a news helicopter which crash landed on Father's ranch after one of his remarkable courtroom victories. Father hated reporters, but when a mountain lion was drawn by the scent of the injured men, Tito said he had to choose between killing a 'perfectly innocent lion', and the more obvious choice of 'lettin' nature take its course'. The decision to save the reporters, Tito said, haunted Father for the rest of his life. It was a light moment in a sad time.

Jenny helped me through those days as much as she'd tried to help Father before them. More than once she reminded me of what he'd done not just for her family, but for others. Better still, she helped get us back to the last assignment he'd wanted to complete, the one for Mrs. Locke.

I had trouble sleeping on the nights after the funeral and one early morning got up at five and went down to Father's study. Jenny and Mr. Oneal were already there, sipping coffee while going through more of the voluminous materials which had come in while I'd been in Italy. I took a stack of materials and pulled up a chair to join in, and we worked without anyone saying a word.

The papers I went over that morning contained further responses by the government to our Freedom of Information lawsuits, reports of Mr. Oneal's associates on Arizona medical and veterinary clinics, copies of old newspaper articles someone had unearthed from archives thirty years before, and a file with background information on Mrs. Locke. I still have that file, and still remember sitting in Father's library that morning, reading it for the first time.

Perhaps it was the sad circumstances about what just happened with my father, but for some reason it was the first time I really began to appreciate the difficulties Mrs. Locke must have faced after her husband was killed.

Mr. Oneal had told me their daughter Molly was born with cerebral palsy and Down's syndrome, and a little about how Mrs. Locke handled her husband Nathan's death, but the file had details about how she then spent year after year battling doctors, nurses and educators, refusing to accept their suggestions that Molly be put into a special facility for such children, and trying instead to get the best treatment and schooling for her. It explained how Molly did so well right up until the year before she died, but also showed how, after all that, having lost her husband and now burying her daughter, Mrs. Locke then turned back to Laura Spinali. That morning was probably the first time I felt any real sympathy for her. It was another reason why I forced myself back into the work on her case.

The Freedom of Information Act materials were mostly just pages with a lot of redactions. Large sections were blacked out, and all of it appeared to be more dead end and wasted money, until I came to a list of government reimbursements for patients who'd been at facilities we'd already called. At first even that seemed useless; not a single name had been produced, and the count on one of them was wrong.

"Find anything?" Mr. Oneal asked.

I held up the page. "They don't give any names, and they're wrong."

"How are they wrong?"

"This says ten patients, but we were told eight."

"Which facility?" He came over to look at the page.

I flipped back to the first page. "Madonna. But they told me they never heard of Laura Spinali."

"Who did you talk to?"

"The director, I can't remember his name … Braga, I think it was."

"Let me see it," he said, and I handed it to him. He stared at the page for several seconds, and then picked up the phone.

"It's four in the morning back there," I said.

"Just as well. Sometimes you can get more from the graveyard shift."

He checked the page then dialled the number … I heard a click, someone's voice, then listened as Mr. Oneal began to speak:

"Hello, I'm calling from Virginia regarding the Department of Health, Education and Welfare in Washington. I realize it's early, but we're trying to reconcile two sets of information that affect funding to facilities in Maricopa County. We have some discrepancies here and are wondering if you may not have been paid enough … Yes, I said Maricopa County … Is that your county? … Sure, I'll leave a message for the director, but it's such a simple matter I'm not sure we even need to bother him … Well, one set of records says you're being paid correctly, the other says you're not … Yes, I understand that completely … and if you want me to call back in the morning I will. It's just that it really just amounts to a count of your patients, and somebody there must know your count … Right … of course. No, that's correct. Just the count … Ten? So you have ten patients, not eight or nine? … By the way, what about patients Rankin and Spinali? Did they pass away last year? … Rankin … *Maurice* Rankin … All of them? Oh … right, I see it. All females. So of course, that would mean no Maurice—What about Spinali—Laura is

134

the first name. Did she pass away last year, or is her funding supposed to go on?"

I held my breath.

"All right. Look, I'm sorry, but I can't thank you enough … I'll make sure the changes are made, and hope you can get a revised draft for future payments … No problem. I hope not to have to bother you again. … I wish we could too, but I'm afraid this will be a long day … I hope so too … We appreciate it."

He put down the phone and looked up.

"She's there, and she's alive."

CHAPTER ELEVEN

Laura measured intervals between inspectors' visits with the state of her gown. It changed colour each day, for the concrete had been cheap and the work quick, and within days of the inspection cracks allowed mildew to peek up over edges and around drains, and from there over the floor and up the walls, until the colour of her small room changed from light to dark. Since the excitement over Eight had died down, Laura had renewed her battle with it, fighting the mood with her story and the colour with her fist. She did them mostly for her friend, using her fingers to clean the small space of wall in which she appeared at night, then using the gown to clean her fist. But in this dank place mildew was relentless, and the battle such a constant one, that within three weeks of every wash her gown was blackened in every place she could reach.

The flies were another signal. Within days of inspectors' visits they started to gather to the rim of broad pipe that served as a toilet, and from there to circle on erratic little journeys which sometimes ended on her face or arms or legs. As their numbers increased she knew the next visit was coming.

All the older women did. They especially looked forward to it, for the visits brought the older ones their only relief from the grimy rooms and filthy gowns. The rooms of younger women were kept clean, and they were bathed regularly, but the rest of them, and the flies in their rooms, waited on preparations for inspectors.

When the morning finally came the clanging of equipment announced it. The creak of beds followed as the women slowly got up. One by one their doors opened and they were given extra medicines, always by injection to prevent their being hidden under tongues or vomited out, then a fat hose was brought in to suck out their toilets, followed by a thin one that peeled off the mildew and flushed it to the floor drain. Then, and only then, the women were taken outside, into the sun and fresh air, for a cold wash and clean gowns.

The wash three weeks ago was her first glimpse of Eight. She was about fifteen, with a beautiful young body and a face which was pretty but already paling towards the chalky look everyone else had. She was groggy with extra medicine and needed help standing when the spray came to her, so Laura helped. She dutifully undressed and helped cleaned the girl. The orderlies fell quiet as it happened, then heightened the effect with the spray. Laura grunted softly as it went on, and, as the men had never understood her, began that very first time to try to explain her plan.

"Eight, I'm Nine. I will help you get away from this place," she began, and she tried to explain the strategy and tactics. She was sore for days because of what then happened.

Eight became nervous with Laura's grunts and was frightened by the spray. Laura tried to shield her but the orderlies stopped that, until she showed affection. Then they watched, ignoring Laura's grunts until the small one bored of it and yelled and the big one focused the spray like a nail into Laura's side. She'd thought for a moment of trying what her friend had years before, but

137

didn't for fear that what occurred then might happen again. No, this time would be different, and she'd follow the plan precisely. So she took the hard water until the orderlies' ire spent itself. Then the water finally stopped, and they were given fresh gowns.

Through it all Eight's response had been simple and abject fear. But Laura wasn't discouraged, not yet. Eight needed time to get to know her. She might still learn.

The inspector had arrived a few hours after the wash, fat and brusque and quick in most rooms before he chose Eight's to spend time in. He stayed almost an hour, then he left, the doors clanged shut, and their meals came. After eating most everyone fell asleep, but Laura's side had been too painful.

That was three weeks ago. She brushed a fly from her forehead and studied the wall. There was another smudge there. She rubbed it with her fist, and turned to her gown. It was getting difficult to find a clean spot. The inspectors must be coming again soon. She'd have another chance.

Mrs. Locke took news of her friend's likely survival with less relief than resolve to get her out. I didn't actually meet her until almost two more months passed, but Mr. Oneal said she wired a second million to the firm the very afternoon we reported our discovery, and then offered a *third* as soon as Laura was out. He said she began to tap into the office almost daily to check on the status and to insist that things be moved more quickly. Oneal was never one known for undue restraint, but this time he urged more caution than she seemed able to stand.

"She's sure Laura's being held against her will and is ready to go in with guns blazing," he smiled to me wearily after the first week. "She wanted me to hire the people that made *The Great Escape* a few years ago, to break Laura out. I told her we can bend laws but not break them."

"How did she take that?"

"She told me to bend over so she could kick my ass."

Our research showed getting someone out of Madonna would be very difficult, and perhaps impossible, as it had never been done before. We found virtually nothing on the facility in medical texts, newspaper articles or periodicals, but government records showed the building was initially established as a 'home for wayward girls' shortly after the Civil War, and sometime later converted to a facility to house and care for 'criminally insane'. In the past half century court records showed only three cases in which a family had tried to extricate a patient. Although the records on each were sealed, two of those files were very thick—which suggested trials had taken place. The final orders showed both efforts to extricate patients had been rejected. From those materials it was obvious, not just that Madonna wouldn't freely release Laura, but that they had formidable legal talent.

We spent just over seven weeks deciding how to proceed. Mr. Oneal had the firm's best minds working on the problem, and they debated and discarded several strategies to find one that might work. We were eventually left with only one, a plan that involved a lot of bending of the rules. Unfortunately, my role was initially once again that of dog walker. The very first week Mr. Oneal informed me that Mrs. Locke insisted we find, buy, and 'renovate' a home near Madonna, which she planned to use to hide her friend once the rescue was complete, and because of my real estate expertise I was given the job of arranging everything needed towards that end. I was disgusted by the assignment and ready to revolt at that until Jenny stepped in to help. She saw completion of this project as fulfilment of my father's last wishes, and, I have to admit, her presence was calming during the aggravatingly mundane work.

I didn't finally meet Mrs. Locke until nearly two months had passed, and I remember that day quite well. Mr. Oneal warned me ahead of time that her opinions had 'all the flexibility of cured concrete', and despite the sympathetic material I'd reviewed after Father died I expected the kind of belle or shrew we sometimes saw among the firm's wealthy clientele. But I saw neither—at first, anyway.

One of my indelible recollections is of being in Mr. Oneal's office before sunrise that day, and the knock at his door. Mr. Oneal looked past me and said hello. I turned, and there she was: a small, white haired woman in pale western clothing, her tiny hands folded over a silver horse-head cane, looking so calmly at *me*, and I still recall her first three words—"I know you!"—without so much as a hello. Another thing I remember is how she said it, I mean, with the kind of certainty that meant if I didn't remember her, it had to be a failure of my recollection rather than a mistake in hers. It's a strange recollection, because I remember how quiet it felt all of a sudden, how the room seemed to hush and how part of me seemed to hesitate, and I felt as if a tiny hand of memory was waving somewhere in the back of my mind, making me wonder whether she was right. But I knew she wasn't.

She was there that day because we were ready to go, and I was there because my next part in the plan was to drive her out to the newly built house. And still today, all these years later, I remember every ripple of that trip. She looked so old and small in the rear-view mirror, with her head resting near the bottom of the car's window, looking so resigned to life passing her by instead of being so determined to change it.

It was her first time back to that part of the Southwest in decades, she told me, and while driving from Phoenix out towards the town of Apache Junction I wondered what she must have thought, seeing all the changes to her memories of that place after—what, fifty-something years?

Arizona seemed so let go in those days. As you passed out of the city, the buildings quickly became older and less painted, then there were weedy fields between them, then for a short time the fields became more native, with sagebrush and a few cactus and saguaro, but just that little hint of original desert ended with a wrecking yard, and then another, then a string of rusting hulks and stacks of bald tires lying in sand, then a field with more weeds again, and some other crumbling structure, and a gradual increase in clutter, until finally a worn sign explained what was happening:

"Welcome to Maricopa County"

From there we dipped into a shaded valley of ramshackle structures before the road climbed back up and broke into blinding sunrise. I had to put on sunglasses, but then the road turned, and I saw in the distance those red layers that staggered up two thousand feet to form the Superstition Mountains. They were the only thing able to fight off all the creeping squalor, and the only part of that area that impressed me.

I admired it for a while, but then glanced at the clock. It was getting on to late morning.

"Have you eaten?" I asked her, but there was no answer.

I checked the mirror again. Mrs. Locke's head was still against the side window, but leaning forward, with the fine white hair fallen around her face.

"Mrs. Locke?" I said.

There was still no reply.

I looked over my shoulder. I still remember that in a parting of the white hair there was a thin streak on her cheek, as if she'd been crying.

"Mrs. Locke?" I asked again, but there was still nothing. I looked back and forth between her and the road. There was a pull-out ahead. I lifted the accelerator and began to brake, and just that change in momentum stirred her.

She coughed and asked, "Why are we stopping?"

"Just checking to see if you're still with us," I said, accelerating back up to speed.

"Don't be too quick to bury me, sonny," she sniffed, and wiped her cheek.

"Nobody's burying you."

"You just said you were."

"I didn't mean—"

"I know exactly what you meant."

I bit my lips together.

"I don't understand why we can't get her today," she complained.

"We explained that," I said, hiding a sigh. Our work had been extraordinary, risky, even a little dangerous, but she had this 'what have you done for me lately' air that was irritating. Despite the sympathy I felt and all the money she was spending, it was really irritating. And she kept it up.

"Don't take a tone with me, sonny," she said.

142

"I didn't mean to," I replied. "I'm just saying we have to wait until the morning. It's our best chance."

"So you'll delay it, then bill me for the delay? You lawyers all stretch things out, don't you? To make the bills so much higher."

"Look, lady—"

"Don't call me that," she snapped. I tried to shut up, and for the moment she was quiet, at least long enough to catch her breath. "I hope you at least have the home ready?"

"We do, pretty much."

"Pretty much! You mean they're not finished?"

"They're just doing a little touch up painting, and a little unpacking."

"So you're late on this too."

"Mrs. Locke—"

"What about the medical? Did you at least get that done?"

"A team will be there tomorrow."

"Couldn't they come tonight?"

"They won't be needed until—"

"Do you always put everything off until tomorrow?"

"Please, Mrs. Locke!"

"Please what?"

"Mr. Oneal explained. Our best shot is in the morning," I said it to the rear mirror, feeling angry, but her expression caught me. She was back in her seat, head against the window, exhausted by the brief exchange, so we drove for a while in silence, and my irritation subsided enough that I asked again, "Would you like something to eat before we get to the house?"

"Everybody needs to eat," she replied quietly, wiping her eyes.

"Everything all right?" I asked again, but when I checked her again in the mirror she definitely looked as if she'd been crying—and so I asked again, "You sure you're all right?"

"I told you, I'm fine," she snapped.

"Are you hungry?"

She sniffed as if I'd insulted her, but then replied, "There used to be a diner on the far side of town, on the left, just beyond some railroad tracks."

"Yes," I said slowly, remembering the place. It was hard not to remember, a dump I'd never set foot in.

"Is it still there?" she asked, digging through her purse.

I stared at her in the mirror, "Yeah, but—"

"We'll eat there," she said, searching out her features with a small compact mirror, and wiping something on her cheeks. "But there's another road that went into a place called Shanty Town, before the one that goes to the house. What about that? Is it still there?"

"Yes," I replied, frowning. That was the worst part of this whole squalid stretch.

"Take that," she said, and clicked the case shut. "There's a special place I want to go first."

Special place? I thought, with disgust. I vaguely remembered Father using the term, but that was him telling some back story I couldn't remember, where this was real. She wanted to go into the most dangerous part of this whole territory, a slum cum ghetto that could be deadly. People were killed out there. The diner was bad enough, but this? "It's a dump now," I told her.

"What do you mean?"

"I mean its bums, homeless drunks, and some gangs out there."

"Hasn't changed, then. Turn there."

"You don't want to go there. It's a bad spot."

"I'm not interested in your opinion."

"You should be. I know the place."

144

"Just do as I say. Turn right there."

"It's dangerous, Mrs. Locke."

"Enough arguing," she said more quietly, as if she were no longer paying attention.

"I mean it. It's dangerous, Mrs. Locke."

She didn't answer.

"Mrs. Locke?"

"I heard you."

"I'm just saying its danger—"

"I know what it's like!" she exclaimed with sudden acid in her voice. "My family lived there. *We* were the bums you just insulted. And that's where we're going."

"I'm just trying to warn you—"

"Are you deaf, or just dumb?" she exclaimed. "Just do as I say!"

That did it. I braked sharply and pulled to the shoulder, and as a dust cloud enveloped the car I turned to face her. "I can hear fine, lady—"

"*What?*"

"I'm your lawyer, not a tour guide, and I'm not taking you sightseeing through some damn slum—"

"I didn't ask you to go sightseeing."

"I don't care what you call it—"

"You're my lawyer!" she cried.

"I won't be if you waste more of my time."

Her eyes stayed with me for a moment, then she shrugged, grasped her purse and cane, and opened the door.

"*Mrs. Locke!*" I cried, as she struggled to get out. "Mrs. Locke … Jesus Christ!" I jerked the shifter to park while imagining Mr. Oneal's words—*and what exactly did you say to her?* I jumped out and ran around the front of the car. She was outside, straightening her skirt. I stood before her. "Mrs. Locke you can't …"

"You're fired."

"You can't walk fifty feet on your own!"

"You'd be surprised what I can do." She motioned quaveringly with the cane. "Get out of my way."

"Look, lady, it's too far!"

At my use of that word again the steel rose up in her eyes. She pointed the cane shakily towards me. "Don't *ever* call me that!"

"It's ten miles!"

"I don't care how far it is. If you won't take me I'll walk," she said, struggling with her cane.

"All right! All right! All right! I'll take you, all right? Just get back in the car!"

We stared at each other for several moments, then the mettle seemed to drain out of her. She reached up and patted my cheek with just enough care that it wasn't a slap, and moved past me to the open door.

CHAPTER TWELVE

There had been three opportunities for escape before, but each had ended in disaster. The first was when Laura was roomed with another woman, and an orderly, drunk even before he came to join them, passed out with his keys there for the taking. He'd assumed what everyone knew, that with miles of hot desert to the nearest road, they were essentially marooned. But being as young as both women were then, the temptation had been too compelling. So they'd taken the keys and made it out. But it was torrid outside, and impossible. They lasted several days, before Laura was captured. By that point her roommate was dead.

Both the second and third opportunities took place during the wash outside. Both attempts were sparked by a spur of emotion instead of any planning or thought, but this time each of her companions had been Indian women who were used to the desert. In the second her companion was faster and more sure-footed, and disappeared, never to be heard from again, but Laura broke her leg and was caught. In the third her companion had given in to anger, and, after attacking a doctor and setting fire to the place, she'd stayed to watch just long enough that the sheriff arrived.

In the end they'd all failed, and those allies were all dead. The deaths of the first two women didn't bother

Laura any more than yesterday's weather, because of the noises they made—they took those sounds with them—but the third companion had been Laura's friend, and that memory was singed with so much guilt that every day she tried to soothe it with her story.

But now there was Eight. Her arrival had once again brought hope, and though it had begun faintly there now was real progress. After protecting Eight in the first wash Laura had done it again in the second, and then after that, as she lay sore in her room later that night, after resuming the story to her friend, when at one point she stopped her sounds to take a breath, a sound came.

At first she couldn't believe it.

It might have been—must have been—something else, a cough, perhaps, maybe the scrape of a bed, but no, the short noise was different. Laura held her breath and waited, hoping silence might bring it out again. And sure enough, it did.

"Hello?"

Despite all her experience and years here, Laura suddenly had trouble breathing.

She struggled fiercely to control herself, drew in a deep breath, then tried to form sounds which might be understood. Her reply was pathetic, beyond the comprehension of almost anyone, but had the right cadence.

"Hell-o."

For several seconds it was quiet. Laura was unsure whether to try again, or whether to add a question—"Do you understand me?"—but she waited, with her heart pounding, and eventually more came through the wall: a whole sentence.

"Thank you for helping me."

It rocked her. For several moments she couldn't speak. She began to reply, but couldn't, and then, with her throat choking, said in sounds no one could have understood,

"You're welcome."

And it was quiet for the rest of the night.

The very next day she thought it must have been a dream, but after Eight's 'visitors' finally left, when the moonlight crept in and Laura's friend returned to the wall, Laura had, in her halting, grunting way, begun a new thread in the story.

"—the day after, she got another letter, this one on peach-coloured paper. It had a stamp with a crown and a silver tipped staff, and writing that flowed like a lovely ribbon on the envelope. It seemed familiar somehow—"

She'd paused, thinking of how to phrase the next part, and in the pause it happened.

"Hello?" came through the wall.

There was no mistaking it this time.

Laura caught her breath. She thought for several moments, then, as carefully as she could, she twisted out her reply.

"Hell-o."

And now, with just four more words, Eight said so much more.

"I like your story."

It was astonishing. She could count on one hand those who'd understood her before, but now there was Eight.

Ellen Ruth Parker was her real name, and Ellen poured out her own story for nearly a week before Laura began to teach her the plan.

Ellen was pregnant. She planned to run away with her boyfriend until he met another girl and left. Their original plan was to go to a music festival on the East Coast, and after he left, Ellen decided to go there to find him. Without money she began to hitchhike, trading

149

favours for rides when necessary, until the sheriff picked her up.

In the second week Laura began to teach her the plan, and it was good. Ellen knew how to drive, and had a brother was a paramedic. So she had some very good suggestions to add to the plan. And through it all, and best of all, she'd never made the sounds.

They worked on the plan together, finished it last week, and began right away. Each had her part to play. Laura followed Ellen's progress through the pipes and concrete for a week and a half, and then, just three days ago, she said she was ready.

The road Mrs. Locke wanted me to take was really just two ruts of sand that led into a slum. At first the only signs of life were broken bottles and rusty cans I had to avoid, but after a short distance there was movement in my periphery. I turned and saw an emaciated woman with caramel skin, dressed in torn coveralls. She had a hold of a naked boy's arm, and was pulling him away from our approach. She stopped and followed us with suspicious eyes as we passed. I had to turn to avoid a broken shopping cart, and there was another woman, a younger one with the same coloured skin. She called over her shoulder, and a pony-tailed young man emerged from a plywood shed with a shotgun. I swerved back to the ruts and floored the accelerator, and we escaped with no shots being fired.

When we were out of range I slowed again, but the sand thickened and I nearly got stuck. We made a gradual turn and in the bend saw some toughs with tattoos and two grimy old men on a broken sofa. One pointed at the car with a hand that was missing two or three fingers. A dog exploded from behind the sofa to chase after us but I accelerated again, and we got away.

"Just exactly where are we going?" I asked, checking the rear-view mirror. The dog was right behind.

"Straight," was all she replied.

"How far?"

"Just keep going until I tell you."

I lost the dog but then had to slow for two boys, seven, maybe eight years old, both naked, walking between the ruts away from us. They ignored us until I honked and the taller pulled the shorter to the side. They fell in behind and began chasing us. Another child appeared, then another. Mrs. Locke waved at the small posse, but I nudged the gas, wondering if parents were nearby with more guns. The kids fell back, and the signs of life thinned. There were fewer sheds and no more people. Even the trash disappeared, no more scraps, no more bottles and cans. I followed the ruts for several more minutes, then slowed to a stop. A rusted gate was sunk in the sand ahead, blocking our path, with a wooden sign wired loosely to the top that said: 'STA OUT AN BE QIET'.

"I don't suppose you have any ideas on how to get out of here alive?" I said, shifting to reverse.

"Wait! Stop!"

"It's closed." I said as we began moving backwards.

"Open it!" she cried. I stared at her and stopped, more because of her expression than her words. There was anger, but less bitterness, and something sad in her face. It reminded me of Father's urgency about wanting to help her.

So I pulled forward and stopped again, then got out and began towards the gate, but the children caught us. They came past the car and stood around me panting, the two oldest with their palms turned up and begging. I hesitated, unsure for a moment of quite what to do. Then I said, "Excuse me," and strode through them to the gate. They shrugged and headed back towards the car.

The bottom of the gate was buried in sand. I bent and scooped enough from the lower portion that I was able to shove the whole rickety thing open. When I returned to the car, Mrs. Locke's door was open, and she was handing the children paper bills while saying something. It's another of those little indelible things I remember, the smallest boy nodding shyly at whatever she said before he let her pull him close and hug him. I'm not sure why that moment caught me, but it became another of those small effects that softened my disposition towards the brittle Mrs. Locke.

I went to the passenger side, scattering the children back a little more gently, closed Mrs. Locke's door, and went around to the driver's door. When I got in the children had crowded back against the car, and little hands were cupped against Mrs. Locke's window. They followed us to the gate, then stopped just where it had been, as if it was still closed, and we drove on.

"What's so special about this place?" I asked, as the car ploughed through sand.

"You'll see," Mrs. Locke replied, adjusting herself to the centre of the rear seat. She leaned forward and braced herself on the front seatback as she watched out the windshield, but there were only shallow dunes ahead, flecked with cactus and jimson. We came to a fork with a small metal sign and I stopped. It had a crude picture of a rifle with an arrow beneath that pointed left, and another arrow pointing right, with the word "Rest" above it.

"Turn left," she said, so I did. The way swept up and we were soon into the shade of a shallow hill. The sand was thick at the bottom and the tires began to sink. I nudged the accelerator, but the tires slipped and spun until one caught a rock. It lurched us forward, and I tried to keep our momentum going, but the tires sank and we began to slow again, until we reached a place where the road hardened. I had to gun the motor to keep the heavy car moving, but the incline relaxed and our pace smoothed out.

As we were traveling up further, the ridge ahead caught my attention. It was jagged, with a strangely toothed crest. When we got within fifty yards the silhouette became obvious. It was a mass of grave markers. As we got closer I saw a scattering of them, graves with only shambly pieces of wood nailed into makeshift crosses or chunks of slate with pale paint, or even nothing at all. The Lincoln broke over the ridge amidst a forest of them and I stopped, feeling it suddenly hard to breathe.

We were at the edge of a wide, shallow crater filled with thousands of graves, among cactus and mesquite and a few guard-like saguaros.

"Go," Mrs. Locke said.

I hesitated. It was the dreariest cemetery I'd ever seen.

"Go!" she said again.

The road headed straight down, but after a few yards I stopped again. A splintered sign stood before us, with three faded picket arrows, one pointing left for 'Coloured', a second pointing straight for 'Mexicans', and the third aimed right, for 'Indians'.

"This is a segregated … cemetery …?"

"Turn left."

"How long has this been here?"

"I said turn left."

"How long …?"

"Since before the Civil War. Now turn left."

I caught a headstone out the window, an old one with fresher paint. The top line read *Pfc. James Walker* ... "Jesus ... somebody buried a *soldier* here!"

"They're all soldiers."

"This is ... *military*?"

"They being soldiers this would-be military," she said wearily. "Now would you please move this car?"

"They should be at Pioneer, or National. There's a black member of my platoon who's buried at National."

"You should have paid more attention in your history classes."

"I did."

"Then you must have had a public education. Blacks weren't allowed at National back then."

"This is Arizona, not Alabama or Mississippi."

"Right, and Arizona used to be called the Western Mississippi."

"What are you talking about?"

Her voice took on a note of exasperation. "It was the same here as in the South. If a black man died and his parents asked about burial at Pioneer or National they were told there was a special place for them. This is it."

"But ... what about Arlington? Arlington takes everyone. Even in basic they tell you—"

"These families couldn't afford to travel to Virginia for funerals."

"What are you talking about?"

"Maybe we should've stopped to get you coffee."

"What's that supposed to mean?"

"You don't see the signs? They're all around us. See, there, the ... what is it called? Semper ..."

"Semper Fi?"

"The Semper Fi decals, the Ranger flag?"

"Come on! I can't believe they're ..." I began, but my words fell off, and I felt a sudden wave of depression. The graves all around us had small crossed swords or rifle insignias or cannon; most were painted, some had been scraped into rock, a few were carved into wood. She was right. It was military, but the poorest military place I'd ever seen. A few sites looked tended— their stones or crosses were erect, some even had cans of fresh flowers at their base—but most had been overwhelmed by neglect and the desert. It was a junkyard compared to Arlington.

"It's disgusting," I said quietly.

"Don't be disrespectful."

I surged the car left, and drove slowly along a row of graves until Mrs. Locke made me stop to get her bearings. She finally cried, "There!" and pointed towards a huge saguaro cactus with a single arm that reached up on the right. I drove to within thirty yards of it before we were blocked by graves all around. We got out and headed towards it. I began across a barren stretch but she stopped me.

"This way," she said, and we walked around the patch. We came to another apparently empty area but once again she led us around it. At the saguaro she led me to a smaller area of desert a few yards beyond it and began poking the ground with the tip of her cane. "It's here somewhere," she said, trying to move the sand with the silver point. "It has to be … here," she said. She got frustrated and turned towards me. "Don't just stand there."

I knelt and scooped sand with both hands. My slacks were quickly covered with dust, but I kept at it until I came to a hard edge. I worked at it, shovelling and brushing the sand until a two foot mostly square piece of sun-bleached shale was exposed. There were some edges in it, engraving, but sand was caked like mortar into the gaps I used the key from the Lincoln to scrape it away until an inscription showed:

'sabel … tura Mays, bor … … pril … 832,
Died … vember 2 … 190 …'

Mrs. Locke knelt beside it. For several moments she was motionless, then she kissed her fingers and touched them to the letters.

"Who is it?"

Her voice dropped to a whisper. "Isabel Mays."

"The woman …?" I began, remembering Father's story.

Several seconds passed before she stood and brushed off her long skirt. "She ran a brothel."

I stared at her. She'd said the word without any concern, and was staring reverently at the stone.

"You mean … the Buffalo Equine Ranch?"

She nodded. I was quiet. Father, my research, the newspaper archives had mentioned the place, but here was something that made it real.

"You … were you a …?" I stopped, not sure how to ask it.

"I was never a whore," she sighed quietly, "but she took us in. We lived in the white part of what we passed through to get here."

"The white part?"

"It was segregated too then—into parts called Blanco, Baja, Blackton and Apache Junction—that's where the town got its name. We lived in Blanco. My father needed work. He got a job at her ranch. She took us in, put us up in a barn."

"My father had a lot of respect for her."

"Your father was a good man," she said.

So I've heard, I thought to myself.

Mrs. Locke's eyes moved to the area of crater nearby. There were mostly blank spaces among a few ancient, slanted headstones. "The sand confuses things here."

"What do you mean?"

She motioned with the silver tip to another broad empty space nearby. "There are bodies everywhere here, but the sand plays tricks. The day we brought Mrs. Mays' body here we started somewhere over there but kept coming across other remains—skeletons. In some places there are layers of them; men were buried on top of each other."

I stared, my chest aching. The whole place was depressing. These were soldiers, buried in shabby surroundings, sometimes with *one on top of the other*! But for some reason our surroundings made Mrs. Locke more willing to talk.

"These families didn't have a dime between them," she said. "None of us did."

"Beg your pardon?"

"My parents were runaways. They got married when my father was fourteen and she was twelve. They had nothing …"

"So where did you get your money?" I asked, but I immediately felt embarrassed.

"You think I didn't earn it?"

"No … I mean—"

"Yes you did." She looked up. "And for once you're right. My money came from the settlement of my husband's death and my father's inheritance, and what your father did for us."

"I didn't mean that."

"Of course you did." Her voice rose against the quiet of the graves. But then she stopped, sighed and was quiet.

"Really, I didn't. I was … just curious."

"Any other personal questions?"

My eyes retreated from hers to the headstone." You said it was military. What's she doing here?"

She walked a few feet to the right side of the grave and began to prod her cane into the sand. "Her father's here somewhere." Her voice softened. "Right … around here, I think."

I joined her. It took a few minutes to find another flat lying stone, bigger than the first, buried beneath a foot of sand. I was drenched with sweat by the time I'd scraped out the top. I stood back and rubbed my face on my sleeve, then stared. "Is this …" I began, but my words trailed off.

"Lift it up," she said. "Soldiers' headstones are supposed to stand."

I heaved it up, braced the base into the sand, and then crouched with my eyes on the top. "Is this for real?" Top and centre was a crude relief image someone had carved, of a buffalo. Just below that there was an inscription, its first letters shallower than the rest, and mostly obliterated:

'C … p … Josi … …s, bor … ed …
CW, SA-SJH, MH.'

"Who was he?" I asked her.

"Corporal Josiah Mays. He fought in the Civil War and the Spanish American War."

"So CW and the SJH?"

"Civil War, San Juan Hill."

I remember feeling it hard to breathe there. These were names I'd learned in books and heard again in the army, but seeing the letters on a headstone drew up a depressing reality of what happened in those places.

Here was proof those battles really happened. Here were some of the men who'd died fighting them. It was gloomy there, but somehow…somehow holy—to me, anyway. We were standing over the remains of soldiers, young men who'd died in battle, American soldiers.

"And the MH?" I asked dully.

"MH?"

"The last two letters." My finger underlined them on the stone.

"Medal of Honor …"

My finger jerked back.

"… He was shot at Fort Wagner—"

He was at Fort Wagner. We were in the presence of a hero someone had buried in a junkyard. I looked around at the depressing place and shook my head, "This is wrong. It's too … little."

"He wasn't a big man."

"I mean it's … sacrilegious for him … for them to be here."

"It's a special place," she shrugged.

She stood and began back towards the car. I stayed, staring at the headstone, but the sound of her struggling interrupted my thoughts. I got up and took her arm and helped her to the car, helped her inside and began to shut her door, when a nearly horizontal marker nearby caught my eye. It had the same crude image of a buffalo at the top, but leaned almost to the horizontal. I went over and heaved it up, reworked the sand at its base, then started back towards the car, but then saw another. I righted that one too, then spotted more, and couldn't help myself. I couldn't stop. For the next half hour I sweated over nearby gravesites, while Mrs. Locke said nothing, and just watched me through the open door.

CHAPTER THIRTEEN

An Indian whore came into her dream last night. She held the hand of a tiny blonde girl. Laura reached towards the child but the whore moved between them. The whore smiled, but then her face became anxious and afraid, and her fear spread over the dream, filling Laura's mind and blocking the child. Laura's mouth moved to speak, but only grunts came out. The whore pointed towards the child, but the girl was gone, and in her place was a blue steel revolver. Laura tried to grasp it but before she could the gun began to float, moving away and up into the dank air, turning as it rose, until it faced her at eye level. Laura's hand rose, but the trigger moved, the cylinder turned ... and she woke.

The images broke apart as dreams do upon waking, until there were only small pieces left, along with a feeling of dread. At the back of her mind she wondered whether it was an omen, whether their tool would change to become a gun, not a knife, and whether they might die tomorrow. She wouldn't mention the dream to Eight; that could serve no good purpose. Worse, it might lead to hesitation, and that had been fatal to other allies.

Everything was ready now. Eight had learned the inspectors were coming two days, so there'd be a wash tomorrow. She used yesterday's visit to get the knife and

with Laura's help decided where she should hide it. Now
everything was ready. More than ready.
    The wash would be tomorrow.

Once back through the gate I drove more quickly,
but our exit was less threatening than our entrance had
been. The children were distracted, kicking a rag ball,
and though there were dozens of men out now, they were
busy starting small fires. Only a few looked up. There
was no sign of the man with the shotgun. Near the main
road I even found myself nodding to a withered man in a
faded cap, but he didn't respond.

The diner Mrs. Locke insisted on was up the road,
just beyond abandoned railroad tracks. It was easy to
spot, with three rusty poles holding a sign in the shape of
an ancient grey cowboy on a mottled horse, his once red
bandana faded feathery pink, his outstretched right hand
holding a white pistol from which exploded the letters,
"Buf ... lo Caf..." Off to the side two old *Arizona
Eastern Railway* cars were hooked to pipes
cauliflowered with lime. They faced a dozen dirty autos
and trucks. The cars and diner looked equally filthy.

I was repulsed by the place, but stayed quiet while
parking. The cemetery had gone from my thoughts and
my new feelings of calm with Mrs. Locke were
overcome by a little disgust.

An older Indian waitress headed toward us as we
entered. Her skin had the shine of someone who'd
served hot plates for long hours, but she smiled with a
shiny, tired face.

"Chu like a booth?"

Mrs. Locke nodded, and the waitress led us past a
linoleum counter filled with dusty workmen, along

161

booths crowded with Indian and Mexican families, to an empty one in the far reach of the place.

Mrs. Locke peered at the waitress name tag as she sat. "Are you Pia?"

"'Av we met, Senora?"

"Yes, yes," Mrs. Locke replied, but her face seemed to fall a little that the waitress didn't remember. "It was a long time ago, I suppose," she said.

The cook shouted from behind the counter, cutting off a response. The waitress gave us two plastic coated menus and left. Mrs. Locke craned her neck to follow, and I looked around. There were four small tables in the aisle with couples that leaned towards each other in low talk, or leaned back and eyed other couples. The walls were covered with framed photographs—colour ones of Elvis and Brando, black and whites of Ramon Navarro and Hedy Lamar.

"So it's first thing tomorrow?" Mrs. Locke said, resting her menu.

"We'll try our best," I said, glancing at mine before I put it down.

"After all the money you've spent, you're still not sure it will work!"

"We explained that there can't be any guarantees, Mrs. Locke."

"You're not a very good lawyer."

I began to respond but the waitress returned with a carafe of coffee. She poured us each a cup, tucked back strands of hair, then pulled out her pad and pencil to take the orders. Mrs. Locke turned towards her. "Pia, do you remember anyone named …Louisa Lewis or Laura Spinali?"

"Are these ladies from aroun' here?" the waitress asked.

"Do you remember Mrs. Mays? Isabel Mays?"

162

The waitress' eyes jumped a little. "The lady of horses?"

Mrs. Locke nodded. "I lived there too, with you. It was a long time ago. You were four … five. We helped take care of you. I did, and Laura Spinali."

Her words produced a broad smile of recognition. "My father and mather say about you," she said, becoming more excited. She grasped Mrs. Locke's hand with a knowing look. "Es destiny that we are meeting again, Signora!"

"What's become of you?" Mrs. Locke asked.

Pia smiled with a little pride. "I am nurse in the hospital in Phoenix, but my parents are sick and I come back to help. But the years come and they die," she said, with a shrug, "and they leave me thes diner, and I am here and stay."

"A nurse?" Mrs. Locke said reflectively.

"Ches. Tell me, Signora, when you were born?"

"What?"

"What day you were born?"

"The second of December, 1893, but why is that important?"

"Es always important—" she began, but the chef yelled again. Pia took our orders hurriedly and left. Mrs. Locke turned back in her seat, and took a sip of coffee. I was quiet.

"Tell me more," she finally said, staring at me.

"About what?"

"About where you spent all my money."

"I've told you what we did, and what we found."

"Mostly you bragged about how you lost in some lower court before you won in Washington. Mr. Oneal said it cost a half million dollars of my money, all for— what did you say—a few pages of records?"

I took a sip of coffee and looked out the window without responding, thinking. More than half her money was already gone. I turned back and studied her face, still without saying anything. Some of the brittleness that left her in the cemetery was back, but she was so pale, and already so tired. *How is she going to deal with what happens tomorrow?* I wondered.

"And don't pout," she said. "Just tell me what happened."

"I'm not pouting, Mrs. Locke," I said quietly. I studied her a moment longer while choosing my words.

"It's like I said. She was caught by a group of Indians that still lived around here. She was with them for several years before the Army rescued her."

"You have this lawyer-like way of not answering a question."

"I did answer you."

"Don't treat me like a child!" she said, leaning forward, and she lowered her voice. "I want to know! Was she tortured, beaten. Was she …?"

"We … don't have all the details."

"Do they have courses on dodging questions in law school?"

"It's not a nice story."

"I'm a big girl."

You're tiny, and ancient, I thought, but I decided to tell her. "It's everything you could imagine," I said quietly.

Mrs. Locke's mouth opened slightly as if to speak, but nothing came out. She sat, waiting for me to go on, so I did. For the next ten minutes I gave her the edges of what we'd found, Laura's flight into the mountains after her mother died, and a battle army cavalry had with Indians before her rescue ten years later. I left out the army's conclusion that Laura had been regularly beaten and frequently raped, but by the time I finished, Mrs. Locke was wiping her eyes.

"You must have been really good friends to go to all this trouble to find her," I said.

She put down her napkin, and, staring at the markings of sweat and dust on my shirt, spoke in a softer tone. "The last time I saw her we were in the dirt road in Shantytown. We needed to go, my family, I mean. I so wanted her to come with us, but Laura wouldn't leave her mother, and Sophie couldn't travel. We'd lost everything and had to go, but Laura and her mother couldn't. They stayed with some of Mrs. Mays' women. I swore I'd come back."

"And that's—"

"That's the reason."

"I was going to say that's it? You must have been some good friends."

She bit her lips together, and for a moment seemed unable to go on. "She said we'd meet in the after."

"In the … what?"

"I think we both thought we'd never see each other again. She was certain of it."

"So the 'after'…?"

"The after world. The spirit world, after death and before our next life."

"Reincarnation?"

"Indians believed some part of you is inherited, and goes on when you die--your soul, your essence—it goes on to the after world first, for some while, before it returns in another form. She said we'd just meet in the after."

My face must have shown scepticism.

"You don't believe in that sort of thing?" she said, and when I didn't reply she added, "You needn't be afraid of a little old lady."

"I'm not afraid … all right, no, I don't believe it. You live, you die, and you're dead. People can't deal with what they don't know, so they invent religious or psychic explanations like that to make themselves feel better."

"And what's wrong with that?"

"You're joking?"

"I'm serious."

I shook my head dismissively. "People turn faith into conviction. It's like never growing up. Besides, you have to admit this whole concept can be very unfair."

"Why unfair?"

"Well, how fair would it be if I had to argue a case against someone whose essence came from Daniel Webster, or if you came from Florence Nightingale and your brother came from Jack the Ripper? Some people would have huge advantages."

"You're a very shallow young man."

I tried to smile, but still remember by that point, despite some sympathy for her and her friend, that I was tiring again of her prickliness. "You know, Mrs. Locke, I'm trying to help you in the best way I can—"

"Oh, did I hurt your feelings?"

"Do you have to be such a pain in the ass?" I blurted.

Strange, but she seemed to smile. Then she looked away.

"I'm sorry," I said. "I just think the whole concept is completely irrational and very unfair."

"Maybe with all this young wisdom you can explain to me when life was ever fair," she said quietly.

"Well … sure, but all those things—reincarnation, predestination—teach you to resign yourself in life. If you were bound to be a drunk, then why try sobriety? How can you believe free choice and fate?"

"I'm not talking about fate. Besides, everyone makes choices, and not just about what to order in a diner. Even you could change. Maybe someday you'll become more respectful."

"But—" I stopped as the waitress brought our plates. Four pieces of toast and a jar of cactus jam for her. A salad for me; it was mostly iceberg lettuce. I pushed it away.

"Pia," Mrs. Locke called as the waitress turned away. "Please talk to me before we go."

"Chure," she smiled wearily, and she left.

"So you really believe all this stuff about reincarnation?" I asked.

"I never said that."

"After what you just said, now you're telling me you don't really buy into it?"

"I never had it so hard that I felt the need for something like that."

That's not what I heard, I remember thinking, but I kept the thought to myself. For several moments we both stared out at the dusty parking lot without reaching for our plates. The shadow of the large cowboy sign was touching the Lincoln.

Mrs. Locke turned back and reached for the jam. "How do we know they're not lying, just collecting money when she's been long gone ..." she said, struggling to open the lid.

"She's there," I said, motioning. She handed me the jar. The lid was congealed shut. I tapped it on the table, unseated the lid and handed it back. "They have inspections every so often and record a census, including the names."

"And this Judge Warren, he promised we could get her out tomorrow?"

167

"Chief Justice Warren. He gave us what we needed to set up the plan," I began, but then I stopped. Her attention was wholly on the bread. She used her knife to slather the thick spread to its edges, then scraped off excess at the margins. When it was finished she cleared the knife on the rim of the jar and sat back without taking a bite. "And he said we could get her?"

"He gave us enough to try. The problem is these facilities hardly ever give up their patients. This one never has."

"Never?"

"Three families tried, but the clinic fought them. They've got a team of their own lawyers, and have doctors who insisted the patients have to stay for their own good. The judges went along with the clinic."

"They couldn't have been very good lawyers."

"Don't kid yourself, Mrs. Locke. It's going to be very hard. The general rule is that the longer someone's there the harder it is to get them out, and your friend has been there for more than three decades. It's why we're doing what we're doing."

Her face paled a little at that, and once again we slipped into quiet. She cut into the toast, and while I sipped my coffee she took a couple of bites.

"What will you do if it works? If we can get her out?" I asked.

"I'll take her back to California."

"You have a facility in mind?"

"She'll stay with me," she said, motioning for the check. "Meet me at the door, will you? I'm going to talk with Pia."

I took the check from the waitress, was rung up by the cook, then went back to help. Mrs. Locke was writing something on a napkin while speaking earnestly with Pia. They embraced each other and she put the note into her purse. Pia went past me as Mrs. Locke fished out two bills, both hundreds. She left them on the table.

I helped her out the front door and towards the Lincoln. When we got to the car I opened the door. She started for the opening, then stopped ... and surprised me. It was a simple thing, but unexpected: she reached up and patted my cheek, gently this time. Then without another word she turned back to the car.

The home she'd had us buy was on a road bordering Bureau of Land Management land, and though I'd been there only two months before, its transformation surprised me. It had been an old house, a small one, but we'd added a new section with a basement. Jenny's Bentley was parked in front. She met us at the door, looking tired but attractive in a simple white blouse, long denim skirt and boots, and introduced us to an older heavy-set man she introduced as Jim, the general contractor she'd retained for the work. He had thin wisps of white hair going every which way over the shiny dome of his head.

"Are you finished?" Mrs. Locke demanded.

Jim looked a little warily at her, but Jenny smiled.

"There's still some unpacking, but come on," she said. "We'll show you."

They led us through the front room, past several large boxes and wrapped packages, down a long hallway and past three new guest bedrooms to the master. Jim turned on the lights before closing and locking the door. The room was large and furnished with wall paintings lit by brass down lamps, a walnut four poster bed, an elaborate Persian rug beside the bed, and two bergère chairs and a coffee table on the far side of the rug. Jim crouched and rolled back the rug, revealing a satiny expanse of dark wooden flooring. He went to the window, pulled a brass hook from the drapes' draw string and used it to pull up the edge of a floor register near the wall. "There's a lever in here," he explained, and he reached inside. A deep click came from beneath the middle of the floor, then a hydraulic sigh as three edges of a six by four foot rectangular section appeared as if from nowhere, then hinged slowly up to reveal steps that led down into the basement. Jenny flipped a wall switch next to the bed, lighting a table lamp next to the bed. She flipped it twice again in quick succession, and lights blazed deep in the hole.

"Right this way," the contractor said, and he led us down the stairs.

I took Mrs. Locke's arm but paused at the opening to run my hand along the edge. The steps, the bannister, even the vertical portion were made with perfect mahogany carpentry and were beautifully polished. The steps led down to a smaller hallway that split to a full bedroom done in the same style as that above but with two double beds; a separate bathroom with tub and shower, and a small kitchen done in granite and marble.

"Who knows about this?" Mrs. Locke asked, seeming pleased.

"Only my sons," Jim replied. "We dug it, built the forms, poured the concrete, did all plumbing, electrical, hydraulics, even the wallpaper before we allowed any other workmen in. Nobody will find you here."

"And none of this is on the plans?" I asked.

"No one has any idea," Jenny said. "Not even the city."

"What about ventilation?" I asked.

"It has its own system," Jim replied, "but it should be cooler down here even with the door closed."

"Good," Mrs. Locke allowed. "Now let's clean the mess upstairs." I helped her up and went out to get her bags. When I returned Jenny was helping Jim hang a huge living room picture of a mountain valley.

"A little right," Mrs. Locke ordered, standing back. They complied, but it was just the start of several hours of work. She had us unpack almost all remaining boxes while she tapped her cane around the home, interrupting to order us to adjust pictures, move chairs, and clean nooks. But after four hours she tired. She was pulling at the last large box in the living room when her cane slid out and clattered to the floor. "Oh God—help me," she moaned. Her legs began to buckle. I was moving a chair nearby and jumped over to catch her. I helped her to the sofa. She lay back with a look of disgust. "Sit with me," she whispered, and she motioned to the chair. I pulled it close and sat. "I want you and Jenny to stay here this week," she whispered, nodding as if to prime my response.

"I made reservations at a hotel in town."

"Cancel them, and cancel the medical team, except for Dr. Wisler. Get Pia instead."

"The waitress?" I frowned. "Don't you want professionals?"

"She *is* a professional. She's a nurse and offered to help. Hire somebody to take her place in the diner; buy it if you need to. Pay her whatever she needs, but I want her. The number's in my purse," she said, motioning.

"But—" I began, handing it to her, but her expression stopped me. "All right. What else?"

"I'm going to need your help well beyond this next week, probably for at least another month."

"You really won't, Mrs. Locke," I said, shaking my head. Our plan, if it worked, would be to extricate her friend in the early morning, have a doctor come out to examine her and prepare a report that very afternoon, then let Madonna air their arguments in a full-blown court hearing the following week. "I'll be basically done this week, Mrs. Locke. Besides, I've got other clients."

"You're my lawyer."

"I'm theirs too.

"I need more help than they do," she cried, as Jenny came in. She glanced in our direction but took Jim to the door, then came back and sat next to Mrs. Locke. The old woman seemed near tears.

"I'll stay with you," Jenny said, after Mrs. Locke explained her distress.

"I want him too!" she cried, pointing a wavering finger in my direction. "He's my lawyer. He … you know my case."

"There are others in my office who know it. Several others."

"Not like you!" she yelled, grasping my hand. "Please! I'm crossing rivers here!"

I stared at her small white-knuckled hand, then looked up at her. The brittleness seemed worn down, now as much by exhaustion as…well, some inexplicable fear. She was afraid of something. I took in a deep breath. "I'll call Mr. Oneal after we get back tomorrow to see about a few more days—"

"At least a month, and call him now."

"You won't have phones until tomorrow," Jenny said.

"We passed a gas station," Mrs. Locke told me. "Go back and call Pia, then call Oneal … please."

I suppose I was just tired of arguing with her, but I agreed, figuring Mr. Oneal would agree with me. Then again, part of me felt truly sorry for her. She really had seemed to be just one of those people who tilt at windmills, but her friend had turned out to be alive, and I had begun to feel concern about how she'd react to what was coming: seeing her weaken that evening only made it worse. So I left, took the Lincoln to the gas station and called the waitress, then made the call to Mr. Oneal.

His reaction was not what I expected.

"Not a problem, Paul. I can have the partners handle your cases."

"She doesn't need my help for all this. Once we get back from Madonna I'm coming back. I'll drive out here again for the hearing next week. We can send another associate if she really wants someone."

"What's she got you doing?"

"Basically nothing. She had me drive her to a cemetery, take her to a greasy spoon for toast and jam. Now she's got me moving furniture and hiring a waitress. Next thing I'll be sweeping the porch."

"If that's what she needs."

"I'm not a babysitter."

"You don't know what Madonna will do if you are able to take out one of their patients."

"That's a big if, but I'm not worried about that. They'll put up their usual effort but then, hopefully, take some kind of settlement offer to drop anything further."

"Maybe so, but even if all that does happen, those women may need help in ways you can't predict."

"My aim is to become a trial lawyer, Mr. Oneal, not a general practitioner."

"Remember what your father used to say about how seldom a lawyer gets a truly good client?"

"Oh, come on!"

"Seriously, after everything that happened to her family, and her husband, she spent all that time on her child only to have her die, and now all she's thinking about is this other woman. You could try a lifetime of cases and not find anyone like her. And the hard part's about to start—"

"What she needs is a concierge, not a lawyer"

"What she needs is somebody to help her with anything she'll face for however long she has left. And if you never set foot in another courtroom—"

"What do you mean?"

"You'll both end up a hundred times better off—"

"How long?" I demanded. For some reason I hadn't spent time thinking about her illness.

He didn't answer.

"Mr. Oneal?"

I still remember his long sigh, before he explained. "She has leukaemia. It's stage four, Paul. It's already in her aorta and liver."

I pressed the phone harder against my ear. "How long?" I demanded, staring up at the moonlit mountains while thinking about the small, brittle woman.

He didn't answer, at first, but then he said, "Months … if that."

For several moments neither of us said anything else. Then I took my own long, deep breath. "What do I charge for sweeping her porch?"

He chuckled. "Are you ready for tomorrow?"

"I guess," I replied.

"You really think it'll work?"

"If their lawyer doesn't get up too early."

"You're leaving her behind, I hope."

"I've got to get back," I said, and I hung up. I walked slowly back to the Lincoln, but once on the pavement found myself speeding back to the house.

A rustling noise woke me at midnight. There it was again, from inside the house. Someone was in the living room. I got up and padded to my door. The rustling became louder. I stepped to the end of the hallway and peered around the corner.

It was Mrs. Locke.

She was on the sofa, in a long terry cloth robe, bending into the last big packing box. The table beside her held two statuettes and a tarnished silver bridle. Crumpled sheets of newspaper were scattered at her feet.

"Why aren't you asleep?" I asked, stepping to the chair opposite.

"How can I sleep?" said a muffled voice from inside the box. She pulled out a small package.

"Go to bed," she said, but she handed it to me and bent back inside.

"What are we looking for?" I asked.

"A wooden box," came her voice.

I unwrapped the package. It was a grey soapstone statuette of a swayback horse, unsaddled but with a halter that hung from its head to the base. I set it aside and gently pulled her back. "Let me," I said. I pulled out several more paper-wrapped packets, before I found what she was looking for.

It was an old wooden box with rough dovetail joints and a cardboard top sealed with masking tape. I set it on her lap. She unfastened the top. Two layers of newspaper were inside, and beneath, three thin packages neatly wrapped in more newspaper. Beneath them lay a rectangular package wrapped in pale blue paper and tied with flattened silver ribbon.

She undid one of the thin packages. It was a silver-framed photograph with a yellowed corner note. She handed it to me. "My daughter Molly," she said. I had to smile. There, in the midst of a throng of cap and gowned students was a grinning oval eyed girl in a wheelchair.

"Graduation … in Pennsylvania, I heard. Was it Mercersburg?"

She nodded. Her brittleness seemed gone again, at least for the moment.

"I heard you even got her an internship—was it for Senator … Fishburne?"

"We met his family at the Special Olympics …" she began, but her voice trailed off as she unwrapped another package. My eyes went to her daughter's picture, and to the frame. It was exquisite, with silver vines and a perfect little hummingbird perched in the corner.

"Nice frame," I said, eyes on the hummingbird. It was poised, wings out, head down, as if hovering for the best view of Molly.

"Laura gave it to me the last time I saw her. Her grandfather made it. That's his writing," she said. The little note bore foreign script:

"*Alla mia dolce figlia con amore*'"

I turned to ask what it meant but stopped. With the light behind her Mrs. Locke's hair was darkened, her skin smoothed, and her profile—forehead, mouth, and chin—looked young, sharp, and struck me with a sudden sense of familiarity. I still remember thinking that maybe she'd been right that first day, maybe we had met, or maybe I'd seen a picture of her somewhere; or maybe there was something else that did it, because there *was* something very familiar about her. *What is that?* I wondered. My eyes went back to her hands and the plain wedding band on her finger. Even that seemed familiar, but I'd been distracted. She was talking.

"What?" I asked.

"You're not paying attention. Is it past your bedtime?"

"I'm sorry, I was just thinking." I looked back down at the picture, thinking that despite her wheelchair, a segment of Molly's smile had her mother's beauty—the same sharp curve of the upper lip, the same thinner line of the lower.

"You should go to bed, instead of staying here with a mean old woman."

"May I ask you a question?" I asked.

"You can always ask," she shrugged. "I may not answer."

"Why are you doing this?"

"We didn't finish," she said, motioning to the box.

"No. I mean this work—my research, the court case—everything we're doing to get Laura. You only knew her a short time, I mean, one or two years, and that was a half century ago? And you had no contact since, so why all this?"

"Are you trying to make me feel old?"

"Well ... I just wondered."

"I told you, I made a promise, and I keep my promises."

"Don't tell me you kept every promise you made as a child."

"Don't tell me you haven't."

It was my turn to shrug.

"You should keep them. I haven' always been able to, but I've always tried," she said.

"But that day Laura shot her father. My father said you were pretty upset then too."

She glanced at me and looked down. "She just shot her father, for God's sake."

"I know that, but ..." I stopped, thinking back on what Father had said. He'd said the room was empty except for Gino, lying there. And Mrs. Locke—then a young girl—was right outside, crying, looking a mess. It suddenly hit me. Mrs. Locke looked up. Her face had darkened.

"I'm sorry," I said, feeling suddenly ashamed.

Several seconds passed before she spoke, and her voice came in a whisper. "You don't have to know everything, Paul," she said, and she looked down at the next package. It was still wrapped, cradled in her hands. Some hardness came back into to her voice as she began to unwrap it. "I'm not going to sit home and knit booties while she's in some institution."

"I truly am sorry," I said. "That part's none of my business. Look, will you at least stay here? This won't be pleasant, and if either of us says the wrong thing, or gives the wrong impression, they could just tell us to go to hell."

"No one is telling me to go to hell."

"I mean—"

"I know what you mean. And I haven't come this far to leave without her."

She handed me the next picture. "You have a girlfriend?" she asked.

When I didn't answer she looked up. "You're the one who got personal."

"Did you talk to my father or Mr. Oneal about this?"

"No. Why?"

"I've had a few."

"A few like three or four, or thirty or forty?"

"A *lot*, I guess, but never a real serious thing … Who's that?" I asked, pointing to the picture in her hands, and hoping to change the subject.

"My father, after he started to do well. He began a ranch, a rental string."

It was a good picture of a handsome middle-aged cowboy. He was leaning back against a lodge pole fence, looking with slitted eyes off into a sunset. There were fine wrinkles around his mouth, and a faint smile in his lips.

She unwrapped the last package, and her eyes became wistful. I put the image of her father down and she handed the last one carefully to me. "My Nathan. We were in Carmel."

It was a cheap frame of cracked wood, containing a faded photograph that was torn at the bottom, but her husband had been looking into the camera with strong eyes when it was snapped. I was caught by the impression, enough that once again I didn't notice Mrs. Locke was talking.

"I'm sorry?"

"I said you both have those dark eyes. Probably why you always reminded me of him. And he could be every bit the pain you are, but was someone you wanted on your side."

For several moments we sat, me staring at Nathan and her watching me, until the silence became awkward. My eyes went to the dovetail box still on her lap. The small blue package was all that was left. I was suddenly curious. "What's that?"

"A gift from Nathan," she said, without any sadness. "He was bringing me this when he died." She pulled it out, put the wooden box on the floor and held the blue rectangle in the cups of both hands.

"You never opened it?"

"It doesn't matter. There was another gift he was bringing me. Your father told me later. Nathan was going to tell me we'd turned the corner. He had a new position, with better hours. He'd even begun looking for Laura. And he was going to give this to me ..." she said, and her voice trailed off.

"Why didn't you open it?"

She shrugged and began to put it back in the shoebox.

"I'd have thought he'd have wanted you to."

She frowned at me, hesitating, but then pulled it back to her lap. Her fingers teased the flattened silver ribbon for a moment, then pinched its end and pulled it taut. The knot stuck with years of heat and fixation. She tugged harder; enough that the seal finally separated, the bow slipped through the knot, and the ribbon fell away. She unfolded the stiff paper. A blue velvet box sat inside. Her fingers went to the lid; she took a deep breath and pushed up at the front.

The lid angled back with a *crack,* and reflected light glimmered into her face. Her eyes narrowed, staring for several seconds, then her right hand came up and stopped short of her mouth. "I know … this piece …!" she whispered. She bit her lips together, and clenched her eyes shut, and in a moment the brittle, angry, dying woman was crying. I had always felt unsure of myself around her, but not then. I took her hand, and pulled her closer. A moment later her head was buried in my shoulder, and the only sound was her quiet sobbing.

CHAPTER FOURTEEN

Laura's previous plans hadn't worked out, no matter how much thought and effort she'd put into them, because of the other women she'd involved. Now, even this one, to whom she'd given more thought and effort than ever before, threatened to ruin everything—all because of something she hadn't anticipated. Where two of the other women had become too cautious, last night Eight had become reckless. It had taken days before to convince her to let them to use her one last time, and after all that, just when Laura was sure she'd succeeded and that all was well, now this. And now, the whole plan was in danger. She understood why Eight did it, but spent the rest of the night in anger.

There were clouds outside and the light was dull this morning, but it would eventually wake everyone to what happened. She stretched towards the wall and opened her eye. Her friend hadn't appeared last night, probably from disgust. She brushed her fingers across the irregular surface and sighed. There was a chance the orderly might not be missed until they were out for the wash, for Eight had shoved his body completely under the bed, but when they cleaned the room he'd surely be found, and God knows what would happen then.

The hall door clanged open and closed, then the morning orderly's footsteps sounded with the squeal of a

cart. Breakfast. The noise proceeded a room at a time,
bringing a chain of other noises at each door—keys
jingling, locks turning, room doors clanging open, then
thin, empty metal plates being lifted and full ones put
down; and the door sounds reversing themselves and it
all moving down from one room to the next. The
procession marched slowly past One, Two, and Three.
When it reached Eight Laura held her breath, but the
plates were exchanged without incident, and the sounds
left Eight and came to Laura's room. Her empty plate
was taken, a fresh replacement put on the floor, and the
door clanged shut.

She ignored the meal long enough to hear the
crackling noises of Eight slipping up from her bed,
retrieving her meal, then the crackling as she sat to eat.

Laura retrieved her own plate. It contained the same
small portions of white and brown slurry as every meal
since she could remember, together with a Dixie cup of
apple juice. Small clumps of white powder were
incompletely mixed at the top of the juice. Laura
scooped the thicker pieces out and added them to what
was already in the seam of her gown, then poured the
remaining juice in the toilet. She waved off the flies and
ate the food, smeared her fingers around the edges of the
plate and sucked them clean, then returned the plate to
the foot of the door and laid back.

"Are you ready?" Eight asked, as if nothing was
wrong.

"I am. Are you?"

"Fucking A." There was no mention of the orderly.

Several minutes passed in quiet before the sound of a
car came through the wall. Laura's head turned. It was
a different sound than the staff vehicles, deeper,
smoother. The sound disappeared. A door opened and
closed, then another. There was a knock on the lobby

door, then pounding. The big nurse yelled, then there were footsteps, then it was quiet.

I got up at four-thirty, but Jenny and Mrs. Locke were already awake. An ambulance arrived by five. We led them east in the Bentley until our headlights came to a small junction. There were lights blinking on two federal marshals' vehicles on the other side. They took up the lead and drove us another three miles before slowing at a small sign with faded lettering—'State Facility'. An arrow pointed to a strip of broken concrete that led off into the desert. They stopped and we got out for a short conference, then we returned to the Bentley and fell in behind the marshals. We drove along the broken road into the desert for more than six miles, when the road dropped into a deep wash and climbed over a small rise, and there, in the dull light, there it was, blocking the end of the road.

It was a simple structure in the way military and prison structures are simple, three hundred feet wide, flat-roofed, pale brown stucco and concrete, with forty feet of sagging wooden porch at its centre, and at the midpoint, a large front door of pockmarked metal. A dusty green Mercedes and four older cars were parked in a dirt lot at the right side, and before them a four by five foot sign of white painted plywood announced the place:

'Madonna Hospital and Sanatorium
Formerly, Madonna Home
Est. 1884, by Hon. Frederick Augustus Tritle,
Governor of the Territory of Arizona,
Rebuilt after fire in 1937.
Visitors by Appointment Only. (480) 982-2111'

183

We parked close to the entrance. "You sure you wouldn't rather wait here?" I asked, but Mrs. Locke was already exiting the car, using her cane but with no sign of last night's fragility. I spoke again briefly with the marshals, then we left Jenny with them and the paramedics and went to the front door. It was unlocked, and opened to a ten foot square lobby lit with fluorescents. There were faded chairs inside, a coffee table littered with old *Look* magazines, and another door on the far side, with a reception window beside it. I knocked at the door, and when that produced no response pounded on it with my fist. A muffled yell sounded deep inside the building. A few seconds passed and then footsteps echoed. They grew louder until they reached the wall beside the door.

The reception window clicked and slid open. "We're full up," a woman's voice said, and the window began to close.

I stuck in my hand to stop it. "I've got a court order for production of a patient."

"That has to be cleared through our lawyers."

"They've been notified, and she's to be produced now."

"*When*?"

"Right now. There are marshals outside." I passed my card and an envelope through the window. A pale hand with bright polish snatched them.

"Who's the patient?" the voice demanded.

"Laura Michele Spinali."

"Just a minute." A phone was picked up, a dial turned three times, and a moment later fragments of conversation could be heard through the opening:

"It's me … A lawyer's here with a court order … a lawyer … wait … Rankin somebody … he says they brought a marshal ... says they were notified … no, no

.... I haven't ... Number Nine ... I have no idea ... Right."

There was an audible click, a rustling movement, and on the other side of the door a deadbolt slid aside. The door opened and a heavyset blonde woman in a tight nursing uniform appeared. "This way," she said brusquely. She led us down a grey painted corridor and into an office with walls of grey concrete, a grey linoleum floor and a bank of four grey metal filing cabinets. Against those drab surroundings there was a mahogany desk with elegant inlay at the far end, with a sage tapestry hung behind it. A large golfing photograph hung on the side wall, showing three men in a small arc on a golf course green, their clubs angled toward the camera.

There was a strange assortment of seating in the room—an expensive chair of blue leather behind the desk, another of simple cane wood in front of it, an opulent red leather wingback beside the cane chair, and a sofa of crushed brown velvet in the corner. A golf bag leaned against one side of the sofa, and next to the other side a dusty trophy case held two plastic golfing trophies.

The nurse left without a word. Mrs. Locke gripped my arm but neither of us spoke. The door reopened, admitting a slender little man in a rumpled polo shirt and Levis. He was in his sixties, barely taller than Mrs. Locke, with dyed black hair swept wetly across a bald spot. My envelope was in his right hand, its unfolded contents in his left.

"I'm Dr. Braga," he said. He smiled as he spoke, but above the smile his eyes seemed impatient.

"We have a court order requiring production of a patient—" I began.

"I'm afraid someone has given you the wrong impression about how things are done here," he interrupted. "This patient—" he glanced at the name on the papers, "—is here on a prison sentence as well as a medical hold."

Mrs. Locke's grip tightened on my arm, but she said nothing. I'd explained to her that Laura's confinement was on both grounds, but that because of the confidential nature of the details, which were still stubbornly sealed against us, we had no idea what the criminal charges had been.

"Her criminal status is irrelevant," I said, trying to keep my voice calm, though my heart was pounding. "A federal Judge has ordered her released."

"We have orders from the state saying we can't do that."

"They've been overridden by the federal Judge."

"You can't just waltz in here and expect me to take your word for it. Our lawyers need to be involved, there has to be a full hearing, a lot of things need to be done."

"You needn't take my word for it. The order is in your hand. You can have a hearing—there's one set for next week."

"Well there you go," Braga waved the papers with a quick, smooth gesture. "You've got the cart before the horse. We can discuss this again when that's concluded."

"She's to be released pending the hearing."

"Letting her out before then is impossible."

"Then you should collect your things. There are two marshals outside, with instructions to take you into custody if she's not produced."

"You can't just come in here and remove her that quickly!" he sputtered, snapping his fingers. "She's one we've … taken care of for a long time. We need to be sure … she'll be handled appropriately."

"We have paramedics with us to make sure she will be, and there's a medical team ready to take over her care."

The doctor snorted. "You'd deny our right to counsel in this matter?"

"Your counsel was served thirty minutes ago."

His eyes narrowed over me, then he shook his head. "I won't do it."

"You're saying you won't produce her?"

"Absolutely not," Braga said, folding his arms.

I reached inside my coat, pulled out a miniature recorder, clicked it on and laid it on the desk, then checked my watch and began an announcement:

"This tape is being recorded at the Madonna Hospital and Sanatorium in Apache Junction, Arizona at 6:05 on Monday morning, June 15, 1968. I am Paul Rankin of the Rankin law offices, attorney for Mrs. Louisa Jeannette Locke. Mrs. Locke is the petitioner in *Re the Matter of Laura Michele Spinali.* Mrs. Locke is here with me in the office of Dr. James Braga, the director of the Madonna home. Dr. Braga is also present."

"Doctor, I just served you with an order which was entered last Friday afternoon by the Honorable Jamie Jacobs of the U.S. District Court in Phoenix. It specifically names you and your lawyers. A process server delivered it to your law firm about thirty minutes ago. You have it in your hand. I assume you've read it. The order is self-explanatory but I've told you it requires the immediate release of a patient named Laura Michele Spinali. You've acknowledged she is present on these premises, but you've refused to release her. I'm therefore notifying you again, this time on tape, that the order requires you to produce the patient, and I quote, 'immediately upon presentation of the order'. Those last six words are directly from the order. I've further explained that we've brought federal marshals to enforce the order, but despite my explanation you continued to refuse. I've warned you that you'll be arrested and confined in a federal prison if you don't produce her. Do you have anything else to say before I get the marshal?"

"I can't believe this!" the doctor exclaimed. "You give me five minutes' notice on a patient we've had over thirty years! You can't expect miracles, counsellor—"

"If she's here, it shouldn't take a miracle."

The phone buzzed. The doctor punched the speaker. The nurse's voice came into the room. "There are two federal marshals in the lobby," she said. "They're telling me … they say they've been ordered to pick up either patient Number Nine or you, Doctor."

"Tell them to wait!" Braga snapped. He glanced at his watch and turned to me. "How can you expect me to give up a patient before talking to our lawyer? It's barely six on a Monday morning. No one's going to be there."

"That's not my problem, but I'll give you five minutes to try to reach him," I said, and I held my breath. Braga put the receptionist on hold and began to dial. I motioned Mrs. Locke to the sofa, and sat facing Braga in the wingback chair. He listened to the phone for a moment, then pulled the handset close to his mouth and spoke rapidly.

"Leona, I need to reach Bob … You'd better. We've got a lawyer who just walked in with a federal order to produce a patient … right now! … I said they just walked in … he says your office was served with the order a half hour ago … I know that … All right." He hung up and looked at me with sudden calm. "They're tracking him down."

"How long?" I said sceptically, checking his watch.

"I called his secretary. It shouldn't be long."

Quiet came over the room, and we waited at least two minutes in silence, until Mrs. Locke spoke.

"How is she?" she asked, from the edge of the big sofa.

"Fine," Braga said tightly. "With our help she's ... been fine."

"Can we talk to her while we're waiting?" Mrs. Locke said.

"I'm afraid that's impossible. She's brain damaged, retarded if you will—"

"What! What have you done to her?" Mrs. Locke cried, starting up. I motioned her back.

"Nothing," Braga said, focusing on her. "... I mean ... we've provided good medical care, treated her with medications and counselling, and she's a little better now, but she's been that way since birth. She doesn't understand, can't communicate, and can't even think properly."

"You're a terrible excuse for a Doctor!"

His smile disappeared. "I've practiced medicine for almost forty years, Mrs ...Locke, a lot of it handling patients like ... Miss Spinali for the state."

"If you can't communicate with her it just means you haven't really tried."

Braga's eyes drifted to the grey silk of her blouse, then to the silver horse head of her cane. "What's the source of funding here?"

"What are you talking about?" she asked.

He turned to me, looking suddenly recharged. "We're entitled to payment for what we've done for patients, before they're released. Have you brought a bond, anything to secure our interest?"

"I thought you were paid by the state!" Mrs. Locke said, but he didn't answer. He was once again studying her. As he watched she got out her check book.

"You can put that away, ma'am. A personal check won't do. But yes, we have the right to recover for what the state has paid, on the state's behalf, and quite a bit more, I'm afraid. There's been a lot more spent on her than just what they give us."

"You can't delay production based upon that," I snapped.

"We've supplied more than thirty years of care, counsellor. We're entitled to be paid."

"Then file a motion for payment. I told you, the hearing is next week. You'll have plenty of time," I said, reaching for the recorder. "Doctor, your five minutes are up. I'm going to advise the marshal that you will not produce her. You're going into custody."

"Now wait just a moment—"

"No, *you* wait. You've been served with a direct order. So far you've done nothing but waste our time. I'm getting the marshals." I clicked off the recorder.

The doctor leaned forward to speak, but the intercom buzzed. His arm darted out. "Yes?"

"It's the lawyers," the nurse's voice said. I tensed. We'd timed this in the hope they wouldn't be available until after we had Laura.

"Put them on," he said quickly. He picked up the receiver, sat and swivelled his chair away, and began speaking in a low voice.

"There's a lawyer here with marshals and paramedics, and a court order requiring production of a patient … *Where* …? We've got state confinement orders but they say their order is federal … yes …yes … all right," he said. He turned back to the desk, flipped back to the front of my order, cleared his throat and began reading passages out loud:

"'*To the Madonna Hospital and Sanatorium, also known*' … all right … wait … Here it is … '*You are*

hereby commanded and directed to immediately—' ...
Yes ... it says ... *'immediately'* ... Ok '*... to immediately produce and relinquish custody of the person and possession of the effects of Laura Michele Spinali, and to transfer custody and possession of said person and effects without delay to the Petitioner Louisa Jeannette Locke and the law offices of Rankin, Luckhart ... ,'*"

My stomach churned as the reading went on. The doctor flipped to the last page.

"*'... Honorable Jamie Jacobs, presiding judge of federal district court for the district of .... Dated this tenth day of April, 1968'.*"

He listened several more seconds. "Yes ... yes ... how soon can you get here? ..." He looked up at me. "He can be here in an hour."

I shook my head and he went back to the phone.

"They won't ...all right," he said. He clutched the phone to his chest. "He says you can't do this, and he'll file contempt proceedings against all of you."

"File away," I said, getting up again. "I'm getting the marshals."

"Wait ..." he pleaded. He spoke briefly on the phone and looked up again. "I need your IDs."

"You have them," I said. I pretended to fume but felt myself sweating.

"Picture IDs?" he demanded.

"In the envelope."

Braga spoke into the phone again while watching me. He paused, listening, then swivelled his chair around. I wiped my palms at the sides of my trousers. The doctor spoke too softly to hear more than fragments.

"There's no bond but ... must have ...And then what? ... You think we can ... that? ... sure? ... Rankin office … Yes …When can you start? … Tell him to hurry …All right," he said.

He swivelled back fully around and hung up the phone, wiped his chin carelessly with the back of his sleeve, took a deep breath and stood.

"You can have her, for now," he said and he shrugged, as though all that had happened to this point was unimportant.

CHAPTER FIFTEEN

Laura heard a door close in the distance, followed by footsteps. She could tell where they were—along the corridor from the doctor's office. There were at least two sets—no, three. The heavier were both men; one was the doctor. But there were softer sounds among the louder—a woman? Yes. Another woman, in heeled boots, moving slowly, as if already drugged. And tapping—what was that? She wasn't sure. The doctor's steps paused from time to time, but each time they did, for a few moments, the tapping continued. Laura began feeling nauseous. With Eight's arrival the rooms were all taken. This woman was a replacement.

She heard the creak of other women getting up, and felt their nervousness, then heard Eight get out of the bed next door, getting ready, but for what? Eight wouldn't understand. She didn't know enough to worry. Besides, she didn't have to worry—she was young and pretty. When replacements came they were always for the older ones, and for two years now Laura had been the oldest.

Another door opened and closed, and the sounds came more loudly. Strange, that tapping, of something hard against the linoleum, in rhythm with every other step of the woman's walk. It was beyond Laura's experience. The sounds came to the door at the end of the corridor and stopped. A key turned, the door screeched, and Dr. Braga's voice burst in; he said something about the air. The footsteps moved, then stopped, and the door clanged shut. The steps took up again inside the corridor. They settled into a rough collection that moved past One and Two, then Three and Four, but without pausing. Laura tensed. Three and Four were the only other aged women here, and the sounds hadn't even hesitated there.

They were coming for her.

Replacement happened so rarely here, only six or seven times during her stay here, always to older women who'd been there for decades and one day up and disappeared. It always started with these kinds of noises—footsteps that included a new woman, arriving in an already full corridor, the clank of a door opening, the whisper of a syringe being unwrapped, and after a few minutes of quiet, the last steps of someone who left without departure—without any sounds of a car or a truck, without any noise of a motor or siren, with nothing to signify a person had been taken elsewhere.

They could only be coming for her, but her mind went to Eight. What must she be thinking? Probably she thought someone heard her last night and told, or perhaps the orderly was already missed? She could hear Eight moving, her bed creaking; she was checking to make sure she shoved him far enough beneath the bed, or hiding the knife. But she was wrong.

They were coming for Laura.

The steps slowed somewhere around six, and an unfamiliar man's voice spoke. He asked a question in tones too faint to discern. The doctor replied with a curt voice, using something that ... sounded like a name, a woman's name. Not a number, a name. And his tone— that was strange; he was normally gracious with *newcomers and 'guests' alike, not like this. They were past Six now. Hers and Seven's were the smaller rooms. They ... they were approaching Eight. Eight's bed creaked. She must have the knife. The footsteps approached her door, but didn't slow.*

Laura's fingers clutched at the wall. She was too old to fight. Oh God. Please, she thought, and her nails scraped the concrete. Please!

The doctor stopped at the door to let us catch up, then led us out of the office and down the same corridor we'd walked before. He moved slowly and everything seemed to take longer now; that same short stretch we'd travelled before seemed twice as long. He stopped and looked back at Mrs. Locke a few times, as if waiting to let her catch up. It became obvious he was stalling.

"What are you doing?" I demanded.

"Just waiting for Mrs ...Locke."

"I'm keeping up just fine," she said.

He shrugged and went on just as slowly, leading us through another door and along a shorter hallway, until we reached a thickly painted grey metal door with fat rivets along its perimeter. He pulled out a ring of keys, sorted to one and fit it into the door. It turned and he rotated the handle with a loud metallic clank. He pulled the door open said, "We've had some problems with ventilation recently, so the air is a bit close."

A strong smell billowed out, hot, humid, with the faint scent of urine. "Last room on the right," he said, motioning while standing there.

I put my arm out to block Mrs. Locke. The hallway stretched like a narrow cave for ninety feet ahead of us, with weak light from caged ceiling bulbs that barely illuminated the narrow walls and dark floor. There were nine or ten doors on the right side, each with a small, heavily framed mesh window. A dirty red extinguisher was hung halfway down the right side beneath an old sign that said, 'Fire Extinguisher', with an arrow pointing down. A mop and yellow slop bucket sat nearby.

I turned to Braga. "Lead the way." He smiled one of his cold half smiles and obliged. Our footsteps sounded tacky on the stone floor. I took in the first small, thick, wire meshed window on the right as we passed. It was too dirty to see through.

"Are there patients in these rooms?" I asked.

"I can't discuss anyone here but Laura Spinali, counsellor," Braga called over his shoulder. "You should know that."

We passed the first eight doors without slowing before Braga stopped at the ninth. He pulled the ring of keys, found one and fit it into the lock. It screeched through a full revolution. He took hold of the door handle, drew in a deep breath, then turned his head and pulled the handle. There was a loud metallic click, and the door to Laura's room swung open.

CHAPTER SIXTEEN

As the door opened Laura cringed to the wall. There was coughing behind her—it sounded like both a woman and a man were coughing. The light steps tapped in slowly, still coughing. They stopped. It was still for a moment, then a rustling noise. The light steps rushed out. A woman shouted. There was anger in her voice. The light steps returned, and a heavier pair followed them into the room. The rustling of clothes sounded nearby, then a scent of lemon came to her. The woman's voice spoke closely, softly, calling a name she'd heard before. A man coughed nearby her, paused, and then left.

Laura searched the wall for her friend, but there was nothing but concrete.

The woman called the name again, her voice quavering. There was some sort of fight going on outside, then it was over. It was all over. They were taking her to god knows where? For god knows what? She readied herself, wishing they were dead.

Please!

And the name came again. The woman's voice said it.

"Laura?"

Braga had, without thinking, held his breath, but Mrs. Locke and I were surprised by the thick smell. It was putrid, horrible, and we both began to cough. I pulled a handkerchief and tried to hold it to Mrs. Locke's mouth, but she shook her head and jerked away and still coughing went inside. I started after her, then stopped. She was already back out, struggling past me towards Braga.

"You *bastard*!" she cried. She shifted the cane to mid shaft and raised it towards him. She was going to throw it. I stepped between them. "*Bastard*!" she screamed hoarsely around me.

"We're a state institution," Braga said. "We got next to nothing for air conditioning, ventilation, or anything else, so it's hard to get everything we need—"

"Damn your state institution!" she cried, and turning back to Laura's door she shouted over her shoulder: "Damn your words! You bastard!" And she went back inside. I followed, but after only two steps had to stop.

The room was a concrete rectangle no more than five by six feet, dimly lit by what came through a small and dirty window. At first I saw only a fat drain pipe that came up from the floor on the left side of the room, but then I took a step inside and saw the bed. It was tiny but took up the whole right half of the floor. There was an irregular shape on the bed, up against the wall. As my eyes adjusted I made out the shape of an old, gaunt woman. Her long white hair was matted and dirty, and the right side of her face looked scarred with web like marks that stretched from the right eye to her nose and ear. Her hands were up against the wall, groping its pitted surface. There was mildew everywhere, on the floor around the pipe, up all the walls, except for a small, clear space right next to the woman's face. She was clutching at that space, her fingers slowly stretching and tightening over the concrete.

Mrs. Locke knelt beside the bed and reached out. Her hands approached the figure, but hesitated inches away.

"Oh, Laura, honey," she whispered brokenly. The gaunt woman groaned away from the sound, and the skin of her arms sagged with the movement. Mrs. Locke turned towards me, her eyes welling.

I'll never forget that sight, nor the effect it had on me. My irritation with Mrs. Locke had faded after our visit to the cemetery and was mostly gone after the emotion of last night, but I was still an irritable young man, and whether the spark came more from witnessing her friend in this miserable place or seeing the impact it had on Mrs. Locke, it lit me up more than anything had in a long time.

I used what self-control I had left to pat Mrs. Locke's shoulder, then turned and strode out to where the doctor stood.

"She's right, you know," I said tightly, while walking towards him. He stepped back with a puzzled expression, but moved too slowly to get away. I grabbed him by the collar, clutched him up and yelled into his face. "You *are* a bastard."

"Get your hands off me!" he gasped, but then I hit him. It wasn't a heavy blow, nothing like a roundhouse; it was more the sort of jab we used in basic training to set someone up, but it knocked him back against the door on the other side of the hallway. He stood there, holding his jaw, until I hit him again, harder this time.

He grunted and fell, but I picked him up by the collar. My voice dropped to a whisper.

"What did you do to her?" I demanded, and my hands tightened.

"Please!" he gasped, and I hit him a third time, this time in the stomach. It doubled him over, and he fell again. I pulled him back up, got my hands around his throat, and began tightening them.

"PAUL!" Mrs. Locke's voice came from just behind me. Then she was beside me, pulling at my arm. I remember turning towards her, seeing her face, and that pleading look of hers broke the spell. I turned back to Braga.

"Get some people in here!" I shouted, shoving him back. He gasped for breath.

"NOW!" I yelled.

He pulled a walkie talkie from his hip and began gasping commands. In less than a minute two orderlies had a gurney in the hallway. They tried to get Laura out, but that was difficult. She began to struggle violently, and to scream the strangest noises. The orderlies backed away, circled her warily, moving their heads to dodge her hands, then one got behind her and jumped in. He wrapped his arms around her. She tried turning her head to bite him, but he bent away and the other grabbed her legs.

They got her to the gurney and were able to strap her down. It was then that I was able to see her features for the first time. I wasn't sure at first if my eyes were playing tricks, because everything was so chaotic, but while the right side of her face, though drawn and dirty, looked relatively normal, each time she turned the other way I could see a cratered, web like left socket where the other eye had been.

They rolled her down the hallway, with her shouting and twisting against the straps, and with us following. We passed out the heavy metal door and into the outside corridor, along that to the lobby door, and then through the small lobby and out into the morning sun.

Laura screamed with the sunlight, but kept fighting. The marshals and paramedics stared at the struggling, shouting woman being wheeled onto the rickety porch.

"This is the patient!" I yelled at them. "This is Laura Spinali!" They finally moved, but it took several moments before they managed to get her to the cars. We were still thirty feet from the rear of the ambulance when the nurse came running out, waving her arms.

"Doctor!" she yelled. "Mr. Janoff is on the phone! He says don't release her. He's coming."

"Wait!" Braga shouted. "*Stop!*" Everything seemed to slow, and even Laura stopped her noises.

"Don't listen to him!" Mrs. Locke shouted. She shoved her way past an orderly, and began to undo the strap around Laura's legs. That woke me, and I began to undo the others, but then Laura came to life. She grabbed at my face as I swept her up in my arms.

"Laura, no!" Mrs. Locke cried, but her fingernails clawed at my cheek. I lost my grip and tripped on a strap, and we both fell to the ground. Laura began to crawl back towards the building. I grabbed her from behind and tried to lift her, but now the orderlies had begun to move. They clutched at my arms. I let go of Laura and swung at one of them. A fight broke out, until a gunshot stopped everyone.

One of the marshals had his pistol in the air. "This is a court ordered removal," he said, advancing towards the orderlies. "Now don't interfere."

"You don't know who you're dealing with!" Braga yelled, but marshals took up places blocking the orderlies. Unfortunately, the ambulance was behind the paramedics. I grabbed Laura from behind and lifted her towards the nearest vehicle. It was the Bentley. Jenny had the door open.

We got her into the back seat, and, with her clawing at my face, I knotted the seatbelt around her waist and slammed the door. Laura screamed inside and clawed at the window, but Mrs. Locke got in the other side of her and I ran around to the front passenger seat. With the doctor's muffled yelling behind us Jenny spun the tires and headed back towards the highway.

CHAPTER SEVENTEEN

Laura yelled whenever we hit a pothole or thick crack in the pavement and even when we got onto the smooth pavement every so often would burst out with a scream or yell. But she tired, and by the time we arrived at the home she seemed exhausted. She let me undo her belt but when I lifted her up she began to claw at my face. Jenny grasped her wrists and I was able to get her up into my arms. The paramedics got out of the ambulance, but Mrs. Locke shooed them off and we were headed up towards the door when the waitress from the diner rushed out.

"Madre dios!" she exclaimed, unsure of what to do. She crossed herself and fell in behind us, repeating her *"Madre dios!"* more quietly as Mrs. Locke led us to the basement.

Jenny began a warm bath and with only the floor of the tub wet I eased Laura in, still in her gown. She thrashed weakly at first, but Jenny and Pia helped me hold her and her struggles quickly subsided. We gradually let go of her arms, and she brought her hands up to cover her good eye against the bathroom's fluorescent light. Mrs. Locke turned it off, leaving the hall light on, but then Laura moved away from us to the edge of the tub nearest the wall, and turned her head in small jerks, as if searching for something. I stared, not sure at all of what we were doing, until Mrs. Locke shooed me out.

There was a knock at the front door about thirty minutes later. It was a tall, older doctor named Wisler. He had me fetch two large satchels from his car and then followed me downstairs. The women had removed Laura's filthy gown, daubed her clean, drained the tub with her still in it, then dried her and put on a soft new gown. Dr. Wisler's mouth tightened at the sight of her, but he started in right away. Laura let them take her into the bedroom where they tried to lay her on the first of the double beds, at which point she began to struggle again.

"Laura, honey, don't!" Mrs. Locke said, but her words made no difference. Laura had some new strength in her and was flailing, trying to hit anyone near her. I tried to intervene but things only got worse. She began to scream in the most guttural way. It was a little unnerving, and confused everyone.

"Try letting her go," Dr. Wisler called, so we backed away. Laura hesitated for an instant, as if unsure she was free of our grasp, then scrabbled off the bed, across the floor and to the bed nearest the wall. She got on the mattress on her hands and knees and crawled to its farthest edge, clutched the wall awkwardly, as if hugging it, but then began to move her eye over its surface, as she had over the wall in the tub, with small jerky motions, as if she was searching for something. This went on for several minutes. The doctor eventually moved a satchel next to her bed and withdrew a bottle of alcohol and packages of gauze. He made a motion to indicate the gown should be removed, so Pia and Jenny tried to get it off. Laura struggled at first, but then let them take it. She was clearly less anxious near the wall, and more intent on studying it. The doctor wet a piece of soft gauze and began to daube the sores on her back. She flinched, but let him, and he cleaned and dressed her sores with ointment and soft bandages while she moved her eye in tiny up and down increments over the wall. When the dressings were complete she let Jenny and Pia clothe her in another cotton gown, but all the while kept her face at the wall.

Dr. Wisler removed syringes and two bottles from his bag and prepared injections. I moved closer, expecting a fight, but Laura took them without protest. The doctor took blood samples and began an IV with a chrome stand next to the bed. By this time Laura had tired again. She slumped away from the wall but caught herself and struggled back up to it. It happened twice again before the doctor put his hands gently on her shoulders, and spoke in a very quiet voice.

"Sleep, Miss Spinali. You're tired, and no one will hurt you here." She struggled once more but he repeated the words and she allowed him to lay her back. Within seconds her lips were fluttering with faint sleep noises. Dr. Wisler brushed the matted white hair from the left side of her face and examined the scarring. Then he motioned us to the other bed, then cleaned and bandaged my cheeks and forehead, and took out a pad and pen.

"Do you know how she was hurt—in the face, I mean?" he asked in a low voice, while motioning around his own eye, indicating her injury.

"No idea, Doctor," I replied. "We just got her out an hour ago."

"It's an old injury, but a severe one," he said, while writing. "She needs to be in a hospital."

"We're in a very unusual situation here, Doctor," I whispered, shaking my head. "Whoever did this will try to get her back. If she's in a hospital they're much more likely to find her."

The doctor shook his head disapprovingly. "She needs medical attention, and not just for the eye. But it looks like the socket was crushed, and the eye is gone."

"Thes *pur* gurl," Pia whispered earnestly. She crossed herself again, then suddenly asked, "When che was born?"

"What?" Mrs. Locke said.

"When che was born—what month, what day?"

"That doesn't matter, Pia," Mrs. Locke sighed.

Wisler shook his head sadly. "I gave her a tranquilizer and started her on antibiotics. We'll keep her on that and fluids until I get the test results."

"When will that be?" Mrs. Locke asked, pulling her check book.

"I'll be back in a few days."

"I want you here every day," she said, looking up.

"That's not necessary."

"Every day!" she cried.

"Mrs. Locke, I have other patients, and can assure you, it's not going to do any good."

"I'll pay whatever you want."

"She means it," Jenny whispered.

"Che meens et," Pia nodded.

Dr. Wisler glanced at Mrs. Locke. She was writing a check. "I can come in the evenings, about seven o'clock?"

She nodded, still writing.

"You can call anytime if you need to, but here's a couple of lists, one for what to watch for, the other for supplies," he said, and he gave it to Jenny. She gave it to Pia.

Mrs. Locke gave him a check. He stared at it and blinked. "This is a lot more than I charge, Mrs. Locke."

"I want your best, Doctor."

"You don't need this to get it," he said, tearing the check in half. He dropped the pieces on the bed.

"Wait!" she commanded, grabbing them up, but the doctor was already headed up the stairs.

CHAPTER EIGHTEEN

Nothing yet. Nothing. Her friend was gone from the wall, but Laura was still alive. She kept searching the wall at the corner of the room, moving slowly, up and down, side to side, but there was no sign of her friend. With all this light you'd think she'd have appeared, but she hadn't. Perhaps she was frightened, or angry. She'd always been a little fearful, despite the smile. Maybe it was the wrong kind of light—strange, this place, no windows, but so much light.

She settled back on the bed, and used the beginning of a new plan to shut her mind to the old woman. She'd be easy to overcome, but there were two other women, an Indian who acted pleasant but was strong, and another, younger woman who would be difficult to fool. There was another person, a young man who looked strong, but he'd come in just twice so far.

The younger woman left after a while, leaving the old one and the Indian. The old woman babbled on in a soft voice and stroked her hair. 'Lou' she said her name was, as if it should mean something.

The women remained downstairs while I called the office and reported to Mr. Oneal on what had happened.

I left out having hit Dr. Braga, and described the abysmal conditions we'd found at the clinic. We discussed further papers to submit for the hearing next week, and I was working on an affidavit of what I'd seen when I heard cars outside. I looked out the window. A green Mercedes and a sheriff's cruiser had pulled up outside. Jenny answered, but through a window I saw Dr. Braga and an orderly climb out of the Mercedes, and a hawk-faced sheriff exit the cruiser.

I went out and opened the front door.

"Can I help you?"

"Are you Paul Rankin?" the sheriff asked. He held several papers in his left hand.

"I am."

"Are you holding a woman named Laura Spinali on these premises?" he asked.

"I don't have to answer that."

"Well I'm Bill Damon from the Maricopa sheriff's department," the sheriff said, frowning. "I believe you know Dr. Braga?" I nodded without smiling. The doctor stared back. The sheriff stepped forward. "I've got a couple warrants for you." He handed papers to me

"For what?"

"To search the premises, and for your arrest."

"What's the charge?" I demanded, turning the pages. The search warrant we'd expected, but an arrest? The image of my striking Braga flashed through my mind, and sure enough …

"Battery. On Dr. Braga."

I went back to the first warrant and shook my head. "The search warrant's no good," I said, turning the page. "It allows you to search premises of Mrs. Locke or Ms. Spinali, but this home doesn't belong to them."

"Move aside, counsellor," the sheriff snapped, and he started towards me, then froze, staring over my shoulder. I turned. Jenny stood in the doorway with a rifle casually across her arm, the barrel pointed towards the sheriff's feet.

"Get off my property," she said.

"What do you mean, *your* property?" Braga asked.

"This is my home," she said, patting her pocket. "I've got the deed right here."

"Lemme see it."

She pulled a folded paper from her pocket, handed it to me, and I handed it to the sheriff. The sheriff unfolded it into the light, read it, and then looked up. "This says it's yours … until what? Until Louisa Locke dies?"

"It's called a life estate," I said.

"And you haven't recorded this yet?"

"That doesn't matter, does it?" Jenny said, glancing at me.

"Not a bit," I said. "Sheriff, your warrant doesn't authorize the search of this woman's premises, or even authorize you to be on this property. If you take a step inside it will be an illegal search. And if Dr. Braga does you'll be witness to a criminal trespass." I turned to Jenny. "Will you want to pursue it?"

"Of course," she said.

I turned back to the sheriff. "So you may have to arrest Dr. Braga. I expect you understand that if either of you do step inside we'll have a lawsuit on file by tomorrow morning."

The sheriff frowned at me, turned and shook his head at Braga.

"Get out of my way!" the doctor said, starting up the steps. Jenny shifted the rifle until the barrel pointed directly at Braga's chest.

Braga turned towards the sheriff. "They're obstructing a warrant"

"We'll need another one, Joe," the sheriff said reassuringly, "maybe two."

"Do it now!"

The sheriff shrugged and headed back to the cruiser.

Jenny and I looked at each other without saying anything. Mr. Oneal had foreseen all of this, all, that is, except my arrest for battery.

When he was finished the sheriff called out from the car door. "Don't suppose we can wait inside?"

"Afraid not," I said.

"I'll have to ask you to stay where you are," the sheriff said.

"What if I need to use the bathroom," I said.

"Do it out here."

I sat on the porch. Jenny sat next to me with the rifle. Barely an hour passed before another cruiser and a forensics van pulled up. A deputy got out of the cruiser and handed papers to the sheriff. He scanned them, nodding, and handed them to me. I read them and nodded.

The sheriff stepped past me, and stopped. Jenny was in the doorway with the rifle.

"We're in a different world now, Ma'am," the sheriff said quietly. He pulled his sidearm and casually chambered a round, and holding it at his side said, "You'd best lay that weapon down."

She looked at me. I nodded. She set the rifle against the door and stepped aside.

The sheriff motioned and two men exited the van. They pulled cases from the side door and followed him into the house. They took two hours to reach the master bedroom, and spent another half hour there, without discovering the basement entrance.

"Where is she?" Braga demanded, as the sheriff came back out, shaking his head.

"I don't have to answer that." I said. They looked at Jenny, but she shook her head.

"You going to arrest this sonofabitch?" the doctor said to the sheriff, staring at me.

The sheriff reached for his handcuffs. "Want your rights?"

I shrugged. "I'll get my jacket."

CHAPTER NINETEEN

Laura woke several times through the night and searched again, but her friend hadn't come. She began another plan. The man and the smart one were gone. The old woman was asleep in the next bed. She would be an easy matter—they even brought a knife in with her food! It was still there, next to a fork on the tray.

She shifted her head and glanced at the old woman. There was a large purple vein at the side of her throat. The tray was still there, untouched on a chair between the beds. But the Indian was probably in the room at the top of the stairs. She was stronger, and for the smartest of the three she would need something else.

Her eye crept over the wall again. Still nothing there. Her mind touched the story but immediately moved to her plan. The old woman would be simple, but the Indian would take more thought.

I was handcuffed and taken to the Maricopa County jail. At nine the next morning the sheriff escorted me to a crowded courtroom. The judge was on the bench, listening to the arguments of two other lawyers. Braga stood near the front of the audience, beside a tall, thin man carrying a leather briefcase. Seeing the sheriff, the thin man waved to the judge. The judge interrupted what he was doing.

"Paul Rankin here?" he asked, without looking at notes.

"Yes, sir," I said, as the sheriff took me forward. We went to one of the counsel tables arranged in front of the judge's bench. Braga and the thin man took their places at the other.

"I understand you took one of the Madonna patients out of their facility yesterday?"

"We executed a federal order requiring her release," I replied, "in the presence of a federal marshal."

"Is that right, Mr. Janoff?" the judge said to the thin man. "They had an order?"

"Served by ambush, Judge," he said. "Came in the dark yesterday, while everybody was still sleeping."

"Gave us all of about ten minutes' notice," Braga said.

"That true?" The judge looked at me.

"It was at daybreak, Your Honor, and they've had her more than thirty years."

"She's there on a criminal insanity ruling, Judge," the lawyer said.

"On what charge?" I demanded.

"That's sealed and confidential."

"Not if you're objecting to her being out on that basis." I turned to the judge. "Your Honor, I'd like to know the basis for their objection."

The judge hesitated, and while staring at me asked, "Is she still insane, Doctor?"

"Yes!" Braga exclaimed.

"When was the hearing on whether to release her?"

"There wasn't one, Judge!" the thin man said.

"A federal Judge ordered her released pending the hearing, Your Honor, and it's set next week," I said. "So

…" the judge mused, turning to me, "you convinced a federal judge to release a criminal defendant who's confined to a state institution on an insanity ruling without notifying the institution, their lawyers or the state?"

"We had no idea until this morning that she was in on an insanity ruling—they wouldn't release even that, Your Honor."

"I told them she was!" Braga said. "I told them as soon as he came in the office, but he threatened to have a marshal cart me off to Phoenix."

"Is that right, Mr. Rankin?"

I shifted. "Yes, but we still don't know what the underlying charges were, and she was in that place for more than three decades"

"Because she's insane!" Janoff snapped. "Now they've got an insane criminal defendant out in the public, without proper supervision or medical care."

"She's not any more dangerous than you are," I said, "and she's getting far better medical care than she was getting in their prison."

"Ask him what happened to his face, Judge," Dr. Braga said. I had gauze bandages over both cheeks and my forehead.

"I don't have to answer that," I said, turning to the judge, but I stopped. The judge was holding up his hand.

"That's enough. I'm ordering her back."

"There's a hearing on that next week in federal court," I said.

"Pending the hearing I'm ordering the patient back to the Madonna facility."

"You can't do that!"

"Just watch me, son," the judge said.

"You don't have jurisdiction over a federal case!"

"But I have jurisdiction over Deputy Damon, and he's far more likely to follow my orders than those of some Phoenix Judge. Isn't that right, deputy?" He turned to the sheriff as muffled laughter came from the audience.

"Absolutely, Judge," the sheriff smiled.

"Where is she?" the judge demanded.

"I won't answer."

The judge sighed. "What's the charge against this defendant, Mr. Janoff?"

"Assault and battery on Dr. Braga," the thin lawyer replied.

"How do you plead, Mr. Rankin?"

"Not guilty."

"Bail?"

"One million dollars, Judge," Janoff replied.

"On an assault charge!" I exclaimed. "I'm a member of the bar, and absolutely no flight risk. How about letting me out on my own recognizance."

"Are you going to tell us where the patient is?"

"I can't do that."

"Bail is set at a million."

"*Your Honor!*" I cried.

"If you return the patient I'll suspend the order, but for the time being it stands."

"But—"

"Next case," he said, and he slapped his gavel.

The sheriff escorted me back to the jail.

Mr. Oneal showed up just before noon with a federal order requiring my release and two federal marshals. He was obviously upset about the assault, but said little during our drive back to the house. Jenny handed us a large manila envelope when we came in. "This came an hour ago."

"What is it?" Mr. Oneal asked, as I tore it open.

There were two documents, one thicker than the other. I scanned the thinner and shrugged a little uneasily. "We're ordered not to remove Laura or anything which may belong to her from Apache Junction."

"That was quick," Mr. Oneal said, as I handed it back.

I began to read the second. "These … are papers for our hearing next week," I said, flipping through it. I stopped. "They're asking to be paid … and … they … already have affidavits …three … four …there are at least five affidavits here, doctors, nurses, an orderly—"

"What do they want?" Mr. Oneal asked.

"That's impossible. Nobody could do all that in…what, six hours?"

I flipped to the last page. "They're asking that she be ordered back … and for … three million in expenses for what they've done over the past … thirty-two years," I said soberly.

We exchanged glances and I handed him the second document.

"Aren't they going to an awful lot of trouble over just one patient?" Jenny asked.

"They smell money," Mr. Oneal replied, reading. "Maybe we should let them know Mrs. Locke's is almost all gone."

"You're kidding," I said.

He shook his head. "She's got maybe two million left, but they can't seriously think they can get at whatever she's got," he wondered aloud. He left the thought hanging and turned the page.

"They've done a decent job, here," he murmured, reading. "Did you ever find out why they tried so hard to get their patients back?"

"We couldn't. Everything was sealed in the cases we found. The families told us they couldn't afford to keep fighting and had to give up. Our guess is Madonna is milking the system somehow, and has reasons to make life difficult for anyone who tries to rattle their cage."

"Speaking of that," Mr. Oneal said, turning to me, "would you please explain why in God's name you assaulted their director?"

CHAPTER TWENTY

They all came downstairs for a while, the old woman, the Indian, the younger woman and the man. She pretended to sleep but listened carefully. The old woman was sad all the time, crying even. The Indian wanted to know when everyone was born and was ignored by all but the other woman. The smart one. She was younger than the others, and didn't say much. They called her Jenny, and she took the tray away.

The man responded to the others in short sentences that contained a lie. She wasn't sure where the lie was, or why he was lying, but it was there, somewhere there, she could hear it in his voice. He left and went upstairs as well. Laura sensed he was still in the building, doing something upstairs. He would be the most difficult, and now she didn't have the knife.

There was uneasiness in the house that first night, and it got worse—for me—over the next several days. The others, though, didn't seem to notice as much. Laura seemed oblivious to us. She showed no sign of recognizing Mrs. Locke, no relief at being out of Madonna, and no grasp that she might be better off now. She just stayed near the wall at the far side of her bed, peering over it every so often, as if searching for something, but without making a sound. She was unresponsive to everyone who came near, whether it was Pia and Jenny while bathing her, or even Mrs. Locke.

But Pia brought a strange kind of rhythm to the house. She taped a schedule to the refrigerator for Laura's bathing, meals and sleep, and by the very first evening had begun to sprinkle little bits of glamour and religion everywhere you looked. In the living room she hung a photograph of Grace Kelly between drawings of St. Jude and Joan of Arc, in the kitchen she attached a large magnet showing the image of someone named St. Lidwina to the refrigerator, and one morning while Laura was in the bath she hung a velvet painting of 'St. Dymphna of the Possessed' above her bed. Mrs. Locke had her take that one down, but the next day she replaced it with a large wooden crucifix and a picture of Angie Dickinson. I found another crucifix hanging above my bed that day, along with a picture of Paul Scofield on my desk.

Jenny brought sanity to our surroundings. She was pleasant and calm with everyone, helping Mrs. Locke bathe Laura each morning, dressing Laura's sores and changing the bandages on my face and arms, and taking her car to buy and food and other supplies. In late mornings she'd come into my room to bring meals or supply me with fresh coffee, and later still, sometimes quite late in the evening, when she thought I should quit for the day, she'd bring me a glass of wine and sit, and we'd talk about how the day had gone. I enjoyed these scraps of time together, and began to look forward to them. And she seemed pleased to see me, and occasionally patted my arm or shoulder before she left. But she only asked once how things were going with the legal issues; it was on that very first day, and after I replied with a noncommittal "fine," she never asked that question again.

But then, on the third morning, I received a discouraging call from Mr. Oneal.

"We need to send her back," he said.

"What are you talking about!"

"The District Attorney called me. He's an old classmate. They found a young female patient and an orderly dead in the room next to hers, right after you left. The woman was strangled and the orderly's throat was cut."

I was stunned. "You can't seriously believe that …that feeble old woman could have done that!"

"It's pretty damning, Paul. The knife was found in Laura's bed, along with the orderly's keys. She'll certainly be charged with both murders. But this isn't the first time, Paul. Now that she's out the confinement orders were unsealed. The DA is sending me copies, but he says she was in there for three other murders."

"What!"

"Maurice was right about her having killed her father, and even about the only reason being that she was mad he cheated on her mother. That's worse than manslaughter, Paul, and there were two other murders during a riot at the clinic in 1936. The DA remembers the case because of how bizarre it was. She strangled a state inspector with a garden hose and burned the clinic director to death. Two other patients died. Laura would have faced the death penalty, but her lawyer—she was appointed a public defender—accepted an insanity deal."

"Jesus!" I sighed. It seemed impossible to believe. Laura was even weaker than Mrs. Locke, far weaker, but then my thoughts went to Mrs. Locke. She was in the room below, reading a book to a convicted murderer.

"That's not all," Mr. Oneal went on. "Madonna served a dozen subpoenas on our office and our homes, including your flat and my house. They were knocking on doors by six in the morning; they brought deputies, investigators and their own lawyer, looking for everything we have on any financial resources available to Laura. And they filed even more impressive papers than that first day. We've been served with a small encyclopaedia that basically says they have to get Laura back, for everyone's sake. There's a full-blown memorandum of points and authorities and even more affidavits from four pretty well credentialed doctors on a very impressive safety and wellbeing argument—they paint a pretty convincing picture that says she's dangerous--very dangerous."

"I ... I just can't believe it. She's harmless."

"Is that why your face is such a mess? Look, you need to have a talk with everyone in the house, especially Mrs. Locke. There's no question she'll be sent back. By the way, Judge Jacob's clerk said the judge is pretty upset about our having talked her into letting a triple murderer out before the hearing. I swore that we've got her confined and that the community is safe, but there's no question Laura's going to be ordered back."

"But—"

"And another thing. The DA warned me that Madonna's lawyers can be relentless. He's dealt with them before on other matters."

"Why are they doing all this?"

"The only answer we can come up with is money."

"But she doesn't have any! She had a public defender, didn't she?"

"We're wondering the same thing, and the only answer we can come up with is to try to get more money than the government has already paid them. They're overstating what they've spent, but the reimbursement rights probably are at least two million. Maybe because our firm is involved, maybe they checked out Mrs. Locke, maybe the two of you dressed too well, but the subpoenas are all about assets, and they put some thought into it. They're arguing that since we had Mrs. Locke appointed Laura's conservator they should be able to tap an equitable interest in anything Locke has. I told their lawyer, Janoff, that Mrs. Locke has already run through more than half of what she had, but they want any present or future rights she may have in real estate, bank accounts, anything, and every home or business that could have any connection to her or Laura. It's thin, but inventive; and you better let Mrs. Locke know she'll have to sell her ranch in California if she wants to keep going."

"And the hearing?"

"Three days from now."

"Christ!" I muttered, and while taking notes my hand shook a little. *Three days.* "Maybe we can get Dr. Wisler to testify that they made her a mess, that there was physical abuse."

"That's nothing against what they've got. I talked to the District Attorney about convening a grand jury on patient abuse, but he can't start anything against them without more evidence, and that would take a lot more time than we've got. He also says Madonna passes inspection from State and Federal Health Departments every year—"

"I can't believe that! You should have seen the place!"

"Somebody's probably tipping them off to the inspections. But look, they have more than enough to convince a Judge to send Laura back. And besides, she may be better off there."

"Don't say that. Mrs. Locke can testify … *I* can testify to how that place looks."

"Anything either of you say would be undercut by bias."

"Maybe we can get a speech therapist, somebody who could understand her. Maybe *she* can testify."

"They're saying she's incompetent, remember? Fits in nicely with the argument that they need to take care of her."

"So what do we do? Just give up?"

"Depends on Mrs. Locke."

"She'll never give up."

"Well … I brought in another law firm that specializes in diminished capacity issues, including involuntary confinements. They've already started doing their own research but the senior partner isn't optimistic about keeping her out. They have an expert on hospital administration that they used in a New York case; they're bringing him out to inspect the place, but Madonna's lawyers insist on the full thirty days' notice for inspection. Laura will be back there long before he sees it."

"So what do we do?"

"I'm not finished. There's more."

"What?" I asked helplessly.

"The DA says Madonna's going forward with a criminal complaint against you."

"On a simple assault?"

"They say it was a full-blown battery. You hit him, right? And more than once?"

"Well …"

"And obstruction. They found her fingerprints on the front door jamb of the house. Janoff believes you're concealing her from the sheriff."

"Which we are ..." I began, but my throat went dry.

"You broke up there, Paul," Mr. Oneal said, his voice forced. "You need to be more careful. They're pushing for charges of obstruction and concealment, and if a judge or jury says yes to a single count, Madonna's lawyers say they're going to institute disbarment proceedings ..."

"Oh, come on!"

"Their lawyer says they're dead serious. They've got two lawyers working on you alone, and he says they fully expect felony charges."

"When ...?" I stammered, finding it hard to breathe.

"When what?"

"How long do I have before that happens?"

"About the time the sheriff shows up to take Laura back the state police will be there to arrest you. But look, Janoff comes on like gang busters, but reading between the lines I think they'd back off on the criminal matter *and* the disbarment issues if we turn Laura back over before the hearing."

"We can't do that!"

"These people aren't above gutting a young lawyer's career, Paul, and they're going to get her back sooner or later. Sooner is only three days' difference, and if it's later you'll lose your license and have a criminal record. Even if none of that happens, if we don't give her up you'll never work in the firm again, and probably not in the State. But remember, I get the feeling they'll give in on most and maybe all of this if they get Laura back. We really should send her back."

"I have to think about this."

"You better do it quickly, and in the meantime tell Mrs. Locke. She needs to understand what's going to happen—*and* how much it'll cost. This other firm isn't cheap and I've put four extra lawyers on all this; it's going to take a lot more time, and money."

"She won't care about the money."

"She'll need to at the rate we're going through it. We're going to lose, and we'll be spending a lot more of her money now. If she waits for the hearing it's going to be even uglier, and then you won't be around to sweep her porch anymore."

I glanced towards the door. Someone was knocking at the front of the house.

"Tell her to be careful," he said. "And that Laura will be sent back," he added, as Jenny passed my room. She was headed for the front door. "And everyone may be better off if she is."

"I know, I know," I said. I hung up and headed for the master bedroom.

CHAPTER TWENTY-ONE

The old woman was reading her a story, but Laura wasn't listening. She was working on her plan. She'd start tonight by trying to enlist the Indian. Her name was Pia. That one had been a puzzle, the way she helped them and didn't hurt her. They all pretended to be pleasant, of course, but Laura's experience with Indians hadn't shown them to be as good at deception. So she wondered about Pia, and wondered if she might help.

Laura had difficulty deciding on the old woman too, not at first, but the longer that woman talked, the more some seed of doubt grew in her mind. It came from the voice. She'd heard it for hours now, telling simple stories about beautiful places, fantastic worlds that had castles on hilltops and fields of gold and green. They weren't very good stories—not like those Laura told her friend—but there was something about the quality of the woman's words, not the pitch or tenor so much as her conviction about every part of what she said, a firmness that was familiar, somehow. That same quality was there when she talked about other things, even simple ones like the weather, and especially more complicated ones like the lies she told about Laura being lovely. She was convincing, even when she lied, and it was strange, impressive even, how someone that old and weak could pretend to have such kindness and strength. That too was somehow familiar. It was something Laura had heard before, but nothing she could quite remember.

But the issue of familiarity was too vague to waste time on, and the woman so weak that Laura set that part of the plan aside and went on to the others. She was thinking of what to do about the lawyer when he came in.

"We should talk," he said, and his voice said it was about something important.

The old woman closed the book. "What is it?" But before he could say more others came down the stairs. Jenny walked in, then Pia and the doctor who was here before.

There were subdued greetings, then it was quiet, then her bed creaked with the doctor's weight. An instrument clicked, her gown was moved and a disc cupped against her back. It stayed a long time, then moved a little and stayed a little, several times in several places. Her bed creaked again with the doctor's weight, and she could smell his scent of antiseptic.

"What is it?" the old woman asked, this time of the doctor, and now with less patience.

He replied in a soft voice. "These sores are stubborn. I want Pia to give her more baths—two or three every day. I brought a powder to put in the water, and after each bath I want you to use this cleaner on the sores, then the ointment I'll leave you. Understand? At least two or three times a day."

"I unnerstan," the Indian said. "I start it right today but you show me now before."

"I can help with that," the Asian woman said.

"Use alcohol and the gauze, but don't rub them, not even to dry after the bath. Just blot them as gently as you can," the doctor said, "Like this." Something cool

daubed on her back. Then something creamy, and soothing. It happened again three times in different areas—her shoulder, her buttocks, her leg.

He touched her with his fingers, making her flinch. "It's all right," he said quietly, as if he was talking to her. Then he tapped her with something rubber—he tapped her elbows and wrists and her knees and her feet. He asked her to lie back; she ignored him, so he laid her back and she let him.

"Doctor, please?" the old woman said.

He still didn't reply. The bed creaked again. His breath was on her cheek. He waved a bright light in her eye, then moved it to the other side of her face.

"Doctor, will you answer my question?" the old woman demanded.

And with his mouth still close he finally spoke. "She has some kidney and liver breakdowns—"

"Thes pur gurl," the Indian murmured from the other side of the room.

"—and an infection of some type."

"What can you do about it?" The old woman spoke now as if to take charge. That tone! It reminded her again of someone, or something, but it was too far back. She stretched her memory back as far as she could, but couldn't find the source.

The bed moved, the scent left, a case snapped shut and the doctor spoke with his back to her, but Laura had stopped paying attention. She was trying to place the old woman's voice.

The doctor was saying something about getting a specialist involved, and the Indian kept droning on with her 'thes pur gurl's under his voice, but the others were quiet. The doctor finished speaking, told the Indian to start a bath with the powder now, and left with the

229

lawyer and the smart one. The Indian and the old woman remained.

Laura's mind touched back on her plan—she would start with the old woman, then enlist the Indian—but then the old woman spoke again.

"Not too hot, Pia," she ordered, and Laura heard her leaving up the stairs.

That voice ... the old woman's voice. What was it about that sound? she wondered. There was something about it.

She turned weakly. They were all gone. She heard Pia muttering "Thes pur gurl" in the next room, and heard the sound of water. A bath was being drawn.

I tried to focus but couldn't. A half hour later Mrs. Locke came in, looking haggard. Her face was grey, her eyes dull. She took the chair beside my desk and held the cane between her knees. "What did you want?" she asked, but the words were just out of her mouth when a sound interrupted from below.

A shout—Pia's voice.

I helped Mrs. Locke to the master bedroom and down the stairs. Jenny was at the door to the bathroom.

She let Mrs. Locke past but kept me outside. I heard the tub water sloshing, and Pia talking excitedly:

"... Es good ... Djew pur gurl. Es good. We makin' steps, good steps."

Jenny kept me around the corner, but from there I could hear Pia explain what had happened: "Che is in the wall, in the water an' in the wall. I am daubin' the sores on her back like Dr. Wisler say an' I hear a soun', a small soun' from her. Not like ches afraid soun', but like che feelin' goo'. So I say what did djew say, djew pur gurl? An I keep daubin' the sores an' che make the soun' agin, but louder, so I say *'Icaroles!'* a little loud because I *unnerstan* the sound she sayin'! I unnerstan she sayin' et feel good an' when I say *'Icaroles!'* she jump and she splashin', but then I sayin' 'Don' be afrai', djew are makin' good steps. Ever step is a good step,' and she calm down, and che thanks me! An che sayin' somesing, Meeses Locke!"

It was quiet for a moment, then, from around the corner, I heard Mrs. Locke speak in a soft voice. "Laura?"

There was no reply.

"Laura, honey, it's Lou," she said, in the same tender tone. Do you remember me, honey? It's Lou … Louisa. We were children. I was a little girl everyone called Lou? You remember? You always called me by my real name, Louisa."

And now I heard water rippling in the tub.

"You remember me from when we were children, from the school, from Mrs. Mays' ranch?"

The water rippled again, and I heard grunting syllables that had a faintly hopeful tone.

Mrs. Locke's voice broke. It was quiet, then she spoke: "Sure I understand you, honey. It's Louisa," she replied, choking. I peeked around the corner. Mrs. Locke was kneeling at the edge of the tub, with Pia and Jenny standing back from her, and between the two standing women I saw Laura's back, naked in milky water, her white hair wetly scattered to her waist. Between the clumped strands I could see a strange, bizarre disfigurement in Laura's body, a strong bend of her upper body, with bruised skin rippling on one side and taut on the other.

"Laura, honey," Mrs. Locke said, and her voice had become hoarse.

Laura grunted again, and suddenly moved. It startled everyone. I took a step inside, but before I could reach them Laura had turned, brought her arms up and moved them, clutching, them towards Mrs. Locke's neck. But then her hands went past the neck, past her shoulders, and her arms wrapped around Mrs. Locke, and pulled her close, and they embraced.

I stood there, unable to say or do anything but watch and listen as Laura made her noises again and again, each time the same noise, and Mrs. Locke, crying, each time answered, "That's right, honey."

CHAPTER TWENTY-TWO

The house was thick with emotion that day, but while it was good for the women, to me it seemed poised and uncertain. I was still unsure about so much then—about Laura's nature, about everyone's safety, and about what might happen at the hearing. That was only three days away. But right after the breakthrough, once Laura's bath was finished and she was dressed, Jenny brought me back in and explained who I was.

"Hello, Laura," I said quietly.

She was in a soft white gown, sitting on the bed with her head tilted away, and though her skin sagged and she looked very, very old, with her damaged eye away from us it was clear she'd once been quite beautiful. Her features were sharp, her profile classic, and the uninjured right eye was deep black against the wrinkled white skin. But at first she said nothing.

"He found you," Mrs. Locke said, with more tenderness than I'd yet heard from her. "He got you out."

Laura turned slightly, searching my face with a quick, flat glance of her good eye. It was just a moment, then she turned away, obviously suspicious.

"He got you out of there, honey," Mrs. Locke repeated.

Laura bent and grunted two syllables in a harsh tone, followed by a cold nod, without turning again towards me.

I looked at Mrs. Locke blankly. She mouthed the words '*Thank you*'.

"I'm sorry it took so long, Laura," I said. Laura nodded without smiling.

Laura let Mrs. Locke take her hand, and Mrs. Locke put it to her lips, and one by one kissed each of the old fingers. And with just that Laura seemed to soften. She looked shyly at Mrs. Locke, then withdrew her fingers from Mrs. Locke's and moved them up to her friend's cheek. She seemed genuinely harmless at that moment, and these two sick women seemed so grateful to be reunited that I couldn't bring myself to reveal Mr. Oneal's news.

It was the beginning of much sadness I had to hide, about the position they were in. "I better get back to work," I said.

"Go," Mrs. Locke agreed. I paused at the door. Laura's hand was still at Mrs. Locke's face. It brushed the cheek again, then withdrew to Laura's lap. It was, I suppose, some last remnant of my stubborn and irritable youth, but watching them I felt anger at what Mr. Oneal had ordered me to do. And then Mrs. Locke made it worse. She moved next to Laura, put her arm around her friend's sloping shoulders, and kissed her cheek. Laura took in a deep breath, bent slightly, then forced out a string of harsh, questioning sounds.

Mrs. Locke shook her head and said, "You'll never go back there, honey."

Laura bent and grunted again.

"You're staying with me," Mrs. Locke said. Then she began to reminisce. "Laura, honey, do you remember Mrs. Mays' ranch?"

Laura nodded.

"Do you remember those wonderful old horses?"

She nodded again.

"Remember that morning you first came out there, as the sun came up?"

Laura grunted in the tenor of a question.

"Sure, weren't you?" Mrs. Locke answered.

Laura nodded and flexed more syllables. "I wondered that too, the way the ground shook ..." Mrs. Locke said, and she wiped her cheek with the back of her wrist.

I spent the rest of that day trying to find solutions that turned out not to be there. We had less than three days left before the hearing. I called the firm to organize staff lawyers into new tasks and to have them deliver more research sources right away, then made calls to a couple of ex-Navy friends who had gone to work in the State Department. The research arrived less than an hour later, and I tore into the texts. But by midnight neither I nor anyone at the office had any progress to report. I lay down and tried to sleep, but after tossing for twenty minutes I went back to my desk, worked until just past four in the morning, and then tried again to get some sleep. I was drifting between anxiety and light sleep when I heard a strange sound from the rooms below.

I turned my ear away from the pillow, and it came again, a guttural sound that began low but rose like the growl of a wild animal being approached. I raised my head. The sound faded, and it was quiet again. I lay back, listening, and just as it seemed all was quiet a scream jerked me up. I jumped up and rushed towards the master, but by the time I reached the stairs the sound was gone, and there was only a low murmur. As I descended the stairs I recognized Mrs. Locke's voice, saying something in low tones, but then Laura yelled. Then it was quiet, and Mrs. Locke's voice resumed.

I crept to the corner of the downstairs bedroom. Jenny and Pia were clustered around Mrs. Locke, who sat on the bed stroking Laura's side. Laura was more on the bed than in it, her covers kicked to the foot of the bed and her pillow thrown to the floor, crouching on her knees and turned towards the wall, clutching the smooth surface, moving her face in small, jerky increments against it. She was crying, whimpering just beneath the levels of Mrs. Locke's voice, and now I could hear Mrs. Locke's words distinctly.

"It's just a dream, honey," she was saying in a low and kind voice. "It's just a dream, and that's all the bad you'll ever have again, honey, and when you wake from them you'll always be safe. I won't let anyone hurt you again. Nobody will take you from me. You're safe, honey, it's just a …"

It took several minutes but eventually Laura's whimpering subsided. She relaxed from the wall and allowed Mrs. Locke to lay her back on the bed, let her stroke her forehead and caress her cheek, then listened as Mrs. Locke began another story, this one about Pia's mother. Did she remember the time that Daisy …?

It was touching, I suppose, but I felt sick, watching them, knowing that without some solution to keep them together not only would these two be separated again, but Laura would live out her life in that awful place. I went upstairs and back to work, and stayed at it the rest of the night, but still couldn't find a solution. It was maddening. At dawn I called the office. No one had come up with an answer. Jenny came in a half hour later with coffee and Mrs. Locke. They both looked exhausted, but this time Mrs. Locke asked how things were going.

"Fine," I said, tensely. Jenny frowned at me. I hesitated, then asked Mrs. Locke, "Sounds like you had a rough night?"

She didn't answer, studying me.

"You're not telling us something," Jenny said. Mrs. Locke nodded.

I tried to shrug. "There's a problem, but I'm handling it."

"What is it?" Jenny said sharply, but Mrs. Locke interrupted, as if she'd had enough of this talk. "Do whatever you need to," she said dismissively. "Use whatever it takes. Spend every penny I have. She's not going back. I'm keeping my promise. If you can't do it I'll get someone else, take her myself—"

"I'll deal with it," I interrupted. I was surprised I said it, but then I said it again. "Don't worry. I'll deal with it … Look; I've got a lot to do." And though Jenny was obviously bothered by my responses she took Mrs. Locke and left for bed.

At nine-thirty Mr. Oneal called. Before he could ask his first question I explained that there'd been a breakthrough between the two women, and that Laura seemed competent.

"That's fine, we can have Wisler do another exam, even get a psychiatrist in there before she goes back."

I didn't respond.

"Paul, have you told them?"

"I'm working on a solution."

"Oh my Lord, Paul! What are you thinking! They need to know, Paul! And you have to tell them! It's a losing case, and your career is on the line!"

"It's not that simple."

"Of course it's simple; it's just not easy! Goddamnit, Paul! You *have* to do it! If you don't then I'll drive out there tomorrow and tell them myself."

"All right, all right," I said. I hung up feeling even more dread and irritation, then went back to my desk and kept at the research. I put in another call to my friend at the State Department and had another conference with the associates over lunch. They worked a few new approaches, but by nightfall the only solutions anyone had come up with posed even greater risks to all of us. At midnight I lay down and tried to rest, but went back and forth between the bed and desk for another three hours before I finally fell asleep.

An hour before dawn I woke, and there, somehow, it came to me. It's another of those incredible, indelible moments of my life, when I suddenly knew precisely what to do, and that Mr. Oneal was right. It wouldn't be easy, but the answer *was* simple.

And suddenly the ties to the rest of my life slipped apart.

CHAPTER TWENTY-THREE

She was in a dress, the first she'd ever worn. It was yellow and fit tighter than the gowns she was used to, but was soft, and comfortable. But they'd given her a bra—her first of those as well. That was very strange, uncomfortable, unnatural, to cup her breasts like that. She took it off the first time they let her go to the bathroom by herself. Louisa asked her to put it back on, and gave her a pair of sunglasses to help with the bright light, and said she looked beautiful. Pia said she looked like a movie star, and even Jenny smiled at her. But as soon as Louisa and Jenny left she took the bra back off. Pia didn't stop her.

In the late morning they gave her a warm bath with some kind of powder, and fit her in a clean gown. Jenny combed out more tangles from her hair after each bath, and there were fewer of those today.

Late in the afternoon of the third day they all came back, Pia and Jenny and the lawyer—Paul they called him. He brought the doctor. It was the first good look she'd had at the doctor. He wasn't as fat as Braga—he was thin, in fact—and wasn't nearly as confident. He pretended to be pleasant, but he was a doctor and she knew not to trust them. He brought a second doctor named Bassett. He also pretended to be pleasant, and with two of them there she went back to the wall.

"We have a problem," the one named Bassett said. He didn't seem to care that she heard.

She felt Louisa's hand on her shoulder, "She understands you, Doctor. You can speak to her, and address her as Laura."

"Okay ... good. Well Laura," he said, though her back was turned, "I'm afraid there's a problem."

She kept her face to the wall, and for a moment no one spoke.

"What is it?" Jenny asked. He didn't answer. All the room was quiet, but then he took a deep breath and began to speak.

"She has ... You have an illness in your blood." He said it softly, but the words felt like stones. Once again it was quiet.

Laura bent and grunted three syllables to the wall.

"What illness?" Louisa translated.

Bassett let out a sigh. "You've probably already started feeling the sickness, the weakness?"

She shrugged a little, with her head down, then turned. From behind the sunglasses she took them all in. Louisa and Pia sat on the edge of her bed, staring at the ground. The doctors were in chairs. Jenny and the lawyer stood in the corner by the hallway, their eyes on the tall doctor.

"You must have been feeling nausea for a while now?" he asked.

She shrugged again.

"Sweating at night?"

She forced a nod.

"It's a type of lymphoma ... "

"Ayee," Pia murmured, and she clasped her hands beneath her chin.

"There are blood cells inside her ... inside you which are broken. They're multiplying, crowding out the

240

healthy ones. With your test results I expect the symptoms have already been severe."

She shrugged again, and felt their stares, the doctors, and those of Louisa, Jenny, Pia, everyone but the lawyer. His eyes had drifted to the floor. Paul. Him she still couldn't trust; he hadn't looked at her once since he arrived. He was a liar, hiding something, maybe planning something.

Louisa reached out and brushed long strands of hair from her face. "What can you do for her?"

"Not much, I'm afraid. I'm sorry. America is leading most countries on these diseases, but we still don't have a cure."

Laura clenched out two syllables. Louisa stared, bit her lip, then wiped her eyes without saying anything. Laura made the noises again. Louisa looked towards the taller doctor without speaking. Pia had begun crying. Louisa finally translated.

"She wants to know how long she has."

The tall doctor took in a long breath, pushed his lips outward, and then sighed. "We can make you more comfortable, Laura."

She slapped his hand so suddenly he cried "Hey!" Then she twisted and repeated the noises.

He looked at Louisa.

She said, "She wants you to answer her question. How much longer—she asks this way—how much longer does she need to go on with her life?"

The doctor looked surprised, and was quiet. Laura sensed sadness in the room. She didn't understand that, but then, finally, the doctor seemed to understand.

"Not much. A few months, maybe."

She grunted another question. Louisa translated, her voice strained. "She wants to know what to expect. How will it happen?"

241

He hesitated, then nodded and spoke quietly. "The symptoms will cascade. You'll have some trouble breathing, and more pains, and you'll need more medicine, but then a short time after that ..." His voice stopped, and the last fragment hung in the room. Louisa wiped her cheeks. Pia mouthed words to herself. Jenny drew in a deep breath, and let it out with a sigh.

"What else is there?" the lawyer asked.

It surprised her. Why was he asking that?

The doctors looked at each other, but neither replied.

"You said America is ahead of most countries in this," the lawyer said, raising his voice. "Who's ahead of us? What other doctors are there, anywhere, who might help?"

Dr. Bassett rubbed his jaw. "I don't want to cause false hopes here ..."

"Tell us," Louisa said, wiping her eyes.

The tall one tented his fingers beneath his nose, then raised his chin to their tips. "The French and Italians have done some work ... One of my medical school classmates works at Sloan Kettering and heard about an experimental treatment being carried out at a clinic for patients like Laura."

"Where?" the lawyer asked, pulling out a small pad of paper and a pen.

"It's completely unproven, and controversial. There are medical associations trying to shut it down—"

"Where, Goddamnit?" Louisa interrupted, her voice breaking.

"Somewhere on the continent. I'm not sure exactly where, but that kind of therapies aren't for everyone, and even when they work they're only of marginal help. They may only extend things a few months—"

"What's it called?" the lawyer asked. "This place it's being done—what's it called?"

Bassett rubbed his jaw again. "Altobahn ... Alto ... something," he said. "I can find out." His eyes shifted from Pia to Lou to Laura, then they seemed to give up and went to the floor. Laura shrugged again, because none of this was important.

I spent the rest of that day and several hours of the night on the telephone with my friend at the State Department and two foreign investigators, then with several medical sources in France and Italy. I'm not sure when I drifted off, but Jenny eventually woke me; I was at my desk with pages of notes scattered under my arms, lists with dozens of names and numbers with most entries crossed off. She found an empty spot and put a cup of coffee down. I ground the sleep from my eyes, then took a sip.

"Paul?" she asked.

"Morning," I murmured, still partly asleep.

"It's twelve-thirty in the afternoon," she said.

I stretched my arms, then wiped my forehead. I'd been sweating. She left for a moment and came back with a damp towel. She wiped my forehead, then handed it to me and sat.

"What was it you wanted to tell Mrs. Locke?" she asked quietly.

"What do you mean?"

"Yesterday, you came down and said we needed to talk."

"It doesn't matter," I said, stretching.

"It did then. Why not now?" she asked doubtfully. I stared back. She was in another of her long western skirts, with another tailored white blouse. Then I remembered she'd said it was noon. The hearing was tomorrow morning. We had less than a day.

"It doesn't matter," I said.

"You're a terrible liar."

"Thank you, I think."

"You're hiding something."

"I just need a few more hours. Then I'll explain everything," I said, but before she could respond the telephone rang. I picked it up.

"Hello ...hello, Doctor," I answered. I listened several seconds while Jenny watched. Just then Mrs. Locke came in. She looked exhausted but happy, and took the chair beside Jenny as I picked up my pen. "Go ahead," I said into the phone. I began to write quickly. "Thank you so much, Doctor." I hung up and smiled, tired but relieved.

"What is it?" Mrs. Locke asked wearily. Her cheeks were hollowed, and the skin along her jaw was pale and sagging.

"They found it. That clinic in Europe."

"Who?"

"Dr. Wisler and Dr. Bassett. They found the facility, and made a call. They'll see her."

"When?"

"As soon as we can get there." I began to get up, but Mrs. Locke was shaking her head.

"Can we get passports, visas, things like that?"

"I have them ... I had them delivered," I said, opening my desk drawer. I pulled a manila envelope out and laid it on the desk.

"How is that possible?" Jenny asked, studying me.

"I talked to a friend at the State Department a couple days ago." I tapped a folder on the desk. "He's arranged everything."

"But you just found out!" Mrs. Locke exclaimed, confused. "What's going on?"

My eyes went back and forth between the two women, then I sighed and leaned back. "We have to go, and right away."

"Why? We're just—" Mrs. Locke began.

"The hearing is tomorrow, and we're going to lose."

"What do you mean? I thought—" she said, her eyes filled with concern.

"If we stay they'll take her back. I've looked everywhere for a solution, but there isn't one. The judge will order her back tomorrow. I needed her out of here. We need to leave."

"We? You ...?"

"She'll need help where she's going."

"And where is that?" Jenny asked.

"We were going to go to Brazil, but now we're going to Europe. I'll change the reservations. We're going this afternoon, if I can get a flight."

"*We* ... meaning who?"

"Laura and I. We're the only ones who need to go."

"*I'm* certainly going," Mrs. Locke exclaimed, "You can't even understand her."

"We're all going," Jenny said quietly.

"I thought you might say that," I said, opening the envelope. There were passports and tickets for everyone. "I did them all, just in case."

"I can't believe you haven't told me!" Mrs. Locke said, struggling out of her chair. She made her way around the desk towards me.

"I was going to tell you today ... this morning, actually, but I ... overslept."

"You overslept!" she said crossly. She leaned back sternly on the edge of the desk right next to me. For several moments she stared at me, and it was silent between us. Then she leaned down and pulled me forward, and kissed my forehead. She got up, and while heading to the door raised her voice hoarsely. "Pia, get the suitcases out!"

I picked up the coffee and leaned back in the chair, already exhausted.

"How long have you known?" Jenny asked quietly.

"Known what?"

"That she's going to be ordered back?"

I sighed. "Two days."

She came around the desk to me, and leaning back stared down softly. "Can't you get in trouble for this?"

I didn't answer.

"Did Mr. Oneal agree to these steps?"

I frowned, but didn't answer.

"You haven't told him?"

"I couldn't, Jenny, and I won't, not yet. He'll just raise hell with me. But no one has come up with any other ideas except to send her back. It's the only way left." I hesitated. "Jenny, you really shouldn't go. You'll get in trouble—and I mean a lot of trouble—if you go along. Mrs. Locke … the women … they don't have that much time left to live, and she won't listen to me anyway, but you—"

"I won't listen to you either, Paul. You're probably going to get in more trouble than anyone but Laura. You're all going to need help."

"But not from you. I mean, I appreciate everything you've done, but you could be arrested. If they discover you helped, you'll be charged for aiding the commission of a crime. You and Pia both—she can't go either, or shouldn't."

"She'll insist on it too, and they'll need a nurse." She stared at me a moment longer. "You're very much like your father."

I shook my head. "He'd never have broken the law like this."

"Of course he would have, and he probably did several times. I know he was willing to, at least for my parents, until my father stopped him."

"What are you talking about?"

"I told you about what he did for my parents. After they were interned and mother got sick Maurice was willing to do anything—he was going to bribe guards and even offered to hire people who would break them out of the camp—but my father knew what might happen to Maurice if he did it, and wouldn't allow it."

I shook my head sadly. It was another story I'd never heard about my father.

"You could do a lot worse than to be compared to him," she said. She leaned forwards as if to kiss my forehead as well, but I looked up at the last moment. It brought my lips even with hers. She hesitated, but I didn't. I leaned forward and kissed her. It was a short kiss, and took her by surprise. She pulled away reflexively, but then stopped with her face a few inches away.

"You're a good man, Paul," she said softly. She patted my cheek and turned to go. But she stopped at the door. ... "Where are we going, anyway?"

"Italy, to a village in Northern Italy," I replied, pulling my pad. I'd scrawled the name there and underlined it twice. "A place called Lucca."

PART TWO

Lucca, 1969

CHAPTER TWENTY-FOUR

The phone rang twice while I was packing. Jenny answered both times. She came to the door of my room after the second to tell me it was Mr. Oneal.

"I told him you were out."

"Thank you. What did he have to say?"

"He wanted to make sure everyone knew what was going to happen. I told him we did. Then he said Laura and Mrs. Locke both need to be present at the hearing tomorrow. He suggested we all meet at his home at seven tomorrow morning. I told him I'd make sure everyone got the message."

I didn't call him. The phone rang again about an hour later, but it was just as we were leaving, and I didn't answer. The five of us—Mrs. Locke, Laura, Jenny, Pia and I—took a four o'clock flight out of Phoenix. I still remember how the plane banked over the city after take-off, giving me a clear view of the firm's building. There was a possibility I'd never see it again, and but I was relieved Mrs. Locke and Laura were leaving.

I'd booked first class but it was a long flight for everyone, with a lengthy stopover in New York. Mrs. Locke slept through most of it, but Laura couldn't. Pia fussed over her with a commentary that was part medicine and part superstition; it seemed surprisingly interesting to Laura, but was wearing for Jenny and me. Between Pia's chatter and Laura's grunting talk I was very tired by the time we landed in Pisa.

We arrived just before daybreak. Jenny had hired a car and driver, and the road took us along a succession of hilltop towns and lazy vineyards until we reached the scattered suburbs of Lucca. Our route took us directly into the large walled section of the town, over several cobblestone streets, then out past the eastern wall and down the mountain. We crossed a stone bridge over the river before the road curved into a forest of black oak. A short distance into the trees an old iron fence jutted up from the left. It angled back and forth along the curving road for nearly a half mile before it parted for an opened wrought iron gate. The driver slowed and turned. A tarnished brass sign stood to the right of the gate, with heavily raised letters that said, simply, 'Clinica Altobelli'.

The crunchy driveway took us beneath a canopy of oaks for nearly a hundred yards before it opened to a meadow of wildflowers that spread as far as I could see. Another quarter mile along that we turned slightly left, and there ahead was a gradual bluff. Up there, on the bluff, poised like a crumbling Sphinx, sat a large, old villa, broad, broken at the edges, and of sienna-coloured stone. The road broke into a circular driveway in front of the building, with lawns and curving walkways on every side. There were several patients in wheelchairs being moved slowly along the walks by uniformed attendants. Seeing them gave me an uneasy feeling; although the grounds were lovely the patients were pale, and wore hats or hairpieces whose obvious spines went mostly front to back.

A tall middle aged woman in a white nursing uniform was waiting with two male attendants and wheelchairs at the front of the building. She introduced herself as Signora Soliven and helped Laura and Mrs. Locke into the chairs, then led us into a marble-floored lobby with a large, low round walnut coffee table surrounded by leather chairs. Another attendant brought a silver tray with coffee and we sipped while the Signora explained the clinic's routine and resources, as well as a little about its history and setting. The building itself was 'only' four hundred years old, and had originally been a summer home of the Medicis, but was leased to the Altobelli family in exchange for their work for paediatric hospitals in Florence and Pisa. It had four wings, one each for patients, testing, treatment, and administration.

"The doctor will explain the treatment 'ere but there will be several testings before it may begin."

"We can begin right away," Mrs. Locke said wearily, but just then she looked even worse than Laura.

Signora Soliven nodded and smiled, then stood and led us along a broad marble hallway to another long corridor. She came to a door on the garden side of the hallway and ushered us in. It was a marble-floored private room with two beds and a private bath. There was a dresser and a tan velvet sofa along one side, and on the other, a broad window overlooking the front gardens. We were putting away the women's things when Signora Soliven arrived with the doctor, another woman she introduced as Dr. Altobelli.

She was a blonde woman in thick glasses whose sentences tended to hesitate, then stop between the half and three quarter mark, as if enough was given by then for any listener to decipher the rest. She began by asking Laura, "An' the Signorina is been told that we canno' promise you …?"

Laura shrugged.

She turned to Mrs. Locke. "An' your condition, Signora Locke, es— …"

"We're here for Laura," she interrupted.

"But Signora, you 'ave …? Es et no …?" the doctor began while bracing the clipboard against her hip and turning several pages. She came to a certain page and running her index finger down it to a relevant entry, said, "I 'ave been told you yourself are 'ere for treatment. Is it not …?" She lifted her chin just enough to peer in my direction over her glasses. "Signore, you are the consigliere who …?"

I nodded. The others turned towards me.

"Ded you no' inform us about due Signoras …? Es these no …?"

"What did you tell them?" Mrs. Locke demanded.

"I just thought they might as well check both of you over—I mean, since you're both here," I said, trying to sound nonchalant.

Laura grunted a question of several syllables.

Pia shook her head disapprovingly in Mrs. Locke's direction. "Meeses Lou, why you say nothing about thes?"

"It doesn't concern any of you," Mrs. Locke said, staring at me. The others turned in my direction.

I sighed. "She has lymphoma."

"You're not supposed to tell anyone about a client's condition!" Mrs. Locke exclaimed.

"So sue me," I said quietly.

She glared, then turned to Dr. Soliven. "Don't pay attention to him. We're here for Laura … for Signorina Spinali."

Dr. Altobelli shrugged and crouched down before Laura. "We will begin with examination and testing, but it es … tiring, not very pleasant, and et will take …" she began, finishing the explanation with a long wave of her hand. "We wait until tomorrow, no? Or perhaps …"

Laura bent out several syllables of noise.

"No!" Mrs. Locke said.

Laura forced out several more insistent grunts. Mrs. Locke hesitated, then nodded reluctantly. The doctor looked back and forth between them.

"She wants to start now, Doctor," Jenny explained.

Laura grunted again, and this time Mrs. Locke translated. "But she won't unless … you start with both of us."

The doctor smiled tightly and turned to me, "The Signoras they can stay, Signore, and we will discuss the fees with you, perhaps another moment, perhaps …?" she said, punctuating the words with an offhand gesture towards the door.

I hesitated, feeling a surge of protectiveness about the older women, but Jenny patted my shoulder and walked me to the door.

"You have much more to do?" she said quietly. I nodded. I'd been trying not to think of what was happening in Arizona, and being with the women had at least been a diversion from that. And then there was Jenny, and what I sensed was growing between us. She'd sat next to me on the plane, and at one point fell asleep with her head on my shoulder. Standing there at the door to the hospital room she gave me a smile, pulled me closer, then kissed me on the lips. Then she patted my arm and gave a gentle shove.

"Now that we're here, perhaps you can find out more about Laura's family."

I nodded.

"And call Mr. Oneal. He deserves to know."

I frowned at that, but she'd gone back into the room. I paused another moment at the door. The other women

253

were in a half circle around the doctor, looking up at her, and from the fragments I could understand she was beginning to describe radiation treatments.

CHAPTER TWENTY-FIVE

The driver took me to Lucca and helped me find a street side pension. I rented a second floor room and arranged for a phone and a car. When the phone became available I finally called Mr. Oneal.

"*Where are you?*" he asked, sounding as upset as I'd ever heard him.

"Italy."

There was a long pause. "Please tell me you're joking."

"We're in Italy," I said again. "There's a clinic here."

"You know we're in the hearing right now? I mean *now!*" he yelled. The line buzzed but I could feel him struggling for restraint. When he spoke again his voice was almost a whisper. "There are at least fifteen people here, and every damn one is wondering where the hell Laura and Mrs. Locke are."

I didn't answer.

"Why are you doing this?"

"You said we were going to lose, and that they'd send her back."

"You're giving them even more ammunition, and not just against Laura, against Mrs. Locke, and *you.*"

"You said Mrs. Locke had *months* left, sir. That's what the doctors say about Laura, too. I'm not letting them spend that time back there. ..."

"Who gave you the right to make that decision?"

"This is the only place in the world with any hope for her."

"They're clients, Paul! *Clients!*" he cried through the scratchy line. A roaring sound came through, then distant conversation. "Hold on," he said, and he left the line. I stretched the cord to the window and looked below. The pension was on a narrow cobblestone street, with myrtle trees pollarded like topiaries. An old couple between the boughs idled at the window of a *patisserie* on the opposite side of the street.

"Paul?" Mr. Oneal's voice brought me back.

"I'm here."

"I asked for a recess until tomorrow."

"We're not coming back," I said.

For several moments he said nothing: "It's ...it's ..." he began, but then he stopped. it was one of those few times I remember him being unable to finish a thought. He gave up trying and asked sadly, "How are they?"

"They're running tests. They'll set up a treatment plan and then start on Lou ... Mrs. Locke."

He didn't respond.

I searched for another subject. "What are *you* doing?"

"Judge Jacobs is in one of her sustaining moods, so I've been objecting to everything."

"How's the opposition?"

"Their lawyer, Janoff, is easy to light up," he said, in a less heavy tone. "Dr. Wisler is here, and Dr. Bassett, but they've got twice that many doctors, plus state and federal inspectors, a nurse and several orderlies, who all say it's a country club. So … we're getting our asses kicked."

"I'm sorry, sir."

"Oh, hell, Paul. We'd be losing even with you here."

"How is the money holding out?"

"It's not. We're almost to the end of her retainers."

"The entire million?"

"Two million," he corrected me. "Since the Supreme Court appeal and the second firm Charlie got to help us we've had to use the firm credit line. She'll need to sell the ranch if she wants us to go on."

"She won't care. I'll talk to her about it, but I'm sure it'll be okay." I forced the subject from my mind. "What about my indictment?"

"They're not pushing that as much as they are Laura's return to Madonna. I spoke with the DA, and he'll wait on the grand jury until this hearing is over, but it'll happen. And if you don't show up it'll be worse."

I tried to ignore that. "I appreciate everything you're doing."

"I know that. Listen, Charlie says Madonna was investigated a few years ago."

"For what?"

"He has a friend who used to work for the Government Accounting Offices. He told him someone complained years ago, one of the families that tried to get a daughter out. When they failed at that the girl's father called and accused Madonna of welfare fraud. He said they were signing up patients for everything, AFDC, social security, food stamps, and more from at least a dozen overlapping state programs in Arizona, California, and Oregon. There were allegations that they were duplicating benefits, and scuttlebutt that between state and federal programs they were netting close to fifteen grand a month for each patient they had. The justice department got involved, but Madonna got the whole thing shut down and all those records sealed too. I'm not sure we'll have any more luck getting them unsealed than we did with the other cases, or that there's any way we can prove what the justice department couldn't, but we're trying."

"That's something," I said.

"I suppose, but … listen …" His voice trailed off, then started up with reluctance. "They served me too, Paul. They're calling me as a witness …on you. They'll ask where you are."

"It doesn't matter."

"I won't answer."

"Forget it, sir."

"I owe a lot to your father."

"But you'll end up in jail too, and for no good reason. We used regular passports, so it won't be hard for them to find us anyway. Answer whatever they ask, and don't worry about it."

"They'll track you down, and quickly."

I thought about that for a moment before responding. "Maybe, maybe not," I said.

"These people are relentless, Paul, and almost every country in Europe is part of our extradition treaty. They'll find you and bring you back."

"That'll take a while," I insisted.

"Don't be too sure." He laughed wearily. "You know, this is exactly the kind of crazy stunt your father would've pulled."

"That's what Jenny said."

"She's right."

CHAPTER TWENTY-SIX

I went to the patisserie and had a coffee to mull over Mr. Oneal's words. The longer I sat there the more uneasy I became, so after an hour I called for an interpreter and had the driver take me to the nearby town of Pistoia. We parked at a large stone structure that housed the district records office.

The interpreter was waiting in the lobby. He was middle-aged, surprisingly well-dressed in a sharkskin jacket and black slacks, and introduced himself as Signore Esposito. He'd brought help in the form of two young men who wore inexpensive shirts and pants that were too tight. He introduced them as Antonio and Piero.

"We're looking for information about a couple named Sophie Durer and Gino Spinali," I said. "They would have lived in Italy in the late 1800s, then immigrated to America." I snapped open my briefcase on the lobby table and pulled out a file.

"Who ware thes' people, Signore?" Esposito asked, producing a pad and pen. He began to write.

"I believe they were aristocrats. They owned real estate somewhere in Tuscany, and I'm hoping that they had surviving relatives, someone who's still alive and can help us."

"You mean childrens, grand childrens?"

"Yes, but not just relatives, friends too, anyone who might want to help a descendant," I said while flipping through several pages of notes. I came to those I'd made after our second hilltop conversation with Father, and went on. "The Spinalis might have had money around the turn of the century, but lost it because of a recession, a robbery or maybe both. Maybe neither."

"Seventy-five years es long times, Signore. Thes will take several weeks."

I looked up. "Your income each month is what, Signore?"

Esposito thrust his lips together, unsure of the forward question.

"I'll pay you three months' salary if you find what we're looking for within the next week."

He blinked, but then realized I was serious. He had a loud and disorderly discussion with Antonio and Piero, then turned back to me. "There are others who can help … but …"

"How many?" I asked, swallowing hard.

"Nine, ten more, Signore."

"All right, but if it takes more than a week their pay comes out of yours."

Esposito set his jaw. "We will do thes, Signore." He phoned for reinforcements, then summoned a file clerk.

She led us down a metal stairway to a cavernous room filled with records. There were more than four centuries worth: records of births and deaths, marriage and business licenses, property transfers, wills, and bankruptcy filings, were all contained here. Six library tables stood at the side beneath fluorescent lighting.

Esposito split up the help, suggested a number of shortcuts, and we set to work. Every table was shortly covered with boxes and papers and every one of us was quickly moistening fingers and riffling pages. We worked through the day and into the night, but by one o'clock in the next morning no one had found anything. Coffee was brought in, then sandwiches, then reinforcements arrived to join us. Esposito divided them among the various tasks, and we kept at it. I was struggling with Esposito over a heavy leather volume titled *Morti nel, 1886,* when Piero called from the other table.

"Hallo!"

He'd been combing licensing records from 1862, and found entries under the name Spinali—seven vineyard properties listed in faded but beautiful calligraphy. We were reviewing the writing when Antonio's crew found an 1894 bankruptcy, a filing under the name *Spinali, Genovese Alberto.* Esposito reviewed the entries.

"Et lists two properties, Signore," he said. He called for a map, studied the old handwriting, then pointed on the map. "The first es no' far," Esposito said. "Es is … right. Here," he said. It was on the outskirts of Pistoia. "The other is …" he moved his finger past small dots labelled 'Montecatini' and 'Capannori', then stopped. "Lucca," he said quietly.

"Lucca," I murmured, wondering if there might be neighbouring families who knew of the Spinalis.

"Perhaps we go to *Le Figaro?*" Esposito suggested. "Es better there. They 'ave records goin' back before Garibaldi … Come. We leave Piero and others here, and take Antonio. And I will get my bonus."

So we did. The driver took us across town to the local office of *Le Figaro,* where records were kept on microfiche. Esposito had them pull *'Crimine'* reports beginning backwards from the date of bankruptcy. Antonio was taking me through a series of murders in 1899, when Esposito murmured "*Aha*" appreciatively from the next cubicle.

"What?" I said, from the next cubicle.

He gestured triumphantly to the screen before him. "Genovese Spinali!"

I pushed myself up and went to Esposito's machine. "What does it say?" I asked, peering over his shoulder.

The interpreter motioned towards the screen. "Signorina Spinali's grandfather. He was …"

"Grandfather?"

"Si," Esposito said pointing. There were photographs.

I leaned forward. "Read that," I said quickly, pointing to script beneath a large picture. "Tell me what that says."

Esposito began, turning the thumbwheel haltingly as he went through the article. By the time he was half through the story a picture came up. I stared at the grainy photo, then shook my head with surprise.

"Jesus Christ!"

CHAPTER TWENTY-SEVEN

We worked at *Le Figaro* until five o'clock the next morning, when Esposito called the district records office and put a stop to his small army. He helped me call an investigator and a jewellery house, then I called Signore Scipio at the Rome law firm we'd used to find Moffatt, and arranged to have documents delivered to the jeweller. With that completed I took a thick folder of papers back to the clinic.

I arrived as the eastern sky showed the morning's first glow of orange behind the old estate. An attendant showed me in. Pia was on the sofa, reading. Mrs. Locke was asleep in the hospital bed near the window. I did a double take, for she looked worse. Her skin had paled; her eyes were sunken. On the wall behind her was a large and elaborate crucifix beside a picture of what looked like the actress, Jessica Tandy. The other bed, nearest the wall, was empty and freshly made, but behind it someone had hung another crucifix, this one next to a picture of Angie Dickenson. Two small cots had been placed in the broad expanse that remained of the large room; they were empty.

"Jenny is weth Mees Laura, gettin' another treamen'," Pia said, looking up from an astrological magazine. I sat next to her on the sofa. She had placed a small crucifix statuette and brass pentagram paperweights on the small coffee table, along with several movie magazines and loose, glossy pictures of Paulette Goddard and Veronica Lake.

"How did Mrs. Locke's treatment go?" I whispered of Mrs. Locke.

"Es hard for her," Pia said. She leaned closer and whispered, "What day you ware born?"

"What?" I whispered back.

"I need to know more of you 'cause Meeses Lou make me promise I gon' take care of you too now."

"I don't need to be taken care of."

"You don' know thes, Meester Paul. An I promise Meeses Lou, when che dies, so what day it is you ware born?"

"Christ, Pia!"

"Tell me, Meester Paul."

"Jesus! September. The twenty-seventh. Now just tell me what's happened here."

She gave a meek shrug. "They treated Mees Laura two times yesterday, an' again this morning now. Yesterday they treat Meeses Lou too, but it was very hard for her."

A rustling came from Mrs. Locke's bed. I stood and went to her.

"Mrs. Locke," I whispered, touching her hand. It was cold and white.

"Ches berry tired."

"I'm awake," Mrs. Locke murmured, without opening her eyes.

"I need to talk to you," I said. I pulled my briefcase onto the foot of the bed and snapped it open.

"What is it?" she asked, struggling to sit up. I took pillows from the cots and used them to help brace her. With that done I pulled a sheet from my briefcase and tried to smile.

"Laura's family goes back almost seven hundred years. And her mother was a Durer."

"Durer? As in the artist?" she said, opening her eyes. "That's right. A distant relative, and out of an Austrian line, not the German." I pulled another page of notes and began to read. "Her maiden name was Sophie Durer; she married Gino Spinali in 1888. They lost their first child. Sophie got pregnant again right before the robbery."

"The robbery—the one that injured …"

"Right. That happened in September of 1893."

Mrs. Locke shook her head wearily, trying to keep up. "Was that … when?"

"Right before Laura was born. There was a depression called the *diaspora;* they still teach about it in schools here. A million Italians immigrated to America. The Spinalis lost most of their wealth, which was mainly in vineyards, but they borrowed against the family home and sold belongings to ride it out, and they would have—until the robbery. But her grandfather was the interesting part."

"Who?"

I frowned. Her eyes were fluttering back towards sleep.

"He was a master jeweller, one of the best."

She blinked, and mumbled, "She … You mean she has money?"

"I'm trying to find that out. But anyway, her grandfather worked for a jewellery house called Castellani. They're the Italian counterpart to Faberge, and still around. He had a will, and it may have had a trust in it. Everything her parents had was wiped out by the depression and robbery, but the trust is apparently still there. It's been accumulating interest for more than seventy years. I'm trying …"

I stopped. Mrs. Locke's eyes were closing.

"What?" she murmured dully.

"There's something else."

"I'm very tired, Paul."

"I think … I'm not sure but I think he made that piece of yours."

"What …piece?"

"It was in the papers. When Sophie Spinali lost her first child, the grandfather and his friends … It was in the papers. There were others that helped … Some of the world's best jewellers …"

Her eyes came open slightly. "What are you talking about?"

I pulled a photograph from the file. "You tell me if this doesn't look familiar," I began, and I placed it in front of her.

Mrs. Locke's eyes opened fully at the bluish picture. It showed six men in dusty looking clothes, each wearing a leather apron, arranged behind a wooden easel, and on it …

"Signore Rankin?" a female voice interrupted us.

Dr. Altobelli was coming in the door, followed by a tall, uniformed police officer and a stocky older man in a tweed sport coat.

"Bonasera," the older man said gruffly, and he stuck out his hand. He had some sort of postural difficulty that bent him forwards and made his head tilt up, but despite the appearance there was an air of importance about him. "I am Lieutenant Dominichi, and this is Officer Astranza."

I shook both their hands, as Dr. Altobelli spoke apologetically. "I am sorry, but the Lieutenant, he es talking about—how does one say—a … an American proceeding legale…?"

My mouth went dry. "Litigation," I said.

"Yez," the lieutenant said quietly in his stoop. He pulled an envelope from inside his coat pocket. "The American embassy, she has given … a … order by extradition, for Signorina Laura Spinali. The Signorina must come with us."

"What are you saying!" Mrs. Locke said, struggling to sit straighter. She turned to me.

I felt sick. "This wasn't supposed to happen … yet."

The lieutenant shrugged. "Et 'as 'appened, Signore. The Signorina must go back …"

"Back where?" Mrs. Locke cried hoarsely.

The lieutenant pulled a paper from the envelope and glanced at the top. "To 'ospital Madonna, in Eritzona."

"No! No!"

"An' you are, Signora … Locke?" the lieutenant murmured, glancing at her over the paper. She didn't respond.

Dr. Altobelli came past me towards the bed. Mrs. Locke was completely white. As the doctor reached her side Mrs. Locke shuddered, then her eyes closed and her head fell to the side. Dr. Altobelli began calling for nurses, but the lieutenant ignored that. He approached me and went on as if nothing was wrong.

"Your client, the Signora Locke, will also be sent back, to be examined as to her moneys. There is another order," he said, pulling a second paper from the envelope. "She must produce everything which may belong to the Signorina Spinali."

I stared past him. Orderlies were wheeling Mrs. Locke's bed out, with Dr. Altobelli and Pia. I cleared my throat, "You have the order in English?"

"Yez of course," the lieutenant replied, pulling another envelope from his pocket. He handed it to me with a small flourish. He paused, staring at me as I pulled out the orders. "'Ave we met somewhere before, Signore?"

I glanced at his features. They were dark, craggy, and distinctive.

"Unless you've spent time in the States I've never seen you before."

Dr. Altobelli came back in, looking irritated with what had happened. The lieutenant turned to her. "Doctor, where es thes patient, Signorina Spinali?"

The doctor frowned and stood back. "She es …"

"Wait!" I said, pointing to the paper. "It says ten days. *Ten days!*"

The lieutenant turned slowly to face me. "At Madonna, Signore. To produce at Madonna."

"Nonsense," I said sharply, pointing to the order. "It says, 'to be produced within ten days', so we're *not* producing Miss Spinali right now. It also says she can have a hearing if she wishes, and she does." I turned to Dr. Altobelli. "Doctor, I advise you not to respond, at least not *yet.*"

The lieutenant heaved a great sigh, then moved towards me until we were inches apart. He put his hand on my shoulder, turned his head up and whispered with an almost affectionate tone. "You 'ave been in hearings before, Signore. Es et so?"

I said nothing.

"Come now, Signore. Es a simple question. You are consigliere. You 'ave been in court?"

I nodded.

"As I thought. And you 'ave given … how you say … *argument finale?*"

"Closing arguments. Not yet, but—"

"No matter," the lieutenant smiled. "You 'ave learned of such arguments, and perhaps seen them. Of course you 'ave. And you will in your life give good finales—very good finales, I am sure—yet to come. But can you imagine what you will do if someone interferes while you give such a good finale?"

I was silent.

"Come now, Signore," the lieutenant said, tightening the grip on my shoulder. "What will you do when someone does this to you, when they interfere and are wastin' your time, Signore?"

"What's your point?"

The lieutenant's fingers were like a vice on my shoulder. He was deceptively strong. "Come now, tell me. What do you think you will do when someone interferes weth you?"

"I'll object. I'll ask the judge to stop it."

"Just so. That would be the right choice. I, on the other hand, am merely polizia, and 'ave no judge 'ere to 'elp me." He replaced his copy of the order in the envelope; put it back in his pocket, then from the other side pulled out a dull blue pistol. Holding it sideways as if to examine it, he said. "But I 'ave thes …"

I tensed.

"One might say et es my own tool for use with those who waste my time." He looked up, studied my face, then broke back to a friendly smile. "Do you know 'ow it works?"

I felt myself pale, but nodded.

"Let's review, Signore. See now?" He moved the barrel to the side of my head. "You feel the canna di fucile—the barrel of the gun?"

"What in God's name are you doing?" Dr. Altobelli exclaimed.

"Donna interfere!" Officer Astranza ordered, and he took up a position between us and the doctor.

"I asked a question, Signore," the lieutenant said quietly. "Do you feel the barrel of the gun?"

269

I was beginning to perspire, but nodded.

"If I now pull the grilletto ... how you say grilletto, Signore?"

I answered hoarsely, "The trigger."

"I will pull it—" I flinched, but nothing happened. He lowered the gun between us and moved his finger to a small lever at the side of the weapon. "You see thes? 'Et es the *sicura*. When out like this, the gun is ... inoffensive ... how you say ... safe? But you push it in, the gun is active." He pushed it in, then raised the gun to my chin. "You understand the gun is now active, Signore?"

I stared back.

"Signore, you mus' answer me."

I swallowed, and nodded.

The lieutenant lowered his voice to a whisper, "So if I activate the grilletto, the gun can fire. Es et not so, Signore?"

I shut my eyes and nodded ...

"Now since you waste my time, since you interfere, I must object to you in my own manner. I 'ave moved the sicura and will now active the grilletto ... the trigger." I cringed, and before I could speak, the lieutenant pulled it.

There was a harmless *click.*

The lieutenant chuckled under his breath. He patted my cheek. Stepping back, he pulled a magazine from his belt, slapped it into the butt of the weapon, pulled back the slide and released it with a sharp metallic sound. He holstered the weapon and gave me a knowing smile. "Please you do no' interrupt us again." He turned towards Doctor Altobelli. "Doctor, you will produce Signorina Spinali?"

The doctor said nothing.

"Doctor?"

270

"Per'aps next week you come, Lieutenant'," she said, "and then we ...?"

The lieutenant clucked impatiently and retrieved the order from his pocket. "Doctor, you 'ave an order right 'ere. 'Es very importan' to obey such orders."

"I 'ave little control over thes matter, until I speak with my own consigliere."

"Don' be foolish. If you don' tell me where thes' patient es I will 'ave to arrest you." He motioned to Astranza. The taller officer pulled handcuffs from his belt and approached the doctor.

The doctor shook her head warningly as Astranza pulled her arms back. "Perhaps then you will explain to the Inspector General why I could no' treat his grandchild?"

Astranza hesitated. Dominichi tilted his head up. "The Inspector ..."

"Perhaps you know 'im?" she asked evenly.

The lieutenant's smile was gone. "His granddaughter?"

"You canno' take me from my patient, lieutenant', without alarming their familie ..."

Dominichi looked down irritably. He motioned to Astranza, who released the doctor's arms. "I 'ave no desire to waste the Inspector General's time."

"Then perhaps if you come in *due settimane* an' there is no problem, then we will do what ...."

"That es too much time."

"Due settimane. Two weeks, Lieutenant." She shrugged, as if those words were enough explanation.

The lieutenant pocketed the order. "Ten days," he said. He motioned to Astranza and stalked out.

When their footsteps faded Dr. Altobelli turned to me. "Thes man canno' be ... how you say, taken without weight."

I nodded grimly. "Can you introduce me to the Inspector General?"

"I do not know the inspector, Signore."

"But his granddaughter? Maybe I could speak to her parents?"

"I 'ave no such patient, Signore."

CHAPTER TWENTY-EIGHT

My nerves were shot for the rest of that day, but after meeting privately with Dr. Altobelli I called Senior Scipio, the senior partner at the law firm which helped find Moffatt, to make sure he'd demand a full-fledged extradition hearing. He seemed genuinely dismayed at what had happened—including this news about the robbery which occurred on my last visit to Italy—and agreed to help with the hearing. He had several further suggestions, and they seemed good ones.

My next call was to Mr. Oneal to explain the bad news. He was in a meeting, but called back a few minutes later. They were in the second day of hearings on Laura's case. I told him what had happened. He wasn't surprised.

"I told you, Paul," he said. "These people are relentless."

"What's happening back there?" I asked, still feeling sick.

"A lot," he replied, "and none of it is good. I won't waste your time with details, but you already know Judge May ordered both women back. We're in a hearing now to decide what happens to you, but we're going to lose there as well."

"What does that mean?" I asked tensely.

He hesitated before answering. "The DA is going to charge you with obstruction, and disbarment proceedings will start right away."

I couldn't think of anything to say.

"Paul? Did you hear me?"

"Yes, sir."

"There's still a chance they might drop some of this if you bring them back now," he said quietly.

"They're not coming back unless…the lieutenant…succeeds," I said simply.

"Isn't that just a formality, Paul? We've got an extradition treaty—Italy will have to honour that, won't they?"

I didn't answer, because something else had just occurred to me.

"Paul?"

"We're not coming back," I said, and without waiting for him to say anything else I hung up the phone.

My next call was to Signore Esposito, the translator, then I drove directly to his office. We laid out all the materials we'd copied at *Le Figaro,* and spent the next hour going through them before I found what I was looking for. I made several additional calls, including two to a bank and another to a realty office, then had Esposito take me out, first to the bank, and from there to the real estate office. The owner of the realty was waiting.

Signora Fortuia was her name. She was in her sixties, with silver hair and wearing a handsome tweed suit. She had already prepared a number of documents for us, but seemed hesitant. "I 'ave found thes place," she said. "Et es old, and no longer in the Spinali name. I can show you other villas, Signore."

"I must speak with the owners," I said.

"Es no' for sale, Signore," Signora Fortuia said. "And there are other places which are much more … pleasant."

"I *must* talk to them."

Signora Fortuia sighed. "But et es no' for …"

"Will you help me or not, Signora?" I snapped.

She shrugged. "I will call them, Signore." I paced while she made the call. Two minutes later she was back. "We can go," she shrugged, then she murmured to herself: "But et es no' for sale."

We left Signore Esposito and drove for twenty minutes back to Lucca, crossed the small river bridge and wound our way up into the historic part of the village. She turned onto a rundown cobblestone street lined with unkempt cypress trees. After a half mile or so the trees changed from cypress to olives and a smaller cobblestone road broke left into a thick olive grove. We travelled barely thirty yards along the olives before a rocky driveway branched left again, this time through crumbling stone walls. Signora Fortuia parked just inside and went to the door, while I waited next to the car.

It was a much older home, with walls of marred stucco and old yellow stone, a roof that sagged in places and was missing tiles, and a courtyard which, though it spread at least a hundred and fifty feet around the entire house, was overcome with weeds. Here and there were olive trees that looked as if they'd been untended for years. A single Acacia stood nearer the villa, in a similar state of neglect.

Signora Fortuia came back to me, shaking her head. "They don' want to sell, Signore."

"I need to talk with them," I said firmly, as a barrel chested older man came out of the house.

"They weel talk with you, signor, but they don'…" was all I heard as I walked past her and greeted the older man. He was shorter than me, but heavier, dressed in tight navy swim trunks and a shirt opened to thick chest hair. He motioned to a wooden table beneath the Acacia. We walked there as the villa's front door opened again. A tall woman in a Ferrari sweat suit appeared, carrying a tray with glasses and a pitcher of lemonade. I bowed to her and waited as she placed the tray on the table. Her husband began to pour.

"Signore Rankin, these es Signore an' Signora Basso," Signora Fortuia said. We shook hands, and sat. I pulled papers from my pocket and thrust them into Signora Fortuia's hands. "Tell them I represent a woman whose family once owned their lovely home," I said.

She frowned at the words, glancing at the house, as I accepted a glass of lemonade from Signore Basso with a smile. I took a sip and waited.

Signora Fortuia translated. The Bassos glanced towards me as she spoke.

I pointed to the copy of an old news clipping. "Tell them … this describes what happened to my client's parents. Laura's mother and father. Then read it to them."

"Signore," Signora Fortuia protested, as she flipped the pages. "Thes is quite long."

I reached into my briefcase and pulled a crisp stack of bills still in the bank's paper banding. I placed it on the table and shoved it towards the Bassos. "This is theirs for listening."

Signora Fortuia's eyes widened at the money.

"Go on," I told her.

She blinked, motioned to the money and the article, and explained.

The Bassos looked at each other, and at me, as Signora Fortuia began to read out loud.

It took twenty minutes. As Fortuia finished Signora Basso began to shake her head sympathetically. She whispered to her husband. He nodded and spoke to the realtor.

Signora Fortuia turned back to me. "They say you can keep thes money, an' they are very sorry for Signorina Spinali. Very sorry. But they are 'appy here. They do no' want to sell their home."

"Thank you," I said, "but I'm here to buy it, and I will pay …I will pay …any price they ask."

Signora Fortuia shook her head. "Signore, thes house is their 'ome. The Signora is … she 'as become *incinta*—" she said, motioning to her belly.

"Pregnant?"

"Si, and with twins. They 'ope to 'ave children 'ere …"

"Thank you, and congratulate them on the twins," I said. I took a sip of lemonade and sat, thinking, then looked up. "All right. Now tell them I have an offer which I believe will interest them."

Signora Fortuia shook her head. "Signore, thes' house is their home. They 'ave---"

"Ask them … as a favour to my client, please just listen to my offer," I interrupted.

"But they 'ave already said—"

"Tell them," I insisted. I smiled at the Bassos and took another sip of lemonade.

Signora Fortuia studied me for several seconds, then turned to the Bassos. She spoke three sentences. Signore Basso replied quickly to Signora Fortuia. She repeated herself, and both Bassos turned towards me with sympathy, but shaking their heads.

I thought for several moments, then nodded to the Bassos. "I believe you will find my offer very interesting. But there are certain conditions."

Signora Fortuia translated. The Bassos shrugged and sat back expectantly, as we spoke.

I nodded and went on. "I will pay to have their home appraised. They may choose the appraiser. Then—if they agree to my conditions—I will pay its full value, to buy it, for just a short time."

"You mean to rent, Signore?"

"Not exactly."

"But you will…buy for a while?" I nodded. "And the price?"

"I will pay what the home is appraised at just for the privilege of using it for a short time. A few years, perhaps, five years at the very most. I will also pay to restore it, to fix the roof, improve the grounds, take care of everything which it needs to make it as it once was. I will also pay their moving costs, hotel bills, and what it costs to find them another home, and help them with whatever it costs to obtain a replacement. If they agree to this, then after the period of rental, which as I say will be short, I will then return the home, with all its improvements, to them."

"And the sum you would pay for the rental—it would be the full purchase price?" she asked, incredulous.

"You heard me. That money would be theirs to keep."

Signora Fortuia's jaw had dropped. She stared at me. "You mean …"

"You heard me," I said quietly. I took a deep breath. The scent of pine and *rosmarino* was in the air. "Now tell them," I said.

CHAPTER TWENTY-NINE

I spent the rest of the day working in the law firm's office in Pistoia, using the interpreter and realtor to make several telephone calls, doing additional research, then took Signora Fortuia and drove to the villa for another meeting with the Bassos. With that finished we returned to the law office, where I spent the evening preparing paperwork with two of their attorneys. It was midnight before I got back to the Altobelli clinic.

Mrs. Locke was asleep. Jenny and Pia were dozing on the cots. Laura was awake, looking at pictures in a magazine. Her white hair had been replaced with a wig of long black locks, which with the sunglasses highlighted the bleached look of her skin. She was even paler than before. She looked up as I entered, and stared at me without a smile or even a nod. I assumed that meant she'd learned about the lieutenant, and tried to smile. But there was no reaction—just the cold stare.

"I'm sorry, Laura," I said quietly.

Her eyes narrowed, then she made a noise—a quick, short grunt, and went back to the magazine. I stood there, feeling almost if I'd been slapped, but then the sound of rustling covers came from the other bed.

"Paul," Mrs. Locke murmured.

I pulled my briefcase up onto the foot of Mrs. Locke's bed and snapped it open. "I need your signatures," I said, as the others got up. Jenny came and stood beside me. I pulled three documents from the briefcase, gave one to Laura, and handing her a pen pointed warily to a signature line. "Your grandfather worked for the Castellani House in Viareggio; they set up a trust for you."

"A trust?" Jenny asked.

"That's right, but we need to take a few steps to make sure they don't find it. I've made a few changes," I said.

Laura signed without reading it. I went back to Mrs. Locke and gave her the other documents. "Sign ... here, and here," I said, pointing.

"What is this?" she sighed. She took the pen, but it dropped from her hand. I picked it up, brought the documents closer, and guided her hand to a line at the bottom of the first. She signed without reading. "What is it?" she asked again, as I helped her sign the other.

"I just took all the rest of your money," I said tightly. It's another moment I remember, not saying that so much as guiding her hand—she still had the plain gold wedding band on her finger—and seeing the thin outline of her legs beneath the white sheet, and how they were almost like a child's.

Her eyes flickered up, then she shook her head weakly. "Fine ...I don't care ...But the lieutenant ... he's coming soon."

"Eight days," I said. "I checked."

"But the treatment is ...a month ..."

Longer than that, I thought to myself, but I told her, "I found a place. It needs some fixing up, but workers are already there," and I checked my watch. "Jenny, can they spare you here? I could use your help in Lucca."

"Of course."

"Is this ... will this help us?" Mrs. Locke asked.

"I think so."

"You *think*!" she whispered, then she said it again. "That lieutenant is coming soon."

"I know, I know," I sighed.

"So what are you doing about it?"

"I can't tell you about it, not yet, but I've got some ideas."

Jenny put her hand on my shoulder. "Why don't you lie down? You look exhausted."

"I'm fine, but there's something else," I said, as I pulled a stapled copy of a newspaper article. "I want to read something to you ... to both of you. It's about Laura's parents."

Laura put the magazine down.

"It's an editorial that appeared in *Corriere della Sera*, an Italian newspaper, about sixty years ago. Right before you were born, Laura." She sat up. "I had it translated. The title means *A Pleasant Visitor to Our Pleasant Village.*" I cleaned my throat, but stumbled on the first words.

"I'll read it," Jenny offered. I nodded gratefully and sat beside her as she began:

There has been no great love between the citizens of Italy and Austria at any time since the Celts invaded our lands, but there is now in our home one of their descendants, a woman who gives great hope for better relations between us.

Those who search long and hard enough might perhaps find isolated instances of kindness in the Austrian world, but a rare example of such character can be found in one Sophie Elena Dorothea Durer, the young niece of the skilful painter by that name. Princess Durer (for she is such) has now wed one of our

Spinalis—the son of Genovese the Elder, no less, and it appears a blessed event.

It's correctly assumed by those who know of the marriage that both their families at first either avoided or condemned it. The Elder refused to attend and Sophie's Austrian parents reportedly disowned her, but soon after the nuptials the young bride volunteered her services at the paediatric hospital in Firenze, where she quickly became a favourite of the children, the deaf ones in particular, and is now loved by hospital staff

Gino tells this writer his wife's warmth even melted the cold demeanour of his father, who became understandably reclusive after the death of his wife some years ago. Sophie not only forgave the refusal of the Elder's blessing on their wedding, her sympathies led her to take him on as a mission. The very weekend after the wedding she stopped in Viareggio on her way to the hospital and sought out the pitched Danish roof of the old man's shop, which is located near the large Castellano factory building. There was no answer to her knock on the door, but finding it open she went in. Gino says she described what she found thusly:

"There was clutter and dust and the strong smell of burnt metal, but no one to be seen, so I went in further until there, in the building's darkest recess, hunched over a tiny galaxy of light, I found a small man in a thick leather apron, using the fine point of a brazier's flame to melt threads of silver into the wings of a hummingbird. It was a magical bird, so tiny it would be outmatched by my fingernail, yet with perfect proportions of feathers to wings, and wings to the body!"

She told Gino she admired this sight for several minutes, and finally murmured, "Such a perfect bird!" but as was his sad habit since the death of his wife, the Elder said nothing in response. Nevertheless, Sophie

*introduced herself, told him she'd brought him pears,
and as he still didn't even look up, she left the fruit on
the edge of the bench and departed. After visiting the
children's hospital for several hours she returned with a
wedge of cheese and bottle of port. The Elder was still
bowed over his workbench, still fixed on the same
project, but now was attaching a diminutive vine laced
with small leaves to a silver picture frame. Nearby lay a
shorter vine, which, on its stem, bore the finished bird
from before.*

*When Sophie marvelled, "Such perfection! The bird!
And these leaves and vines are treasures! Where will
they go?" the Elder finally looked up, and said
brusquely, "I don't need fruit". Sophie told Gino that
beyond the words she saw pain in the man's eyes, and,
more importantly, that one of the pears was gone. True
to her nature, she murmured a pleasant reply, "Just as
well that I brought wine and cheese instead." For the
next twenty minutes neither said more, and the only
sound was the hiss of blue flame. Sophie left with no
other conversation.*

*That was the beginning of twice weekly visits she
made to the hospital. On each she stopped by to see The
Elder. She brought bread and cheese, fruit and wine,
and more importantly, her kindly nature, until finally
more gruff words trickled out of him. With time the
words grew to sentences, then small paragraphs, until
one day, on her arrival, there were two glasses and a
bottle of the family's grappa waiting.*

*Looking back Gino says the real breakthrough, if
something so glacial could be described as such, came
when The Elder learned she might bear him a
grandchild. Gino would never forget his response—his
father, uninvited at the front door, with his silver-tipped
cane and wooden workbox. The maid barely opened the*

door before he tapped his way in and up to the guest room, unpacked his belongings and took over the house. He proved to be a godsend. Gino knew nothing of the workings of maternity or fatherhood, and The Elder directed him and the aging villa through both. A nurse was hired, and a cook, then even a gardener. A groom was retained for their horses; repairs were undertaken to the villa; and it became a home again, run as if the old man never left it. Gino and his Father settled into the sort of uneasy truce which can rise between proud men, and life threatened to become grand.

The catastrophe of Sophie's ensuing miscarriage shook The Elder as much as it did his son, but the old man began spending time at Sophie's bedside, teaching her Italian fables of princes and princesses, and stories that spoke of life lessons. When not by her side he spent more and more time in the villa's small barn. He set up a room next to the horses' stalls with a sign—'Non Entrare!' scrawled in black paint on a stone tile at the door—and worked late into the nights. Visitors began to appear—old man, all of them, and all from the Castellano factory. They brought valises with small presents for Sophie and supplies for what was happening in the barn.

For six months only the horses knew about the small mystery in the converted stall, but on the first birthday after her recovery, the old men gathered in the villa's living room, and with gruff pride presented their present: La Crime Sophie, the newspapers called the fabulous necklace.

The old man went back to Viareggio soon after and came less and less to Lucca, so Sophie visited him more and more, bringing Gino with her, until four years after Sophie met him, one evening back in the room above his dingy shop, the once angry jeweller scrawled out a sweet letter in which he apologized for not being there to greet them, but he was leaving to find his wife. They found him in bed, and on the table next to him a bottle of grappa and two empty glasses, as well as three gifts: some of his works in a marquetry box which required a block and tackle and twin horse team to move, the old man's long used silver horse head cane, and a note to Sophie—'Alla mia dolce figlia con amore'— tied to a small package wrapped in burlap and twine. When Sophie unwrapped it she cried, for the humble package contained the hummingbird picture frame. The young princess treasures that even more than the much more valuable necklace.

"I still have that frame," Mrs. Locke sighed, looking over at Laura. She turned back towards us. "She gave it to me when we left Apache Junction."

Jenny brushed her eyes. "There's a picture of it."

"Of the frame?" Mrs. Locke asked weakly.

"No, the piece they called *La Crime*. It looks beautiful." Laura grunted, and Jenny showed it to her. "Your grandfather must have really loved Sophie." Laura was quiet, staring at the photograph.

"Mrs. Locke has one just like it," I said. They all looked at me. "Show the picture to Mrs. Locke." Jenny brought it over to her, and her eyes widened.

"It's very much like mine."

I nodded.

Laura grunted in the tone of a question. Mrs. Locke sighed. "Nathan saw one like it. We were looking for a stroller or crib, I think. at, a collective run by our church. Nathan saw me admire it, then went back later. He was bringing it to me when— …"

"I have to go," I said suddenly. I was fighting exhaustion, trying hard to stay awake.

"Where?"

"I have to go to Rome," I said, but then I had to hide a great yawn.

"You haven't slept," Mrs. Locke yawned too.

"I'm fine," I said quickly, but the excitement was slipping away. In truth, I'd slept less than three hours over the past two nights.

"Lie down and rest," Jenny urged, motioning to the cots.

"There's something else I need to do. Besides, I've got a stack of documents to go over, and meetings to prepare for."

"Nonsense," she said, and she led me to the cot. She pushed me down gently, and I let her. It was too inviting. "Sleep, Paul," she said, slipping a pillow beneath my head. She stroked my forehead and said something else, but I can't remember what—I was falling into a deeper sleep than I'd had in weeks.

CHAPTER THIRTY

I left Jenny at the villa in Lucca and headed to Rome.
The work there took longer than I expected; I had
enough experience in American real estate transactions
that I considered them no more complex than any
number of dog walker tasks I'd been assigned, but the
Italian counterparts had a remarkable complexity to
them, and that required extra time to learn as much as
possible about the rules. With that more or less done I
made two trips to the Castellani House, then joined
Signore Scipio in an Italian courtroom for an appearance
before a magistrate. After another day spent wrapping up
details and a long telephone call to Mr. Oneal, I left
Rome and raced back to Lucca.

A week had passed since I'd been to the clinic. I got
there just before two o'clock in the morning, and tiptoed
in the door of the women's room. It was dark but for the
faint glow of a tent lamp near the sofa. Mrs. Locke and
Laura were sleeping. I was disappointed at the sight of
them. The skin around Mrs. Locke's eyes was dark, and
both women's cheeks were sunken in on the bones.

I went to the cot against the wall, where Pia snored
quietly. I sat beside her and nudged her shoulder. She
turned and opened her eyes to slits.

"Meester Paul," she sighed, pulling herself up. "Chu
look terrible."

"What's happening here?"

"Meeses Locke she es afraid," Pia said, stretching her arms. Her face became sombre. "Che very afraid of the lieutenant. Dr. Altobelli say he came again two days ago, and tell her to have Mees Laura ready—" She hesitated, looking up at the clock with alarm. "He es coming today!" she said, and she began to raise herself up.

"I need to talk with you about your parents, Pia."

"*My* parents?"

"That's right. Daisy and Lalo."

She nodded, puzzled by the question, but said, "Chure." Someone stirred behind us.

"Paul," Mrs. Locke murmured.

I stepped to the bed. "Hey there," I whispered, forcing a smile. She focused unsteadily on me.

"What time is it?" she asked.

"Just after two in the morning."

"When?" she asked. Her eyes brimmed with worry and then seemed to slip into confusion. Her gaze stopped above my shoulder, and seemed to focus there. "Mrs. Locke?" I asked uneasily. She looked terrible. Pia came and stood next to me, watching.

"Ches no feeling good," she said.

"Mrs. Locke?" I said again.

Mrs. Locke raised her hand towards my face. It stopped, trembling an inch from my cheek, as if she were unsure of distance. Then it moved again, and touched my cheek. The contact seemed to bring a little strength into her. She smiled weakly, and her lips moved.

I couldn't hear. "What?" I asked, leaning my ear to her mouth.

"*Nathan ...*" she whispered.

"It's Paul," I said, feeling suddenly uneasy.

She brushed at my cheek, and whispered, "Help her." Then her hand fell back to her waist. She seemed to want to move it, but couldn't.

"We're here," I said, sadly. "Pia and I are here, Mrs. Locke."

She didn't seem to understand. Her hand was trembling, as if trying to move, to gesture in some way. I felt Pia's hand on mine. She moved my hand gently to Mrs. Locke's. I patted the fingers.

"It's Paul," I said again.

She said something, but I couldn't hear. Her mouth was moving, and then her hand moved slightly up. She was motioning me closer.

"What is it?" I asked, bending closer. Her lips moved again, but I only made out the last part of what she said. "—will you help me?" was the fragment I heard.

"Of course," I whispered back. But then she said it again, and I heard her plea from the beginning:

"Nathan, will ... you help me?"

I tried to speak, but my throat was suddenly too dry. Pia put her arm on my shoulder. "Chu say et," she whispered. "Chu be her Nathan."

I glanced at her and frowned, but bent back down and did it.

"Sure, Mrs ...Lou. I'll help you. I'll take care of it, Lou."

And that little bit seemed to help Mrs. Locke. She settled and seemed a little less anxious. I took her hand and said it again.

"Of course I'll help you ... Lou."

This time she squeezed my fingers, but then her hand grew heavy. I guided it back to her waist. It stayed there with the other hand, her eyes closed, and in seconds her chest began to rise and fall in sleep. "Ches berry sick,"

Pia whispered. "Ches afraid. Mees Laura don' care, but we afraid because the lieutenant, he's coming today."

"I understand," I said, turning to leave. "I'll be back in a little while."

"Where is Mees Jenny?"

"She's working," I whispered, and that was all I said. I wasn't sure what the lieutenant might do to them if they were caught. "I have to go, Pia, but we need to discuss your parents."

"Chure. Go, Meester Paul, but remember the lieutenant, he's comin'."

"I know that," I said, and I walked out.

CHAPTER THIRTY-ONE

I drove back through the forest, through the vineyard leading to the river, and across the bridge and up into Lucca. I reached the cobblestone streets of the old section when I first saw the glow ahead. It brightened as I passed through the cypress grove, and when I reached the lane of olives, began splintering through their branches. I turned the last corner and saw a chiselled blast of light through the open gate of the villa. I stopped in the grey apron outside its edge, put on a pair of sunglasses, and stepped into the light.

Klieg lights had been erected in several places around the villa's courtyard, with beams that extinguished every shadow and bleached every surface. Dozens of ghostlike tradespeople were trailing in and out of the home and working around its sides, chalky plumbers, electricians, carpenters, masons, metalsmiths, seamstresses, and landscapers. Signora Fortuia stood in the centre of the courtyard, trying to calm two gesticulating masons. She saw me and waved them off impatiently, then we met by the old Acacia tree.

"Thes' es a nightmare, Signore," she cried, gesturing upwards.

"You must finish," I said, concerned that so much looked undone. I turned on her, shielding my eyes. "I mean it. You have only a few hours left."

"We 'ave been tryin', Signore. For six days an' nights. But eet is madness …"

"If you want your bonus you *will* do it." Three workers passed us, carrying mouldings and cans of varnish.

"Si, si, et weel … probably be done."

"Where is Jenny?"

"She es in the back, Signore."

"Paul!" Jenny's voice called from behind. She was coming from the rear of the villa. Her eyes were red, but she looked determined. She motioned three workmen with paint cans towards the back, then approached me.

"Will you finish?" I asked her.

"By sunrise," she replied, nodding. Signora Fortuia rolled her eyes. "We will," Jenny repeated. "We've even got the painting."

"And the other property?" I asked.

"It's done, Paul. What about you? Do you need more help?"

I hesitated, unwilling to explain the rest of my plans. I'd have liked to tell someone, but there was too much risk to anyone who knew what I was doing. I shook my head, and led her out to my car.

"Can *you* get everything done?" she asked in the grey apron of shade. It was quieter there.

"I'm trying."

She nodded, then let me kiss her. She stroked my cheek. "You look terrible."

"Thanks," I said, holding her. "I can't say the same back to you."

She let me kiss her again, then I left. I drove back to the pension. I made a call to Mr. Oneal. It was lengthy, but interrupted by a call from Signore Scipio. We spoke for nearly an hour before I was ready. I had barely enough time to shower and change. By the time I turned back through the clinic gates, the sun had begun to stretch over the eastern mountains. As I came out of the oak grove my lights hit an anonymous looking delivery van coming towards me. For a second the driver's face was clearly illuminated, and I could see it was Pia, wearing a blonde wig.

I was in Dr. Altobelli's personal office forty minutes later when news came that the stooped Lieutenant Dominichi and Officer Astranza were pulling up in the front driveway, followed by a marked police van. We met them in the Clinic lobby. Dominichi, Astranza and two other heavy-set officers were waiting. Dr. Altobelli nodded stiffly to Dominichi. "Buongiorno, Lieutenant," she said without smiling.

"Buongiorno, Doctore," the lieutenant said from his bowed frame. He showed a little smile. "You know why we are here," he said.

"But she is gone, Lieutenant."

He stared at her for a moment, then turned to me, "Where es she?"

I shook my head. "She's a client now, Lieutenant. You can shoot me if you wish, but I can assure you, I will not respond."

Dominichi clicked his tongue warningly. "Les' no play games 'ere," he barked, and he whirled on Dr. Altobelli.

"Es not a game, Lieutenant," the doctor said. "I donna where she is." That was true. I hadn't told her.

The lieutenant glared at her for an instant, then his right hand swept up with remarkable speed, and he slapped her. It was a hard blow, and knocked the doctor back. I started forward but Astranza grabbed my arm.

One of the other officers held me back as the lieutenant went after the doctor. He struck her again with the back of his hand, and just as quickly grasped her by the blouse and slapped her twice again. "You waste my time by concealing a fugitive, Signora."

"Hey!" Two large orderlies approached.

Astranza drew his revolver and motioned them to stop.

Dr. Altobelli put her hand to her mouth. There was blood at the corner. She stared back angrily. "I am not concealing anyone."

"Where are they?" he shouted.

Dr. Altobelli jerked her head around them. "You may search anywhere. She es no here."

"Where have they gone?" the lieutenant yelled. He spun at me and swung. I leaned back, avoiding the blow, but then Astranza hit me from the side. I fell, and turned just as Dominichi went after the doctor again. He grabbed her collar and clutched her to his face. "*Where are they*?" he yelled.

"Please!" she said hoarsely. "Please! I only know there is another clinic in Paris …" And it was true. That *was* all she knew, because it was the only information I'd given her.

"Es et so?" he demanded. "When did they leave?"

"Not an hour ago, Lieutenant."

He shoved her back. "You made a mistake, you two," he said coldly. Then he pulled Astranza's arm roughly and the other men followed them out.

I spoke with the doctor for a few minutes, then returned to the pension and tried to get some sleep. Less than two hours later I was roused by long and hard knocking. It was Dominichi again.

"Lieutenant, Officer," I said, trying to stay calm. It was in some ways a failing of mine, though, that I usually felt less fear than anger at the way people like the lieutenant handled themselves. Unfortunately, that day when this failing helped little, and hurt a lot.

"Signore, we must speak," Lieutenant Dominichi commanded up at me from his stoop. He eyed the room behind me, then his gaze narrowed back upon my face. He smiled tightly, and spoke with much more calm than before. "I wonder if the Signorina and her companions did not board the plane, Signore. What do you think?"

"I can't say, Lieutenant," I replied, glancing past him. A commotion of loud voices and heavy steps was coming from the hallway, but Astranza shut the door. I turned and padded to the bed, sat on its edge, and held my breath. I glanced up. More noises could be heard through the ceiling, doors being pounded and thrown open, men yelling.

The lieutenant pulled a chair and sat directly in front of me, shaking his head disappointedly. "You take me for a fool, Signore?"

"Why would I do that, Lieutenant?"

"Tell me, Signore. Where is your client? Did you hide her in one of the rooms 'ere?" he said, gesturing upwards as a crashing noise came through the ceiling. "We are searching, you know."

"You have a warrant?"

The lieutenant laughed. "This is not America, Signore."

There was a sharp knock at the door. Astranza opened it. Another officer was outside, breathing heavily. They spoke in low tones. Astranza turned back and shook his head to the lieutenant.

Dominichi leaned forward and raised his voice at me. "Three aero tickets were purchased to Orly under the name Spinali this morning. The Sûreté is searching for them, but I wonder. Did they go? Was it a trick, Signore?"

I didn't answer.

"Where is she, Signore?" he demanded.

"She's not here."

The lieutenant leaned forward. "You know the Signorina contacted several clinics? There is one outside Paris, another in Berlin, and a third in Barcelona? Is she to become a patient in one of those places?"

"I can't tell you, Lieutenant."

"I told you, Signore. I am not a fool." He pointed his finger into my chest. "Did you tell the Signorina Spinali to flee?"

I stared at the stubby digit. "To flee?"

The lieutenant leaned forward. "Do no' play games with me, Signore. Did you counsel 'er to flee?"

I felt a flash of anger. "How could I? Hasn't Madonna told you she's brain damaged? Haven't they said she cannot communicate with anyone?" The lieutenant hesitated, and I leaned forward. "Have they said why they want her? What they're going to do with her?"

Dominichi shrugged. "I canno' say, Signore. I am merely polizia … but *you* must know have known thes things? You must know where she es?"

I stared at him, then took a deep breath. "I canno' say, Lieutenant. I am merely *consigliere*."

I should have expected what happened next, but I didn't. Dominichi simultaneously leaned forward even further, and, more quickly than I'd have expected, curled his hand into a fist and swung. I felt a dull crack at the side of my face and fell sideways towards the wall. My cheek burned, blood flowed from my nostril. I rose, furious, as the lieutenant examined his knuckles.

"Get the hell out of here," I yelled.

Dominichi sighed, smiled a little, and lowered his voice. "Signore Rankin," he said, shaking his head. His right hand shot out to grasp my neck. I brought my hands up around his wrist, but it was like a thick branch. His fingers tightened, choking me. I struggled to pry them loose, but he was too strong. I took a swing at him, but Astranza caught my fist and pulled my arm around behind me. Dominichi brought his other hand up around my neck, and his fingers closed more tightly. I gasped. He forced a tight smile and spoke with little strain. "You thought we wouldn't find it?" He let go, and I slumped back, coughing. "We know there was … what you say, *fondo fiduciario …*"

"A what?" I asked hoarsely.

"A trust," Astranza offered, and he snorted.

I tried to remain calm, but their discovery staggered me.

"A *trust* … " the lieutenant repeated, smiling tightly. "I know you have been to the Castellani house in Viareggio. We discover what they did. Since you are consigliere you surely know that under *American* law her amounts belong to the Clinica in Eritzona which 'as done so much for her. And we 'ave it now," he said, flipping his hand matter-of-factly. "All of it, and all of it will go to Clinica Madonna."

I tried not to show it, but remember feeling my resolve collapse with disappointment. "Bastard," I muttered.

"Come now, Signore. You know there is more, do you not?"

"What are you talking about?"

"I am talking of something taken so many years ago?"

"Where did you get this information, Lieutenant?"

"I told you, Signore, I am merely polizia, Signore, and not an open book." He leaned forward. "But the jewellery, you know what 'appen to et?"

I stared back at him, and seeing his craggy, corrupt face, felt my anger return. Only now it was the same reckless kind of rage I'd felt at the Clinic. I took another deep breath, and said it again,

"I am merely consigliere, Lieutenant, not an open book."

The lieutenant leaned forward again, but this time I was ready. His fist shot out, but I blocked with my left and swung with my right.

Sitting beside me Astranza reacted with unfair speed. He caught my hand, twisted my arm around over my shoulder, and pulled me upright. As suddenly as that happened he loosened his grip, and I looked up just in time to see Dominichi swing again. This time his fist came straight on. It flattened my nose and knocked me back. My head cracked against the wall. I recall dimly that Dominichi muttered something in Italian, and suddenly Astranza was all over me. He rained blows across my face and chest for what seemed like a long time, but was probably no more than a minute. The last thing I recall before I lost consciousness is Dominichi muttering again, and that Astranza began to strip off my shirt.

When I came to, my jaw and chest burned. I was naked. I felt my face. My lips were broken and swollen. My nose and chin were still bleeding. I heard voices, and realized with a start that Dominichi and Astranza were still there. The lieutenant sat in the chair, his sidearm carelessly in his hand, the barrel towards my feet.

"Jesus," I moaned.

"Jesus canno' 'elp you, Signore, but, you can 'elp yourself," he smiled. "Just tell us where she is." He

298

pulled a clip from his belt, showed me its end to display the cartridges, slapped it into the butt and chambered the first round.

"You know I can't tell you that," I said, thinking, *he can't shoot me. He's a policeman.*

The lieutenant used his free hand to grab my hair and pull my face close. "Signore, do you know the first time I fire a gun at something?"

I shook my head. He let go of me, then leaned back with a tight smile. "I was a little boy, just a little child when my father gave me a small ... fucile—" He hesitated and turned to Astranza.

"Rifle," the big man said.

"Just so. He gave me a rifle, and there was a bird, a pretty bird, in a tree in our yard, making the songs birds sing, and so I shoot et." He laughed, then waved the gun in a descending circle. "And the bird flapped ets wings an' try to go off, but it couldn't because of a wound from the bullet. It flap an' flap, making a circle, tryin' to go away but fallin' lower an' lower until it finally came to ground at my very feet. And you know I look down and the bird es still movin', so I shoot it again, until it died right before me." He held up the gun, chambered a round deliberately, then moved the barrel to my lips, pushed them aside with the end and bent his head as if to examine my mouth as he went on. "You know what I hated most 'bout thes business with the bird?" He moved the barrel from my lips to my chin, but instead of answering I shut my eyes.

"Look a' me, Signore," he said quietly.

I opened my eyes.

The lieutenant moved the gun from my chin down, past my chest to my waist, then down along my leg, to my right foot. "Do you know what it was that I hated most?" he asked, smiling that same tight smile. "It was the waste of time. To thes very day I remember how the bird wasted my time, flapping its wings, trying to stay alive even though it was dying. It is why I shot it again. And do you know what?" he asked, pressing the gun to the top of my ankle, "You are no more than a little bird to me—a little bird, but an irritating one. Can you guess just what it is that irritates me so 'bout you, Signore?"

I shook my head.

"Et's when you fly aroun' and aroun' in circles before me, Signore."

"Go fuck your—"

A sharp explosion interrupted my words, and I felt a sudden, white hot pain from my foot. I screamed and clutched at my foot, but my hands slipped over blood.

"You motherfucking—" My words were cut short by a *crack* of the pistol hitting my face, and the world went black.

I awoke with a horrible pain within my foot, and feeling freezing cold. I was still naked, but my foot was in a deep metal basin, filled with red water and ice cubes.

"You ere awake, Signore?" the lieutenant asked. His voice had regained its calm. I looked up. He was still in the chair, with the gun in his lap. He gestured to the bowl. "I 'ave 'ad Officer Astranza bathe your foot, to slow the blood and help you. You see? We are no' without pieta. You can appreciate this, no?"

I shook my head numbly.

He leaned forward and held the gun towards my groin. "You were about to tell me of the Signorina?" he said softly.

My eyes closed. I tasted blood in my mouth.

"Signore?"

I shook my head numbly.

"Les' return to my discussion from before," Dominichi said softly. "Do you recall what I say that I 'ate most about my work, Signore?"

I said nothing, and tried to keep from thinking what might happen next. He raised the barrel of the gun towards my forehead until it touched my skin. "Come now. I shot you inna foot, so your mouth remains in order. Do you know what it is that affects me so?"

I shook my head numbly.

"No? Well then, I will remind you. What I 'ate most is when someone wastes my time. We 'ave a small police department here in Lucca, Signore, and it es especially upsetting 'ere." He pressed the barrel more forcefully against my forehead, then slowly, deliberately cocked it. "You donna wish to upset me, so you?"

I shook my head.

"Tha's good. Then tell me, Signore, where are the women?"

I shut my eyes, wondering for a bizarre moment why I'd given up walking dogs back in Arizona. Then it happened again. Something clicked inside. What was left of that anger came up again, and for the last time in my life what remained of my foolish, reckless and angry self took hold. I opened my eyes, and whispered back, "I am not an open book, Lieutenant."

He studied me for two, maybe three seconds, then shrugged, lowered the gun past my eyes, my mouth, my chest, down towards my waist, and fired again.

CHAPTER THIRTY-TWO

One of the few blessings of my failing memory is that the details that have slipped away were more often about pain than about pleasure. I assume that's why I can't remember much about the days after I was shot. Jenny told me later that an ambulance took me to a small hospital in Lucca, but I don't recall being there, just as I don't remember her then getting me moved to the Altobelli clinic. I also have no recollection of Dr. Altobelli operating on me that night, nor of the second surgery one of her colleagues performed on my foot the third day. I do have a vague recollection of waking up in the clinic, in the bed which had been that of Mrs. Locke, and seeing Jenny asleep in that which had been Laura's.

I insisted on leaving the clinic after six days, despite Dr. Altobelli's objections, because there was much more that had to be done to protect the women. The doctor drove Jenny and me back to the pension and the two of them helped my landlord get me up the stairs. By the time I was in bed, my stitches had loosened, and blood had seeped through some of my bandages, soaking my trousers. Dr. Altobelli restitched and redressed me, then helped Jenny attach an embarrassing apparatus which would help with my bathroom needs until my own parts mended. By then I was exhausted, and the other plans I had would have to wait until at least the following day.

Even then, I was very weak, and in quite a bit of pain, so I had to stay in bed and rely mostly on Jenny.

There was a lot she had to do. She took notes, ran errands, and got meals for me. One afternoon she returned from buying groceries to warn me that a vehicle from Lucca's small police force had followed her to and from the market, and that Astranza was now parked in another car in front of the patisserie across from the pension. I assumed they were listening to our calls, and even to our conversations in the room, so we were very careful in what we did and didn't say. We knew enough to stay away from Laura and Mrs. Locke, but they still weren't finished with their treatment. Fortunately, the lieutenant didn't know that, so we were able to use Dr. Altobelli, and through her Pia, to make sure the women were cared for.

One very late night in the second week after Laura and Mrs. Locke disappeared, a 'Spanish' nurse with blonde hair drove an ambulance into the clinic grounds and was let into one of the carriage stalls behind the facility. Attendants who'd been carefully selected removed American actresses named Dickinson and Tandy, took them to treatment, then placed them in a furnished basement room. The room was kept locked, and only Pia and Dr. Altobelli had keys. The actresses stayed for five weeks before the Spanish nurse arrived with the same ambulance, and in the dead of a rainy night, took them away.

Pia and Jenny were godsends in those weeks. Jenny, in particular, played a personal and kind role for me, helping me at night with my more embarrassing functions without a single word of complaint. The first two nights she slept on the sofa, getting up whenever I needed help. After helping me several times on the third night, she lay down on the covers of my bed, bracing herself with her elbows as she took notes about a few things that I felt needed to be done, but at some point while I was talking she fell asleep. I let her lie there and fell asleep myself, but when I woke later she was under the covers with me. I was harmless, of course, but I laid there awake for a while, enjoying the sensation of having her so close, dressed only in a pale cotton nightgown.

She ended up beneath the covers again after helping around midnight the next evening. This time she got under without either of us saying a word. Things went like that for about a week before I no longer needed night-time help, but Jenny stayed in my bed. I certainly wasn't going to object, and enjoyed having her close, never mind the feeling of her occasionally brushing my elbow or bumping my leg. It became a new normal neither of us spoiled with talk, but then one night I woke to find her asleep with an arm across my chest and a leg over mine. Then she woke up, and we discovered I was no longer harmless.

A lot of the memories which have stayed with me about the next weeks are about her. I suppose it was inevitable that something of a relationship would develop as it did, and not just because of everything she did for me, but due to our working together to keep Laura and Mrs. Locke safe. But it did blossom. I began to feel protective about Jenny in ways I hadn't experienced with anyone before, and while neither of us said much about it, it became obvious that she felt the same way, if not even more strongly towards me. Looking back over my life many years later I can honestly say I don't believe I was ever capable of the kind of love written about in poetry or books, but there was certainly more than just friendship. Those memories still stand out from others, but I do recall that things were crumbling around us. The trust set up by Laura's grandfather had been seized by Italian authorities, and since parts of my plans depended on funds from it and Mrs. Locke, we were running out of money. The women were for the moment 'safe' in the Basso villa, and though Dr. Altobelli's tests showed the treatments were working and would indeed extend the women's lives, that increased the risk they might not be able to live them out here.

It was about that time I got a call from Mr. Oneal. It was, unfortunately, more bad news.

"Since the women didn't obey Judge Jacob's order to come back, Madonna has been able to get a judgement of more than two million dollars against them jointly."

"Jesus!"

"That's not all," he said, hesitating.

"Before you say more, you should know the lieutenant has probably tapped our phone."

"I assumed that."

"Then what else can you tell me?"

"You've been indicted."

"Well ..." I began, but my throat was dry. He'd warned me that might happen, but that was then, this was now, and now it had.

"It actually happened several days ago, so the fact Dominichi hasn't come back to arrest you may mean you're worth more to them there than you would be back here. You have any idea why?"

"They think I might eventually lead them to Laura and Mrs. Locke."

"Sure, but why is getting the women still so important? They have the judgement, and the trust, but they have teams looking in France, Germany and Holland. Why are they doing all that?"

I was uneasy with the question, but couldn't think of an answer. The line was quiet for several seconds.

"How are you doing?" Mr. Oneal finally asked.

"Better," I said, "but under the watchful eyes and ears of the lieutenant."

"How much time do you need?" he asked carefully. I knew what he meant was *how much time does Dr. Altobelli give them to live?*

"Maybe a year, possibly two," I told him.

"Can you hold out there?"

"The money is running out."

"Talk to Scipio about that too. He filed a request to have some of the Castellani trust released. You might get something there—it won't be much, but it'll be something. But apart from the funds, how long can you stay?"

"I'm not feeling real confident about that," I said, and I wasn't. I'd done a lot to hide the transaction at the villa, but with the increased effort Dominichi was putting into the search, and the time he now had, my efforts were beginning to seem less fool proof.

"Are you well enough to move?"

"I … I suppose."

Mr. Oneal was quiet for several moments, before he made the suggestion. "Talk to Signore Scipio about Mr. Fuentes."

"Who?"

"Your father's old hand."

"You mean Ti—"

"I mean Mr. Fuentes," he interrupted quickly. "Ask Scipio he knows anyone like him who might put you up. There has to be somebody like him that could help us."

"I have no idea what you're talking about."

"Just do what I said. Don't discuss it until you get there, but tell him what I said, and get back to me in a few days."

I had no clue about what he meant, but the next day Jenny drove me to Rome.

CHAPTER THIRTY-THREE

Signore Scipio's office was in an ultra-modern building of glass and stone, with a few classical touches—downlit statues and ancient paintings. His suite was huge, with rich wood panelling and a thick antique carpet. He was expecting us, and had coffee and croissants waiting. He poured our cups himself, and we all sat around a leather coffee table at the far end of his room.

"I spoke with Signore Oneal this morning," the tall man said, frowning at me. I wore bandages on my head, limped noticeably, and still had a shiner and bruises. "It is terrible what 'as 'appened to you. Disgraceful!"

"Thank you. I spoke with him last night. He wanted me to come here directly to speak with you, but didn't really explain why."

Scipio nodded. "He was very ... cautious in his conversation with me. I take it he thinks Madonna has ... *sorveglianza*—"

"I beg your pardon?"

"His phones, and yours?"

"Oh, right. We're being monitored, and he certainly is."

"But you may speak freely here, Signore," he said, waving his hand.

"Thank you."

"But I cannot say that I understood what he suggested we discuss," Scipio said, shaking his head.

"I'm sorry to hear that, because I'm not sure what to tell you. All he said to me was that I should ask you about one of my father's employees, a man named Fuentes. I'm not really sure why, but he wanted to know if you knew anyone like him."

"Tito? The old cowboy?" Jenny asked. I had followed Mr. Oneal's instructions to the letter, including not mentioning any of what he said to her while in the car.

I nodded. "He's the only Fuentes I know of."

"But I do not know this Mr. Fuentes," Scipio said. "How can I then say whether I know anyone who is like him?"

"What exactly did Duncan tell you?" Jenny asked me.

"Yes," Scipio said, leaning forward. "Precisely what did he ask?"

I thought for several seconds, then spoke slowly. "He wanted … he wanted me to ask … if you knew of anyone like Mr. Fuentes, anyone who might help us."

"Thes Signore Fuentes, his first name is Tito?" Scipio asked thoughtfully, glancing at Jenny.

"That's right," we both replied.

"And his precise request was that you ask me if someone *like* Signore Fuentes might be of help?"

We sat silently, sipping our coffee. I put my cup down and tipped my head. "That's what he said. He wondered if—"

"He meant another Tito," Scipio said, looking up with sudden confidence. "The Signora and Signorina are in danger here, and you hope to give them time here—to protect them from extradition. And there is another Tito less than two hundred miles from us--*Marshal* Tito—

309

who has already helped us. Just last year he opened his country to any immigration, and Yugoslavia does not extradite!"

"So he's saying we should move them there?"

Scipio nodded approvingly. "It's a very good idea."

"How long would it take?"

He shrugged. "Considering the Signorina's legal difficulties, perhaps six months, a year at the most."

"They may not make it that long, but even if they do, I think Dominichi will discover where they are well before that."

"We will try to act more quickly," Scipio said, obviously already thinking through what needed to be put in place. He began to smile. "Dubrovnik is a lovely city, and the weather is wonderful there. The Signora and Signorina will be very happy there." His mood changed suddenly to a more serious one. "But there is much to do, and it will take time, and the lieutenant, he will not wait idly." Quiet came over the table for several moments, then he began nodding gravely at his coffee while thinking. Jenny and I sat, waiting, but then he looked up. "Perhaps you can give the lieutenant other things to do, while I work on this."

"How do you mean?"

He sat back again and waved his hand dismissively. "The Lucca polizia is not large, Signore, but the lieutenant has what, at least four or five people on your matter?"

I nodded.

"And I have already seen that you have a certain ability with … *operazioni immobiliari*."

"I beg your pardon?"

"I'm sorry. You have shown some skill with … legal matters, with properties, with American trusts, and even the Castellani matter. Perhaps you could do more of the same—for the women, I mean."

"I'm not following you."

"It will require funds."

"We don't have much left," I said.

He frowned, then almost immediately brightened. "We did obtain a favourable result from our effort to 'ave some of the Castellani trust moneys be released. It es not a large amount, but it should help."

"How did you accomplish that?" I exclaimed.

"You are still avvocate for Signora Locke, and the Signora is conservator for the *beneficiario* of the trust. You 'ave the right—no, the responsibility—to use such moneys as are needed for her benefit." But he seemed suddenly disappointed. "Es not much, I fear. Perhaps fifty thousand American." The room got quiet again.

"I have money we can use," Jenny said softly.

"Yes? 'Ow much, signorina?"

"About a half million."

I frowned at the idea, but she gave me a warning look, as if to prevent any argument.

I turned back to Scipio. "So what do you have in mind?"

"What I 'ave in mind is to have the lieutenant—how do you say—chase a wild goose?"

"You mean …" I began, thinking.

He was nodding. "Just so, Signore. The lieutenant is a thorough man, and has already shown he is checking records. Give him more to which he might devote his limited resources."

"But …"

"It could be done 'ere, and in other places we know Madonna is looking." He rested his elbows on the arms of his chair and folded his fingers thoughtfully on his lap.

"Where do you suggest?"

"Wherever they suspect the women may go, or may already be. He already 'as the Sûreté watching in France, the polizei in Germany, and in Belgium and, I believe Holland, Signore; and of course, the lieutenant is searching very diligently here," he said, getting up. "I suggest wherever they suspect, we heighten the suspicions." He walked back to his desk and picked up the phone. He said several things in Italian, then put it down.

I got to my feet. "Signore Scipio, I have to tell you, we don't have that many resources of our own." As soon as the words were out of my mouth I could feel his disappointment that I'd said them, not to mention Jenny's eyes on me. Scipio was shaking his head at the remark.

"We will 'elp you there. But Signore, you must know 'ow to use whatever sums you 'ave and we provide in several places, to use …'ow do you say it?"

"Leverage," I nodded as there was a knock on the door. It opened and three other attorneys entered—two were older men, the third a middle-aged woman.

"Just so," Scipio said. "May we begin now?"

"Right now," I said.

And we did.

CHAPTER THIRTY-FOUR

We spent the next two days preparing legal documents and making telephone calls. Scipio had one of his partners help us with contacts in France and Germany, while the other two worked with firms in Belgium and Holland. Early the third morning Jenny and I flew to Paris. A driver took me to an apartment in Fontainebleau, where I met with the owner and manager while Jenny made trips to a nearby shopping district for the sort of bedding and bric-a-brac which would be appropriate to two older women. By the time the lease-purchase documents were signed and sent off for immediate recording Jenny was back with delivery people and a *de corateur* to furnish the flat; and before we left it was clear to the owner, manager and several neighbours that the place was being prepared for a pair of elderly females who looked forward to living in the City of Lights.

The following morning we took a train to Berlin, where we made similar arrangements for a two bedroom house in the suburb of Wilmersdorf, making sure to record the documents right away. We spent the rest of that week doing essentially the same things in Luxembourg and Amsterdam, after which we took a flight back to Rome. We spent another day there, meeting with Scipio's banking contacts and partners to arrange financing details and transfer of the lease-purchase documents to an Italian corporation we'd decided to name *Spinalocke*. With those steps completed Jenny drove us back to Lucca for a meeting with Signora Fortuia.

The Signora had spent the previous week searching for other properties around Florence, and had found several. We spent the next week visiting some of the more lovely Tuscan communities, and in the process bought a small home in Viareggio, an apartment in Assisi, and a tiny villa in Perugia, using the same lease-purchase methods which would allow for minimal down payments, quick occupancy and instant recordings. We were on our way back to Lucca when we passed another property on the outskirts of Montevarchi. Jenny saw a small sign that said '*In Vendita*' nailed to a pristine white fence along the road, and stopped us. It was beautiful. Signora Fortuia made a couple of telephone calls, and we drove back to inspect it.

It was a rectangular parcel that stretched back several lovely miles across creeks and rolling meadows to a main house, then from there into a forest. The owner lent us a closed, horse drawn carriage and drew lengthy directions, and we followed a dirt path that wandered further into the woods, then split to six separate wood and stone cottages scattered around the forest; each had a kitchen, a bath and two moderately sized bedrooms. The owner offered the carriage and a small herd of horses if we kept on his tiny staff. It was far too expensive, but Jenny insisted. We both felt there was something especially lovely about the place. So I called Signore Scipio about it. He was surprisingly unconcerned about the price, and gave us another idea his banker had suggested.

The next day Signora Fortuia quietly put the Viareggio and Perugia properties back on the market, and we bought the Montevarchi farm. Signora Fortuia made sure the purchase was registered at once, but had strict instructions to delay any recording of the sales in Viareggio and Perugia. Jenny followed up with her usual deliveries to each place we'd bought—even the two we were now selling—and within the next week it became clear that Signore Scipio's suggestion was working. The lieutenant was taking the bait.

We started to receive calls from managers and neighbours at the properties in France, Belgium and Germany, then from people connected with the Italian properties, notifying us that police had been by, asking about the new buyers, and in particular wondering when they'd arrive. The *Guardia,* in particular, went further, and stationed vehicles nearby our properties and were watching them day and night. Then the foreman at the Montevarchi farm called to say Lieutenant Dominichi himself had gone there, closely questioned him and his staff, and even borrowed a horse to ride out to the cabins. He'd eventually left, but within two hours another officer, who from the foreman's description had to be Astranza, had parked on the street and was watching as anyone came or went.

We continued the process, buying or renting with quick transactions, and selling others with much more drawn out closures. By the end of that month Signore Scipio's contacts learned that Dominichi had come under criticism from neighbouring police departments for requisitioning their staffs for his surveillance, and then one day it finally happened: the *Guardia* patrol was gone from its station outside the *patisserie* across from our pension in Lucca, and we were no longer followed when Jenny drove me to Dr. Altobelli.

It was clear to me that Scipio had been right. We'd stretched the lieutenant's forces so thin they'd broken, and I was sure that if we were careful it might even be safe to visit Laura and Mrs. Locke. I had wanted to see them all along—Mrs. Locke, especially, and not only because she was still technically my client. It is still strange, thinking about it these years later, that I'd felt so close to that old woman, but I did. I wanted to see her, to speak with her, to reassure her that she was safe and would remain that way, and, secondarily, to assure her that her friend would be just as well protected. I wanted to see them—and at times I felt I *had* to see them.

Jenny suggested we stay away, but then something else happened to tip me over the edge. It was during a follow up visit to Dr. Altobelli. After finishing her examination of my wounds the doctor told me that both Laura and Mrs. Locke were better, and that recently they'd become more worried about me than they were about themselves. She said Mrs. Locke, in particular, had been concerned. The doctor made it clear a visit was out of the question, but they at least wanted me to have a gift. And from behind her desk the doctor produced a long, thin package, wrapped in silver paper.

I was touched, even before I unwrapped it, but it turned out to be Mrs. Locke's horse head cane, the one Laura's grandfather had used, then given to Sophie. Though the same cane had then been used so brutally *on* Laura's mother, it had been used by Mrs. Locke for quite some time now. It was beautiful, that cane, and, despite its mixed history, has proved a useful present. What was most significant to me at that time, though, was that Mrs. Locke was the one who'd suggested I have it. That touched me more than anything had in a long time, enough to make matters far worse.

CHAPTER THIRTY-FIVE

We arrived at the villa with a truck and trailer one morning, shortly before dawn. There wasn't enough light to be able to tell much about the villa's exterior renovations, but the gate looked brand new, and the parts of the front door and wall which were illuminated by our headlights had been fixed and looked newly painted. Pia met us as we unloaded the trailer, then the truck and trailer rumbled out and she took us inside. In my anticipation I forgot a bag from the car, and after Pia and Jenny helped me up the stairs I asked Pia to retrieve it. She left us in the hallway, motioning to the bedroom towards its end, where an open door showed a fire's light snapping over an inner wall.

We crept in quietly. The room was tall and wide, with tones of sage. A huge four poster bed off to the left fit the room's proportions perfectly, leaving more than enough space for a comfortable seating area in front of a stone fireplace. The fireplace was flanked by two large windows that opened to what I assumed was the garden. Wingback chairs and a small sofa were arranged about a low coffee table that faced the fireplace. Laura and Mrs. Locke were seated in the chairs, talking quietly, but they heard us and rose.

"Ladies," I said, and I had to smile. They looked better than I'd expected, in nicely tailored white and yellow dresses. Though wigged and despite Laura's sunglasses it was obvious their gaunt expressions were gone, helped by weight and colour. I knew then they'd outlive whatever safety I thought I'd secured for them in Italy, and that our efforts to distract Dominichi wouldn't be enough. We would surely have to go forward with the move to Dubrovnik.

Mrs. Locke was especially pleased to see us—especially, it seemed, to see me—but Laura grunted something which I couldn't understand. She seemed upset. Mrs. Locke glanced at her, then seemed to choose her words carefully.

"She wants to know if it's safe for you to come."

"Perfectly," I said. "The lieutenant is probably a hundred miles away."

"Searching in Assisi today," Jenny added while we took our seats.

"And the Bassos?" Mrs. Locke asked, about the couple who were still registered as owners of this lovely place. "Can we trust them?"

"The lieutenant has no idea about the Bassos, and they're quite happy" I replied.

"Mrs. Basso is expecting twins," Jenny said, smiling. She embraced both women as Pia came back in with my bag. Laura snorted something in my direction. I turned to Mrs. Locke, but she looked down, and the room went quiet until Jenny patted my hand.

"Paul made sure the Bassos won't tell, and that you won't be discovered. He's done a lot for you."

"I'm sorry it took so long," was all I could think of to say, and but for the snapping fire it was quiet again. My eyes went to the coffee table, then beside it. An old shoebox lay on the marble floor. It looked like the same one Mrs. Locke fished out of the packing in Arizona, the one with Nathan's last gift to her.

I motioned to the box. "Did you show it to Laura?"

Mrs. Locke shook her head sleepily. Laura grunted something with the cadence of a question.

"It was her husband's gift," Jenny said.

Laura grunted and beckoned. Mrs. Locke nodded reluctantly, so Jenny picked it up and brought it to Laura. Laura pulled out the blue velvet box and nodded, then opened it. Her glasses brightened with the reflection of the stones, and her face filled with admiration.

"We were in a collective, looking for a stroller. I couldn't help admiring it, and he must have seen. He was always looking for ways to … spoil me. He went back to St. Vincent's later to buy it for my birthday. He was on his way—"

"St. Vincent's?" I said.

"Right."

"St. Vincent's …" I murmured, remembering where I'd heard the name. Jenny clutched at my arm. She knew right away.

"Were there ever any other collectives by that name?"

Mrs. Locke shook her head. "There was only ever the one St. Vincent's."

I explained what Moffatt had told me about his son's friend, and the man's wife having donated items from Sophie's robbery. I left out the more brutal parts, but the news brought quiet over all of us for the longest time. Laura finally began to twist out lengthy grunts, with a gathering determination.

"Don't be silly," Mrs. Locke whispered, but Laura took the sparkling necklace in her hand and motioned towards me, then towards Mrs. Locke. Mrs. Locke continued to protest, but Pia and Jenny agreed wholeheartedly with what Laura was trying to do. Jenny handed me the cane, and helped me up.

"It was your mother's!" Mrs. Locke cried, as we approached. Laura put the necklace in my hand and motioned again. I started to move but then she jerked my wrist. I turned to face Laura; she stared at me through the dark glasses, then brought my hand close enough that I felt her breath on the backs of my fingers. She kissed the back of my hand once, grunted something, then pushed me towards Mrs. Locke.

"No, Paul!" Mrs. Locke insisted, trying to shield herself with her arms. But I put the cane aside and moved her arms, then leaned forward with the necklace. She shoved her head back stubbornly against the head of the chair. I shifted the necklace to my left hand, and with my right reached to the side of her face. She frowned, but let me move her head forward. I laid the necklace around her neck, and fastening it, whispered, "Happy Birthday, Lou."

"Thes right!" Pia cried. She spoke with her voice breaking. "You 'ave the present from Nathan, from Laura, from all of us. Feliz cumpleaños, Meeses Lou."

Mrs. Locke looked up at me, and with the firelight behind her reminded me again of how she looked the night she first opened the box: so ageless and lovely. Her eyes were welling up. She grasped my hand and whispered, "Thank you."

I couldn't reply; my throat was very tight just then. It seemed we were all having trouble talking. Jenny helped me back to my chair, and I sat, holding the cane between my knees, and feeling as satisfied as I had in quite a long time. We all sat there for several minutes, listening to the snapping fire, until Mrs. Locke turned.

"What was all the noise about?" she asked. My eyes crossed to the sack Pia had retrieved for me. Pia had laid it beside the coffee table.

"I nearly forgot," I said, pulling myself up with the cane. "We have a surprise for you ladies." I motioned to Jenny, and she got up, smiling.

"What is it?" Mrs. Locke said, as Laura grunted.

"They're outside." Jenny picked up the bag and motioned Pia towards the window.

"They're?" Mrs. Locke whispered. Laura bent a single questioning syllable.

Pia opened the windows. The garden scents drifted in, and the courtyard sounds. For several moments there was nothing but the morning chatter of birds, but then another noise drifted up from below. It was strong, and deep, and brought Laura forward in her chair. It came again, across the windowsill, this time in two distinct parts that were joined in a low, disconnected harmony. She stood, twisting out excited noises.

"You didn't!" Mrs. Locke cried, but Pia was already pulling apples and carrots from the bag. The women helped me out the room. We made our way down the stairs, out the front door, and back, through the garden, past the Acacia, and to a small clearing of lawn, where two horses were pulling at the lawn.

CHAPTER THIRTY-SIX

That next month was the best of my life, and it seemed, of any of our lives. Laura and Mrs. Locke were transformed. Laura was becoming accustomed to freedom, and began chattering away more and more with her bends and noises; especially with Mrs. Locke, with Pia, and, strangely enough, even with the horses; while Mrs. Locke, who'd been so bitter and quiet before, now was pleasant, even kind, especially with her friend. She offered suggestions whenever Laura seemed at a loss, listened with interest whenever she didn't, and, because Laura needed lengthy rests each afternoon, she began spending that time in the garden with me. It was the first and only time she ever seemed truly happy.

I came out one afternoon shortly after we arrived and found her sitting on the bench beneath the Acacia, watching some of the birds which seemed attracted to the big tree. We greeted each other, then she invited me to join her. I was a little reluctant at first, but she seemed so genuinely at peace, and made me feel welcome. We began to talk about Laura, then the villa, then about any of a number of subjects which came to her. We did it again the next day, and the next, until it became something of a routine for us. I was more listener than talker in these conversations, but in her much more pleasant and relaxed moods that was perfectly fine with me. Our discussions were rarely, if ever, about the risks we faced by staying in Italy, nor very often about anything else that was more stressful or less pleasant; but it didn't seem to matter. Mrs. Locke was obviously as aware as I was that the time she had left was limited, and had no desire to spend what she had left in any other way. No, though she did sometimes talk sadly about things she or Laura had lived through, our conversations were much more often about what pleasant things there'd been in her life.

She had seen some—with her daughter and her husband, and then, of course also with Laura. She talked often about things they'd done at Mrs. Mays' ranch, and especially about things Laura had told her—stories she made up to pass the time, memories she had about what she knew of her family, and then, of course, about her mother, Sophie. I enjoyed those conversations a great deal, not just because of what was said, but also because I grew to truly enjoy spending time with Mrs. Locke.

The villa seemed the perfect setting to live out those days. Its exterior was newly set with stone and fresh terracotta, the shutters had been fixed, repainted and refitted to all the windows; and a newly laid sod lawn stretched broadly around the house, all the way to the rear of the property, its lush green interrupted only by a flagstone path bordered with lavender. There were several olive and lavender trees to go with the Acacia, and of course, the wall that circled the grounds. Its stones had been replaced and recaulked with fresh masonry, and a row of younger olives had been planted just inside its footings. Even the old Acacia tree had been neatly pruned to a much healthier state, and its bright yellow flowers towered over us as we chatted.

Laura was much better, but remained weak through those weeks. She got up slowly and came out late, spending her first waking moments out in the garden, usually with the horses. She'd bring them a carrot or an apple and grunt small phrases or even little stories to them, while stroking their foreheads or the skin around their ears. The others began to go out when they'd hear her sounds—especially Pia and Mrs. Locke—to sit and listen as Laura told little grunting tales. Jenny and I would sometimes join them; although she could follow the gist of Laura's meanings I never could understand any of Laura's sounds; but they had a cadence that drew me in, a rise and fall that seemed to describe a mood all by themselves, sometimes gentle, sometimes building suspense.

To be honest, even the horses seemed to enjoy it. They certainly liked Laura. Whenever she paused her petting or interrupted what she was saying they'd wave their heads or nicker back, as if asking her to go on. It was enough to convince Pia, at least, that there were conversations going on. Mrs. Locke would translate Laura's stories to me later, and a much larger part of my afternoons with her were devoted to stories about the Spinali and Durer family ancestors than about any of the difficulties this last of their line had faced.

It was a good time for Jenny and I then too, for a while. We were obviously a couple by then, and Pia put us in another upstairs bedroom. It was remarkable, in hindsight, how quickly our relationship had grown, but the villa property was large enough that we had what privacy we needed, yet also whatever time either of us wanted with others. And there was that, for sure; I always felt that despite our intimacy there was still some distance between us—as if the fondness we had for each other was more a closeness between two different souls than the sort of love poets say unites them.

But then one morning while we laid in bed, sipping coffee and listening lazily to birds through the open window, Jenny rolled over, and almost as if wondering about the day's weather, asked the question.

"Would you like to get married, Paul?"

It took me completely by surprise. I'd never thought of marriage in my life to that point, not even since our relationship had begun. I may have been foolish not to, I suppose, and I was obviously a clod about the subject then.

"That's a surprise?" was all I could think of to say, and I lay there, not sure how else to reply, until she spoke again.

"You don't want to marry me?" she asked softly.

"I'm sorry," I said, stammering now, "I ... I ... just never thought about it. I haven't thought much of anything except protecting Laura and Mrs. Locke."

It was Jenny's turn to be quiet, and her silence lasted long enough to sting. She finally turned towards me.

"Well think about it now. Think about *us* for a moment, Paul—and about me. I'm offering you marriage."

"But now? I don't know ..." I said, stumbling lamely. "I mean, I'll think it over, but I appreciate that," I said lamely.

"Good to know," she said, with a little bitterness in her voice. And she rolled away.

"Why are you asking now?" I said quickly. "What brought this up?"

She shook her head dismissively and got up. I watched her move. "Wait a minute!" I said. Her gown had slipped open. My eyes went over her figure.

"You're pregnant!"

She forced a smile.

"That's not why I'm asking."

"Of course it is."

"It's *not* what I want to base a marriage on."

"I'm sorry, Jenny," I said, and I got up. I went to her and pulled her close. "I'm such an ass. Please forgive me. And I do want to marry you."

"So good of you," she said, still with an edge, but then she softened, and we kissed. I was lucky Jenny didn't just walk away then, given my first reaction—but she didn't. And over the next weeks my thoughts of protecting the older women shifted, and I started thinking seriously of becoming a husband, and a father. I began to consider what to do as an ex patriate somewhere in Europe, what jobs I could still obtain, where we might live, and how we'd raise the child we were going to have. It was an awakening, something that became both exciting and daunting—to me, anyway. Jenny was calmer, even casual about the whole thing. She'd suggested tying the knot, but to be honest, she showed none of the excitement I began to feel with this step. At times she seemed to think the marriage was just a friendly trip we'd be taking together.

Looking back over what memories I still have of those times I've sometimes wondered about the feeling between us, and whether it really was enough. There was a great deal of affection and friendship, of course, but we never had the sort of glassy-eyed infatuation the poets consider so necessary to true love. I discovered that even Mrs. Locke sensed that, because of the doubt she showed when I announced our engagement.

I had been restless the night before, and got up early the following morning. Jenny was still sound asleep. I showered and went outside for a walk down the olive lane, past the cypress, to view the river. It was early dawn, and the water was grey. When I got back to the villa Mrs. Locke was up, dressed and standing near the gate, looking out towards the olive lane while sipping coffee.

"Morning," I said. She nodded but didn't speak. She looked as if she hadn't slept much either. It was quiet for several moments, then she shifted.

"I hear you're getting married," she said, but she said it with a distant tone, with what seemed almost more like sympathy than happiness.

"What's the matter?" I asked.

She didn't respond right away, but then she murmured, "Why?"

"Why what?"

"Why are you getting married?" she asked quietly, looking off towards the sunrise.

"Because we love each other," I replied.

She smiled and nodded, but it was a thin smile, and a brief nod, and the reactions—the question, her tone, and the look she gave me—were disappointing. She and I had become close friends those weeks, and this sudden change irritated me. I left her without saying more, and didn't mention her reaction to Jenny.

Pia, on the other hand, was thrilled that an event with rituals and religion might need her help. She began to organize everything, making lists, planning the ceremony, and even consulting astrological sources to schedule the date and hour of the wedding. Her focus was intimidating, but gathered momentum as the day got closer. The week before the event took place she took her lists, donned her Marilyn Monroe wig, and set off to school the minister.

On the days leading up to the ceremony Laura prepared a small story especially for us. The evening before was a perfect setting—it was clear and warm, and Pia brought out chairs so we could all sit beneath the Acacia. Laura wore a very pretty yellow dress; Mrs.

Locke sat beside her in a white one, and Jenny, looking especially lovely in a dark silk dress with hand-painted orange flowers, sat between me and Pia.

Laura began with three sentences of sounds, then paused to let Mrs. Locke translate. Mrs. Locke smiled back at Laura, then turned to us:

"Laura says *I'm very happy for both of you. I'm glad I can be here with Louisa to celebrate your wedding. I'm especially glad you're getting married here, because it's here that my mother was married, almost eighty years ago.*"

Mrs. Locke paused, waiting. Laura spoke longer pieces, gesturing with her hands and head as she went on, interrupting from time to time to allow her friend to translate, and at one point taking Mrs. Locke's hand affectionately; and I remember hearing Mrs. Locke tell it:

"*My mother, Sophie was one of the kindest people who ever lived. You know the story, how soon after she married she volunteered to work in a children's hospital in Viareggio, and how soon after that she started going to see my grandfather. Mother grew to love him as much as anyone she ever knew—even more than my father did, I believe.*

"*When she met him Grandpa was making a small treasure, a beautiful thing that Mother admired a great deal. Later on, when he died, he left it to her. When we moved to America I met another of the kindest people who ever lived, a girl named Louisa—*"

I gather it was her she'd reached over for Mrs. Locke's hand.

"*Louisa loved me as much as Grandfather loved my mother, and loves me still. She became the best friend of my life. But one day long ago she had to leave me, so I took the treasure Grandfather had given my mother, and gave it to her. I'm sure my mother wouldn't have minded.*

"When that happened I never thought I'd see Louisa again, and many years passed before I did. But then it happened, partly because of you, Jenny, and you, Paul. And I'm so grateful. I can't show you how grateful, but I am very grateful. And I hope the two of you will have just as much love between you as my mother and grandfather had between them, as much as Louisa and her Nathan did together, and as much as Louisa and I have had between us.

"I don't have much else to give you, but since you've done all you did and are getting married tomorrow morning, Louisa agreed that what Grandfather gave to Mother and what I gave to her, we can now give to you."

And she handed Jenny a small package wrapped in gold paper. Jenny smiled, looked at me, then opened the package.

It was the hummingbird frame. Molly's picture had been removed, and it was gleaming, waiting for another photograph.

It was a lovely gift, a lovely story, and a lovely moment.

I remember the next morning better than any in my life. It was early spring, the sun was out, and had dried the morning dew by the time Pia and the women brought Jenny downstairs. She was as beautiful as I'd ever seen her, in a long but simple cream-colored gown with an Asian motif of pale flowers. A table was placed on the lawn, covered with white linen and laid with lilac and heather from the garden. There was fruit in a bowl and a plate of croissants, and preserves Pia had shipped from Arizona. Signora Fortuia was late, so we sipped

Champagne while waiting for her. I remember being so pleased with how things had gone, at least for those moments.

There my memory breaks, and there are only shards of the rest. I remember Mrs. Locke and Laura feeding the horses and some low talk in the courtyard, then the sound of racing engines spilling over the walls. A pair of Lancias tore into the courtyard, and I glimpsed Signora Fortuia through the rear window of the first car. She was crying, dishevelled and bleeding; then the front doors opened, and Lieutenant Dominichi and Dr. Braga got out.

CHAPTER THIRTY-SEVEN

I can't fully describe the rest of those moments, though they happened directly in front of me. I remember that I grabbed the cane and began hobbling forwards, but it was like one of those dreams where you're moving in quicksand. Pia rushed by me, followed by Mrs. Locke, Jenny, and finally Laura. There was a glint from Laura's hand; she was holding a knife. Other officers jumped out of the second car, and people converged a few yards ahead of me. There was yelling, and suddenly, above the yelling, Laura screamed.

It wasn't like other screams I've heard in my lifetime, but one with the most awful, angry, and vicious heart in it. I still couldn't move very quickly, but Mrs. Locke told me later that Laura had passed everyone and was headed towards Braga with the knife; that she and Jenny tried to stop her, until a gunshot stopped everyone. I still remember hearing that sound, and then another scream, that went on and on, until the scream stopped, and it was quiet.

I hobbled through the others and saw the lieutenant holding his gun, Laura being restrained by two officers; and everyone was staring at the ground. I turned, and looked, and there was Jenny's body, with a deep red stain spreading over the pale flowers in her dress.

We were all taken to the Lucca police department and booked. Pia and Mrs. Locke were put in cells someplace there, but I was taken to another jail outside Florence. The guards told me Laura was relocated to a psychiatric prison, where she was kept in restraints and confined to a padded room. We were scheduled for extradition, but Signore Scipio demanded a hearing, and that request was granted.

The hearing would actually be a trial, and would take place in ten days' time. Mr. Oneal flew out to help, and he and Scipio were able to get Pia and Mr. Locke released. Pia spent the first day making arrangements with Jenny's American relations for her remains to be flown to San Francisco; I could do nothing about any of that, but at least that part was being taken care of. The extradition hearing, however, was going to be a problem, partly because I felt too broken and demoralized to do anything but let it play out.

Laura was the other problem. Only her attorneys were permitted to see her, and not only could neither Scipio nor Mr. Oneal understand her sounds, she refused to cooperate with either of them. Scipio convinced a Judge to let Mrs. Locke try to communicate with her, but even with her friend in the room, Laura wouldn't speak with the men.

"She does no trust any man, it seems," Scipio explained. "We are not able to get anywhere with 'er."

I didn't respond, though I could fully understand Laura's reaction.

"Et es a problem, Signore. Signora Locke says it is because there were … things which 'appened at other times with other men, but she will 'ave nothing to do with me, or Signore Oneal, or any other man except,

333

perhaps—Signora Locke says—except perhaps … you. The Signorina must be our chief witness, so it is important to both of you. So I 'ave requested a hearing this afternoon to ask that you be permitted to assist."

"I won't do it," was all I said, because I wanted nothing more to do with anyone. I shook my head. "I've made everything worse."

"Signore, I understand 'ow you feel. But from what I 'ave been told you made nothing worse and everything better. You 'ave suffered great loss, and 'ave much pain, but it would scarcely make your anguish better if we now added a lifetime of regret because of what you decide now. It would truly be a mistake, Signore, to give in to your grief. An avvocate canno' abandon a client, even in such times, especially in such distress."

"You can't say that. I … haven't abandoned anyone."

"Not yet, et es true. But your pain asks you to do just that in the coming hearing. Donna listen to it, Signore."

I shook my head, unwilling to agree. He argued, but I refused his suggestion to speak with Mr. Oneal or even Mrs. Locke. But the next day he brought them, and Pia as well.

I felt even worse. Every bit of Mrs. Locke's progress over the past months seemed to have vanished. She was pale and weak. She struggled to keep up with what was being said, and sometimes lost her train of thought. Mr. Oneal stood sombre and subdued, and said nothing that seemed to matter. Pia seemed determined as ever to help, but had no idea how to.

"Meeses Laura needs your help," she said.

"I just screwed everything up."

"No one could have helped that," Mr. Oneal said quietly.

"It's not true."

"It is. You gave her a reprieve."

"He's right," Mrs. Locke said with her voice quavering. "You gave her life when she was dying, life out of that place—"

"And now she's going back!"

"Not necessarily," Mr. Oneal said, "and remember what your father said? Good clients are like good friends. You're lucky—"

"You're not helping, Mr. Oneal," I interrupted, shaking my head numbly.

"Look, we just need to regroup."

I turned to Mrs. Locke. "This whole thing was a mistake."

"What are you saying?" she asked in a whisper.

"I'm sorry, but it would've been better not to have gotten her out in the first place. I've just made things worse."

She stared at me, then, weak as she was, a faint bit of hardness came into her eyes. She struggled to speak, but did, weakly, in a few halting sentences.

"You haven't … made anything worse … but you will …if you just sit here …Your work isn't done. You still have … responsibilities … After the freedom you gave her, you can't just sit here while they try to take it away."

I frowned at her, feeling horrible. She leaned forward and took my hand, looking as if she hadn't slept in days. And then all she said was, "All right. This was my doing, Paul, not yours. Let's go." She struggled to her feet, then bent down and kissed my forehead. "Thank you, Paul," she said, and without more she began to leave. She was barely to the door when I heard her moan. By the time I looked up she had fallen to the ground.

It's another moment I can't forget, and not just because what happened after was chaotic—a commotion of yells, people crowding into the prison hallway, Pia trying to resuscitate Mrs. Locke, then paramedics taking her out on a gurney—but, though I'd been consumed with grief over Jenny and Laura, somehow this was too much. Seeing Mrs. Locke's tiny form on the cold floor staggered me. I stared as Pia worked on her and the paramedics removed her. Then everyone was gone, and everything was quiet.

That afternoon I had Scipio bring me the files.

He came with a paralegal lugging a handcart and three large boxes.

"How is she?" I demanded, before touching any of the materials.

He replied sadly while shaking his head. "Es … fundamentale—how you say?—very serious, but they will do whatever can be done. Just as we must do what can be done for her friend, Signore."

"How much do you know the case?" I asked, opening the first box. I recognized files on top from my father.

"I know some of it, of course," he said, "but there's much I've not yet been able to review. But you may rest assured that I will read it all, Signore. I will be prepared."

"Good," I said, "because you better be."

"I would no use thes word '*good*' to describe what we face," he replied, settling onto a small chair. "But we can perhaps make it better."

"What do you suggest?"

"We can do nothing for her unless she cooperates, and she will not with any man, it seems, but you, Signore—or so we hope. But getting you to see her will be difficult, for you are accused of arranging her escape."

"You know why I had to get her out of there?"

"Of course, but nonetheless, it is not likely the court will take a risk with you ... *unless* we offer measures to reduce it. You would not object to being—how do you say? Bound and chained?"

I stared, wondering if this was his attempt at humour.

"I am serious, Signore. Do you object to ... manetta—manacles, I think you say, around your arms and legs, if they would be necessary to obtain permission for you to assist?"

"No, no. Of course not."

"Then I will try this very afternoon. You read these materials, especially the second box. It 'as the procedures for our trials."

"And what do you think of our chances?" I said, pulling the second box from beneath the first. "Will we be sent back?"

"Of course," he said. I looked up. He was staring over his glasses at me, looking deadly serious. "You yourself have had a great loss, Signore, but you are avvocate, and understand I must tell you things not pleasant to hear?"

I nodded, and he settled back in his chair.

"I must review everything, Signore, but there are several things which seem clear without reading any of it. First, Signore, 'es my opinion you will be returned to America, no matter what we do. You will 'ave another trial in Arizona, after which *you* will most likely be sent to prison. However, your time there should not be so long—perhaps two or three years—though it es most

337

likely you will lose your ability to remain avvocate, because of other proceedings that are in place. Signore Oneal agrees, and you should prepare yourself for thes."

"Go on," I said, swallowing as he took another long breath.

"The Signorina's situation is more serious than your own, I'm afraid. She 'as been already convicted of quite serious crimes in Eritzona, omicidio—murder of the secondi degree, you call it—and more than one il giudice—*judge,* I think you say—has made orders that she should certainly be returned and committed, to thes place Madonna."

"You know what they did to her?"

"But it is an 'ospital in America you accuse, not a gulag in Russia, and Signore Oneal says they 'ave many more doctors and inspectors to dispute the two we may bring. So we will try, Signore, but I'm afraid her return is far more likely than yours, and that your own is probable."

"So what is the point?"

"The point, Signore?"

"The reason? Why are we trying if we're bound to lose?"

"You are at the moment still an avvocate, are you not?" he asked, looking over his glasses.

"Yes, yes."

"And your client, Signora Locke, she 'as asked you to assist the Signorina?"

"She … yes. She has."

"Then you should not need a point, Signore. Et es your job."

It was a depressing start, but Scipio was at least successful enough that afternoon that the next morning guards manacled my wrists and ankles and Astranza drove me to Laura's psychiatric lockup. It was on the

338

other side of the Arno River in Florence, in an East bloc looking building with barbed wire along the top of its walls. Astranza and an orderly took me into a tiny, padded room and sat right outside the open bars while I crowded in with Laura, Pia, Mr. Oneal and Signore Scipio. It was one of the more surreal experiences I can remember, gathering in that depressing cubicle, with Astranza sitting a few feet away, listening to everything we said.

Laura was in a grey hospital gown, with her wrists and ankles in leather bindings. Her sunglasses had been taken away, and even apart from the web-like scarring of her eye, she looked as if her months of progress had been seriously damaged by the past few days. Outwardly she seemed more concerned about Mrs. Locke than herself, but I felt a seething anger beneath her composure. With me there though, for some reason, she was finally willing to help us try to put together a defence, and we worked at it for several hours that day, and into the night. They put me in a separate cell to sleep, but it was hard; my thoughts kept going to Jenny, and Mrs. Locke, what had happened to the one, and what was happening to the other.

Early the next morning I was taken back to Laura's room. The others were already there, including Astranza, sitting, as before, just outside our room. We worked for hours again that day and into the evening, and that night it was harder to think of anything but the hearing. It was slowly taking over my mind, which was probably a good thing. That change went on the next day, then progressed further on the next, and not halfway through our preparations I already had trouble focusing on anything else. By the time we were finished we'd spent a total of eight days and nine nights immersed in the work, while Astranza sat outside, listening to all that was said.

PART THREE

Trial

Florence, 1969

CHAPTER THIRTY-EIGHT

When the first day of trial arrived I was allowed to change from prison garb into a suit, before two *Guardia* escorted me to the courthouse. It was, in retrospect, a beautiful setting for this ugly proceeding, an historic marble building with white columns outside, and inner walls of dark wood that stretched up twenty feet before curving into a dark beamed ceiling. There were four huge steel and brass chandeliers spaced around the large room, giving a stately and dignified air. But the beauty had an oppressive, even ominous atmosphere to it.

The guards sat me directly beneath one of the chandeliers. Two female officers brought Laura in and seated her next to me. She had leather wrist restraints and manacles on her ankles, and yet they'd let her wear one of her nicer dresses—a pale blue one—as well as a pair of sunglasses. She nodded in my direction and sat.

A door at the front of the courtroom opened, admitting the man we call the prosecutor and they referred to as the procuratore. He was a thin man, about Laura's height, dressed in a grey wig and black robe. Signore Scipio and Mr. Oneal came through the door, Scipio dressed like the procuratore in a wig and robe, while Mr. Oneal wore one of his dark trial suits.

A door banged at the back of the room. The bailiff was letting in dozens of people—men, women, teenagers; a crowd that only aggravated the tension. Pia came in. Signore Scipio seated her just behind us, and explained to Laura that she would help with translation.

She grunted a question. Pia held her shoulder and leaned towards us. "Che wants to know who are all thes people?"

Signore Scipio patted Laura's arm. "You 'ave become famous, Signorina. I 'ave 'ad calls from *Le Figaro* and *Corriere della Serra* already, wanting to speak with you. There are many familiar with the old Spinali familie, and you are … as you say, the last of the Mohicans?"

"How is Mrs. Locke?" I asked.

"Che's no good," Pia said gravely.

"Why?" I asked, and Laura turned, obviously concerned.

She hesitated.

Laura grunted.

Pia nodded reluctantly. "Dr. Altobelli es bringin' a heart surgeon, but she's very weak. They're goin' to choose an operation for this afternoon."

Laura bit her lip, but then the doors banged again. Lieutenant Dominichi walked in. He was followed by Dr. Braga and Braga's lawyer, Donald Janoff. Braga looked more confident, impressive in a conservative grey suit, but Janoff had that slightly disreputable appearance even well-dressed lawyers seem unable to escape.

Braga caught sight of Laura and stopped. She stared at him. The moment stretched between them, but then she turned and looked at me for what seemed even longer, without any sound or change in expression, until a door opened just off the judge's bench.

The bailiff barked, *"Tutta l'alba!"* and everyone stood. The judge entered, wearing his own wig and dark robe. He had a thick folder under his arm. He strode up to the bench and sat, put on reading glasses, and glancing over them, said in heavily accented English,

343

"Signore Raadi, Signore Scipio, are we ready to proceed?"

"Si, Suo Onore," both counsel said.

"Because the Signorina and so many of those on both sides are from America, and as avvocate from America will be permitted to 'assist' on both sides in this very unusual proceeding, I 'ave been asked to conduct the proceedings in English. Does everyone agree?"

"It es acceptibile with us, Il Giudice," the procuratore said.

"And with us," Scipio said. "I will also 'ave an interpreter present during the Signorina's testimony."

The judge nodded. "And we 'ave an English-speaking court reporter, and staff which understands both English an' Italian."

"Grazie—thank you, Il Giudice," both counsel intoned.

"Then as you are procurator, please present your side of thes matter, Signore Raadi."

Scipio surprised me by interrupting right away. "Pardon, Il Giudice, but I must object to the proceedings taking place at all. My clients are here only because Signorina Spinali escaped the brutality she received in America, at a place which threatened her life until she quite sensibly fled from it. She sits 'ere today, already in the last months of her life, only because a member of our own *Guardia* beat one of our citizens to discover her whereabouts," he said, raising his voice as Raadi got to his feet. "We should not reward such behaviour with a proceeding that threatens to return my client to that awful place."

"Il Giudice, if you please," Signore Raadi countered calmly, "The witness who 'helped locate the Signorina was attacked and robbed not by *Guardia,* but by others who are being sought by them—"

"Pardon," Scipio said, "but thes man who attacked her has come into thes courtroom!" he said, pointing at the lieutenant. "He is, I must add, being investigated for 'aving shot the Signorina's avvocate, who sits beside me still suffering from—"

"Come now, Signore Scipio," Raadi interrupted. "You know quite well *investigazione* is not evidenza, or, might I ask, if we may dispense with the formality of thes hearing because its own investigation makes evidenza unnecessary?"

"But of course not—" Scipio began.

"Well then," Raadi interrupted, raising his voice. "Evidenza is what is required both 'ere and with respect to the avvocate's shooting, and what evidenza exists on that subject will show the avvocate himself attacked the lieutenant, and a witness—an officer, in fact—can verify the lieutenant shot only to defend himself, and that he fired to injure, not to kill."

"Then my client should be grateful for being shot?" Scipio snapped.

"For being alive, Signore!" Raadi said, turning to the judge. "Il Giudice, this is nonsense. These officers will easily prove the arrests of the Signorina and her avvocate were proper."

"Signore Scipio," the judge said, "have proceedings taken place proven what you claim?"

"That es only a matter of time, Il Giudice," Scipio replied.

"Do you have witnesses who support your assertions?"

"We have the victims themselves, Il Giudice."

"Of course you do. But Signore Raadi says there are at least two *Guardia,* including a lieutenant, who dispute thes' claims. Do you 'ave any *independent* witnesses?"

"These *Guardia* are no more *independent* than those they injured, Il Giudice. They themselves arranged their attacks in such a manner to exclude other witnesses."

"Will the officers testify 'ere?"

"Si, Il Giudice," Raadi replied. Scipio shrugged.

"Then, Signore Scipio, you may question them as they appear. Since time is of some essence in thes hearing we will proceed. If the victims are convincing despite witnesses against them, and if you meet your burden of showing proof as to such matters, then we will suspend our work and refer the matter to Crimine Court. If not, we will proceed to the issues of estradizione with no unnecessary delay or duplication."

"Si, Il Giudice," Scipio said, resuming his seat. I exchanged glances with Mr. Oneal. Scipio had started out more aggressively than we expected. It was a little encouraging.

The judge turned to Raadi, waiting.

The procuratore was studying his file. He nodded to Scipio, then faced the judge, and pausing from time to time to choose his English words, explained his position.

"The State of Eritzona an' the United States 'ave presented applications for arrest an' extradition of a *retardato*, Signorina Laura Spinali—"

"Scusarsi, Suo Onore," Scipio interrupted again, getting slowly to his feet. "But whether the Signorina is of such defect to be considered *retardato* is a matter of contest in this proceeding."

"I am aware of thes question, Signore Scipio," the judge replied, "But let him finish. He may speak and present evidence, just as you may question whatever he does. But do so as the evidence enters, Signore Scipio, not now. Proceed, Signore Raadi."

"As I was sayin'," Raadi resumed, "we 'ave American applications for arrest and extradition of the

Signorina so that she may receive treatment from those best able to deal with her, and that the claim she has ... *equilibrio,"* he said, hesitating.

"Sanity," the clerk offered in perfect English.

"Grazie. It appears, Il Giudice, that the question of her sanity has already been investigated so thoroughly, and found so wanting, that it may easily be said that thes woman who sits like a lamb 'ere before us has within her the nature of a wolf, one which has already killed some and injured others. Within her is a force which, except for its uncontrollable nature, would require that she who is so cursed to suffer it would serve life sentences for charges of 'omicidio and ... *scompiglio,"* he said, turning to the clerk.

"Mayhem."

"May-ham," he said. "There are also testimonianza from hearings in the State of Aritzona, affidati from doctors who worked for that State and for the United States governmen' itself, and doctors from the 'Ospedale who know the Signorina best, who will show that to this very day she has yet great violence inside her. She 'as attacked people several times, even in her advanced years, even a lieutenant of our own *Guardia.*

"For such crimes in America she was arrested, but because of her mental condition she was not held within the brutal walls of a prison, but instead delivered to the more kindly and careful attentions of a medical facility. 'Ospedale Madonna is thes place, and it is not what Signore Scipio said earlier. We will show the 'Ospedale does much to help patients and did much to help her, and for a great while at least, succeeded in calming the Signorina's violence and soothing her mind. But the doctors will prove what we all can imagine, that it es a delicate business to care for such a person, and that lacking their attentions she has already regressed, and will surely do so further unless she is sent back." He paused to review his notes, then looked back up.

"With respect to the Signorina there is another issue. Since her escape it has been discovered that this patient received quite expensive care and treatment at the expense of the 'Ospedale and the United States, because she was thought to be ... without funds of any kind, when in fact she 'as all along possessed—but concealed—ample sources to recompense those who provided her care or paid for such provisions. An American Judge much like yourself has ordered the Signorina must therefore pay for what she received from her ample resources, and we therefore ask that you, Il Giudice, should order that enough of the possessions and wealth of the Signorina be turned over to repay the sum she owes." He turned a page and read. "We will provide ... precise *contabilie*—" He looked down at the clerk.

"Accounting," she said.

"—Accounting of the expense, with adjustmens for such things as inflazione and increase in costs."

"Finally, Il Giudice, there is also application seeking return of the Signorina's consigliere, Signore Paul Rankin, to face charges of creating false evidence to arrange her release, interfering with an order for her return, arranging her flight to escape lawful orders, and for his own violence against the 'Ospedale director." He turned and frowned at me, then sat.

"Signore Scipio," the judge said.

"Grazie," Scipio replied. He stood, removed his glasses and pinched the bridge of his nose, then replaced the glasses. He motioned to Laura and began. "Signore Raadi says this aging woman sitting here so delicately poised between inner peace and uncontrollable violenz should terrify us by her very presence, but it is not true. The truth, and we will show it, is that we should be grateful that the Signorina, who is the last survivor of one of our oldest and most respected families, was saved from horrors none of us should endure, and is back where she belongs. We will show thes' so-called 'ospedale' is a place which with such … *sacrilegio,*" he said, turning to the clerk.

"Sacrilege," she nodded.

"Grazie, Signora. We will show that thes place which, with so much sacrilege masquerades behind the name 'Madonna', practices less medicine than it does stupro—" He turned again to the clerk.

"Rape."

"Si. Grazie. Less medicine than it does rape, and less kindness than it does cruelty, out there in the wilds of America." He walked behind Laura's chair and rested his hands on her shoulders. "Thes woman faced great 'horrors abroad. Kidnap, rape--repeated, incessant, and inhuman rape, as well as brutal beatings, and confinement at the very Ospedale which 'as snuck into our country and now tries to convince Il Giudice to give her back. She fled that place as anyone with … how do they say, *un cervello nella loro testa?*—" he turned to the clerk.

"With a brain in their head."

"Just so, with a brain in their head would have, for her own survival, and returned to our country—to *her country*—where she simply asks we let her live out what little life remains to her. Thes woman who would already have died by now remains alive only through efforts of our own doctors because of the …*cancro …*" He turned again to the clerk.

"Cancer."

"Grazie, cancer, which even now eats its way through her frail body. Our doctors gave her a little more time—perhaps a few more months, but the so-called

'Ospedale which already subjected her to unspeakable horrors has followed her over a great ocean and hired corrupt detectives to recapture her. And why, we may ask?" He turned and waved to the audience. "Do they truly fear she will rise up from her chair and strike us all dead?" He shook his head wearily and reached into a fold of his robe to retrieve a ten thousand lire note. "No. What brings them all thes way es the simple matter of greed." He waved the note, then returned it to his pocket.

"Il Giudice, the proof here is simple enough. It will show these claims are but a disguise for avarizia—" He turned again to the clerk.

"Avarice."

"Si, grazie. Il Giudice. Their real wish is for those millions of American dollars. They care nothing about the life of thes precious survivor of our own country, thes' woman who wants only to live out what little time she has left, and then die here, in her home, in *our* home."

I exchanged another look with Mr. Oneal. It was a decent opening, but one of few bright spots we could expect.

CHAPTER THIRTY-NINE

Despite Scipio's opening, the next days were an example of how the worst of times can become even more awful. Raadi started his case with some of his strongest ammunition—the orders American judges had handed down on the subjects of Laura's murders, her escape, and her flight from America—and as the evidence piled up its effect on Laura became a matter of concern to us all. Each morning she looked paler and seemed less alert, and each night she required more help just to get out of the courtroom. And then, on the third morning of trial Pia reported that though Mrs. Locke had survived emergency surgery, she was doing so badly that Dr. Altobelli thought she might not survive.

Back in court Signore Raadi and Donald Janoff started their next attack with a damning presentation from Dr. Braga himself. It was depressing just to see the small man walk up to be questioned, looking so professional, and pretending to be humble when he had previously been so much of a thug. The only clue this was the same man I'd attacked were his eyes, which above his otherwise ingratiating expression, showed glimpses of the cold lack of feeling I'd seen that day.

But he was well prepared, and Janoff, who was allowed to bring out his testimony, didn't waste time. After gilding Braga's qualifications with the number of patients he'd 'helped', he went straight to Laura's case, focusing on her 'crimes' and 'retarded' condition.

"And how did you first meet Miss Spinali?"

"She was a patient when I took over the clinic," Braga replied calmly. "That was about thirty years ago."

"So, about 1938?"

"That's correct."

"And was she ever the victim of rape or brutality such as Signore Scipio mentioned in his opening?"

"Yes, but not at our facility."

"Would you explain?"

Braga took on a note of sadness. "Miss Spinali's history is actually quite heart-breaking. Her parents died when she was a teenager, and there being no programs to help her, she wandered off into the desert. She was found and held by a group of Indians, who treated her very badly, so yes, she was raped before she came to us, and treated brutally."

"Is she what's commonly referred to as retarded?"

"I'm afraid so. Laura was born with retardation that confuses recent and long term memories, and the traumas she then endured were so severe they even now live on in her mind, so vividly they can at times seem to have happened yesterday. So her mind confuses past events with the present, past characters with those today. She relates the trauma she endured years ago to present events and people, attributes wrongs she suffered as a child to people in her present life. If she had the skills to communicate she might very likely believe she was raped by people in this courtroom—even by the judge or members of the audience, people who never touched or even met her before. It's part of her retardation, her mental dysfunction."

"You said 'if she had the skills to communicate. Does she lack such skills?"

"Yes, and again, it's part of her retardation. She's had a difficult time processing her thoughts and a nearly impossible task of trying to communicate with others, ever since she was a child."

"Was she was born with these problems?"

"That's correct. I understand her mother was injured badly just before she gave birth, and that may have caused it."

"And has her retardation led to violence?"

"I'm afraid that's also true. Anger and violence have been a major part of her life ever since she was a child. To be fair, she can't really control herself when she gets these episodes, but her entire life has alternated between periods where she can appear calm and quiet as she is now, and episodes of violence, even lethal violence."

"Did this ever happen at the Madonna Clinic?"

"Several times. The one you're no doubt referring to, the one that brought me to Madonna, happened in 1937. She strangled a guard—killed him—and took his keys, got out and set fire to the facility."

"Are there other examples of such behaviour?"

"Yes, including one when she injured a former director very badly, sadistically, you might say, with a knife."

"Were records made of these events?"

"Yes. There are very thorough records of each, and I've brought them all."

"We 'ave marked them, Il Giudice," Raadi said, getting to his feet. The judge nodded, eying a thick stack on the clerk's desk.

Janoff went on. "Do these records also show what you've done to try to help her?"

"They do."

"Would you briefly summarize it for the judge?"

353

"Certainly. For years I spent—*we* spent—part of every day with Laura, trying to work on her communication, drawing her out, and on some occasions achieving small breakthroughs. What we've tried to do is to clarify in her own mind at least some of her confusion between the past and the present, between trauma that occurred before and the safety and healing of what she enjoys in our facility, but it hasn't always been possible.

"How did you go about trying to accomplish this?"

"It's been very difficult, but what progress we've made had happened mainly through with counselling, therapy if you will, and with the latest medicines. I keep up on developments in both areas—with the latest and best therapies and with medicines that have been developed for patients like her, both in the United States and here in Europe. I've tried for years, and continue to try to find new ways to help her. To whatever extent possible I think we have helped her. Over the years and as newer methods and medicines came available I found there were more times like these, when she was calm, controlled, and where the violence subsided."

"Is she cured?"

"I'm afraid few retarded individuals can ever truly be 'cured', because past recollections and damage stay with them in different ways than they do a normal person. It's a little like trying to remember events through a bent mirror; they're distorted, magnified or minimized in ways that change their reality. We try to put things in context for them, and try to help people understand what's real and what isn't, to accept that what's behind them truly is past, but retardation will always prevent a patient from processing things properly. She has also had severe inability to communicate, and to control herself. She'll always have these difficulties, and they'll always affect her in ways no one can predict."

"And in this case," Janoff continued, "did the Madonna Clinic take care of her not only with housing, food, and clothing, but provide medical care, give tests, administer medicines, treat her for almost three and a half decades?"

"Yes, we did."

"And was it your impression—Madonna's impression—that when giving all this care to her through all these years, that she had no means to pay for it herself?"

"Yes, that's correct."

"But you furnished it anyway?"

"We provide care and treatment for a patient whether they can afford it or not, either by volunteering our help or through government assistance from the United States Department of Health, and from the State of Arizona."

"Did there comes a time when you discovered she had means to pay for what she'd been getting for free?"

"Yes," he said, and he motioned to me. "When Mr. Rankin's law firm became involved we began to check more thoroughly, because their law office is one of the most expensive in Arizona. So we investigated, and found Laura's family left a trust to which she has full access, but hadn't been disclosed to us, and that she has interests in other assets."

"Were you then asked by an American ... Judge to ascertain the value of all you've provided her?"

"Yes, I was."

"Tell us why and how this was done."

"We retained an accounting firm that works both for medical entities and the government of Arizona. We gave them access to all our records, and they made the calculations."

"And what is the value of all you did for her?"
"Approximately ... I'm sorry, I don't know the

conversion to lire, but in American dollars, just for the past year it comes to approximately three hundred and seventy-four thousand dollars. The total over the entire thirty-four years of service comes to just over eight million dollars."

A murmur rippled through the audience. Janoff paused to let it settle, then went on.

"If you discover a patient does have money to pay for the care she received, are you allowed to recover such amounts back, even those the government paid?"

"The government doesn't have its own collection system for these programs. They rely on us to collect their monies back."

"Thank you, Doctor. Now the patient's lawyer, Mr. Rankin," He turned and pointed towards me. "He attacked you, did he not?"

Braga glanced towards me and nodded. "Yes, he did."

"Would you tell us how that happened?"

"Yes. His law firm got a Judge to order her release without explaining her needs or telling him what we'd been doing for her, and without ever giving us a hearing. I understand they have a reputation for such tactics—"

"Il Giudice, if you please," Signore Scipio said, getting to his feet.

"Si. Signore Janoff …, Doctor Braga, please confine your responses to what is asked."

"I'm sorry, Your Honor, I'm not familiar with these kinds of proceedings," Braga said.

The judge waved Janoff ahead.

"Will you explain the circumstances surrounding Mr. Rankin's attack upon you?"

"I'll try. When they came I was surprised—shocked, really. We'd never had anyone … ambush us, if I may use that term, with court orders in that way. He was from the very beginning very aggressive, interrupting, insisting I do whatever he said. I asked him several times to let us talk with the judge, but he refused, then became even more belligerent, and attacked me."

"Did he injure you?"

"Well, not that seriously, but yes. He struck me, several times, and choked me. I would have let it go, but the district attorney and a Judge felt it was so unacceptable that—"

"Il Giudice," Signore Scipio said, shaking his head.

"Never mind," Janoff said before the judge could react. He nodded to Braga. "Thank you, Doctor. Your witness." And he sat.

Mr. Oneal rose to his feet, but before he could speak Laura made a grunting, angry noise. Everyone turned. She was looking at Mr. Oneal, motioning between him and me. She pulled at my sleeve and made the noise more angrily. Scipio called for a break, and we huddled together. Pia translated: Laura didn't trust Mr. Oneal, or Scipio. She wanted *me* to question Braga, and without Mrs. Locke there to calm her she wouldn't budge. Scipio asked to speak with the judge and Raadi, and when they finished Mr. Oneal handed me his notes.

"You wanted a trial," he said. "Just don't lose your temper."

CHAPTER FORTY

Janoff didn't object, except to releasing me from the manacles, and we had another argument about that. It ended with the wrist chains being removed but the ankle restraints left on, and so, still tethered to the floor, I asked questions from behind our table.

Mr. Oneal's notes were cryptic: nothing like a script, no written questions, not even an outline; just a list of four words. The first was something we'd spoken about, their use of the word 'retarded', and since we had discussed it I knew exactly what he meant. But how to frame a cross examination about it? I thought for several moments before starting.

"Doctor, you used the term 'retarded' several times when speaking of Miss Spinali? Doesn't modern medicine avoid insulting patients?"

"I beg your pardon?"

"I mean, don't all leading psychiatrists and psychologists believe that calling a patient retarded is an insult?"

Braga smiled and shook his head. "Some people think that, but I don't pay attention to labels as much as I do to treatment. As I recall even the judge used it."

"Well, you're the doctor, aren't you?"

"Yes, and as a Doctor I wouldn't criticize the judge or anyone else for using the term. We may not keep up on the latest fashion, but I do on the latest treatments."

"You let your staff call the women at your facility retarded, or…or even 'retards'?"

"Well, you're getting into what some people call 'political correctness', which is a fad. And I don't use fads as a guide when treating a patient."

"You follow the latest developments in psychiatry?"

"Of course I do. I just don't keep up on the latest labels."

That triggered something not on Mr. Oneal's list. I put the notes aside.

"Do you keep up on patient's names?"

"I don't understand."

"You've referred to Miss Spinali by her first name in your testimony, by the name 'Laura'. Is that how you know her at your facility?"

"Yes … or …"

"You address her as Miss Spinali, or as Laura?"

"Well … either … as … Miss Spinali, or Laura."

"Don't you assign the women at your facility numbers instead of names, and refer to, for example, Miss Spinali as 'Number Nine'?"

"No … I refer to her as Laura."

"Do you know her full name?"

"Of course," he said, but he hesitated a moment, then sat up. "It's Laura Spinali."

"Her full name, if you please, Doctor."

"We never use middle names—"

"Does she have one?"

Braga hesitated again. "I'm sure she does."

"You have a small clinic, only eight or ten patients, and this one was there longer than any other, wasn't she?"

"Yes."

"Thirty-four years, and yet you don't know her full name?"

"As I said, we don't use their middle names."

I motioned to Laura. "It's Michele. Your patient's name is Laura Michele Durer Spinali," I said, still trying to keep my voice polite. "Her father was a vintner here in Italy, and her mother was a niece of Albrecht Durer, the painter. Did you know she has some well-known people in her family tree?"

"I … yes, I did"

"When did you learn those things?"

"I believe we … we learned them last year."

"So after you met me? It was only after you learned a high-priced law firm was trying to help her that you bothered to find out who she actually was?"

"Objection!" Janoff barked. Both he and the procuratore stood.

The judge nodded and turned to me. "Perhaps you can rephrase yourself?"

"Sorry, Judge," I said, glancing at Mr. Oneal's notes. The next word on his list was: 'Money'. I thought again, and looked up at Braga.

"How much money do you make off the women in your facility?"

"I don't *make* money, Mr. Rankin, at least not the way your law firm does. I do receive compensation for the care we provide."

"You receive it from several sources, don't you? The state or Arizona? And also from the federal government?"

"That's true."

"For each patient?"

"Just about everyone."

360

"And you also take whatever money or other assets the patients have, and even their families have?"

"Well, no. We only take … I mean try to get paid for what we've done, and if our pay comes from the state or federal government and the patient has resources, then we'll try to get reimbursement."

"You take essentially everything they have, don't you?"

"We take whatever we can get, to stay in business, so that we can help everyone we can. It's only fair to those who don't have funds available, that we're paid by those who do."

"It doesn't have to do with paying for your Mercedes?"

"Wait a minute—"

"Objection!" Janoff and the procuratore were back up on their feet.

"And your membership in an expensive golf club?"

"*Signore!*" the judge said crossly. "When counsel object you must allow me to respond."

"I'm sorry, Judge."

He thought for a moment, then waved me on. "But you may continue. The objections, they are overruled."

I turned back to the doctor.

"So you get money from Arizona *and* from the U.S. government for all your patients. And after getting all those funds you also take the patients' money, their homes, belongings—everything they have, is that right?"

"You're mischaracterizing this. We do get paid, but we do an enormous amount for our patients."

"You house them and keep them drugged, you mean?"

"Objection!"

"Sustained."

"And all this money you get from the federal government and the State of Arizona, do you ever actually pay them back with monies you take out of patients' accounts?"

"Il Giudice, if you please," Raadi said, standing. "I fail to see the relevance 'ere."

"He may continue," the judge replied, watching Braga. "Doctor, answer the question. Do you pay it back?"

Braga hesitated. "When they request it."

"Have they ever requested it?" I asked.

Braga looked back and forth between me and the judge. "I'm sure they have at some point."

"So you don't remember them doing it?"

"I'm not sure."

"So you take hundreds of thousands of dollars from the government and from these women, sometimes from their families and you keep it?"

"Il Giudice, please!" Raadi protested.

"Si. Signore Rankin, I believe you've made the point."

"Thank you, Your Honor." I checked the notes. Mr. Oneal's last subject was: '*Conditions*'

I turned back to Braga. "Are you aware of any allegations of unsafe, unsanitary conditions made against your facility over the years? Mould, mildew, sewage in the rooms, things like that."

"Absolutely not," Braga insisted.

"So the open sewer in Miss Spinali's room was what, something I just imagined?"

Murmurs rippled through the audience again, until the judge slapped his gavel.

Janoff stood. "Your Honor—Il Giudice—I object to this as argumentative and defamatory."

"Overruled," the judge said, frowning. He turned to Braga. "You may answer whether there was such an open sewer on the premises."

"Absolutely not!" Braga insisted. But his face reddened as he turned to the judge. "He knows this isn't true. His father asked these same questions in a hearing we had in Arizona, and the judge was convinced it wasn't true." The judge looked at me, his eyes narrowing.

"That hearing was held without Miss Spinali there, wasn't it?" I demanded.

"Yes, but there were inspectors there, who come every month ... or so. State and federal inspectors. I should add that most facilities get their share of criticisms. We're not exempt from that, but we've come a long way, and have regular reviews by federal and state inspectors."

The judge shrugged, and Braga turned back to me, looking as if he'd been vindicated.

"Do you ever entertain these inspectors?" I asked, feeling my anger grow.

"I ... what do you mean?"

"You know what I mean, don't you?" I said, trying to keep my voice low.

"I'm not sure."

"You don't drug the women and then let the inspectors have sexual relations with them?"

The courtroom erupted. The judge pounded his gavel and the bailiff waved his arms at the audience, but everyone ignored them. The chaos went on for a while before order was restored. The judge sustained the procuratore's objection, and when a semblance of order had returned Braga answered with a huff.

"That's absurd and insulting. I can't imagine anything like that happening there."

"It wouldn't require much imagination on your part, would it?" I asked, and I couldn't keep from raising my voice.

"Il Giudice!" Raadi said, rising.

"Signore Rankin, if you please," the judge said.

"Have you ever had sex with your patients?"

"No!" he shouted, but that suggestion restarted the chaos.

When order was restored the judge took the lawyers to his chambers. When they returned he ordered me to sit down, and announced I was finished. I would no longer be permitted to ask questions.

CHAPTER FORTY-ONE

Although we were allowed to present Pia's testimony and to offer an affidavit from Mrs. Locke, during the next few days Raadi and Janoff fought back with overwhelming evidence. Inspectors arrived who complimented the facility; doctors corroborated the inspectors; and everyone, it seemed, refuted everything Scipio and I had suggested. Transcripts were introduced from Arizona which detailed Laura's crimes—including the recent murder of an orderly and strangulation of another young patient. By the time they finished Madonna looked angelic.

Raadi ended with a balding, bespectacled Italian accountant, who introduced records of the value of Madonna's 'services' to Laura; as well as sources Laura had available to repay what she'd been 'given'.

"There es a corporazione which was established to combine the wealth of Signorina Spinali with that of her friend, the American woman named Louisa Jeannette Locke, and with thes fiction they 'ave purchased several properties 'ere in Italia, in France, in Germany, and in 'Olland," he said. "It was arranged to make et difficult—perhaps *impossibile* to locate or retrieve the funds, and thus to pay the Signorina's debt."

"Who created thes arrangement, thes ... *schema*?" Signore Raadi asked him.

"The avvocate for the Signorina. Signore Rankin, I believe."

"'Ave you discovered any other way in which funds may be obtained to satisfy the Signorina's obligation?"

"Si. We 'ave determined that there are at least two."

"And what are these sources?"

"There is a fondo—" He looked down at the clerk.

"A trust," she said.

"A trust, from the Castellani House, which the Signorina's grandfather created. The Signorina became entitled to it upon 'er twenty-fifth birthday."

"'Ow much is in the trust?"

"A *contilibie*—"

"Accounting."

"Accounting—says the *fondo* is now worth ..." he paused, turning a page, "approximate-ely cinque millione—about five million dollars—"

"Where is the trust now?"

"We 'ave obtained orders to ... *sequestrare* et."

"And es there more?"

"Si. We 'ave word there is a valuable necklace, a very famous, fabulous piece, reputed to be *La Crime* itself—"

A murmur came up from the audience.

"And where 'es the necklace?"

"I am told it es somewhere in Lucca. Precisely where we donna know, but we believe the Signorina knows, and if she could speak et would easily make up the difference."

"Grazie," Raadi said, and he turned towards Laura to make a stunning concession. "Il Giudice, we now call the Signorina to testify."

Scipio glanced at Mr. Oneal, then me, then he slowly got to his feet and turned to the judge. "I thought my learned colleague had taken the position this poor woman is *retardo*. Does he now concede that his own witness, this Doctor Braga, has misrepresented the matter to this court?"

"Don' be ridiculous!" Raadi exclaimed.

"Gentlemen, please!" the judge said loudly.

"But Il Giudice," Scipio insisted, "they canno' say capacity exists on what serves them, but not what contradicts! If she is permitted to testify, may she also to the remainder of their contentions?"

"Et es a good point, Signore Raadi," the judge said, nodding. "Do you accept their contention that the Signorina 'es not *retardo* and may testify?"

"No, Il Giudice. But whether the Signorina's condition creates not only violenz but even an inability to speak es something we believe may be debated, or at least deferred, Il Giudice. We will concede that an officer observed her communicating with some effectiveness in her cell during the days before thes hearing—"

"You mean the officer was spying on us?" Scipio asked mildly.

Raadi rolled his eyes. "And as they will present the Signorina anyway, and because Il Giudice seems inclined to accept testimony subject to its being questioned later, we wish to question her first."

"Can she be understood?" the judge asked.

"We 'ave obtained the leading ... *logopedista*—" Again, he turned to the clerk.

"Speech pathologist."

"Grazie. Just so, and she will translate if et es at all possible to understand her."

Raadi's move seemed risky, for both sides, for though Laura would be allowed to testify to what really happened at Madonna, whether she could control herself was an open question. But the judge agreed.

He emptied the room and held a separate hearing with Raadi, Scipio, Laura and the pathologist for over an hour to make sure the pathologist was qualified, and could understand Laura. When we returned he announced that the pathologist, a woman named Signora Agnesi, was able to understand Laura's sounds, and would be able to translate them to the rest of us,

The pathologist was introduced. She was a pleasant, professional woman in her early sixties, with nicely coiffed silver hair, conservatively dressed, and most important, already seemed very sympathetic to Laura. But there was another problem. Laura refused to testify, or even to take the stand.

Signora Agnesi told us Laura frankly didn't trust Raadi, and wouldn't answer any question he asked. The judge called a halt to the day's proceedings to let the sides try to work out a solution, and I was back in my cell until the following morning.

CHAPTER FORTY-TWO

We were ready to start proceedings the next morning, when a loud noise of metal against wood came from the courtroom doors. Everyone turned, and we saw Dr. Altobelli and a nurse pushing a reclined, chrome wheelchair contraption in, with tubes and bags, a chrome pole and some sort of electric box—everything, it seemed, but a patient. But in the chaos that followed turned and came down the aisle towards us, and we could see Mrs. Locke, lying so thin and grey she seemed hidden within the chair. A hospital gown hung on her as a parent's shirt would on a child. The judge called for a short recess and we huddled around the chair.

Mrs. Locke's presence had a dramatic impact on Laura, whose features cracked with worry about her friend, and though she kissed Mrs. Locke's hand she then grunted an angry scold at Dr. Altobelli. The doctor was obviously unhappy that her patient was there, but explained that after being told what happened the day before, Mrs. Locke had insisted on coming.

Once quiet was achieved Mrs. Locke motioned Laura close and spoke to her in an urgent, broken whisper. She went on for several minutes without letting Laura reply. When she finished she motioned the doctor and nurse. They let Laura kiss her, then moved the chair to the side of the audience.

I had no idea what was happening, nor, it seemed, did almost anyone else. But when the proceedings were called back to order Laura rose, walked slowly to the witness chair and sat, staring through dark glasses at her friend. The bailiff seated the speech pathologist next to her, and the judge asked her directly, "Are you ready to begin, Signorina?" Laura nodded and we all waited.

The room was full but quiet, watching. Laura was in a yellow dress Pia had altered for her, and with her hair pulled back her features showed her classic Roman profile, despite the sunglasses.

Procuratore Raadi spent several moments quietly studying his notes. Then he put on his glasses, bending one flexible temple over the right ear, the other over the left, tilted his head a fraction towards the judge, and when the judge motioned, he smiled a small, quick smile at Laura, and got straight to the point.

"Signorina Spinali, do you 'ave the necklace known as 'La Crime'?"

"Objection, Il Giudice," Scipio said, getting to his feet. "The necklace 'as no bearing on whether the Signorina should be returned. If she should not be sent back these questions would prove wholly irrelevant." I tried not to look at him. In between our meetings with Laura I'd told Scipio to have Pia take it. Neither he nor the rest of us had any idea where it was now. We therefore fully expected Laura would answer the question by saying she didn't know where it was.

"Overrule-ed," the judge said, and he motioned benignly to Laura, "You may answer 'im, Signorina."

It was obvious by now that when the judge told a witness 'you may' answer a question he meant they must, but for several seconds Laura said nothing. Everyone waited, and for several moments the only sound in the large room was the tick of a clock on the far wall and an occasional creak of chairs from the audience. It went on for a long half minute while Laura sat, staring at Mrs. Locke. The procuratore studied the end of his pen, then put it down on the table, leaned forward and said, "Signorina, will you answer my question?"

Laura shook her head. Raadi looked up at the judge.

"Do you unnerstan' what 'e is asking?" the judge said.

She nodded, but still said nothing.

"An answer will be necessary, Signorina. Do you refuse to respon'?"

She nodded again, and said nothing.

The judge glanced disapprovingly at Scipio. Raadi smiled a small smile and began to collect his papers. "Then I believe we are finished 'ere. She mus' go back."

"Il Giudice, please," Scipio said, getting to his feet. "Signore Raadi 'as been allowed to present 'is case despite our position that the hearing itself should not occur. May we not 'ave the same courtesy 'ere?"

"Es a different matter," Raadi said, but his papers remained in a pile before him. All eyes settled on the judge.

He toyed with his pencil, then spoke quietly towards Laura. "You are no' familiar with our laws, Signorina, but the procuratore … es correct." He put down the pencil and with a slight cast of sympathy curled his hand outward towards her. "I do not 'ave to remind you 'ow you come to be here, or what you are accused of. Whatever 'appens now, you may be required to go back, Signorina, unless you answer all the questions. Every one."

Laura nodded, still watching Mrs. Locke, but still said nothing. The judge turned back to Raadi and motioned him forward.

"Where es the necklace, Signorina?" he demanded quietly.

She glanced at me but said nothing.

"Does your attorney 'ave et?"

She shook her head.

"You 'ave et, don' you?"

She shook her head.

"Where es et?"

Once again she said nothing.

"Will you not answer?"

She bent and grunted three syllables. The pathologist, seated beside her, took in a deep breath. "She will not."

"Il Giudice," Raadi said, turning to the judge, "we ask the proceedings be concluded at once, and that our requests be granted in their entirety."

Mr. Oneal and Signore Scipio began an argument which went from the courtroom to chambers, where it lasted nearly an hour. When they returned Raadi looked displeased, Mr. Oneal handed me more notes, and the judge addressed us all.

"The Signorina will testify, and the requests by Signore Raadi which relate to the Signorina's refusals will be held … *sospensione*—"

"In suspension," the clerk said.

"Si, in suspension. Signore Raadi 'as been allowed to present much evidence and many witnesses, and Signore Scipio in turn was allowed to question it all. I will give Signore Scipio the same allowance and Signore Raadi the same opportunity. And I will decide the procuratore's requests once we 'ave all the evidenzia. Signore Raadi, you may proceed."

Raadi stood, looking mildly displeased with the ruling.

Scipio addressed the court. "Il Giudice, with permiso I will allow Signore Rankin to conduct."

The judge nodded and turned to Raadi. "Signore Raadi?"

"Et es acceptable, Il Giudice," Raadi waved. The judge turned to me. "Signore Rankin, I will allow you to question again, but please do not use such language as before."

"Yes sir," I said, standing.

So once again I began. Talking to Laura was, strangely, easier across that large room than it ever had been before, but what she said was much more difficult to hear, and seemed impossible to believe.

We began, as they say, very near the beginning.

"Laura," I first said, "do you remember how you came to be at the facility known as Madonna?"

Her gaze left me, rested on Mrs. Locke, and then turned to Signora Agnesi. She began a long series of grunting noises. Signora Agnesi took notes, and when Laura stopped, referred to them as she translated the sounds:

"I lived with my mother and father on a ranch in Arizona, a place called the *Buffalo Ranch.* It was run by a woman named Isabel Mays. She helped us, and our families. But then Mrs. Mays died, and my parents died and the ranch was shut down, I left, and was taken in by an Indian who lived in the area. He took me to his home, and I lived with his family … his tribe … for several years."

"The first Doctor who testified here," I went on, "Dr. Braga, said you were treated badly by the Indians. Is this true?"

Laura frowned at the doctor's name, then had a brief but more animated discussion with Signora Agnesi. When they were done the Signora turned to us.

"It is not true. They were good to me. They were kind to me. They taught me to live, to hunt, to catch food and make shelter, and to survive."

"Were you brutalized by them, as the doctor claimed?"

She shook her head.

"Were you raped by them?"

Once again, she shook her head, and added two short syllables. "Never," Signora Agnesi interpreted.

"How did you come to leave the Indians and get to the Madonna facility?"

"It was near the end of the Indian wars. Soldiers came, and there was a fight. We were on a mountain, on a ledge, and they came from below and behind. The men died, except for one, the man who found me and took me in. Juh was his name. Then he died as well."

"Who was this man Juh?"

She stared back at me. I nodded, trying to get her to speak. She shrugged and flexed out more noises. "He was named Juh. He was my … friend, and he was a holy man."

"A what?" the judge asked, before I could go on.

Laura bent out an explanation. "He was a holy … man," Signora Agnesi translated. "He was a warrior, but he was touched, and he was holy."

"Why … Why was 'e considered so, Signorina?" the judge asked.

She tightened and grunted. "Because he stuttered," came Signora Agnesi's translation. "If your features or speech or mind were different, they thought it was a blessing and that people who were blessed were holy."

The judge studied Laura a little reluctantly, and with a tone of apology asked the next logical question. "Were you 'holy', Signorina?"

She twisted a short sentence. The pathologist stared at her a moment, then turned to the judge and nodded. "Up until then I was, but not after."

CHAPTER FORTY-THREE

I stared at the next question. Scipio had insisted that in this setting and before this apparently religious Judge we might hope for some favourable impact:

"Before we get to the soldiers, would you describe what they did with the bodies of the Indians?"

Laura nodded and made a few grunts. "They left them on the rock."

"No burials?" the judge asked, looking up.

Laura shook her head.

"Where did they take you?" I asked.

"To the tents, tents the soldiers had in the desert."

"How many tents were there?"

Her head tilted up and she seemed to count them to herself. Then she turned to the pathologist and grunted a short response. The pathologist nodded, "Thirty, forty maybe."

"How many of you did they bring back?"

"Me, Lozen and another Apache woman. She was a prophet, and the wife of the leader."

"Who was the leader?"

"His name was Goyale."

"Goyale!" Janoff snorted, getting to his feet. "May I have the court's permission, Judge—Il Giudice?"

The judge nodded. Janoff turned to her and asked, "You claim you knew the Indian named Goyale?"

She nodded and grunted. Signora Agnesi said, "Yes, I knew him."

"Did you like him?"

"What difference does that make?" I snapped.

"What difference!" Janoff exclaimed. "Judge, this man was one of the worst murderers in that region of America. I wish to know if Miss Spinali admired such men, and his methods, and whether that might help explain some of her own violence. Where I come from that's certainly relevant to whether she ever tried to emulate him."

"It's irrelevant!" I insisted.

"I am afraid et is relevan', Signore," the judge said softly. But he turned and motioned not to Janoff, but to the procuratore. "You may enquire."

Raadi had a brief discussion with Janoff, then stood. "How do you feel abou' thes man, the one you refer to by the name Goyale?"

Laura stared back through her dark glasses, then she began to bend and grunt her response. It was lengthy. The pathologist took notes and then began translating: "Goyale's wife and children were killed by soldiers, then he went after the soldiers and their families, then the army came after him. He took warriors to draw soldiers away from the women and children, but most of the warriors were killed or captured. Then the soldiers came after the women, and the women died, except for a blind old woman named Gouyen, and Lozen, Goyale's woman. Goyale left Juh with the women. Juh found me, and helped me, and I helped him take care of the blind old woman Gouyen. I lived with them for several years, so I met Goyale a few times, but each time only for a little while. And no, I didn't like him, at first. I didn't like what he did to the white people, and I was afraid he'd do it to me, but he never did, and Lozen helped me

377

with my fear, and yes, I liked some things about him—not the violence, but I admired the way he never gave up on the women, or even his men."

Raadi had a whispered exchange with Janoff, then shrugged to the court and took his seat.

I stood and went on. "After the soldiers came and got you, did they put both you and the Indian woman Lozen into a single tent?"

"Yes, both of us. We were tied to the centre poles of the tent."

"You were both tied?" the judge said, interrupting with a note of incredulity. "You yourself? A ... a white woman, were kept bound by white soldiers?"

She nodded.

The judge held up his hand to stop me, took off his glasses, and while thinking pulled out a handkerchief and began cleaning them. It was quiet for several moments. He replaced his glasses and peered down at her. His voice dropped softly. "But they knew you were not Indian?"

She nodded. "Yes."

"Why were you kept there?"

"For the soldiers. We were both kept for the soldiers."

"What! ... not! You mean ... for ...you mean for their ... pleasure?"

She nodded and went on as if that were not important, motioning to her face. When she was finished Signora Agnesi touched Laura's hand, then turned to us.

"Lozen was a beautiful woman, and I," Signora Agnesi interpreted, motioning to her own face, "I did no' look like this then. I was ... considered beautiful, so yes, for pleasure."

The judge's face had tightened. "'Ow many men used the two of you in thes way?"

378

Laura flexed out her response. "Not many … at first," the pathologist said. "but later there were more."

The judge stared, and once again the only sound was the tick of the clock. I turned back to Laura, but the judge raised his hand again, and asked, "Who ware thees men? Do you remember, Signorina? Do you remember any of them?"

She nodded, and twisted her response. "It was always the same two at the beginning," the pathologist said. "First the captain, then the lieutenant."

"An' after that?"

Laura twisted out more, now more quietly. The pathologist scraped her chair closer, then turned to the judge.

"After the second week the lieutenant didn't come anymore. But the captain did, and let others in after he finished. By then, sometimes it was five or six, but every night, sometimes more."

"And this 'appen to both you and to Lozen?"

"For two of the three weeks," the pathologist interpreted. "Then Lozen was gone."

"What 'appened to her?" the judge asked.

She looked down at the sliver of floor, uneven with its centuries of wear and refinishing, then grunted two syllables.

"She died," the pathologist said quietly.

"Oh? How did she die?"

Laura hesitated, obviously reluctant. She shook her head. For a moment it wasn't clear whether she meant that as an answer or was refusing to respond, but then she began to speak. The grunts came gently, as if she was dealing with a precious subject. When she was done we turned to the pathologist.

"She just died. I mean, they didn't shoot her. She just died, the way Indians can sometimes when they want to.

She told me one night it would happen, and it did. As the last man left us for the night he said her man, Goyale, was dead. He laughed as though he thought it was a joke, but we believed him. When he was gone Lozen told me she was going to the after to find Goyale."

"The after?" the judge interrupted.

"I believe she means where souls go when one dies, Il Giudice," the pathologist explained. The judge waved her on, and she continued the translation.

"And after she said where she was going, Lozen closed her eyes and went to sleep. When I woke up the next morning she was dead."

The judge was shaking his head, frowning, but he turned back to me and nodded that I continue.

"So after that, were you by yourself?" I asked.

She looked blankly back. The pathologist repeated the question, but she didn't seem to understand. The judge leaned forward. "Do you understand, Signorina?"

She bent out more noises. The pathologist hesitated, and while watching her began to translate, "She understands your words, but not what he means. She says no one was … tied up in there with her, but others came. The soldiers. They came every day, but each one only for a little while."

"How long ware you kept in such circumstances?" the judge asked.

"The whole time. Another three weeks after Lozen was gone."

CHAPTER FORTY-FOUR

The judge was obviously shocked by Laura's testimony, so I pretended to study Mr. Oneal's notes to let the impact settle. When I thought enough time had gone by I looked up at her.

"What happened after the tents?"

Laura twisted a short sentence.

The pathologist said, "We walked to Madonna."

"What do you mean?"

"My wrists were tied and I walked behind one of the horses. I walked for seven or eight days. We were roped and walked between the horses. All of us together."

"Us? Who were the others?"

Laura made few short sounds, and Signora Agnesi translated: "The other girls, from another tent. Three or four Mescalero women."

"Who are the Mescaleros?"

"Another tribe of Apaches."

"And when you arrived at Madonna? What happened then?"

Laura flexed and grunted. The pathologist's face took on a troubled expression. "They cleaned us and put us in the rooms, put me in a separate room, then a man came into my room, an orderly. At first it was only him."

"And he began … more of these assaults on you?"

Laura shrugged and grunted a single syllable.

"Yes."

I kept trying to keep my voice low, but remember feeling anger build in the large courtroom with this testimony. It was all around me, and inside me, but I forced myself to keep from yelling.

"Did you encourage the orderly in any way?"

The pathologist and court reporter exchanged glances. Laura stared at me for a moment before shaking her head. "No."

"Did you ... resist?"

She began a longer response. "The first time, yes," Signora Agnesi began, when Laura finished. "I fought him, and hurt him. But he was a large man, much stronger than me, and he hit me until I couldn't breathe. So I didn't resist after that. He came back two or three times that week, then not again until after we were washed."

"How long did this go on?"

Laura looked up, as if calculating then grunted three syllables to the pathologist. Signora Agnesi stared at her a moment, then turned to the judge:

"Twenty years."

There were probably three hundred people in that courtroom, but it was completely quiet. I let the silence go on for a few seconds, and in the pause Laura began to speak again without being asked. Her noises gradually took on a low anger. When she was finished she stared at Braga. Signora Agnesi turned, glanced at him, then spoke:

"It went on that way for a while, then the army took it over. The captain came, the same man from the tents, and he brought another man. He was another doctor, a very young one. I'd never met him before."

"Is that man in this courtroom?"

She nodded.

"What was his name?"

Laura pointed to Braga and grunted coldly. "Braga. Joseph Braga. The man over there," Signora Agnesi said, motioning.

"And did anything change when he arrived?"

Her mouth tightened, and the grunts began to come bitterly. The pathologist took notes again, glanced at Laura for a moment, then turned to translate:

"Up until then we were allowed to work, to clean, sweep, to do simple things. We were tied, but at least allowed to be outside. But he wouldn't let us work. He made us stay inside, in our rooms. They began to lock the doors. The food changed, and there was less. And it was like the tents again, but there were more of us, and more of them."

"You mean …?"

"There were more women that began to come there, and more men came."

"What other women?"

"There were mostly girls like me, but they were Indian girls. I mean not like me," Signora Agnese translated, motioning to Laura's torso. "But normal."

"How many?"

"Nine or ten."

"And why were the men there?"

Laura grunted three syllables calmly. Her tone seemed to upset Signora Agnesi. The Signora's eyes shifted to the judge, then she drew in a breath and looked down.

"To fuck us."

"Please, Signorina!" the judge exclaimed, holding up his hand. He turned to her, and she looked calmly at him and shrugged as if to ask *What?* He stared at her, then shook his head and asked quietly,

"How long did things go on this way? I mean … with men coming in to do such things?"

She made several brief, grunting sentences. Signora Agnesi bit her lip, then translated. "For me it went on until I got old. For the others it continued until … well, it was still happening when Paul … Mr. Rankin got me out. So…thirty years?"

The judge stared incredulously. "Thirty … years?"

She nodded. The judge turned back and waved me on.

"I am going to change subjects now, Your Honor," I said. Scipio had told me of the judge's preferences with procedure, and suggested this, so I asked, "Should Signore Raadi wish first to inquire as to this one?" It was different from our ways of doing things, breaking up the presentation in that fashion, but Scipio was right. The judge nodded as if pleased with the gesture, and I motioned Raadi, then stopped, staring at Laura. Her old fingers were laced tightly together on her lap, the knuckles clenched white.

CHAPTER FORTY-FIVE

Raadi stood. "The last man who died in the battle on the mountain, Signorina, what was 'is name?"

She twisted a single syllable. We turned to the pathologist.

"Juh," she said.

"You 'ad some sort of ... may I say ... intimacy with ... thes young man ... Juh, either forced or by your consent?"

"Objection!" I said. "That's irrelevant!"

"But you claim she was ... how did you say *stuprare*—raped by white men?" Raadi responded calmly.

"Yes!" I nodded angrily.

"And since consent may be inferred from one's behaviour, surely the Signorina's *invitati* of advances by a savage would be relevant to her acquiescence to them by more civilized men?"

"That's absurd!" I snapped, getting up. "He's using innuendo about her distant past to excuse her being raped at Madonna!"

"A moment, Signores," the judge said, holding up his hand. He pulled a document from his file and looking over his glasses read for several moments. Then he held up the document. "The American attorney general has outlined the proper inquiry. He says in Arizona such matters are relevant to the accusations of stuprare—rape." He turned to Laura. "You must answer the question, Signorina. Did you 'ave intimacy with one or more Indians?"

She stared at him blankly, without answering.

"Signorina, did you 'ave intimacy with the Indian Juh?"

She still didn't answer. Her mouth was clenched tightly.

"Signorina, I 'ave explained before something which is true here as well. You must answer all the questions before any of what you say may be accepted into the proceedings."

She shook her head.

"You ware never married to 'im, were you?" the procuratore added.

She bit her lip, but still was silent.

"Had you 'ad relations weth any other Indians in addition to thes' warrior Juh perhaps—before the soldiers came?"

I motioned to her to answer.

"Signore, you canno' provide your client answers," Raadi barked.

"I'm just telling her she must reply," I said.

Raadi faced Laura and folded his arms. "You say you were raped at Madonna, but do you 'ave any proof of the stuprare? Did you become pregnant, for example?"

She took a deep breath, but once again said nothing.

"The record will reflect the Signorina's refusal to respond," the procuratore said, turning to the judge. The judge nodded, frowning. The procuratore turned a page of his notes, read, then looked back to her.

"Did you live with … prostituiti before thes' matters?"

Laura shook her head with confusion.

"Did you no' live in a bordello, a ... house of prostituzione?"

She began a string of tightly grunted syllables that went on for several minutes. Signora Agnesi took notes again, nodding from time to time as the sounds came out. When Laura finished she began from her paper.

"It was a bad time for women who were by themselves. But the woman at the ranch, Mrs. Mays, would go every week to visit her father's grave in a special place near there, and from time to time she came across the women in the homeless camp she rode through to get to the cemetery. There were two women she found begging, an Indian girl named Rita whose parents had been killed by soldiers, and a white woman named Lula whose husband had been killed by Indians. They were begging together. There were two other women, prostitutes who'd worked in the town, but the man who ran the whores there kept them in a cellar. They got out and ran away, and she found them hiding in the cemetery. She brought them all back to the ranch. There were others, too, a woman named Daisy who was pregnant, and more. And they weren't prostitutes any more, not for a while, but some of them didn't like cleaning up after the horses. Mrs. Mays had two men there and Miss Lula ... said cleaning ... —what is the word 'shit'?" the pathologist asked.

"Merda," the clerk said.

Signora Agnesi turned a page of her notes and read further: "She complained that cleaning shit was man's work. Mrs. Mays became angry with her, but Miss Lula wouldn't do it. She didn't know other work, but she knew some of the soldiers who came to the ranch to sell horses, and she asked Mrs. Mays if she could have them as her own customers. At first Mrs. Mays said no, but then others who'd worked as whores before asked if they could work that way instead of cleaning up after horses. Mrs. Mays finally changed her mind. But she set down rules. They would have to be clean, and dress nicely, and every Sunday all the whores would have to go with her to church to confess what they'd done the week before. And there would be no stealing and no shooting. They agreed, and the soldiers came. The women began to get better clothes, and learn to read."

"Was there truly nothing else thes' women could do?" the procuratore asked, raising his eyes in disbelief.

I stood, "This was the early 1900s, counsel, in Arizona, not New York in the sixties."

"Grazie, Signore," the procuratore replied icily.

But during that exchange Laura had kept going, bending out more. The pathologist listened, then turned to the judge. "They were poor. Most of them had never gone to school. They couldn't read or write or even sew—"

"Can *you* read?" the judge interrupted.

She nodded and grunted. "I went to school for a while."

The judge shrugged and turned back to the procuratore. Raadi nodded. "Il Giudice, may I now be permitted to proceed with the …'omicidio?"

"Signore Rankin, you do not object to 'im continuing?" the judge asked, with a rhetorical tone.

"No, Your Honor," I said. Once again, Scipio had suggested the unusual tactic of letting this come out first through cross examination, because of the possible impact on the judge.

The judge nodded approvingly, then looked at Laura with sudden concern while speaking to us. "'As the witness been advised that if she es determined to 'ave

388

capacity she may eventually be moved from the Madonna facility to a prison?"

"Yes, Your Honor," I replied.

"'As she been advised there is no statuto prescrizione—" he hesitated, looking to the clerk.

"Statute of limitations period?" she offered.

"Just so. That there es no such limitations for murder prosecutions en … Arizona?"

"Si, Il Giudice," Scipio replied.

"She understands that," I added.

"'As she been told she may then 'ave to face charges?"

"She has, and she has agreed to go forward."

The judge motioned to the procuratore.

Raadi chose a kindly tone to start the subject. "When you were still a child, did you fight with your father?"

Laura stared at him but didn't answer.

"You mus' reply, Signorina," the judge said mildly.

She took a deep breath and nodded.

"Did you, when you were just twelve or thirteen, take a loaded revolver and shoot and kill him?"

The courtroom fell completely silent. Laura made a short series of noises to the pathologist, who then turned to the judge.

"He was a bad man. A bad husband and a bad man."

"So you killed him?" the procuratore demanded.

She made a longer series of noises. The pathologist took notes. When they finished the pathologist stared at Laura a moment, then began to translate.

"He was a bad husband. My mother needed his help, and he didn't give it. She needed to be fed and he wouldn't feed her, she needed to be washed and he wouldn't bathe her, she needed to be spoken to, but he ignored her, and he … he … he was unfaithful to my mother. He used whores, and then …" Signora Agnesi

389

stopped mid-sentence, motioning that Laura had done the same.

"Did he not bring his pregnant wife all the way from Italy for a better life?"

Laura shrugged.

"Did he not work to provide you with a home, and with food, and clothing?"

Laura stared at him silently, then nodded.

"Yes, but your mother … she was no longer able to provide him with intimacy of any kind, was she?"

Laura didn't answer. I watched her, hoping she'd go on, but she didn't.

"And your father was still a young man? Strong? Virile?" the procuratore asked.

Laura still said nothing.

The judge again admonished her to answer. She wouldn't, at first, so this time the judge called for another session in chambers, with everyone. Pia even brought Mrs. Locke back. The judge reminded Laura of the importance of responding, and Signore Scipio and I pleaded with her to answer, but she wouldn't, until Mrs. Locke spoke.

"Tell her, Laura," Mrs. Locke said weakly.

Laura shook her head.

"You want me to testify?"

Those words brought a change into Laura. She seemed less resolute than upset. She shook her head slowly at Mrs. Locke, then turned to the pathologist. A series of grunts came out, and the Signora began to interpret.

"I will tell you, but do not bother Mrs. Locke. I will tell you."

We returned to the courtroom and she retook the stand, and, looking down, began to speak. Her sounds came quietly now, with a tone of sadness. The pathologist wrote, and when Laura was done she turned to the judge.

"We were thirteen, and we lived at the ranch. I was looking for my father. He was supposed to be working with us in the barn, but he wasn't there. Daisy told me he said he'd gone to check on my mother, but I'd just come from her and I knew he wasn't there. I knew he'd lied, and I thought he was probably seeing one of the other women, but I didn't care because it meant he spent less time with me."

"How did he spend time with you?"

Laura looked down and didn't answer.

"Did your father have relations with you?" I asked.

Her mouth tightened perceptibly. She looked down, but still she didn't answer. Then she did. She raised her head and began to speak, quickly, then loudly. She began shouting and pointing. The room exploded. The judge pounded his gavel, but for several minutes it was no use. When quiet was finally restored the judge turned to Signora Agnesi.

"Tell us what the Signorina said."

Signora Agnesi glanced in my direction, then looked ruefully up at the judge. "She says that Signore Rankin was not supposed to mention this. She said it was none of his—and she cursed him—none of his business. She said Signore Rankin is just like the others, and ... and ... she said she is goin' to kill him."

"Kill who?" the judge demanded, looking at Laura.

"Signore Rankin. She said he is a bastarde, and that she will kill him."

"Laura!" I cried. "You want to go back there?"

But she only shrugged.

"You want them to take Mrs. Locke back—to steal her money, to—"

"Il Giudice," Raadi interrupted, getting to his feet. The judge held up his hand to stop him. He was still watching Laura.

"Signorina, Signore Rankin speaks the truth here. If you donna answer you will surely be sent back, as will Signore Rankin and, quite possibly, Signora Locke."

She looked up at him. He nodded back. She looked back down and shook her head with disgust. At that point I still believed she wouldn't respond, but then she shifted in the chair, turned to Signora Agnesi, and began her sounds. Agnesi had to take notes again, lots of notes, but looked up twice at Laura as the narration went on. When Laura finished the Signora looked around the court tightly, then began.

"He began coming into my room before we came to Mrs. Mays' ranch. I was nine or ten, and I was pretty. People said I looked like my mother, not like this. Mrs. Mays understood what was happening, and let me stay in the house with my mother. He used to come up there anyway, but Mrs. Mays stopped him. So he began to spend time with other women. Then one day when Mrs. Mays was gone on to Shantytown and the Special Place he started doing it with my friend. She didn't like that, but was afraid if anyone found out they'd have killed him."

Signora Agnesi stopped, took a sip of water, then went on.

"I didn't think he'd ever try with Louisa, but then one day I saw her in one of the horses' stalls. She was on the ground, crying, and bleeding. I made her tell me. I wanted to kill him then, but she warned me that I'd be taken away. I'd never see her or my mother again. I didn't care, but she said he'd just done it that day, just once, and because she said so, that time I didn't do anything. But the next week Mrs. Mays went to the

Special Place and took the two women he liked. I was in the barn and saw that my father wasn't there. Neither was Louisa. She'd gone up to the house for a key, but hadn't come back. So I went up to the house. I got to my mother's door and heard fighting, and heard my friend crying. The sound came from inside—I mean inside my mother's room. There were voices—my father was saying something that he used to say to me, and Louisa was crying, fighting, trying to keep him away. So I went to the case where Mrs. Mays kept her father's gun, and took it, and went in. My friend was in the corner, crying, and he was pushing at her, so ... yes ... I shot him."

It was another moment of quiet in the room. Once again it seemed the whole place was holding its breath, and once again the only sound was the clock

----

CHAPTER FORTY-SIX

The subject of rape was never mentioned again, but the procuratore wasn't finished with us. When we got back from the break he went into another killing:

"Did a fire take place a' Madonna while you were there?"

Laura nodded slowly.

"In 1937?"

She shook her head and bent out more sounds.

"I don't know what year," the pathologist said.

"Two people died?"

Laura's gaze drifted past the pathologist, to the court reporter, then down at the dark wood floor. She bent out two reluctant syllables.

"Four died," the pathologist said.

"Two workers?"

"And two patients."

"Was it ... arson?" the procuratore asked.

Laura's forehead wrinkled with a lack of understanding.

"Did someone burn the 'ospital ... with purpose?"

She shook her head and began to twist out more sounds.

"That was an accident," the pathologist said. "They meant only to burn the men."

We all looked at the pathologist, unsure if we'd heard correctly. Signora Agnesi spoke to her for several seconds. Laura bent out a response, then leaned back. The pathologist stared, blinking, then turned to the judge and nodded soberly.

"Only the men. They only meant to burn the men."

The judge turned and addressed her. "Who set them on fire, Signorina?" he asked quietly.

She grunted three syllables and sat back.

"They're dead now," Signora Agnesi said.

"You must answer the question, Signorina," the judge ordered less softly. "Who set the fire?"

She bit her lower lip inward, then sighed and began.

"Two of the Indian girls … one, really," the pathologist said when she finished.

"Who?" the procuratore asked, readying his pen.

She glanced towards me. I nodded that she should answer, and she turned to Signora Agnesi. She began an easier series of movements and grunts, as if she'd changed to a lighter subject. It went on for a while, and while it went on the pathologist took notes. When Laura finished Signora Agnesi jotted a few more entries, then took a deep breath and began:

"There were two Mescalero sisters there, Nacoma and Zitkala-sa. They sold baskets by the road and the sheriff caught them and brought them in. Nacoma was younger. She was the prettiest girl there, and a nice girl, even there she was nice, to me and to the others. She never made fun of me, and she understood me, so I told her stories about my mother, and ones I made up, and she understood me, and she enjoyed them. She helped me, and helped others, too. She was nice, happy, always smiling, and not at us, but with us. When we … when others were sad her smile helped the sadness. When someone was crying, she always made them feel better.

A couple of women got sick and died while she was there, and when they were sick or dying, she comforted them. She always smiled. But because she was pretty, she got a lot of … attention from the soldiers. One day the lieutenant brought a big man we called the Swimming Man …"

"Swimmin' Man?" the judge repeated uncertainly while writing.

"That is what she said," the pathologist nodded. She frowned at her notes, glanced at Laura and went on. "… a big man we called the Swimming Man, because of how he got on the girls. He was an older man, and a large man, but he wasn't big … there. It was difficult for him, and he had to concentrate. He didn't like you to speak, to make sounds, even to look at him—you had to look away—as you held him. If he caught you looking or you said anything he'd slap you until you turned away, and because he was so big he slapped very hard. The first time he chose Nacoma, he had trouble with the mounting. She didn't know about him yet, and she looked at him, and smiled at him—not to make fun of him, but he didn't know that. He thought she was laughing, and he became angry. He slapped her, and she was surprised, but still she smiled. It ruined it for him. He couldn't go on, and he became very angry. He began to hit her. The lieutenant came and he told the lieutenant, and she smiled at him and he hit her too. One held her while the other struck, then the other held while the first struck, and still she tried to smile, so they kept on taking turns …until she was no longer smiling, and even then they kept hitting her for a while."

The room went rigid with that description, and how it came out. Laura's words had come in an easy tone of low grunts, almost if she'd been describing the weather.

The judge held up his hand to stop the procuratore from asking his next question, and looked at her.

"'Ow do you know thes?"

She gave a brief answer.

"Her older sister, Zitkala-sa, told us," the pathologist said.

"And how did she know thes?"

"She was there."

"She was …? Where?"

"She was in the room while it went on."

"She was in the same room?" he asked, incredulous.

Laura bent out a handful of syllables.

And Signora Agnesi, staring at her, said, "Tied to the other bed."

CHAPTER FORTY-SEVEN

The judge held up his hand again as if about to speak, but his face was frozen. For several moments it was quiet. He lowered his hand, and nodded to the procuratore.

"And the fire? The killing?" Raadi asked, but even he was pale.

Laura looked at me. I nodded back to her. She bent out more sentences.

"Every two weeks or so we were taken outside for the wash. To be cleaned. They had us stand at the side of the building and take off our clothes and the captain sprayed us with a hose—"

Raadi raised his hand. "Were you bound, tied, restrained in any fashion?"

"No."

"So you could have escaped during these washings?"

She shook her head. "The captain had a pistol, and the doctor had a club."

"A club?"

"A golf club," she said.

The procuratore rolled his eyes towards the judge, then turned back to her. "An' what 'appened with the fire?"

She began slowly, but began to grunt more rapidly as she went on. Signora Agnesi stopped her twice to make notes. When she finished the signora went on writing for several moments before she looked up and began.

"The day after Nacoma died was the day for wash. The captain and doctor were gone. It was only the lieutenant and Swimming Man. Swimming Man hadn't finished the night before. He wanted someone, and was waiting for us to be washed before he chose another. Nacoma's sister Zitkala-sa was number eight but the first to be washed. She was at the start of the line. After she was washed and they turned to others, they weren't paying attention to her; so she took the hose and wrapped it around Swimming Man's neck. The lieutenant stopped her. They began to beat her, but then the other girls ...and me ..." Signora Agnesi hesitated, took a deep breath and went on. "We took stones and hit their heads. They became quiet with the stones. We took them inside, into two of our rooms, and tied with their arms and legs to the beds, and began the fires, and then we ran away."

The procuratore stared at Laura for several moments, then spoke with a pause after each word. "How many ware you then?"

"Ten ... nine after Nacoma died."

"Nine against two?"

She nodded.

"How ware the fires started?"

She bent out a handful of syllables.

"Before the fire our beds were made of straw," the pathologist interpreted.

"You started the beds?"

She twisted out a short sentence.

"Just the ones they were in," the pathologist said.

"With them on them ... lying there?" he asked, startled.

She nodded.

"Where they awake?"

She nodded again, and went on with more matter of fact sounds. When she was finished the pathologist stared at her for several seconds before beginning.

"Not at first, but the Mescaleros, they decided … we decided to wait until they woke to begin. They weren't awake, so we took damp cloths and woke them. Then we did it."

"You woke them, and while they were tied there, and awake, you started the fires?"

She stared at him for several seconds, then nodded, and for the first time since they'd begun, the only time it had happened in several hours of testimony, she smiled.

CHAPTER FORTY-EIGHT

The procuratore started back up with a less pleasant tone.

"You ran away after you begin-ned the fire?"

"Yes," the pathologist interpreted.

"All of you?"

"Yes."

"But you were recaptured?"

She grimaced. "All but Zitkala-sa and two others."

"What 'appened to them? To Zitkala-sa an' the others?"

She bent out her response. "I don't know," the pathologist translated. "We never saw them again. One of the girls asked Dr. Braga later and he said Zitkala-sa was killed by wolves."

It was something we hadn't discussed. Mr. Oneal rose with a puzzled expression. "May I, Your Honor—Il Giudice?"

"Of course."

"Were there wolves in Arizona in the 1930s?"

"We never heard of any. There were coyotes, but they were small."

Mr. Oneal sat, and the procuratore shrugged. "Signorina, there was a charge of caos—" He turned to the clerk.

"Mayhem."

"Grazie. Mayhem brought against you, because you stabbed a person at Madonna."

She nodded.

"Was it the Captain?"

She looked back down past the wooden rail to the darker floor in front of her. For several moments there was no answer.

"Go ahead, Laura," I blurted, but still she wouldn't speak. The judge was about to say something when she bent out a series of curt grunts that settled into a longer answer. Signora Agnesi again took notes, and when Laura finished referred to them as she spoke:

"It was after Nacoma died and Zitkala-sa was gone, after the fire, after they rebuilt Madonna. Things were different. We were tied after, with a strap to the bed. One week the Captain came to me. He was older then, and I was too, but not as old as he was, and I still didn't look like this," she said, motioning to her face. "He told me he understood me, the way I speak. He knew I really wasn't ... retarded and didn't think I was stupid. He said I was a nice-looking woman, that with Nacoma dead I was prettier than all the others. He said that except for the bend my body was more beautiful than theirs, and he said he liked me, he would help me if I helped him teach new women to behave. And for a while he did help me, and I taught the new women how not to get beaten, and to get by. He began to visit me, and when he left my room he left me untied. He let me clean my room, gave me more food, and better food than the others got. Then one day he took me to his room. He had a bathtub in his room and let me use it. He cleaned me himself in his bath, and took me for himself, and not for anyone else. And I lived with him for two or three years."

"Did you develop feelings for him?" the judge ventured.

She took a deep breath but said nothing.

"Signorina?"

Her lips came tightly together. She looked down, then twisted out a short sentence. "I began to l … like him," the pathologist said.

"Yet you stabbed him?" asked the judge.

Once again the clock made the only noise in the room. Then Laura looked up and began. When she was finished the pathologist stared at her, then turned to us:

"The last weeks I was in his room there were other girls that had been caught and brought in. Two of them were from the reservation. They'd been like Nacoma and Zitikala-sa, selling baskets at the side of the road, young girls, and very pretty girls. And the captain lost interest in me. He wasn't happy with me anymore. I was put back in my room. I was kept there a week before an orderly came in, and tied me back to the bed. He went as if to leave but instead just closed the door. He turned back and told me the Captain had suggested he try me again."

"The orderly said this?" Raadi said sceptically.

She nodded. "His name was Alan. He spoke as he was getting undressed, but said it as if he were talking to himself and didn't care if I understood. Then he said the Captain had been a fool to believe I could think and speak."

"Did he say anythin' else?"

She nodded.

"What did 'e say?"

The pathologist listened with us, but then the grunts seemed to break. She reached out and patted Laura's hand, then turned and began to translate.

"When he was undressed he said 'let's try something new, Nine'—I was number nine. But then he called me something else, and he said the Captain told him I …

was much better at some of what a man wanted. He made motions of what he wanted, and … began making the sounds …"

The judge had been watching Laura, but now turned, and motioned to the bailiff.

Laura was crying, quietly.

The bailiff got a box of Kleenex and brought it to Laura. She took one and took off her sunglasses and wiped the good, right eye.

Everyone stared at that—the judge, the pathologist, the court reporter—and some in the front seats of the audience gasped at what had been the other eye. With her treatments and loss of weight the skin was wrapped tightly over the broken ridge where a clean eyebrow once was. The orbit beneath was a small irregular hole, and the skin sagged beneath it.

"Do you wish to take a break, Signorina?" the judge asked.

Laura shook her head. He looked at me, then back at her. "Are you sure?" he asked her.

She replaced the glasses, took a ragged breath and began bending out more sounds with a low anger. Signora Agnesi sat up right away.

"He made the sounds …"

"What sounds?"

Her noises came bitterly now, and when she finished the pathologist explained.

"The sounds people made all my life, even children made before my friend came to help me. Louisa," she said. Her tone softened around the name, and it was the first sound I could faintly understand without the pathologist.

"Who es thes?" the judge asked.

I stood. "If I may, Il Giudice?" He nodded, and I motioned to Mrs. Locke. "She's referring to Louisa

404

Locke, Your Honor, the woman in the wheelchair. They were childhood friends. They were separated by … economic times, but Mrs. Locke retained us to find Laura—the Signorina—we were able to … locate her a few months ago."

The judge made a note, then looked back at Laura. "You said children made sounds before Signor … Signora … Locke helped you? What sounds?"

She twisted out the answer with angry tones.

"Like a pig …" the pathologist said, but Laura was still speaking. She went on with fierce intensity, trying to control herself. When she finished it was quiet. The pathologist glanced at the judge and took a long breath.

"They'd snort like a pig. When I was young, children made circles around me and did it like a chorus, called me 'pig girl, pig girl'. It was one of the things I hated. When Louisa came she stopped them from doing it. When Lozen heard the soldiers do it, she comforted me. But they weren't there when the orderly came in. He said the captain told him to try the Pig Girl. And while he was on me he began snorting and laughing, and when he finished he snorted again and said I was a good pig. And I became angry."

Tears had come down her cheek but more of Laura's grunts twisted out sharply. When she paused Signora Agnesi patted her hand again, then turned and translated.

"I'm crying here and I cried there but … I don't cry. Lozen and Juh taught me not to. But when the captain brought me back into his room one day after Alan did what he did I had been crying. And he was different … from before, I mean. He wasn't kind anymore. He was drunk, and he wanted what … what Alan wanted, and what I could give him. He told me to stop crying first, but right then I couldn't. He became angry and began yelling at me. He said what he'd told me before wasn't

405

right. That the nice things he'd said weren't true, that I was just a stupid retard, and a pig. And I couldn't stop and I cried more. So he began to hit me." She stopped and clenched her teeth, then looked down and twisted out more, raising her voice in shouted grunts. "It just made it worse. I still couldn't stop, so he hit me again."

"He slapped you?" Raadi asked.

"No. He hit me."

"With what?" the judge asked. "What did 'e use?"

"His fists," Signora Agnesi said, holding up her own fists. Laura removed her glasses again, wiped her eye, then replaced the glasses and looked up at him. A coldness came over her as she went on.

"He was old then, and drunk. Hitting me didn't hurt, but it made me stop crying. So he stopped and undressed and made me do the things …" Signora Agnesi paused to let Laura go on, but at first she didn't.

She was staring at Scipio. He shifted slightly. Then she began again, bending into quieter sounds. She hesitated, then sat back. Signora Agnesi seemed pale, but while watching Laura, went on.

"And as soon as he finished he fell asleep, and I took the knife from his belt, and used it to …" Signora Agnesi paused again.

"Did she finish?" the judge asked.

She nodded grimly.

"What did she say?"

Agnesi took a deep breath. "She said … she cut his privates."

The judge blinked, then stared at Laura. "Is this true? Did you … Did the mutilare really occur? Did you castra' him?"

Laura looked at him blankly, not understanding.

"Castra! Castra!" he repeated softly, with small circular motions of his pen. When that brought no understanding, he motioned towards his lap, "Did you stab 'im … in the yoke … in the area between …"

"In the groin?" the clerk said quietly.

Laura nodded at that. Her expression relaxed, and she began another response with a tone of satisfaction.

Signora Agnesi shut her eyes as she explained. "He screamed over and over."

"Why did you do thes?" the judge cried. "The captain … he was an old man by then. 'E had given you food, ease-ed your sufferin' somewhat, had 'e not?"

Laura stared at him for several seconds as if she hadn't understood. He began to repeat the question but she grunted curtly to interrupt. The interpreter began to speak but Laura twisted out angry noises on top of her words.

Signora Agnesi shook her head. "You better ask another question, Il Giudice."

The judge hesitated, then drew new words together. "Why … ded you do this to 'im?"

Laura showed him the same cold stare. She twisted out more sounds. The pathologist turned to the others. "Lozen explained when I asked why Apaches killed so many white families, not just soldiers but settlers. Why they killed women. Why they killed children."

The judge looked back sombrely. "What did she say?"

Laura's stare held him for several seconds, then she flexed out her answer.

The pathologist took a deep breath. "Lozen told her something the Apaches have always said, that there are many who go to the after world not from loyalty or courage, but from compassion. They are mostly young, and known there as fools."

CHAPTER FORTY-NINE

The judge motioned that Raadi could resume his own questioning. The procuratore studied his notes, then put them down and removed his glasses.

"Il Giudice, I believe thes concludes my inquiry. She 'as not answered all the questions. But even if you accept her statements, we 'ave met our burden, the allegations are proven and there is good cause to return the patient."

The judge turned to me. "Signore Rankin? You 'ave anythin' to add?"

"I do, Your Honor," I said, but I was concerned. Laura was showing the strain. We all were very tired, but the stress was showing on her.

"Tell us about the other men who came," I asked. "Those who … visited with you before the doctor kept you for himself."

She answered. It was one of the only times Signora Agnesi didn't fully understand. She had her repeat it, then turned to translate.

"There was a Judge, and a sheriff, mostly, and they let me stay with them, if I did what they wanted."

"A moment, Your Honor?" I said, because once again the judge stared at her in disbelief. He nodded to me as Scipio handed me a typed sheet and whispered. I read the list, stood, and studied Laura for a moment. She looked as if she'd been through a war. I measured my words out slowly.

"You said they called your Number Nine?"

She nodded.

"How did that start?"

She bent out her response.

The pathologist said, "There was another man who started that. He had Swimming Man's job before Swimming Man came. He came three or four times a year and counted us."

"Who was he?"

"I don't know who he was, but he worked with the government, with the U.S. government. He was tall and heavy ... and smelled of cigar. He carried a pad of paper. He would come and count us and then spend time with one or two of us, then he would go."

I took a sip of water, then went on. "You were pregnant once in your life, weren't you?"

She stared at me for several moments, then grunted coldly. The pathologist nodded, "Yes."

"What happened to the child?"

She looked away, then down at the table.

"Tell them, Laura," I insisted.

She looked back at me, then back down and twisted several words. The pathologist shifted in her chair. "Dr. Braga took the babies out of us."

"Did you ask him to do this ..." I began, but those first words brought a look of disbelief. I changed my mind and went on. "Were there ever any childbirths at Madonna?"

She shook her head. "No."

"No ... meaning ..."

"No one was pregnant for long. The doctor would stop them."

"How did he do this?"

"We were tied …"

"Obezione—objection!" the procuratore interrupted. "Thes is no' relevant to the proceedings."

"You're joking!" I exclaimed.

"Please, Signore," the judge admonished me. "You may proceed, but no one 'ere is joking."

"I'm sorry, Judge."

I turned back to her. "How did he perform the procedures?"

She began again. The pathologist tightened as she grunted her answer. When it was finished Signora Agnesi took in a deep breath and explained.

"We were strapped to the bed. Then he used his instruments and did it, without much anaesthetic, at least not enough to put us to sleep. He just did it with his instruments, and I could feel it, and then he said, 'Well Nine, I wouldn't worry about that sick feeling anymore'."

"Did any of the women actually give birth?"

She shook her head. "Not there."

The judge stared. "And by that … you mean what, Signorina?"

She grunted out more. The pathologist turned to the judge.

"Mr. Rankin explained that another woman, before I was there … There was another good doctor there, for a short time. He discovered one of the women was pregnant. He had her transferred to a clinic in Apache Junction."

"Who was that?"

"The mother didn't know if it would be a male or female child, but she wanted it to be called Ra-Na-Tana. It means My Worthy Friend. But the mother died during the birth. The child was born, but white families wouldn't take her because she was half Indian, and the

Indians wouldn't take her because she was half white. So she was adopted."

"Who adopted her?"

"Mrs. Mays. The lady at the ranch. Isabel Mays."

"What happened to Ra-Na-Tana when Mrs. Mays died?"

"She was adopted by Daisy and her husband."

"Did they call her by the Indian name?"

"No."

"What was she called?"

Laura took a sip of water, wiped her lips with a napkin, then grunted two short syllables.

"Pia," the pathologist said.

"The woman who testified before me last week?" the judge asked.

"Just so, Il Giudice," Scipio said, rising.

The judge rubbed his face with both hands, then motioned to me to continue.

"One last subject, Laura. I want to go back to the incident with the captain. After he stopped your privileges and the orderly came in and raped you and made the pig noises, after you stabbed the captain, was that when your eye was injured?"

She shook her head and made the noises. "It was after that," the pathologist said. "The next day."

"The day after you stabbed the captain?"

"Yes."

"Who did it?"

She looked around the room uneasily, then dropped her eyes and didn't answer.

I tried a different tack. "Tell us what happened?"

Still looking down, she bent out two quiet sentences. "The captain was taken to another hospital," the pathologist said. "We never saw him again."

"And then?"

411

"The police came to Madonna."

"Did you talk to them?"

She went on with a series of bends and grunts that carried increasing anxiety. When she was finished she bit her lip and looked down. With her eyes still on Laura the pathologist translated:

"I tried to, but the police didn't understand me. They came in with ... with ... Dr. Braga, a different policeman was with them, dressed in brown instead of black. They argued, because the police were going to take me to jail for attacking the captain. Dr. Braga said I couldn't have committed a crime because I was retarded. He said a Judge already knew I stabbed the captain and had ordered that a new medicine be tried on me. The doctor was going to use it on me, and felt sure it would work.

"The police didn't believe him because I'd stabbed the captain just days before. So Dr. Braga went to get the order, and as soon as he left my room I tried to tell them. I told them to take me. One of them wouldn't listen and went outside, but the other tried to listen. He asked me, 'Are you trying to tell me something?' and I nodded and said the doctor was the murderer, just as Dr. Braga came back in and saw what I was doing."

"Thes' is quite interestin' but pleas' can we move on to matters of more pertinence?" the procuratore asked, getting to his feet.

"Sit and be quiet, Signore Raadi," the judge ordered, while staring at Laura. "Go on, Signorina."

"'Ow es thes relevan'?" Raadi pressed him.

"I said sit, Signore Raadi. I wish to 'ere more."

Laura bent out more grunts. The pathologist took notes, and once again began translating as the grunts went on. I remember how the room was filled with those

412

sounds, the grunts, Laura's words, while everyone listened, and how Signora Agnesi then translated:

"Even after Dr. Braga was there I kept telling the police, and they made Braga let me go on, so I did, and told them about everything he was doing to the girls. I begged them to take me. The one started to understand. He told Dr. Braga I was trying to say something. Dr. Braga said it always seemed that way. The officer said it didn't seem like I was that retarded but sure seemed like I didn't want to be there, and Dr. Braga said I didn't want to be anywhere, that they could even take me to the best hotel and I would do the same thing.

"Dr. Braga got angry. He said he'd practiced medicine fifteen years and if the officer was going to claim he could diagnose me and violate the judge's order based on a single question he would lose his job. So the officer hesitated, and I knew I had to do something, so I tried to tell them Braga was lying, and I tried to tell them how he was to me and the other women, and he lets the judge—" the pathologist hesitated, took a deep breath and went on: "He lets the judge come in and fuck us, and that the doctor and people there killed two women. I tried to show them by moving my body and pointing to him, and I said it even though Dr. Braga was there, and he was getting madder as I spoke."

Laura stopped and bit her lips tightly together, before bending out more with a bitter tone. Signora Agnesi wrote again, then turned to the judge:

"Dr. Braga told the officers, 'You see what I mean?' Because I was trying to wave my hands in the restraints and motioning with my hips about the fucking, and the officers had backed away as I went on. And I kept saying over and over, help me, help me, and I was crying but they didn't understand. But the doctor said it always looked like that, and like I was asking for help but it was

413

because I was retarded. He convinced them I was insane. So they left, and I stayed there, with him."

When the pathologist finished their eyes went to Laura. She wiped her face, and her eye, replaced her glasses and sat back, looking exhausted.

"And your injury?" I asked her.

Several seconds went by with her sunglasses aimed at the sliver of floor between the pathologist and the procuratore. She finally took a deep breath and let it out, then looked up at me and twisted out more. "It happened right after the police left."

"Who did it?"

She glanced at Braga.

"He can't hurt you here," I said.

She grunted a question. The pathologist sat back and looked at the others. "She wishes to know whether the doctor will be removed from court."

The judge stared at her, then the doctor, and nodded. "Doctor, if you please."

Braga stood. "She's my patient, Your Honor. It's important for her that I be here."

"This I will decide, Doctor. Now if you would please wait outside."

Braga's eyes narrowed over Laura, then he turned and walked out.

Laura grunted more. "She wants to know whether, if she's ordered back, the doctor will learn of what is said here," the pathologist said.

Raadi stood, looking uncertain what to say.

Scipio nodded, rising. "We can make thes' portion of the testimonia under seal. Signore Raadi, will you consent."

Raadi shrugged.

"All right," the judge said. "I ask all of you ladies and gentlemen in the audience to be excused." And he repeated it in Italian.

When the room was cleared he turned to Laura. "Your consigliere 'as obtained an order that thes portion of thes proceeding es under seal. No one but I and those present can know, and we are all bound by thes order."

She grunted a question. The pathologist nodded. "She wants to hear everyone agree with what the judge said. Everyone."

The procuratore shrugged. "Et es so."

The court reporter nodded. "Yes."

The pathologist agreed. "It is correct."

"Tell them what happened," I said.

She leaned forward and began to grunt more. The pathologist nodded. "Dr. Braga walked the police out, and he came back right after they left."

"By himself?"

"Yes. He shut the door. He was angry because of what I had done to the captain but furious because of what I tried to tell the police."

"Were you still tied to the bed?"

She nodded.

"What did he do?" he asked.

She stared down at the table and without saying anything motioned with her hand to her face.

"How did he hurt your face?"

There was another long silence. She looked at the judge helplessly, then stared down at the floor.

"'Ow did he do it?" the judge asked.

Her face tightened. She twisted herself and made out three short, angry sounds. They turned to the pathologist. She was shaking her head. "With a club."

"A club?"

The pathologist paled and, shaking her head, said, "A golf club."

"Explain how he struck you,"

"Obezione!" the procuratore interrupted, getting to his feet. "I believe we get the point?"

"I'd like her to describe that point," I said, raising my voice.

"Of course you would," Raadi scoffed, "but what the Signorina claims on thes subject es denied by the director, and in any even' es no' pertinent to thes proceedings. Es dettaglio inutile—unnecessary detail. We don' need to be wastin' time on … dettaglio osceno, dettaglio volgare. I'm sorry," he said, looking to the clerk.

"Obscene or vulgar detail," she said.

"You think hearing it is obscene! She had to go through it!"

"That is not the point, Signore. I am simply—"

"Silenzio, per favore," the judge said, waving his hand. "'You may go on. Proceed, Signore Rankin."

The procuratore sat back, shaking his head. I turned to Laura. "Go ahead, Laura. Explain exactly what the director did to you."

She glanced up at me, turned back to the judge and began to grunt the response. The pathologist resumed taking notes, interrupting once to ask a question, then nodded and continued writing. By the time Laura finished Signora Agnesi had gone white. She stared at Laura, cleared her throat, and using her notes began.

"He brought a golf club and while he spoke to me he began poking the head of the club against me. He talked about how good he'd tried to be to me and would poke me as if to punish, or jerk me back if I turned away, and he talked about foods he'd given me and he'd poke harder because he was getting angrier as he spoke, and he said he'd been honest with me and loyal to me and he began hitting me with it, below my stomach, and he said how he'd had feelings for me and hit my chest and my stomach, and I was having trouble breathing and tried to protect my stomach and my privates and he began to yell, and he said all I'd ever given him was trouble and he stood and swung it once and I ducked inside my arms, and he yelled that if there was one thing he couldn't stand it was ingratitude and I ducked, and he didn't hit me, so I looked to see what was happening and he'd been waiting with the club, and when he saw my head start to rise from my arms he swung. I don't remember anything after that until I woke up with pain in my head, and a bandage across my eye. And I was left alone after that."

"When was that?"

"About … fifteen years ago."

"Were you ever taken to a hospital?"

"We were never allowed anywhere but outside for the wash."

"I turned to Scipio to see if he had more. He shook his head in my direction and stood. "Il Giudice, thes concludes our presentation."

"Very well," the judge sighed. He was quiet for several moments, staring at Laura. Then he turned to us. "You 'ave supplied your written arguments to the clerk?"

Scipio and Raadi both nodded.

"Then we will end for today. I will review your submissions this evening and will give my decision in the morning," he said. A bailiff took Laura away, and I was sent back to my cell.

CHAPTER FIFTY

It was the longest night of my life, and I expect one of the longest of Laura's. When I was returned by an officer to the courtroom the next morning she was there, wearing a pale blue dress, and huddled in a corner of the courtroom with Mrs. Locke, Mr. Oneal, and Signore Scipio. Dr. Altobelli and Pia were seated nearby. Braga and Janoff were standing with Signore Raadi. The officer locked my irons to the floor at our counsel table and the others came over.

The courtroom was more crowded than before, now with as many reporters and television crews as interested citizens. Signora Agnesi, the pathologist had been excused from her position at the witness chair but had taken a seat near our table.

The judge came in, looking as grey as his wig. He took the bench, peered over his glasses, and asked both Raadi and Scipio, "You gentlemen 'ave any more to add?"

"No, il Suo Onore," both counsel replied, standing.

"Then I 'ave my decision." He took a sip of water, adjusted his glasses, and began to read from his notes.

"There are four subjects I am asked to decide: Primo ... first, whether the American convictions of Signorina Laura Michele Spinali may be overturned by thes court; secondi, whether the petition to extradite Signorina

418

Spinali should be granted and she should be returned to Ospedale Madonna; tre—third, whether certain sums said to be those of the Signorina should be transferred to the Ospedale Madonna, and its counsel; and lastly, whether the Signorina's avvocate, Paul Thomas Rankin, should be returned to America to face certain criminal and civil charges." He took another sip of water.

"Point une … one: Signorina Spinali's consigliere 'as submitted written challenges of the Signorina's first commitment to the Ospedale Madonna, saying it was arrived at without a jury, without avvocate, and without proper evidenz, and that abundant evidenz exists that she should not 'ave been there in the first instance, that she was badly mistreated while kept there, and that she should therefore not be returned.

"As to the posizione that the Signorina's commitment so many years ago was improper, we do not 'ave the records of what took place then. There es no evidenz of the process through which she arrived to the 'Ospedale Madonna, except a few sentences of the United States militare that shows their proceedings took place durin' the Indian Wars. The procuratore, Signore Raadi, and Signore Janoff argue that one can rarely apply the more meticulous rules of evidenz in times of battle, and that we cannot in calmer times look back to question decisions reached in war, without undermining the certainty of commanders.

"As to thes' point, I find I am not willing to accept the arguments of Signorina Spinali's counsel to refute thes, and will therefore not question what was found by the American commanders in the field. Thes' point, therefore, is denied."

I exchanged glances with Mr. Oneal. He didn't seem concerned at the judge's ruling. Nor was I. We didn't expect that field trials during the Indian wars would be overturned decades later, but had included the argument as a 'throwaway' anyway, a position to be lost with enough grace that the judge might feel more even-handed when, hopefully, he ruled for us on the more important matters.

"Due—two," the judge continued, turning a page of notes, "The Signorina's consigliere also says she should not be restored to the 'Ospedale Madonna because the 'Ospedale is not really a 'ospedale, but a place where at least one woman was killed, others were beaten and the subject of stup—rape—and the Signorina herself was beaten so badly she lost the sight of one eye. Further, the young women called patients there are in fact the victims of ... *rapito* ... " he turned to the clerk.

"Kidnap," she said, looking out to the audience. Small exclamations of astonishment had begun rippling through the audience. The judge motioned irritably to quiet them and went back to his papers.

"Kidnap by the 'Ospedale colleagues, acquaintances, or employees, and are given calmante—"

"Tranquilizers, or sedatives," the clerk offered.

"Tranquilizers or sedatives so they may be made docile victims of stuprare, or rape, by soldiers, citizens, and even by ... a giudice—a judge. Signore Scipio and Signore Oneal provided testimony from Dr. James Wisler, who flew 'ere from Eritzona to say he examined the Signorina five and seven days after she was taken from the 'Ospedale, and found signs of past sessuality ..." He hesitated and looked down at the clerk.

"Sexual activity," The clerk murmured.

"Just so," he said, "And beatings."

He turned the page. "The 'Ospedale Madonna denies all these allegations. The 'Ospedale says the only 'omicidio within its walls ware those in which the Signorina participated. Et says the Signorina's condizione in the face es from 'er own violenz, and that her evidence of sessuality is from her own behaviour; that she sought out intimacy with many others, and that such behaviours appear because she is *retardito,* or *retardo mentale,* or, as the Signorina's American counsel prefers we describe it, from a condition of menomazione psichica—"

"Mental defect," the clerk said.

"Si. Mental defect." He paused, looked up, then went on.

"Signorina Spinali's American consigliere 'as submitted affidati of the Signorina's friends, provided affidati and provided testimony which says she does not 'ave such a condition, that she is not filled with violenz, and did not belong in the 'Ospedale to begin with. And then there was the testimonia of Signorina Spinali herself."

He took a sip of water before going on.

"Signorina Spinali testified before me for two full days. She did not answer all the questions, but many she did, including some which were asked with little delicacy." He glanced at Janoff before turning another page. "She was provoke'ed on one occasion 'ere in thes very courtroom to threaten violenz, and on another, to threaten 'omicidio, even against Signore Rankin, her own avvocate. This I must weigh carefully. The provocation for her threats might 'ave angered many— but not to bring them to violenz. I must also add, however, that during such threats the Signorina seemed concerned for 'er friend, and at other times she was moved to tears by such concern. I must say that the evidenz on this issue es very close, but though it may show a tendency for violenz, I cannot find that such behaviour proves she is *retardito* in any other respect known to me. She is loyal to 'er friend, and quite bitter,

421

perhaps, but loyalty and bitterness do not mean one is *retardo mentale.*" He paused again to take a sip, glanced at Raadi, then Scipio, and went on.

"However, I am not a physician, and there were affidati given to me from several who *are* physicians, two for the Signorina which say-es she is as I found her—with soundness of mind—and even more from the 'Ospedale, including doctors who 'ave known 'er for a much longer time, and say her benign effect is because of their medical effort. These physicians 'ave warned she still has the malattie—" He looked down at the clerk.

"Disease."

"The disease for which she required their treatment."

He turned another page, read several lines, and went on. "For purposes of estradizione the question of whether she es *retarde mentale* is only one of the issues 'ere. We must also decide whether thes' place is as brutal as she and 'er avvocate say, and whether she should be transferred back to it. That and all else I must decide on the evidenz of greatest weight, which brings me to the question of what evidenz I may accept." He turned the page and went on. "Ospedale Madonna says the evidenz against estradizione comes chiefly from the Signorina, and that her testimony must be excluded because she did not answer all the questions. Signore Scipio submits the unanswered questions ware of no significance to thes' proceedings, that they ware personal—about the Signorina's sessuale, or sex habits even before coming to the 'Ospedale, or about a simple necklace.

"Signore Raadi, 'owever, asserts this necklace was not a simple one, and may satisfy the claims of the 'Ospedale." He straightened, and his voice shifted into the rhythm and cadence of axioms:

"One cannot choose for themselves what is relevant in a trial. If proper and important questions are unanswered by a witness, then the remaining testimony is incomplete and must be rejected—in toto. If, on the other hand, the questions which remain unanswered were improper or of less significance, then a court may assept the rest of what was said." He looked up, his eyes swept over us, and he lapsed back to his papers.

"I 'ave gone over all the unanswered questions, and find several of the questions were of little or no significance. Others, 'owever, were of significance."

The air seemed suddenly gone from the room.

"The sessuale questions and the whereabouts of *La Crime,* for example, are both matters of pertinence. On such issues I find the law of Arizona is similar to ours. Here or there, when someone claims stupor—scusi, rape—they cannot avoid questions of their own habits, proclivities or even invitations, just as when a debt becomes an issue, so does one's ability to repay it." The judge looked up at Laura. "I therefore cannot accept what the Signorina has said 'ere."

For a brief, palpable instant the courtroom was dead still, then exclamations burst from the audience. People rose and shouted. Some shook their fists. Pia cried loudly. The judge pounded his gavel and the bailiff yelled. I looked over at Laura. She sat motionless, staring at the judge, and my old anger came back.

I stood, and shouted, "How can you say that! Is this what you call justice?"

"*Silenzio!*" the judge shouted. He looked down at me and lowered his voice. "Sit, Signore."

I slumped into my chair, but then I heard Mrs. Locke.

"Judge … *Il Giudice!*" she said. She'd gotten up from the wheelchair and was holding the low railing before the audience.

"Senora, please," the judge said softly. "It's enough."

Mrs. Locke shook her head. "She'd be far better off being kept in jail here. Keep her in your prison, if you like, but don't send her back to that place."

From the corner of my eye I saw Laura nodding vigorously.

"She wants that!" I blurted out, jumping up again. "Your Honor … I'm sorry, Il Giudice, Miss Spinali wants that! Do you want that? Wouldn't you rather go to prison here?" I asked. Laura nodded and stood, and bent to grunt vigorously. Startled cries came from the audience. I yelled over them to be heard, "She'd rather go to prison than that place! You can't send her back." The noise exploded again. People were on their feet, gesticulating and shouting support for 'le Signorina Spinali!', 'le familie Spinali!'

"Silencio!" the bailiff barked, as the judge shouted and slapped his gavel. When quiet was finally restored Signore Scipio stood, and addressed the judge wearily.

"Il Giudice, my client 'as a point. Per'aps if the pathologist could translate what the Signorina was saying?"

"Et would be pointless, Signore."

"Why?" I demanded.

"I 'ave told you why," the judge said curtly. "This hearing determines whether estradizione should take place, not who receives her."

"Doesn't the fact she'd prefer prison prove she's telling the truth about—"

"Signore, I said enough!" and he slapped his gavel again.

When the room was mostly quiet he went back to his orders.

"Terzo—third: On the subject of recoupamente of sums the 'Ospedale seeks, I believe the fondo from Castellani 'house is for the Signorina and therefore must be turn-ed over to 'Ospedale. The Ospedale also asks that the holdings of the corporazione Spinalocke should be seized. I 'ave examined the documents of this foundation, Spinalocke." He glanced up at me. "It appears the papers were prepared carefully, one may even say cleverly, but well enough to prevent the Ospedale's request. I cannot conclude the assets of Spinalocke should be turned over."

"Quarto—fourth: As to the consigliere, I fin' no great evidence not to extradite him as well. He admits 'aving interfered—"

The rest of what he said was drowned out by more noise. I remember Pia shouting at the judge, and, in a blur of noise and people, saw the lieutenant approach. I remember getting up and swinging a fist towards him, then felt a blow to the side of my face. I fell to the ground, and through a jumble of legs looked back. There was a blue dress, Laura's dress, and Pia. They were on the ground, crawling towards me. Laura was flexing and grunting something.

"What?" I murmured.

She grasped my shoulder and grunted insistent, impatient sounds.

"I can't …" I said, as Pia approached.

"Che es sayin' are you her avvocate?" Pia said.

"Am I her what?" I asked dully. Fights were breaking out around us. Laura grasped my necktie, pulled me to the railing, and grunted the sounds with the tenor and force of an angry question.

"Lawyer! Her lawyer!" Pia said. "Che wants to know if you will stay as her lawyer, Meester Paul. Che says che will be in the after soon, away from Madonna, and wants only one thing from you. But che needs to know if you are really *her* lawyer, and will do what che asks."

"Of course! Of course! Yes. Tell me, and I will do it. Whatever I can, I'll do it."

Laura pulled me next to her face and grunted more loudly than I'd ever heard her speak.

"Mees Laura. Hees—"

Laura snapped at her.

Pia nodded as if rebuked, and turned to me. "Che say swear to it."

"What are you asking?"

Laura slapped my face and repeated the syllables angrily.

"Swear to it," Pia said.

"All right. All right. I swear. Now what is it I'm swearing?"

While still holding my tie Laura grunted several sentences. Pia bit her lips, then shut her eyes tightly against the message.

"What is she saying?" I shouted, but Laura tried to stand. Pia helped her up. She shoved Pia away and took an unsteady step forward, then stretched out her arms.

"What did she …?" I began, turning, and then I stopped.

Braga was pushing his way through the crowd, followed by an orderly who held a set of leather restraints.

CHAPTER FIFTY-ONE

I was taken to another jail near the Arno, where I was kept three days while travel was arranged back to Arizona. They let me make only one telephone call to Signore Scipio, who told me that Laura was in a prison clinic near the Galileo Airport, and that Mrs. Locke was back at the Altobelli Clinic.

Early on the fourth morning I was shackled and taken to the airport. Laura was already there, in a corner farthest from the flight gate, chained in a wheelchair. She wore an oversized grey prison uniform and was surrounded by six uniformed *Guardia*. Her sunglasses had been taken away, and a flock of tittering children had been drawn to her disfigured face. Lieutenant Dominichi and Don Janoff stood nearby. Janoff nodded to me, and even handed me a newspaper.

My guards seated me next to Laura. She patted my hand, then stared at the ground as I spread the paper between my restrained wrists. It was the *Phoenix Gazette* from two days ago. We'd made the front page:

Son of Legal Scion Arrested

Authorities in Apache Junction and Florence, Italy, report that a local lawyer has been arrested in Italy and is being extradited to Arizona to face criminal charges and disbarment proceedings before the Arizona Supreme Court. Paul Rankin, of Rankin, Oneal and Lonhardt, was taken into custody on charges of interference with a warrant, obstruction of justice, and battery, and is scheduled to be flown to Phoenix this coming week. He is reportedly the son of Maurice Rankin, the late but well-respected senior partner of the same law office. The younger Rankin apparently fabricated means to obtain the release of a woman being held on murder charges at the Madonna Clinic, in Apache Junction. A spokesperson for the Clinic says the ruse was discovered as he was escorting the patient out of the clinic, that he then attacked the Clinic's director and staff, and, using falsified documents, spirited the woman out of the country. The patient has also been found and is being returned to the Clinic. She was apparently not harmed. Rankin will reportedly be held in the Phoenix jail for arraignment in Federal Court on Monday. His law firm could not be reached for comment.

Mr. Oneal arrived with Pia and Mrs. Locke in another wheelchair. Mrs. Locke looked even worse than before, but was seated upright in the chair and no longer had as many medical devices attached to her. Pia chased the children away while Mrs. Locke took glasses from her purse and motioned to the Guardia nearest Laura to let her in. He was younger than the others, and turned to Dominichi, who shook his head.

"For God's sake," I exclaimed. "Don, is it really necessary?"

Janoff turned to see what was happening. He spoke to Dominichi, who shrugged and nodded. The young officer let Pia shove Mrs. Locke's wheelchair next to Laura. Mrs. Locke brushed the white hair back from Laura's forehead and ears, and fitted the glasses. I heard her say, "This isn't over," and heard Laura make a short series of grunts. She moved the chain-joined leather straps to pat Mrs. Locke's hand.

I couldn't continue to watch them, because both women began to cry. Laura flexed out soft grunts, Pia said it was something about the 'after'. The little grunting sounds came out halting, and broken. I turned back. Mrs. Locke had Laura's hand to her cheek.

"I won't let you stay there," Mrs. Locke said.

Laura twisted more with a tone of resignation. A woman's voice came over the intercom, announcing our flight. Laura grunted again and patted Mrs. Locke's hand.

"What friend?" Mrs. Locke asked.

Laura bent and grunted softly.

I looked around us. The guards were staring at a group of tight-skirted young women who strained not to look back.

Mr. Oneal took a seat next to me and patted my knee.

"Is Janoff gloating?" I asked.

"Actually, he says they—"

He was interrupted by Mrs. Locke. Her head was down, her voice breaking. Laura stroked her hair, and the chains brushed Mrs. Locke's cheek.

Mr. Oneal leaned closer and whispered to me. "You want to tell me why they took it?"

"What?"

"The necklace. Pia had it. Scipio came yesterday afternoon and took it. He said you told him to. You want to explain why? Janoff says they'll let everything against you go if you turn the necklace over."

I glanced in Laura's direction, then looked back at him. "I can't."

"Why not?"

"I'm Laura's counsel now too, and I promised her I wouldn't." And I explained what had happened in the courtroom.

"Jesus Christ!" Oneal murmured, and we both turned towards Laura. She was stroking Mrs. Locke's head, watching us with no expression.

CHAPTER FIFTY-TWO

Mr. Oneal came this morning, with a speech therapist who translated Laura's sounds. He said Louisa had another plan; she'd ordered Mr. Oneal to tell her. Laura shook her head wearily. It was unacceptable. She knew what was waiting for her, and was ready. She'd lived most of her life here, and would live the rest here as well. She didn't tell them what had happened in the night.

It was different here now, both better and worse. The building had been painted, the dank interior cleaned, the dim corridors and rooms well lit. Even her bed was new, and the thick pipe had been replaced by a toilet that flushed. And there was quiet now—no more voices coming through pipes, no more crying or moaning from the next room. That room was empty—no sign of Free Bird. Even the flies were less. But the orderlies here knew who'd forced those changes, just as they knew very well what upset her the most.

Her first night back it began to rain. She'd searched the wall, but her friend wasn't there. The cracks and seams were like tiny, rutted wounds, but there was no face—nothing. She tried to brush at the concrete, but her strength was slipping; raising her arm was too difficult. It dropped to her side. But later on the rain stopped, the clouds left, and the moon came out. Its light came into the room, and her friend returned. Laura's imagination filled in the dark hair and pretty expression. She laid back, and grunted.

"I missed you."

Her friend smiled back, and they rested together. Laura tried to begin a story, but it was difficult. Speech was difficult, even thinking was hard. She tried to remember where her story had left off, but she couldn't recall. She went back to an old story, but even that was frustrating. It came out slow and halting, and took too much effort. She stopped several times to rest, but her friend seemed to understand. When the moon crept past its zenith her friend faded and left. Laura lay back, and fell into the beginnings of sleep. At the very edge, as her mind slipped to the vague border near dreams, she felt what was happening inside, felt it growing, and moving, then felt it pause, as if it knew she was aware.

"Are you ready?" the feeling asked.

Yes. I'm ready, she thought.

And she was, so ready, in fact, that she wanted it all to end.

Mr. Oneal visited me at the Apache Junction jail at ten-thirty in the morning. A guard brought him a chair, and we spoke through the bars of my cell.

"How are they?" I asked, a little unsettled at his appearance. He'd lost weight. His suit fit loosely, and his features looked grey. He shook his head without saying anything.

"Tell me," I said. "How's Mrs. Locke?"

"You'll see for yourself," he sighed.

"What do you mean? Can you get me out?"

432

"You fled the country, Paul. They'd never allow that."

"Then how—"

"She's bribed them to let her visit you."

I frowned, dreading another meeting with her, and yet I'd been wondering how she was, most of all.

"And Laura?" I asked.

"Pia and I saw her this morning, at Madonna," he said sadly. "She's very weak, much worse than before, but she's still there. She made some noises—I've never been able to understand her, but Pia says she keeps talking about a friend in the wall. I have no idea what she's talking about. The walls are concrete, and have been there for decades; and the next room is empty. There's no friend anywhere there. By the way, the whole facility looks pretty clean."

"They knew you were coming."

"That's true. The paint was still tacky."

His words settled, and we were both quiet.

"How much longer does she have?" I asked quietly.

"Dr. Wisler says a few days, maybe a week."

"What else has happened?"

Mr. Oneal sat up. "We filed another lawsuit against Madonna, but they're moving to dismiss, and they'll win. And they just delivered another of their own, this time for defamation, and having already lost on those issues we may well lose that as well."

"What about the rest of it?"

He stared at me for a few seconds, then took a deep breath. "I'm trying to work on a plea, but you'll spend time in a federal prison."

"How long?" I asked, looking down at the footings of the barred door between us.

"Three years, maybe two if we're lucky. If you give up your license to save them disbarment proceedings, they may knock off a year."

I sighed, thinking of what two years would be like in a place like this. Laura had lived for more than thirty in hers.

"Is Mrs. Locke angry?" I asked him.

He nodded. "Very, but she says she's not finished."

"Why? What's she doing now?"

"She wanted me to unravel your little transactions so she could bargain with more."

"Bargain?"

He lowered his voice. "Bribe, is what she means, but it's taking five lawyers in three countries to unwind everything you did. That'll take longer than either she or Laura have. I'm not sure we'll ever get the museum to give up the necklace, and the way you set it up they don't really have to. But she's ordered me to liquidate anything we can get out of Spinalocke, and whatever she has left."

"What in God's name does she hope to do?"

He glanced around us. The guard was out in the hallway, too far away to be heard, but he lowered his voice. "She wants us to bribe them into letting her take Laura's place," he said grimly.

"Jesus!"

He nodded. "I told her we aren't allowed to commit felonies in our line of work, but she doesn't seem to care. She says if we won't help her she'll find someone who will, and if bribery doesn't work she'll find some way that does. She's going to talk to you about it."

I laughed bitterly. "How is she doing? I mean, how much time for her?"

He nodded solemnly. "Not a lot. I have her at the home you had built for her, with Pia and another nurse, but you'll see." He hesitated. "I fought her on this, Paul, but she's still as stubborn as ever. She's insisted on seeing you. An ambulance is bringing her here as we speak."

I stood and went to the bars. "What the hell can I do?"

"I'm guessing she hopes you'll do whatever it takes. Maybe she thinks since your license will be yanked anyway. But she'll pay them to let you make the calls."

CHAPTER FIFTY-THREE

She got there about a half hour after Mr. Oneal left. A guard opened my door and a paramedic wheeled her wheelchair in. She looked tiny, in her long skirt and white blouse, like a child who'd dressed up in an adult's clothes. The paramedic locked the wheels and stepped out, but the guard stayed at the door. She pulled an envelope from the side of her chair and motioned weakly to him. The guard came closer. She said something too faintly for me to hear. He nodded, took the envelope and patted her hand. Then he closed the door and left.

"Mrs. Locke," I said quietly, feeling so sad to see her. Her pale skin was mottled over her forehead and sagged from her eyes; the areas around her eyes were dark, almost black.

She gave me a slow, abbreviated nod, then motioned with her hand towards me. I crouched next to the chair. Her hand came up to my face and touched my cheek, and she spoke in a broken whisper.

"You...you know...what I want?"

I nodded. "I think so, but I can't."

"You're ... my ... lawyer."

"I was," I said, and I took her hand.

"Still ... are," she said hoarsely. She took in a shallow breath, then began to speak in fragments about what she planned.

I shook my head. "Even if I would agree, and even if they were willing to consider it, we'd need a lot more than we have left. Mr. Oneal says it'll take too long to get the money."

"I have more money now, and the car."

"What car? What money?"

"Jennie's. She left it all … to help Laura."

That surprised me. I'd never thought of Jenny's money, and certainly never expected any of it. But she'd thought of … everything. *Jenny,* I thought. *Poor Jenny.* I looked back at Mrs. Locke. "I can't do what you're asking."

"You're…you're the only one…who can. Oneal says they…they can't, they're afraid…to lose their licenses."

"They would lose them."

"You've…already…lost yours—or you will."

It was absurd. I felt so sorry for her, and so sad about what had happened. Ever since the trial ended, even though I'd been thinking about Laura, about Jenny, and my own problems, Mrs. Locke was always there in my thoughts, as if part of me felt that for some reason, hers was my biggest failure.

But here she was, still asking for my help, and there still was some crazy part of me that wanted to do just that. But I couldn't. She wanted to keep fighting battles we'd already lost. It wasn't possible. I kissed her hand. "I can't help you, Mrs. Locke."

She leaned forward and with both hands grasped mine, and with a raspy breath she whispered. "She's … been there … all this time because of me … for me."

"I'm sorry."

Her fingers tightened around mine, and she whispered. "It was going on … and on … for weeks, before she stopped him."

"Stopped—?" I began, but then I realized what she was saying.

"Please," she said, and her eyes welled. She tried to brush at them, then suddenly lost it. She slumped in her chair. I moved forward and held her up, and called for the guard. The hallway door clanged in the distance and footsteps approached. I felt her breath on my cheek, and heard her whisper one last thing.

"I'm crossing ... rivers here, ... Nathan."

The door opened. The paramedic came in and took her pulse. He yelled down the hallway. A second paramedic came in with oxygen. They placed the tubes and wheeled her out.

"Goodbye, Mrs. Locke," I whispered, but I'm not sure she heard. But as they turned the corner I saw her head move slightly. The paramedic stopped. He bent and listened, then spoke to the guard. The guard came back to me and told me.

"She said she'll see you after."

But I never saw her again.

I didn't learn what she'd started until after midnight that night, when the guard came back with a telephone. He waited while I did what Mrs. Locke asked, and then opened my door and said I was free to go.

438

CHAPTER FIFTY-FOUR

The moon was out, full and strong, but it was just a wall, glittering and translucent in the pale light. No friend, no face, nothing at all. She moved her head slightly, and slowly blinked. It was faint, just a very slight outline, but nothing more. She brushed weakly at the concrete. It didn't budge. She used her fingernail to catch a small imperfection. It dislodged a tiny crumb. She worked for several minutes, but then her arm weakened and her hand dropped to the bed.

When she woke the next time she did it again, more feebly this time. She found a faint crack that wouldn't give, but then higher up, a slight edge. Her fingers rested a moment, then tugged. Another small crumb fell to the bed. It was hard work, and tiring, and before long she slept again.

When she opened her eyes for the last time there was still no face. Nothing like that. But beyond one edge there was a small space, and in that space a tiny curve that hadn't been there before. She moved her hand there. Its sharp edge cut her finger, but she didn't feel it. The strength left her hand, and the hand slipped back down onto the bed.

Her eyes shifted weakly to try again, but her hand wouldn't move. She tried to look up, but her eyes stayed on her hand. She began to lose focus. It was slow, but where her hand had been she saw only a faint outline now, then even that faded. She lay still, hoping for strength, but its last little remnant was leaving her.

A clang came down the corridor, and vibration. Footsteps approached from the far end of the hallway. Her eyes opened a thin crack, and she remembered something. Someone. A tiny shard of memory floated up in her mind, and gave movement to her lips. But she lacked the strength for sound, and could barely form the name.

Laura

The footsteps came closer, but she didn't hear them, didn't hear the keys jangle, the handle turn, or the door being opened. The last bit of life left her. Then the widow of Nathan Locke and best friend of Laura Spinali was gone.

It was after two o'clock in the morning when Mr. Oneal dropped me at the house. In the moonlight there were little vignettes of stone and desert plants and a flowering mesquite. A corral had been built behind the house. Once inside I took a file of work and went straight to the master bedroom. I stepped in the door and stopped, shocked to see Laura. At first it looked as if she'd already died, but then I heard a faint hiss and her chest rose. There was a long pause, then it slowly fell.

I sat in one of the chairs. Pia came in quietly, holding a magazine. She patted my shoulder and took the other chair. We sat there at least two or three hours, trying to read, until Laura stirred. Pia got up and went to her. She was moving her hand. I got up and stood beside Pia. Laura was motioning towards the window. The grey morning light was coming in. Laura made a weak sound.

"Es cold," Pia whispered back to her.

Laura grunted weakly. Pia sighed disapprovingly, but went over and opened the window. An icy breeze slipped in, and noises followed from outside. A horse's snort, and a tapping sound. I got up and looked out. The morning sun splintered itself through the mesquite tree and dotted the dark form of a man. He was rough-looking, and bent next to one of the horses.

"Es Meester Alford," Pia said. "'Ees chuing the 'orses. Wha chu doin', Mees Laura?"

I turned.

Laura's lips began to move again. Pia leaned down and listened. Then she straightened and folded her arms. "I'm sorry, but che's not 'ere."

Laura's eye came open and moved slowly past Pia, to me. She motioned. I went closer. She motioned again and I leaned over her. Her fingers moved up to my shirt, and pulled me even closer, then she whispered something I couldn't understand. I turned. Pia's eyes were shut in a frown.

"What?" I asked.

Pia rolled her eyes and whispered. "Che very upset with you, but che say…che say thank you."

"I'm sorry, Laura," I said quietly, and I moved her hand back to her lap.

The phone rang. I ignored it. It stopped, then started up again. I didn't bother to get up, but when it happened a third time I did.

It was Mr. Oneal, calling from Madonna. His voice was raised, upset, but I could barely hear him because someone was yelling in the background. There were several voices. I recognized Braga's, but not the others.

"Hold on," Mr. Oneal said loudly. I heard him yell, loudly and with authority, in the background. The other voices subsided, then he came back on. He told me what he'd found in the room, and what I needed to do, and then, finally, told me Mrs. Locke had died. I don't remember too much after that, though Pia told me I sat for a while, then made two calls, then went back to Laura's room.

I do remember that. Pia was next to the bed, holding one of Laura's hands. Laura wasn't moving. The only sound was the *tap ... tap ... tap* of the farrier's nails, and then a rustling joined it. The morning air had come through the mesquite, moving its branches, and loosening a thin curtain of yellow petals. Some drifted over the sill and into the room, some went over the edge of the bed and across Laura, and brushed her face as we cried.

EPILOGUE

Lucca, Italy

They never could confirm that the remains in Laura's wall were those of her friend, 'Nacoma', because the reservation nearby didn't have dental records, but we knew it was her. And by the time they finished removing the body they also found a shallow grave just yards to the side of the facility's sign. That body turned out to be that of the young runaway, Ellen Parker, or Eight.

Those finds changed everything. Judge Jacobs granted Mr. Oneal's request for a more exhaustive search, as well as for a forensic review of all Madonna's records. Before Dr. Braga knew it more sets of remains were discovered within nearby walls, and the surrounding desert was pitted with open graves.

The news world was flooded with stories. There followed more indictments than Arizona had seen in decades, and it went on for seven and a half years. By the time prosecutors wrapped up the last case there were several state and federal inspectors behind bars, and Braga and his staff, the local sheriff and two judges, though they filed one appeal after another, eventually had to join them. Janoff, their lawyer, somehow got off with disbarment and a short prison sentence—I'm not sure how he did it, but I was gone by then.

Mr. Oneal was surprised that I showed so little interest in any of those events, or even about my license, but I didn't care. Once my charges were dismissed I spent a week with Jenny's family in California, then flew back to Italy with two sealed caskets. Mrs. Locke had left a letter asking that I make it three, but I never could find Sophie's remains. Some of the people in Shantytown knew stories about Isabel Mays, but none of them had ever heard of the Spinalis. We still have no idea where Laura's mother was buried.

In her letter Mrs. Locke also asked to be buried as close to Laura as humanly possible. That did turn out to be possible, and their graves are now next to each other in a tiny cemetery in Lucca, overlooking the Serchio River. It's just a short walk from the villa.

I'd intended to go back to Arizona after the services for Laura and Mrs. Locke, but when the local papers reported what had happened to the last of the Spinali line I became a minor celebrity. There were stories in the paper and on television, and the city council even had a small ceremony for me. Those few weeks in Tuscany were enough to change my mind about returning to the States. And so one day I drove back out to the farm in Montevarchi. We'd had to sell it and the other properties, but its serenity had always stayed with me. The new owner let me rent one of the cabins. It was away from the road, just through a small forest and beside a stream. I lived there for several years, using it as a base while I began to work for Dr. Altobelli's clinic and the Bassos.

The Bassos have been very kind, and we've grown very close. The Signore and Signora moved back into the villa after their daughters were born, just as we'd planned. Pia was insufferable about that—she clucked endlessly about the overlap of Laura and Mrs. Locke's deaths with the twins' births, for that simple coincidence seemed to validate every bit of astrological nonsense she'd ever read. The Bassos didn't care; they were so happy with what we'd done that they eventually hired me to handle all their affairs.

Forty years later I still work for them. These days it's more dog walker assignments than anything else, but I've grown to appreciate life that's less exciting. I don't wonder about it, and shouldn't, I suppose, considering how much happened to so many people that year.

There was Father's death, of course, but my emotions about him were a little like our relationship had been—somewhat at arm's length, I mean. I loved and respected the man, but always, as I said, more as a parent than a close friend. And yet, in some ways I miss him, too.

But losing Jenny and our child was much harder. The trial and extradition kept me distracted for a while, but when that was over, grief about her joined with sorrow about Laura and Mrs. Locke, and I was overcome. It was a bad time for me.

Those first years were the saddest of my life, especially at night, when, while living out in the Montevarchi cabin, I had nothing but my books and the sound of the nearby stream to divert me. The sadness faded over time, but I still have an ache about those women, certainly Jenny, but also Laura, and, surprisingly, most of all, about Mrs. Locke. I can't really explain why she affected me so, and have tired of trying—but she did. I still feel it, the wake of her presence, and that feeling, and how much she made me want to help a client, even to this day.

In one sense, I suppose, it's never been the same. I certainly never had another client like her, and never even tried to return to more intense work. No, I've have been perfectly happy with more menial dog walking tasks. These past few years I've had a little trouble doing even those, partly because of my age, I suppose, partly because my memory seems to be slipping, and then, also, because my wounds never healed quite right.

A few years ago the Bassos offered to rent me one of the villa's rooms. I liked my cabin, but it brought me much nearer what little work I still do, so I accepted the offer. So I'm back here again. I have a lovely view of the garden, including the Acacia. I like that tree, especially this time of year, when the yellow blossoms in its upper limbs give camouflage to a pair of bright Orioles. I leave the window open so they'll wake me in the mornings, then have my coffee sitting there, and try to pick them out. Every so often I'll hear the clatter of hooves from outside, so I use my cane to pull myself up to the sill, and see what's out there, down below.

It happened again this morning, so I got up and peered out. It was the Bassos' twin daughters, leading their horses in from the gate. It took me a little while, but I made my way down the stairs and out to the great room to greet them.

"Hello, Paul," Gwen said, as they came in. Their English boots clicked dirtily on the dark parquet.

"Ladies," I replied.

"We found some of your things," Gwen said. She handed me two yellowed scraps of old newspaper, then headed for the mail. It was on the dining table. I stared at the scraps, not registering what they were. Julia saw my confusion and offered to help me. She set a tray next to my chair, then went to the table and came back with two books and a roll of tape. She laid the books beside each other and pulled a chair next to mine.

The clippings were articles that had slipped out of the books. Pia left me a scrapbook she titled *Antes Y Despues*. It has a lot of superstitious writings about reincarnation and nonsense like that, but there are also dozens of personal anecdotes and news articles about that year. They're interesting. I read them, then forget, and read them again as if for the first time. I guess one can become more easily entertained with age.

The other book is a leather-bound volume that was left to me by Mr. Oneal when he passed away. It was begun by my father, and finished by Mr. Oneal after I came back to Italy. Both books are smudged with coffee

447

and use; the tape holding articles and photos to their pages has yellowed and lost much of its grip, so some things loosen and slip out, sometimes while I'm out on the bench, reading beneath the Acacia. I was out there again last night, I think, so it must have happened then.

"I'll help you read them," Julia offered kindly, as she took her seat. "You tell me which book they're from." As I said, the Bassos are kind. Julia, especially. She read the first clipping to herself. "It's about Madonna, and the investigations," she said.

"Mr. Oneal's book," I replied. She helped me find its page, then taped it back in.

She scanned the other, and brightened. "This is a translation from your old interpreter—Signora Agnesi. It's from Le Figaro, about the necklace.

"The necklace!" I smiled. I liked that subject. "That must be interesting! Would you read it?"

"She's read everything about that to you several times," Gwen scolded from across the room.

"I doubt that," I said quietly.

"Doesn't matter," Julia said. "We'll read it again … It's dated April 27, 1973. It says,

Paul Rankin, consigliere for the Spinalocke foundation in Lucca, announced the startling reappearance of a necklace known as Sophie's Tears, and its donation to the Galleria Degli Uffizi in Florence. Recent ownership of the fabulous piece is unclear, though a historian at Uffizi says it was crafted by Genovese Spinali (The Elder) and other master jewellers of the Castellani House in the late 1800s for his daughter in law, Sophie Durer, after Ms. Durer's first but unsuccessful pregnancy. It was said to be fashioned from the finest silver and to contain an emerald which in quality and setting was reputed to have been the equal of

*the famous Chalk ring from India, and the Mackay
necklace now in New York.*

*Students of local history will recall that the fabled
necklace and many other extremely valuable creations
by The Elder vanished during a robbery which took
place at the Spinali villa in 1893. It now appears the
necklace had been locked away in a warehouse jointly
owned by the Castellani House and the Uffizi
Foundation. Neither the Castellani House, Uffizi, nor
Signore Rankin could explain how long it was kept there,
nor why.*

*Tazio Ribisi, chief historian for Uffizi, released a
statement saying that "the Gallerie is honoured to know
that a piece so deeply intertwined with our Tuscan past
has been kept here all these years, and will forever
remain available to the public."*

*The remaining jewellery taken in the robbery, which
was conservatively valued in the tens of millions, was
never recovered.*

"Here's the picture," Julia said, holding it up. And it
was. The old Castellani jewellers, mostly old men,
mostly in scarred leather aprons, arranged in a semi-
circle around the glittery necklace. "Which book do you
think it's from?" she asked.

I studied it carefully, then nodded. "Mr. Oneal's."
She helped find its place, retaped it, then took my hand.

"Would you like to go see it again?" she said. "I can
take you tomorrow."

"I don't think so," I said, "but thank you. Maybe
next week."

"Let me know if you change your mind."

"I will," I said, glancing up at Gwen. Gwen tries to
keep me from going. She'll scold me about living in the
past and comment on my colour when I get back, but

Julia understands. Looking at the books starts a small tug that gets stronger each day, until I have to go. So I usually do, even though, whenever I give in, a little commotion comes to the villa: Julia changes her plans, makes me lunch, has my best suit pressed, even has my shoes shined.

But I like Uffizi. The guard there knows me now. Her name is Margherite, I think; something like that. The first time I went, while searching the museum a young woman's voice behind me offered some help. I turned, and here was this pleasant young guard. I bowed a little over my cane and explained why I'd come. So she took me to another floor, then led me slowly down a corridor that wandered through one room after another, to the very last room and to its very last case.

It's part infirmary, and part orphanage, that wing, for broken or less famous pieces. That's why the first piece you come to in this particular case is an old Tiffany mystery clock with two legs replaced by stained corks. Next to that there's a blue and gold Faberge egg, with a hole the shape of Louisiana in its lower shell. And then, finally, there next to the egg, lying on a piece of dusty black velvet, is the necklace.

On my first visit I stood there, trying to picture it on Laura, but maybe because it was Nathan's parting gift to Mrs. Locke, I gradually found myself more imagining it on my client—it seems somehow more fitting to me, there, somehow calming.

The guard stayed and watched while I stood and stared. She probably thought I'd just be a moment, but the moment stretched to minutes, and the minutes even longer. My leg eventually stiffened, and I began to shift, one leg to the other, then back again. So this pleasant young woman—Marge...Mar, something, I think—

brought me a lovely chair, and I sat, watching the necklace as the guard watched me.

Though by then I'd long considered myself a recovered soul, after returning to the villa from that first visit, for a while, up in my room, I was terribly depressed. The next day I came to my senses and decided never to go back, but within the next week I wanted to return more badly than any old man could resist. So despite the emotion following that first visit I went back for a second, and now have gone so many times now that both Julia and Gwen know it's a hopeless thing for me.

And it's always the same. Each time I go up to that floor I tap in to the room until I see the guard, then a small liturgy takes place. I give her a little bow and say, "Bongiorno, Signorina", each time she returns a respectful, "Good day, Signore"; each time I'll explain why I'm here; then each time she nods, as if agreeing that's a very good reason for coming. And then, each time, she takes me to it.

There's a paper with printing that rests in front of it. It says, 'Le La Crime Sophie', and below that the name, 'The Elder'. I read the card on each visit; it's one of my whims, I suppose, but the little ceremony has a way of settling me, like a pleasant introduction can. Then I sit, and the guard stands back, and it's quiet, except for an occasional cough from me, or the creak of the guard's leather belt.

The guard—Marg...something—her name starts with an M—she stays the whole time, but never seems bored. I have no idea why. There's no drama here—age has turned me into one of those people who's always in backgrounds, and I just sit there in my reveries. But she stays, and I like her presence. After a while, though, I take a deep breath and use the cane to pull myself up. I'll

451

steady myself and straighten my coat, then turn and nod my parting to the guard.

"Grazie y arrivederci, Signorina," I'll say.

And each time she smiles and nods back, "Good day, Signore."

Then I tap my way out, vaguely satisfied but very tired. I'll sleep well that night, and the following nights, and will put the visit out of my mind—until the tug comes again. I'll fight it, mind you, with the garden or the scrapbooks, but one thing always leads to the other, and the other is at Uffizi.

"Hey! It looks good," Gwen said, holding up a letter to Julia. Julia joined her. Their voices dropped to more confidential tones, but I heard Gwen say the name "Margherite." I'd heard that name before, but just then I couldn't remember where. Then Julia chuckled, reading the letter. "She's a bit odd. She put in here that she's a Scorpio! But she took some nursing before she got the job at Uffizi."

That sparked my recollection.

"At the Uffizi! I know a Margherite! She works at the Uffizi!"

"That's the one," Julia said more softly. "We're looking for some help, and she's looking for another job."

"You need help?" I asked.

She hesitated, and glanced at Gwen.

"She's going to help around here when we're gone," Gwen said.

"What! Where are you going?"

"To the U.S.," Julia said, "but not for long, Paul. We need someone to watch the house anyway."

The butler came in to announce the arrival of the music instructor. I braced the tip of my cane against a seam in the floor, and tried to get up. But the cane slipped from the seam. Julia came over and helped me up.

"You must be tired, Paul," she said quietly.

"I'm fine," I replied a little too quickly. I tapped my way to the hallway before turning. "Thank you, Julia."

Once in my room I worked on my glasses and faced the computer. It's very complicated, but I used my hunt and peck system to get it going. I drew up a daily report to send to Dr. Altobelli's accountant, but got confused with the email program and had trouble sending the damn thing. I was about to shut it when I noticed a shortcut at the bottom

'Locke'

On a whim I opened it. Subfolders appeared. Christ, there were a lot of them: Attorney General/Arizona; Grand Juries; Inspector General/Rome; Photographs; Properties-Italy; Properties-Arizona; Research-Dominichi; Research-Madonna; Research-Spinali; Travel; Trials-Arizona; Trials-Florence; and several trust folders. Good Lord, there were a lot of them. I moved to the photographs file and opened it.

There were more subfolders. I stared at the third, titled 'Mrs. Locke' and opened it. There was a photograph, taken of a younger version of the woman I knew. I like the picture, but looking at it gives me the same nagging doubt I had the first time I saw her; as if she was right, about having met somewhere before. It's probably something I'd forgotten, I suppose, but I get that feeling when I go to Uffizi and sit there with the necklace. It's much stronger there, that feeling, as if the answer is somewhere just inside the case.

I worked my glasses off, and, using the cane, limped to the bed. I sat for a moment, indulging in quiet. I'm not normally melancholy—not morose, anyway. I smile, though maybe not as much as before; and I laugh, though maybe not as hard; and when I need solace—and there have been those times—there are always my books, or the garden…or Uffizi.

I lifted my right leg to the bed, then pulled up my left, and laid my head slowly back. Then I decided. Tomorrow I'll go back. I'll ask Julia to take me. I hope she can. Maybe this time I'll tap the main halls for a little while, and take in other works. Then again, one needs a measured diet of art, so maybe I'll just get on with what I go for. The guard will show me the way. Her name is … M … Margaret—something like that.

My eyes slipped to the cane, over its gleaming ridge of silver mane at the handle, then down the stock to where the black is mottled with age and use. I never told anyone what it had been used for, and I have no trouble remembering that. For a while after the women died I considered destroying it—not just throwing it away, but burning the wooden stock, melting the silver into the ground, then covering it with Tuscan dirt. But it's just silver and wood, and if such things can in some way be imbued with more, then maybe there's redemption in Mrs. Locke having had it. It's comforting, anyway, knowing that her hand was on that silvery head all those years, and that I can put mine where hers used to be.

I stopped, distracted by other noises, coming from different places. Piano notes echoed up through the floor, a signal that Julia's little girl was at the keys. The instructor was coaxing her over some simple bars of Vivaldi. It was charmingly bad, with bi-dextrous sections that harmonized only briefly before one slipped out of step from the other. Each time the music stopped I could hear the murmur of the instructor's voice, and then the notes went back to the beginning. I like those sounds; they've never bothered me.

But the other sound ... there it is again, coming from outside, through the window. I use the cane to pull myself up, make my way to the sill and look down into the garden. I have to smile. The two women are back outside. Gwen is feeding carrots to the horses, her hand carefully flattened, her lips earnest in speech. Julia is at her side, arms folded, smiling a lovely smile. And the noise I heard, the sound that drifts across the sill, the one that always signals they are out there with them, is from the horses, making their sounds back to Gwen.